PATTI CALLAHAN HENRY

"Will touch your heart and make you wonder about long-forgotten possibilities waiting to be rediscovered."
—*THE CHARLESTON POST AND COURIER* (SC)

"Brings to mind such authors as Pat Conroy, Anne Rivers Siddons, and Dorothea Benton Frank—against whom Henry stacks up admirably."
—ST. JOHN FLYNN, NPR HOST OF *COVER TO COVER*

"Enfolds us in a story that stays with us long after we've turned the last page."—*SOUTHERN LADY*

"Doesn't disappoint in this beautiful novel of discovery and self-acceptance."—*BOOKLIST* (STARRED REVIEW)

"Implores the reader to get to the end for the satisfaction of finding out the answers to those secrets."—*THE HERALD-SUN* (NC)

continued . . .

Where the River Runs

"Books about the journey to self-realization often make us contemplate our own lives and choices. You travel with the character through joy, heartache, and redemption, and when it's over, you have laughed and cried. This book proves no exception. . . . Descriptive language, paired with heartfelt characters, accentuates the story, which is peppered with Lowcountry culture and customs. . . . After reading this tale, cherishing family and home becomes the reader's own mantra." —*Southern Living* magazine

"Quietly reflective and softly compelling, this tale of a Lowcountry woman's reblossoming will touch your heart and make you wonder about long-forgotten possibilities waiting to be rediscovered in your own family and soul."
—*Charleston Post and Courier* (SC)

"*Where the River Runs* is an expression of love between author and story. Readers will instantly fall for Patti Callahan Henry's unique voice and lyrical writing style in this satisfying story of a secret revealed." —*Topsail Magazine*

"A melodious, encouraging tale that upholds memories, friendship, and family."
—*Atlanta Woman* magazine

"As in Henry's debut, *Losing the Moon*, and this beautifully written story, the sheer lyricism of the author's voice transports the reader. Fans of such books as Mary Alice Monroe's *Skyward*, also about the Gullah, and Patricia Gaffney's *Flight Lessons* will add this book to their list of favorites." —*Booklist*

Losing the Moon

"Henry has been hailed as being included in the ranks of important Southern writers such as Pat Conroy and Anne Rivers Siddons. If this debut novel is any indication . . . we can look forward to many years of reading enjoyment."
—*Chance Times Record News* (TX)

"Readers who enjoy the lyrical voices of Patricia Gaffney and Mary Alice Monroe will also be drawn to this talented newcomer." —*Booklist* (Starred Review)

"Patti Callahan Henry's engaging story and compelling characters captured my heart from page one, and stayed with me long after the final, satisfying conclusion. Don't miss this wonderful book." —Haywood Smith

Driftwood Summer

PATTI CALLAHAN HENRY

NAL
ACCENT

NAL Accent
Published by New American Library, a division of
Penguin Group (USA) Inc., 375 Hudson Street,
New York, New York 10014, USA
Penguin Group (Canada), 90 Eglinton Avenue East, Suite 700, Toronto,
Ontario M4P 2Y3, Canada (a division of Pearson Penguin Canada Inc.)
Penguin Books Ltd., 80 Strand, London WC2R 0RL, England
Penguin Ireland, 25 St. Stephen's Green, Dublin 2,
Ireland (a division of Penguin Books Ltd.)
Penguin Group (Australia), 250 Camberwell Road, Camberwell, Victoria 3124,
Australia (a division of Pearson Australia Group Pty. Ltd.)
Penguin Books India Pvt. Ltd., 11 Community Centre, Panchsheel Park,
New Delhi - 110 017, India
Penguin Group (NZ), 67 Apollo Drive, Rosedale, North Shore 0632,
New Zealand (a division of Pearson New Zealand Ltd.)
Penguin Books (South Africa) (Pty.) Ltd., 24 Sturdee Avenue,
Rosebank, Johannesburg 2196, South Africa

Penguin Books Ltd., Registered Offices:
80 Strand, London WC2R 0RL, England

First published by NAL Accent, an imprint of New American Library,
a division of Penguin Group (USA) Inc.

First Printing, June 2009
1   3   5   7   9   10   8   6   4   2

 REGISTERED TRADEMARK—MARCA REGISTRADA

LIBRARY OF CONGRESS CATALOGING-IN-PUBLICATION DATA:

Henry, Patti Callahan.
Driftwood summer/Patti Callahan Henry.
p. cm.
ISBN 978-0-451-22688-4
1. Sisters—Fiction. 2. Family secrets—Fiction. I. Title.
PS3608.E578D75 2009
813'.6—dc22   2009000969

Set in Garamond
Designed by Ginger Legato

Printed in the United States of America

To my dearest friends, who just happen to be my sisters:
Barbi Callahan Burris and Jeannie Callahan Cunnion

ACKNOWLEDGMENTS

This novel is a collaboration of many beautiful voices, which shaped, formed, changed, inspired, and improved the novel. To those voices I want to extend a sincere thank-you.

—To my family: Pat, Meagan, Thomas and Rusk. I love you. I couldn't and wouldn't do this without you. Special thanks to Bonnie and George Callahan, my extraordinary parents, and to Gwen and Chuck Henry, whom I would have chosen as in-laws even if I hadn't married their son.

—To my agent, Kimberly Whalen, who always knows what works and what doesn't. She can also make me laugh—a lot.

—To my editor, Ellen Edwards, and all the people at NAL who make this possible. Claire Zion, Kara Welsh, Becky Vinter, and the formidable PR team of Craig Burke, Rick Pascocello and Melissa Broder, the sales force, production team and amazing art department.

—To the bookstores throughout the country who love books, words and story as much as I do. With special thanks to those who helped contribute to this bookstore story: Patti Morrison of Barnes and Noble in Mt. Pleasant, South Carolina; Tom Warner of Litchfield Books in Pawley's Island, South Carolina; Kelly Justice at Fountain Books in Richmond, Virginia; Cynthia Grabenbauer at the the Vero Beach Book Center; Karin Wilson, Taylor Mathis and Jennifer Calhoun (and her sisters, of course) at Page and Palette in Fairhope, Alabama.

—To my sweet writing friends who encourage, love and always remind me why we write: the power and magic of words.

—To the readers who write, call, read my novels and take the time to visit me on book tours. You inspire me every single day.

—To my encouraging friends who say things like, "You are meant to do this." "Do not stop." "We are on your side." I do not know what I would do without you. I really don't. I love you!!

"Life can only be understood backwards; but it must be lived forwards."

—Søren Kierkegaard (1813–1855)

"I can not live without books."

—Thomas Jefferson in a letter to John Adams (1815)

Driftwood Summer

Driftwood Cottage Bookstore

News and Views From Palmetto Beach

Dear Booklover,

It's finally here—summer. Ahhh…

This time of year brings our beloved summer friends back to Palmetto Beach, and offers a slower pace with more time to slip away to the backyard rocking chair, the beach, Pearson's Pier and of course the Driftwood Cottage Bookstore.

Starting next Friday, we have an incredible season planned. We have been yacking about this special event for over a year now and it is hard to believe it is finally here: THE TWO-HUNDRED-YEAR ANNIVERSARY of Driftwood Cottage. Of course it has only been our cozy bookstore for twelve years, but the house has withstood time, trials and even a move from the plantation to the beach where it now stands.

We have a full week of events planned. There will be a night for everyone's love of poetry, art, nonfiction, book clubs and all that Driftwood Cottage Bookstore has to offer.

You'll find some fabulous new books in the review section of this month's newsletter along with Anne and Ethel's picks of the month. The book club picks are also listed. Don't forget about Anne's art classes and the Kids' Corner activities.

Come eat at our café, grab a good book and enjoy our cozy atmosphere as we celebrate the endurance of DRIFT-WOOD COTTAGE and our local Palmetto Beach community.

Until next time…

Read Well,
Kitsy and Riley Sheffield

Celebration Week—Schedule of Events

Friday night 6 p.m.—*New York Times* Bestselling Author Nick Martin speaks and signs his new thriller set in a winery in Napa Valley.

Saturday night 7 p.m.—BOOK CLUB CELEBRATION. All book club members and guests come join us for a night of fun including a literary trivia contest, prizes and wine and food donated by our local businesses.

Sunday night 6 p.m.—JOIN THE COOKBOOK CLUB in the café, where they'll be preparing their favorite recipe from their pick of the month: *Shrimp & Grits Cookbook* by Nathalie Dupree. Come taste, watch and enjoy!

Monday night 6 p.m.—LOCAL ARTIST NIGHT. Come join us as our local artisans display and sell their original works.

Tuesday night 7 p.m.—POETRY NIGHT. Come hear poets from our surrounding communities read their original work.

Wednesday night 7 p.m.—KIDS' CORNER. Bring the kids and teens tonight for various activities including art, writing and a book signing with our local children's book illustrator, Sally Wentworth.

Thursday night 7 p.m.—LOCAL AUTHORS NIGHT. You know them all, right? And they'll all be here. Buy local. Support our community.

Friday night—CLOSED to prepare for the BIG Party Saturday.

SATURDAY 4 p.m.–10 p.m.—DRIFTWOOD COTTAGE BOOK-STORE ANNIVERSARY PARTY. The biggest party Palmetto Beach has seen in two centuries. Local musicians; food and wine from our local restaurants; raffle to win amazing prizes. You won't want to miss this night.

ONE

*B*ookstore owner Riley Sheffield believed that even the most ordinary life was like a good novel, a tale to be told. Her own life was full of twists and turns, secrets and surprises, with narrative threads that intertwined with the fabric of other people's lives. Her story revolved around a two-hundred-year-old cottage on the beach—Driftwood Cottage Bookstore.

Her mother had bought the old cottage and turned it into a bookstore, and now Riley was raising her son in the upstairs apartment, her days tuned to the rhythm of the tides and the ebb and flow of customers. The sea-infused air mingled with the scents of ink and paper. The ocean breeze coming through the open windows created a symphony with the creaking walls and groaning bookshelves. The same sand that found its way between Riley's toes was also embedded in the cracks between the uneven floorboards, in the creases of the well-worn upholstered armchairs and sometimes between the pages of the books. Every morning Riley awoke with anticipation of another day of stories unfolding—stories in the novels she read and in the lives of the customers she served.

On the first floor of the cottage, behind a wooden door to the left of the checkout counter, Riley's office desk was half hidden beneath the piles of RSVP cards for the party to be held at the bookstore in a week. She avoided the tedious task of recording these responses by walking toward the Book Club Corner—her favorite nook in the store.

Riley sighed as she ran her fingertips lazily across the spines of the books lining the crooked shelves. The stories were old friends that comforted her. The camaraderie of women in the book clubs helped ease the loneliness of being a thirty-two-year-old single mother. Somehow sitting with the women and discussing the novels, then later, their personal stories, had opened Riley's heart to the tenderness of others' hurts. Book clubs acted as a balm on the ache for intimacy.

She stood behind the bookshelf and listened while the Beach Babes Book Club talked over and above one another, each woman speaking in the commanding tone of one who believed that what she had to say was more important than what anyone else had to say. Riley smiled, sensing an impending arument brewing. Listening to browsers and book club members, to authors and would-be authors, she'd become an expert at detecting a negative undercurrent.

She poked her head around the corner.

"Hi, ladies."

Seated on upholstered club chairs, their feet propped up on faded green-and-pink ottomans, coffee cups scattered on the driftwood side tables, the book club waved back and hollered greetings.

"Riley," called Lola Martin, her eybrows raised, "who was your first love?"

"Tom Sawyer," she replied with a crooked smile, slipped a fallen book back onto a shelf. "Interesting question. What book are y'all discussing this month?"

"*Beach Music* by Pat Conroy," Lola said. "The main character never stops loving his first love and we were just wondering who yours was. Tom Sawyer does not count."

"Oh, yes, it does." Riley walked into the Book Club Corner's circle, picked up several empty coffee cups. "For a twelve-year-old bookworm sitting alone on the riverbank, Tom Sawyer made a perfect first love."

"You make it sound like he was real," Lola said.

"He was." Riley glanced out the window to the front yard, to the ancient live oak spreading its branches toward the earth and sky, circles of light nestled in its curves.

"See?" said Ashley Carpenter, bouncing her six-month-old baby on her lap. "True love and happy endings are only in fairy tales or novels. Not in real life."

Riley's gaze returned to the group. Lola shook her head. "I'm not saying all true loves end happily. But some do. Right?" She looked again at Riley.

Ashley laughed. "Well, I'm gonna need some convincing."

Riley smiled at the group as several different conversations started up; she said goodbye and returned to her office to face the pile of work.

Of course Tom Sawyer wasn't her first love: Mack Logan was. She'd kept this conscious knowledge far from her mind, but some memories haunt the heart.

The RSVP cards on her desk brought her thoughts back to the present, to the upcoming party—an ambitious week's worth of events, a celebration intended to draw an influx of cash into the bookstore to help it stay afloat. This party was also in honor of Mama's seventieth birthday—a combination Mama believed just could not fail. But of course it could fall short of saving the store. Profits were down, and on the balance sheets Riley saw an abyss of debt with no way out.

This would be the party of all parties, according to Mama; it would rival the Fourth of July celebration, the mayoral inauguration and the town's very own anniversary. But this was how Mama always talked, as if her grandiose descriptions could somehow make up for the smallness of her everyday life of tea parties, social calls and hours spent on personal grooming before visits to the same people, every day for years on end.

Riley's sisters, Maisy and Adalee, were also coming to the party. They'd all be together for the first time in six years.

The pile of envelopes on the desk tilted, fell to the floor. Riley picked them up, and then caught her hair in a rubber band to begin removing RSVP cards and recording them in the ledger. The stack of letter-pressed stationery (nothing but the best for Mama) had been arranged in alphabetical order. The town's pre-

mier wedding-invitation specialist had addressed the return envelopes in handsome calligraphy—a donation for which Riley
had begged in humiliating fashion. It was important for Mama
to keep up the pretense of opulence. For Riley, each family name
and return address on the top-left corner created an emotion, including a yearning for those long-gone summers of freedom and
joy. She said the names out loud as she drew the cards from the
envelopes.

When Riley had been younger, Mama used to call the names
out loud in this same manner as she addressed the family's Christmas cards. She would utter the name in a singsong voice and then
say, "Remember when Aunt Sis drank too much at Thanksgiving
and knocked over the china cabinet?" or "Oh, sweet Mrs. Dun-
can, she lost her son to that terrible car wreck." Each envelope
evoked a remembrance.

For once, the phone didn't ring and no knock sounded on
the office door as Riley enjoyed each memory conjured up as
she checked guests off the invitation list. Half an hour later she
reached for the next envelope—**Mr. Mack Logan** was written in
slanted block letters. She closed her eyes and said his name out
loud, her tongue now unfamiliar with the sounds.

A soft, tender and well-guarded place inside Riley opened to a
flood of Technicolor memories: Mack's attempt at ten years old to
right the sailboat in the middle of the bay, hollering that he didn't
need her help; at twelve his tousled hair backlit by evening sun at
the end of a day's fishing excursion; at sixteen his body long and
lean; at eighteen returning from his senior year in high school
as an adult. In rapid sequence she saw the images as if they were

pictures in a waterlogged scrapbook. Summer after summer was filled with various images of Mack Logan—her childhood best friend, her ally, the boy who all at once had become a man.

Now he was returning to Palmetto Beach for the bookstore's celebration, and she would see him again for the first time in thirteen years. What would he be like?

She shoved her memory of him down again, but it was like keeping a buoy underwater. Her Mack images were still vivid and complete. She wasn't sure why she'd thought they would disappear because she didn't visit them, like thinking an entire country didn't exist just because she'd never been there.

Throughout her childhood, this very cottage had been the Logans' family vacation home, and never once had she imagined that it would become her own unconventional home. Since her son, Brayden, was born twelve years ago and she'd moved here, she'd built her life around this bookstore, focused all her attention on what was practical, necessary. Her sole escape was the novels she devoured.

A knock came to the door and Riley jumped up. "Yes?" she hollered.

"Riley honey?" called Ethel Larkin, who managed the checkout counter.

Riley opened the door to where Ethel held out the portable phone. "It's Harriet calling from the house."

Riley smiled. This sweet woman—her white hair piled like cotton batting on top of her head, her clothing bright and loose around her tiny body—had helped run the store for all twelve years. Her sarcasm and wit often kept Riley from taking herself or her problems too seriously. Among Ethel's many eccentricities was her habit of wearing white gloves every day as if she were going to a cotillion dance. She waved her hands when she talked, and the gloves punctuated every word. Riley was never sure if Ethel realized that her gloves—every pair—were dirty; not just dirty, but torn in places. But Riley never asked—it was part of the mystery of Ethel, a piece of the Driftwood Cottage Bookstore mystique.

Now Ethel held one gloved hand next to her cheek; her eyes were ringed with worry. "Harriet says your mama has fallen."

Riley closed her eyes, whispered in her mind, *No. Not Mama.* Daddy had died six years before, and the blow still felt fresh and painful.

She grabbed the phone. "Hello?" She glanced through the office doorway to the front foyer, hoping to see the Sheffield matriarch marching in. Evening light fell across the dark floorboards; a young mother and pigtailed girl wound their way among the bookshelves. Mama wouldn't be arriving now—it was martini time. What could possibly have gone wrong during martini time?

Harriet Waters, Mama's housekeeper of forty-five years, spoke in shaky tones. "Oh, Riley, your mama fell down the main staircase. I had to call nine-one-one because I couldn't wake her up. They just took her to the hospital. . . . She woke up before the ambulance got here. She's mad as hell that I called for help, but what was I gonna do with her all crumpled up at the bottom of the stairs with her eyes all but rolled back in her head? For God's sake, was I just gonna leave her there?" Her words tripped one over the other.

"Slow down." Riley grabbed the edge of the desk and attempted to right the room, to understand the words.

Harriet began again. "Your mama's on her way to General in the back of an ambulance. She left cussing me out, hollering and waving her tiny little arms like she's gonna kick my butt. I'm still home, but they're gone . . . gone."

Riley leaned against the counter. "Did she fall before or after her evening martinis?"

"After. I been telling her not to walk around an empty house in high heels, but she's never listened to me."

Sorrow lodged into the space below Riley's breastbone at the realization that Mama was still attempting to keep up the gracious lifestyle of her married life—dressing up for cocktails at five, dinner at eight—without a husband. "I'll be at the hospital as soon as I can."

Riley hung up the phone and faced Ethel over the faded beige linoleum counter. "I've got to run over to General. Can you watch Brayden?"

"Of course," Ethel said. "Is your mama okay?"

Riley shrugged. "I'm about to find out." She grabbed her car keys and looked over her shoulder at the book club still huddled in the corner. They'd have moved on from the novel and would now be talking about their personal lives. Riley believed you could chart the interior lives of the book club members by the books they chose. Right now Riley's life book would be a Southern novel about dysfunctional families pretending that everything was just fine: a drunk mother falling down the front curved staircase, a sister who'd run away to California and another sister with the mistaken assumption that going to a university meant a free pass to all-day and all-night partying.

Riley went over to her son, who'd run in from school moments before. He was leafing through *Sport Fishing* in the periodical section. Her hand on his arm gained his attention. "Gamma had a little fall; she's all right but she's at the hospital. She needs me. Ethel is here. . . . I'll be back as soon as I can."

Brayden looked up at her. "Can I come with?"

Riley shook her head. "No, but I'll call you as soon as I know something."

He shrugged. "Okay."

"I love you." Riley kissed his forehead.

"You, too." He wiped off the kiss and grinned.

Riley hurried through the doors of the hospital emergency room to the front desk. Memories of her father's last days in this place crowded her awareness. The receptionist looked up. "May I help you?"

"Yes, I'm looking for Kitsy Sheffield. She would have come in just a few minutes ago."

"Are you family?"

"Yes. Her daughter."

"She is in X-ray right now, but you can wait for her in the second room on the right. Dr. Foster will be there shortly."

"Okay," Riley called over her shoulder, ran through the double doors and down the hall. The cubbyhole room was empty of its stretcher; she sat in one of two metal chairs and dropped her head into her hands. "Oh, Mama."

"Riley."

She looked up to see Dr. Foster standing in the doorway. She'd known this man all her life; he'd eased Daddy's passing. His white hair spoke of his age, while the lines on his face suggested a quiet sorrow for all he'd seen as a small-town physician.

"How is she?" Riley asked.

"She's already had a CAT scan. She's now in X-ray. But she's awake and hollering, so she seems fine, although Harriet says she did black out when she fell. There are definitely some broken bones. I'll know more in an hour or so."

"Thanks," Riley said, and attempted a smile.

Dr. Foster left and the interminable wait began to grate on Riley like a nail file running across a chalkboard. She paced the room and tried not to think of the million things that could go awry if Mama was seriously injured. She went to the doorway when a quarrelsome voice echoed down the ER corridor. Kitsy Sheffield, lying flat on a stretcher, was being rolled down the hallway, screaming at Dr. Foster, "I am telling you, I'm fine. Just give me some pain medicine and I'll be okay."

Dr. Foster caught Riley's glance and smiled. She ran to their side, followed them back to the room. "Mama, I'm here," she said.

Mama's normally well-coiffed hair stuck up on the right side and was tamped down in a mass of tangles on the left. Her green eyes were clouded and moist. Her face was blanched the same color as the white blanket pulled up to her chin. A dark-haired nurse pushed the IV pole alongside the stretcher.

"Of course you're here, dear," Mama said. "Now tell Dr. Foster to let me go home. Right now. And I mean right now. And this hurts so much. So damn bad." Tears rose in her eyes and she turned away.

"Kitsy, hold on a minute." Dr. Foster's deep voice lowered as the nurse straightened the stretcher and locked its wheels. "Nurse, please give Mrs. Sheffield a dose of the prescribed pain med."

The nurse pushed buttons on the pump and then closed the door when she left.

Dr. Foster sat next to Kitsy. "You have a sprained wrist, a broken femur, two cracked ribs and a bruise running down your hip that makes it look like you fell off a bucking horse. You didn't, did you?"

"Very funny," Mama said.

"You'll be here for at least a day, so just quit your hollering and settle in. You'll need casts, splints and some tests. I promise to keep you comfortable. I'm working on getting you a room upstairs, where you can get into a bed and off this stretcher, so just sit tight."

Mama squinted at Riley. "Why aren't you at the store? Who's there?"

"Mama, I believe you are a bit more important than the store."

"I will be fine. Just fine," Kitsy said.

Dr. Foster glanced back and forth between them. "Riley, I'm going to ask you to leave so I can talk to your mother in private."

Kitsy held her palm out in a stopping motion. "It's okay. We can tell Riley. She will need to know if I am to get through this week."

Dr. Foster leaned down, adjusted the blanket at the end of the stretcher. "Are you sure?"

"Yes."

Riley felt the revelation, not yet spoken, slip into the room like dark smoke. She went to Mama's side, wiped a stray hair off her forehead. Lying in the bed with an IV in the back of her hand, with bandages on her arms and a spot of dried blood on her cheek, Mama had a vulnerability that grabbed Riley by the throat and robbed her of breath. "What is it, Dr. Foster?"

"Your mother found a lump behind her knee a few weeks ago. The tests have come back and she has a bone cancer called chondrosarcoma."

"No." Riley's plea was a desperate whisper. "Not cancer. Not like Dad."

"It's not like that. . . . It's not the same kind," Mama whispered. "My cancer is treatable. They think so anyway. I just don't want to do anything about it or tell anyone . . . until after your sisters' visit, after the bookstore party. Do not tell your sisters. . . ."

"Mama, you cannot wait on treatment. Right, Dr. Foster? She can't wait. We have to deal with this now."

"We're doing all we can, Riley. Obviously these new injuries complicate the situation." Dr. Foster patted the bedrail as if it were Riley's hand. "Your mother has made informed decisions and will begin treatment after the party."

Riley looked down at Mama, her heart reaching out to the childlike woman in the bed, but Kitsy's eyes were closed and the soft sound of sleep slipped from her parted lips. Riley took two steps toward Dr. Foster. "You have to talk her out of waiting. . . ."

"Is the disease what caused her to break so many bones?" Riley asked.

"It's possible. Beyond that, your mother will tell you what she wants you to know. I can't answer all your questions." Dr. Foster looked away.

Riley grabbed the sleeve of his white coat. "Doc, you can. I've known you my entire life."

Dr. Foster took Riley's hand. "She wants to get through this week of parties and festivities before she tells anyone. Can you understand her decision? She wants her daughters together—that's all I can tell you."

"Parties? Festivities? What is that compared to . . . ?" She couldn't say the word "death."

"Everything, to your mother. She will have all her daughters home for the first time in years, and she doesn't want anything to ruin it."

"Maisy and Adalee are only coming for two days next weekend. Two days. They're too busy to be involved in the bookstore or with Mama's care."

"Two days is enough for your mother. Listen, Riley, your mother is strong and I will not go against her wishes. For a year and a half, she has been planning this week of parties and looking forward to seeing all her girls together. I will not take that joy away from her."

"But now she's gonna miss all of it. She'll be . . . in bed."

"Please, just let us treat her and allow her to tell you whatever she needs to say to you, in her own way and in her own time." Dr. Foster stood, held up his hand to stay any further words. "And do not say anything to your sisters."

Dr. Foster shut the door harder than necessary, leaving Riley in the middle of the room, more alone than she'd felt since the day she awoke and found that Maisy had run away to California. She placed her hand on her chest where the thought of losing one more person caused a sharp pain. "No," she said out loud, and then wondered how many men, women, children, parents and loved ones had mumbled the same denial in this place.

She kissed her sleeping mama's forehead and walked into the hall, then reached for her cell phone. She dialed Maisy's number in California. For the past twelve years Riley had convinced herself that she would never need Maisy again.

She'd been wrong.

Two

MAISY

*M*aisy Sheffield ran her fingers over the linen fabric, then held it next to the pale pink paint chip the customer had handed her with instructions to find the perfect match. Maisy pretended to focus intently, picking up swatch after swatch when she knew all along which one she would choose. The customer squinted with a slight smile, as though pleased by the hard work Maisy was putting into the choice.

The fabrics in the Beach Chic store in Laguna Beach were now as familiar to Maisy as her own life. She had studied everything about the store with more diligence than she'd ever applied to schoolwork. Long ago, she'd decided that the harder she worked to establish this California life, the more her existence in Georgia would disappear from her consciousness. So far her strategy had worked well.

After twelve years the memory of the thin sand dollars, white starfish and gray-white shells of coastal Georgia had been replaced with the reality of coarser sand, the sun setting over the water instead of behind it, and light, dry air instead of dense, humid moisture that sent Maisy's hair into a mass of bronze curls. Here the rhythms of nature sang in softer, subtler songs under sleek palm trees instead of in the chaotic chirp of the cicadas under cluttered live oaks. The beaches here were consistently wide and deep instead of narrow at high tide and low, muddy and exposed at low tide.

Maisy had gone to the opposite side of the continent to create a new life for herself in a completely different world.

Maisy closed one eye and held the trellis rose fabric swatch up to the light. "This one, Mrs. Findle."

"I knew you'd pick the right one. You have an eye for these things." Mrs. Findle plucked the swatch from Maisy's hand.

Maisy tried not to look over at her boss, Sheila, to see if she had heard the compliment, but she couldn't help it. Sheila nodded at Maisy, her blond bob barely moving, and smiled.

"Let's go ahead and order the fabric, and then we'll decide on some other pieces," Maisy said.

"I don't need anything else. I just need to cover the lounge chair in my bedroom. I hate the damask on it now."

"Oh, once this fabric is in your room, you will surely want to think about the lamps and the bedcovers." Maisy started off toward the back of the store. "The mirrors and chandeliers will need to reflect your new vision for the room. I don't want y'all to regret that the rest of the decor isn't as lovely as your new chair."

Mrs. Findle fingered the chain on her Chanel purse. "Well, maybe just the lamps, because the ones I have are dark wood."

"Yes, that's a great place to start." Maisy walked toward a crystal lamp at the far end of the room, pointing out other accessories that would work well to give Ms. Findle's room the serene look she desired.

Mrs. Findle stopped next to an oversized ottoman. "Do you think this is too large to go with my chair?"

"I really don't."

"You have the most lovely accent. Where are you from? I've been meaning to ask," Mrs. Findle said.

"Georgia. A small coastal town." Maisy had found that women in southern California had a vision of southern Georgia that was more romantic than real. When she'd first arrived at Beach Chic, she'd tried to hide her Southern roots until she realized it was an asset to be from "the South." Maisy resumed her Southern accent and allowed the women to believe she'd lived in an antebellum world where life moved at a slower pace and the olden song of Southern hospitality whispered across jasmine-scented nights.

Of course that was an illusion. The small Southern coastal town where Maisy had grown up was mostly deserted except during the weeks between Memorial Day and Labor Day, when the "summer people" arrived and the fun began. Her boring hometown was enough to make her crazy. If anyone asked why she'd moved across the country, she said she needed to shake the dirt-road dust and sandburs off her flip-flops and try something new. Only she knew the biggest reason she had left. Only she and Tucker Morgan.

Sheila hollered across the store. "Maisy, phone call."

Maisy turned and smiled. "Can I return the call?"

"I don't think so," Sheila said. "Sounds . . . like an emergency from home."

Maisy ran a hand through her hair, now smooth instead of "puffy," as her mama had once labeled her bad hair. If this call came from Mama, with some faux drama, Maisy would have to tell her not to call the store anymore. Mrs. Findle had the potential to become the best customer she'd had in months.

"I'll be right back." Maisy smiled at Mrs. Findle.

"Oh, go on, dear. I'll just browse for a minute. You've got me thinking."

Maisy accepted the portable phone from Sheila and headed into the back room. She took a long swallow of her cold Starbucks sitting on the counter and then asked, "Okay, what is it?"

"Well, hello to you, too, sis." Riley's voice sounded as though it had traveled from the far end of the world, and Maisy wanted to keep it that way. Jealousy, doubt, guilt and other irritating emotions—she could hold them at bay as long as the Georgia she had left twelve years ago seemed as distant as another planet.

"I'm sorry. I didn't mean to be rude. I'm just outrageously busy. Is everything okay?"

"No," Riley said, then paused. "Mama fell down the main stairs. She's okay, but . . ."

"Sounds like a bad movie. Mama fell down the stairs? All of them?" Maisy pictured their front curving staircase, the same one she had come down every morning of her life, for school, for dates, for cotillion dances.

"Yes," Riley answered. "All of them."

"Drunk?"

Riley's silence was the only reply.

"Was she drunk, Riley?" Maisy repeated.

"Probably. But that isn't the point."

"What is?"

"She broke her left femur, and two ribs, and sprained her right wrist."

"I thought you said she was okay." Out of the dark corner of her mind, Maisy felt something move toward her sight, some vague and dark inevitability from which she wanted to run as fast and as far as possible.

"When I said she was okay, I meant she wasn't . . ."

"Dead," Maisy said.

"You are so crass. She's going to be home, but laid up. . . ."

"No way."

"You don't even know what I'm going to say yet."

Maisy closed her eyes. "Yes, I do. You're gonna say I have to come earlier. Stay longer."

"Yes, you have to come home."

"No." Maisy opened her eyes, picked up a wrinkled swatch of fabric and folded it into a neat square. "I'll help you if I can from here, but I can't stay longer than the weekend. I have a job . . . friends, a life."

"Your family needs you. You know the store won't make it if this week's events don't bring in enough . . . money. It will all be gone. You know that."

"Don't pull the family card on me. I don't remember anyone

coming out here to help me. I don't see any Sheffields in Laguna Beach with Maisy."

"You left."

"Yes, I did. And I'm staying. What can I do to help?"

"Take an early plane. Leave your return ticket open-ended." Riley's voice cracked with the strain of rare tears. "Please."

"No," Maisy said again, realizing her answer sounded like a watered-down version of her *no* of only five seconds ago. She knew how this would go—the negative response would become so weak and insipid that soon it would turn into a *maybe*, then a *yes*. She had to hang up before that happened.

Riley's voice strengthened. "I need . . . *We* need you."

"I was only gonna fly in for the party, fly out. The end. I swear, no one but Mama could have figured out how to coincide her seventieth birthday with the anniversary of a two-hundred-year-old house. And now this."

"Stop it."

"Can't you call Adalee and get her to help?"

"I will as soon as I hang up with you."

Static silence on the line sounded like the incoming tide, the filling of the marsh, the cicadas on the back porch, and the rising song of the seagull on a summer night. "No," Maisy repeated. "I can't." She shoved aside her ingrained good manners and hung up on her sister.

Sheila poked her head in the back room. "Everything okay?"

"Just a little Southern family drama."

Sheila laughed. "Don't go thinkin' that drama is only reserved for the South." Her fake Southern accent made Maisy laugh.

"My drunk mama fell down the stairs, broke her leg and other assorted bones. My uptight sister wants me to come home now and help her."

Sheila's smile dropped. "I'm sorry," she said. "I lost my mother two years ago. You do know you have to go, right?"

"Not you, too."

Sheila smiled. "We can do without you—but not for very long."

Maisy sank into a down-cushioned chair and dropped her face into her hands. She exhaled into the truth: she had to go home to Georgia.

THREE

RILEY

*R*iley leaned against her desk with the cell phone pressed to her ear. Night settled around the closed bookstore, blending the shadows into darkness. Adalee had ignored Riley's last four phone calls; finally she answered.

"Hey, sis. What's up?" Loud voices echoed in the background.

"I've been trying to call you all evening," Riley said in a light voice, attempting to hide her frustration.

"I know. I've been . . . busy."

"Where are you?"

"I'm at my boyfriend Chad's house. A party. Is this important?"

"Yes. I'm hoping you can come home a little earlier than you planned because—"

"No way," Adalee interrupted.

"Let me finish," Riley said.

"Well, then let me go outside." Adalee hollered something to Chad, and Riley heard the slam of a door. "Go ahead. What is it?"

Riley repeated everything she'd told Maisy about Mama, and then took a deep breath. "Adalee, can you come home as soon as you finish your last exam? Isn't that tomorrow?"

"I was gonna to Florida with some friends to celebrate the end of the semester. But if Mama is hurt, I'll come now."

"What about your exam tomorrow?"

"I sorta already ed the class. And a couple others."

"Oh, God, Adal Does Mama know?"

"Yes. She's already lectured me. Yelled at me. Told me the implications of laziness. Don't need a lecture from you, too."

"None planned. come home tomorrow. We'll work together—me, you and Maisy."

"Maisy's coming?"

Riley fought a rising jealousy—Adalee had always looked at Maisy with awe, the cooler sister who lived in California. "Yes."

"I'll leave first thing in the morning, but I'm not working at the store, right? I mean it's my summer, my time off."

"Yes, Adalee, you'll be working at the store."

"Ah, no, I won't."

"Yes." Riley slumped into her desk chair.

"We'll see. . . ." Adalee's voice faded, laughter, and then the click of disconnection.

Riley sat in her dark office and hours of frustration. This she would not do: give in and cry. od and stretched, walked through the dim bookstore toward staircase leading to her apartment. Her thoughts were scattered and unquiet; she wasn't prepared, in any way, to deal with the possibility of giving up the store while taking care of Mama and now working with her sisters, too. Yet through the years, she had learned that life never waited until she was ready before it threw the next change at her.

Riley watched the sunrise from the Driftwood Cottage observation tower, just as she did every morning. Before the cottage was moved from its original location on a plantation, this same tower had overseen a cotton field. Riley's quiet soul belonged to the dawn of each day. Her flashlight in one hand, a copy of *The Screwtape Letters* in the other. She in the sole wicker chair and opened to where the leather bookmark indicated; she was almost finished. She stared out over the void of sea and turned the flashlight onto her page. She did her best to read all the books the book clubs had chosen, but instead of reading, she recalled the conversations she'd had with Maisy and Adalee. How had her relationship with her sisters, especially Maisy, turned so wrong, so inside out for so long?

Often in the months before sun climbed into view, and with a book in her hand, a deep longing would rise inside Riley's heart. Normally the logical realities of life consumed her. Taking care of Brayden and before, her mama, and when she thought of it, herself, her joys. Her to-do list was a fortress against loneliness; but was a balm.

When she thought of losing Driftwood Cottage Bookstore, of possibly having to walk away from the slanted floors and crooked bookshelves, of leaving behind the back porch or inviting café, her insides dropped in a rapid freefall. She shook her head—she would not think about that. Not now. But ignoring the possible loss was like trying to ignore a shrill siren. She climbed down from the observation deck, the sun now fully risen, and stood in the middle of the kitchen, unsure of which task to attend to first. Her thoughts and emotions were as scattered as though someone had blown them like dandelion seed on a windy day.

Mama was sick . . . and for all her idiosyncrasies, Kitsy Sheffield was the backbone of the bookstore.

Kitsy had bought Driftwood Cottage from the Logan family twelve years ago. She had seen the opportunity not only to buy her favorite cottage on the beach and open a bookstore, but also to present her pregnant, unwed daughter with a chance to live her own life. During the first days after the news of Riley's pregnancy had settled into the marrow of the Sheffield home, the long and tearful conversations at the kitchen table had ended in Kitsy's offering her personal dream of owning a small coastal bookstore. Kitsy's aspiration became Riley's refuge.

A few months after Brayden's birth, the transformation from Logan family home to fully equipped bookstore had been completed. Driftwood Cottage Bookstore had opened its doors to the town of Palmetto Beach.

Riley and her baby had moved into the upstairs apartment. She and her mother struck a deal in which Kitsy paid for the renovations and the down payment, but Riley must rely on income from the store to pay the mortgage and her own living expenses. In her worst moments, Riley wondered if the arrangement reflected her manipulative mother's bizarre attempt to keep control over her eldest daughter.

Kitsy came to the store every day before noon, dressed as though she were arriving at the luncheon of the year. She flitted from customer to customer, checking on book club picks and reviewing book orders. Her favorite customers—the woman who only read books with blue covers; the man who only read nonfiction with dogs in the story; the mother who read only books without curse words—were the customers who waited for Kitsy. They didn't take advice from Riley or Ethel.

The only nonnegotiable demand Kitsy made was that she must be present when the sales reps from each publishing house made their pitches for the next season's books. Riley had bristled and fought this request until she realized that her mama had a gift for knowing and understanding the needs and wants of her customers. Mama would find an obscure book in the Penguin catalog, know her clientele would like it, and a hundred copies would be sold within the first month of the book's release.

Yet Kitsy wasn't around when it came time to pay the bills. Through the years, they had added up, and each month brought an exacting of blood from Riley's heart—fear that this would be the month when she could no longer pay enough bills to keep afloat, and her mama would sell the store. They both hoped the week of anniversary festivities would bring in enough revenue to tide them over for at least the next year. Now Riley had a new and more urgent reason to make this week a success—Mama's ill health.

Riley leaned down next to the stairs, which led to the bookstore below, and straightened a stack of fallen books she had meant to take back downstairs. After she yanked her long, unruly hair into a ponytail, she opened her son's bedroom door and stared at his sleeping form. He had kicked off his covers and was curled in a ball with his T-shirt and gym shorts scrunched around his body. When Gamma had given him tractor jammies for Christmas this past year, he'd informed Riley "no more jammies."

His alarm clock screeched, yet he didn't stir. This boy knew how to sleep hard and long, and Riley imagined that he grew with every passing hour, even while unconscious. She turned off his alarm clock, kissed his warm cheek. "Time to get up, buddy. Only one day left of school . . . You can do it."

He groaned without opening his eyes. The shadowed forms of baseball trophies, schoolbooks and fishing poles seemed to capture his boyhood. Riley's heart filled with gratitude.

"Mom, call me in sick."

"No way. Get up." She shook the bed and resisted the urge to kiss him one more time. She flicked on his overhead and bedside lights. "Now."

"I hate school."

"Oh, well. Last day." She headed to the kitchen to make his favorite: scrambled eggs and bacon on a bagel. The sounds of Anne McComus opening the café downstairs joined the smell of the gourmet coffee she brewed. The bookstore would soon come to life.

Half an hour later, Brayden and Riley opened the door at the bottom of their staircase, which led directly into the café. Anne was singing out loud to the Jack Johnson CD playing through the

speakers. She arranged the muffins in the display cabinet; her flap-
ping ponytail and tight T-shirts with various slogans were main-
stays of the café. Today she wore a Driftwood Cottage Bookstore
T-shirt that stated *The Original Laptop . . . Books.*

Anne only worked in the store to finance her hobby of crafting
pottery angel's wings. She had an uncanny ability to make delicate wings out of fired clay and then carve a single word between
the wings. She chose words like PEACE, SERENITY, FORGIVE. A
customer would come in, see her collection in the gift section and
then ask Anne to make them their own special angel. Anne would
do so without ever asking what angel they wanted—somehow she
knew.

Riley returned Anne's good morning hug—Anne would never
let anyone pass without a hug—and then began a checklist in
her mind: finish the bookstore newsletter, check on the Harcourt
shipment, meet with Anne about stationery reorders for the gift
section. . . .

Riley kissed Brayden goodbye, and then the day passed in a
flurry of arranging for Mama's return home, making calls to her
sisters and dealing with other details as irritating as the no-see-
ums that buzzed around the store when the doors were left open.
Late afternoon arrived before Ethel leaned through the open office door. "Hey, Riley, the newspaper guy is here." She pointed her
gloved finger toward the entrance.

Riley squinted at the front door; she needed to get her vision checked, but that task was moving further down her to-do
list. Lodge Barton, the newspaper editor, walked toward the front

desk, dressed in his usual white wrinkled button-down shirt and khaki chinos, his tortoiseshell glasses awry.

Riley ran a hand through her hair. She'd forgotten he was coming. "Tell him I'll be out in a minute."

Riley combed her hair loose of its ponytail and stepped into the bookstore. Lodge waved from across the room. She'd known him since elementary school, and felt a comfort level with him that she shared with all those who'd grown up in a summer-resort town.

Riley stood on her tiptoes to hug Lodge. He was tall, had been since fifth grade when he was hit by an early growth spurt. Now at only thirty-one, he sported premature gray in his goatee and at his temples. His glasses had been crooked since her first memory of him, as if his nose just couldn't hold them straight. He ran the town's newspaper, had won the trust and devotion of the entire population despite their not always agreeing with him. Riley seated herself in a threadbare upholstered chair, motioned for him to sit next to her in a ladder-back chair with peeling white paint.

"You look great, Riley."

"You always say that, you goofball." She placed her hand on his arm.

He shrugged. "Well, it's always true."

"Thanks for doing this article," she said. "I hope it gets picked up by some other local papers and loads of people want to come to the events. I really want this festival of activities to be hugely successful . . . for everyone."

"No problem," he said. "Let's get started. Tell me a quick history of the house and why you're having a whole week's worth of events."

"Let's see—where should I start?" Riley stared up at the ceiling, the stories, the lives of this house running through her mind like a rapid-sequence slideshow.

"How about starting with how old the house is," he said.

She smiled. "Two hundred years old this year. Thus the two-hundred-year party." She poked at Lodge with her elbow.

He grinned with his cute, crooked smile. "Go ahead, smart-ass."

"This structure was the main home of an early-eighteen-hundreds cotton plantation owner. The house had an unusual floor plan for that time." Riley spread her arms as if to encompass the main room. "There is this large center area, and then four corner rooms, which we've made into offices, storage, the café and the Book Club Corner. Then there is the second story, which is where Brayden and I live. And then the observation tower on top, which once looked over the cotton fields." She pointed to each corner of the house as she spoke.

"You look like a flight attendant," Lodge said, writing in his pad. "Here are the emergency exits, and . . ." He laughed.

"Thanks. You're always so sweet to me."

He looked up, straightened his glasses. "I try."

She grinned and shook her head. "Anyway, the outside of the house is made of tabby—a mixture of lime, oyster shells and cement. We've had to add some siding through the years. The house was moved from its original location on the riverbank when a development went in forty years ago."

"How did you all come up with the name Driftwood Cottage Bookstore?"

"When they first moved the house, it looked like a piece of driftwood dropped onto the beach. We just added the word 'bookstore.'"

Lodge tapped his pencil on the side of the chair. "I never knew that."

"That would be why you're interviewing me. I do know."

"Yeah, that's why." His laughter was as full and free as it had been as a child, all those years before he lost his wife.

"And maybe you can use this—Norse myth says that the first humans were made from driftwood."

He nodded. "Isn't there also a myth about the house?"

"The first owner after the house was moved here said that the cottage offered *happy* connections to all those who passed through its doors. She was a big E. M. Forster fan and believed in that epigraph from *Howards End*. You know that one, right?"

"'Only Connect. . . .'"

"A man who knows his books." She smiled.

"So all the families who live here end up happy?"

"It might not look like it at any particular moment because you have to go all the way to the end of the story—you can't just stay in the middle of it. You have to see where the connections go."

"Good point. I'm quoting." He scribbled on his pad, and then glanced up at her over the top of his glasses. "You have done that thing with your hair since I've known you."

"What?"

"Where you brush it off your shoulder. Right before you say something, you do that."

"I do not."

"Okay," he said, leaned back in the chair. "Now give me a story, make this a human interest piece."

Yes, she thought, *Mama might be dying and this is her last hurrah.* The morbid and unbidden thought caused her to shiver. She was quite sure Mama would not want Lodge to include in his article her fall down the stairs, her cancer.

Riley forced her hand to stay in her lap when she felt it lifting to brush her hair away from her face. "Well, coincidentally the anniversary year coincides with Mama's seventieth birthday, so we are combining the celebrations. Mama started the store twelve years ago, and it has offered a home not only to my son and me, but also to the town. This is where we meet friends and discuss our lives as well as books. This is where we catch up on the town news. This is where we bring our children for art classes. It's become a community-gathering place, one of those sacred places for a fragmented world. A refuge. That's what I think this place has always been."

"Refuge," he said. "Okay, who's invited to the festivities?"

"Anyone. Everyone. Most of the town, and we did send invitations to all the previous owners of the house, and to all of the former summer people we could track down."

"Previous owners? How many do you know about?"

"At least three families, then it gets iffy. Mack and Sheppard Logan are coming. . . ."

"Mack Logan," Lodge said, wrote down the name, then looked up and smiled. "Old boyfriend . . ."

"Not mine. . . . That was Maisy."

"Oh." Lodge stared off toward the window, then back. "Well, I remember you and Mack being inseparable."

"Childhood friends," Riley said.

"Of course. Thanks for all the info." Lodge stood, held his hand out to pull Riley upright. "Hey, is Brayden fishing today?"

"I'm sure he is. It's the last day of school. He'll probably be at the pier before the bell stops ringing."

"Well, tell him I'll be down there if he wants to . . . fish today."

"Brayden would fish every day, all day if he could."

Lodge touched Riley's arm, ran his finger down to a place on her right wrist where a fishhook had left a curled, comma-shaped scar. "I once knew a girl who would fish all day, every day, also."

"It's amazing," Riley said, "what we pass on to our kids without meaning to."

"When's the last time you went to the pier?" Logan shoved his notebook into a worn leather portfolio.

"I go almost every day," she said.

"I mean to do more than pick up your son."

Riley had no intention of answering that question. She smiled. "Thanks so much for writing this article. Let me know if you think of something you forgot to ask."

Logan nodded. "Got it."

He walked out the front door, waved over his shoulder without turning around. Riley exhaled and returned to her office, to her work. Constant reminders of who you were as a child was one of the distinct disadvantages of living in your hometown. Her sisters didn't have such worries. They'd been able to start over elsewhere, become someone new and move on. Sometimes, like right at that moment, Riley felt a twinge of cowardice; the farthest she'd gone from home was two blocks. The separate life she'd built rested within shouting distance of her childhood.

The Driftwood Cottage Bookstore's plaster walls, wide-plank hardwood floors, cedar crossbeams and crooked back steps were as much a part of her life now as the Sheffield bones and blood that formed her. Each family that had passed through the rooms of this cottage had its own story to tell—of grief and joy, disaster and triumph. Riley had always thought it fitting that a place that had contributed to so much of the town's story now held volumes of stories from floor to ceiling.

It was, she'd found, only in her favorite books that the world worked out exactly as it should. Family and Brayden filled the lonely places. Work helped, and books healed.

Four

Riley watched Brayden burst through the kitchen door with the grin of a child just released from school for the summer. Riley hugged him. "Come on, punk. I'll walk you to the pier. Then I have to go see Gamma in the hospital."

"Let me change. . . ." Brayden ran for his room and reappeared in record time, wearing a baseball hat, ragged T-shirt and bathing suit, his uniform for the next three months. "Poor Gamma," he said, opening the door to the crooked stairs that led to the bookstore below.

"Yes," Riley said. "Poor Gamma." She followed him down the stairs.

The only way out of their apartment was down the stairs and through the bookstore. When Brayden was a toddler, these crooked and creaking stairs were a nightmare. Riley had been constantly afraid he would tumble down them, break his tiny neck. She remembered the days when she had sat curled and alone in this staircase during those terrible first weeks of being a single mother, exhausted and overwhelmed with the new life she had borne. In the darkness she had allowed herself to weep. In the light, in her life, in her apartment above the bookstore she never, not once, wept over the creation of Brayden Collins Sheffield.

Brayden pushed open the bottom door with his foot and they stepped into the bookstore. Anne stood behind the coffee counter, a smudge of orange glaze on her nose, and placed a steaming cup of skinny latte—Riley's afternoon habit—onto the counter. "Hey, Riley."

Riley picked up the coffee, took a long swallow. "You've got angel glaze on your nose."

"Ah, I made an Angel of Truth for my friend whose husband seems to tell everything but . . ."

"Truth . . ." Riley said, and then did her quick and every-afternoon inventory of the store, making sure everything was in its place. The stationery section was orderly and appealing with handmade cards, journals and small gifts for customers on their way to a baby shower, birthday party or wedding. Anne wrapped these trinkets in the finest hand-blocked paper, and whenever someone received a gift in the Driftwood Cottage Bookstore's signature brown-and-blue paper, they knew they'd received a high-quality or handmade gift.

When Riley finished her bookstore routine, she walked Brayden to the pier, where a group of boys waved him to the end of the long wooden structure. She knew better than to kiss him goodbye, watched him run to his friends and then stood for a moment taking in the scene. Humidity had moved in for the season, but the summer people hadn't arrived quite yet and the beach was largely deserted, the tide high. Riley relished this time before the summer rush, when traffic was light and the sounds of the sea more audible.

Soon enough the two-lane main road would be jammed with the returning crowds. She and her sisters used to love waiting for their summer friends. Every year she'd stood at the end of this very pier, waiting for the arrival of the Logan family, for Mack to sneak up behind her while she fished and slap her on the back, half trying to knock her off her feet. One time, two weeks into summer, he'd found her in the dark on the edge of the pier. . . .

The day had ended as most days did that summer for twelve-year-old Riley—nightfall arriving without her noticing until she was the only one left on the dock. Low clouds pregnant with rain covered the moon and hid the stars.

Then Mack joined her. They lay back on the dock, life seeming simple in its small graces: an evening crafted from the sound of slapping waves, the cooling comfort of shaved ice amidst a heat wave, a mist from unshed rain, a foghorn sounding far off.

They'd stared into the darkness. Their arms and legs touched, sticky with salt sweat, without any self-consciousness. Mack's knobby elbow poked against the soft inside of Riley's arm; she felt his rough scab from last week's skateboard fall. His legs were moist against hers, his left foot underneath her right. His upper arm rested against hers. Suddenly it was as if they had become one body; she couldn't feel where hers stopped and his began. Fear prickled the edge of her thoughts—what if she became lost in feeling him and never felt like her separate self again?

Despite this fear, she couldn't move, the tangle of arms and legs more important than the loss her own being.

He spoke first. "It's so dark."

"I know," she said, her whisper all at once that of someone older.

"It feels like there's only one of us," he said.

She didn't speak again, knowing that this was what she wanted—this oneness—but not able to understand how or why. Time dissolved, and she didn't know how long they stayed that way, only that she didn't speak until he did.

"I'm sorry I punched Candler today," he said.

"Don't be sorry," she said, beginning to feel her own toes, her own skin. Relieved, yet noting the loss, too.

They didn't move for moments longer.

"I know he's a friend of yours from school and all, but damn, he's not allowed to pick on you like that."

"He's done that since he moved here a few years ago—I just think he hates that I beat him at everything."

"He still can't . . . do that. He hit you, Riley. No one is ever allowed to hit you."

"I know, but I would have punched him back."

He moved imperceptibly, a tiny movement that might not have been a movement at all, but then she felt her body: her toes, then her legs, her arms and then her rapid heartbeat. They were separate now and he stood, held his hand out to pull her up.

Their words faded into the darkness as if they were spoken and unspoken at the same time; as if they were important and yet not at all, as if they were two people talking or maybe just one. Darkness, she understood later, easily confused the meaning of words, of skin touching skin.

In their remaining summers together she tried to find that oneness again. When it was all over, when youth ended and he chose Maisy, she understood the lesson from the dock that night: she could never again call her feelings of intimacy and oneness love. Nor would she be fooled again into believing that her love was returned, that a boy felt more for her than friendship.

Riley looked down the length of Pearson's Pier and watched her son bait his hook, reminded herself to live in the moment while remembering the lessons of the past.

The walk to the hospital ran north along the beach, then west at Sixth Avenue for five blocks inland. As she went through the front doors of the hospital, she shoved away the memory of her daddy's last days here with lung cancer, his lucidity returning only briefly before agony followed when one morphine shot wore off and the next hadn't yet arrived. She had rushed her words during those brief respites, in a hurry to tell him how much she loved him, how much he'd meant to her, how she cherished him, all the while wondering why she hadn't said these words all her life.

Kitsy Sheffield's hospital room was on the fourth floor. Riley kissed her sleeping mama on the cheek, and grabbed the chart hanging off the bottom of the bed to read the night's statistics—

temperature, blood pressure and urine output. She'd learned the lingo during Daddy's illness.

Kitsy opened her eyes. "Where have you been?"

"Right here." Riley took her mama's hand and smiled. "And you?"

"Is that supposed to be funny?" Kitsy fashioned her eyes into narrow slits through which Riley had no idea how she could see.

"Unfortunately, yes. That was supposed to be funny. I was working, and then I waited for Brayden to come home after his last day of school."

"I was here alone all night, and then for most of today. What if they'd given me the wrong medication, or . . . forgotten about me?"

"Mama, I can't sleep here—I have Brayden. And I can't imagine who could ever, ever forget about you."

"Where are your sisters?"

Riley squeezed her hand. "They're both on their way. Adalee is driving down from the university this morning; I talked to her last night. Maisy is flying in tomorrow afternoon, five days earlier than she was supposed to come."

Kitsy's eyes opened wide. "Maisy is coming early? You mean, all this time, all these years, all I had to do was fall down the damn staircase to make her come home? So, all my girls will finally be here."

Riley laughed and released her mama's hand, dug into her purse for a muffin wrapped in a napkin. "I brought you contraband—your favorite cranberry muffin from the store."

Kisty attempted to scoot up in bed, but with her ribs wrapped and her wrist in a cast, she couldn't move. She exhaled. "Thanks, darling. Now give me updates on the party."

"Mama, you've only been here for one day. There's nothing new to report."

"I will delegate responsibilities to each of you girls," Kitsy said as she held her muffin in the air. "I have sorted it in my mind and I want to tell each of you what to do. I can still write. Thank God I sprained my left wrist." She held up her muffin. "You'll help me and take notes, Maisy will stay for the summer and Adalee will run—"

"Whoa, Mama. Your only job right now is to get better. We can handle the rest."

"No, you can't. I'm the only one who understands the big picture."

"Just prepare yourself for a couple of reality checks. I highly doubt Maisy will stay for more than a week, if that long, and Adalee sounded like we'd ruined her summer. I'm not sure how much help she'll be."

"Oh, that will change when I talk to them." Kitsy took a bite of the muffin. "You'll see."

Riley leaned back in the hard metal chair and breathed in the scents of multiple flower arrangements around the room. "It's all under control, Mama."

"Now you listen to me, young lady. Just because I'm all tied down in a hospital bed does not mean that I am not in charge. It does not mean you can sass me back or tell me what to do. Do you understand?"

"Mama, quit it. Don't talk to me like I'm twelve years old."

Kitsy closed her eyes. "God, sometimes I wish you were. Then I could change so much about what has happened."

"What is that supposed to mean?" Riley stood up, offended.

"You know exactly what it means. I would never have let you go out that night with a boy who forced himself on you. I would have made sure you finished college, got a degree."

"Mama, I'd like to blame this tirade of yours on some kind of drug you're on, but sadly, I can't. Your hurtful words aren't softened just because you're lying in bed with casts and bruises. No one ever forced himself on me. So stop it."

Mama's anger was legendary. There were rants at the dinner table about her daughters' grades, fiery speeches in the town hall over the installation of the new stoplight and public outcries about Mayor Friscoe's affair with his son's second-grade teacher. The storms always passed as quickly as they came and Mama's remorse was genuine each time.

"Oh, baby. You know I don't mean it. My hip is throbbing with some kind of new pain I've never felt before. I can't roll over. My ribs hurt every time I take a breath and they won't give me any more pain meds until Doc comes in this morning. I didn't mean to take it out on you." Tears formed in the corners of her eyes.

"I know," Riley said, as she leaned back in the chair and closed her eyes. God, how many times had this scene been repeated? Somehow Kitsy Sheffield managed to apologize without ever saying "Sorry" or "Forgive me."

Dr. Foster's presence at the bedside startled Riley. "Where did you come from?"

"Snuck in while you two were bickering." He smiled.

"How is she?" Riley pointed to Mama.

"Don't be talking about me like I'm in a coma," Kitsy warned. "I'm right here."

Riley rolled her eyes at Dr. Foster. "Please tell me that the drugs you're giving her are what's making her so mean."

He laughed, picked Kitsy's chart off the end of the bed. "The meds and the pain—the combination often puts patients in foul moods."

"Stop it," Kitsy hollered, slammed her free hand on the metal bed rail; muffin crumbs landed on the floor. "I'm. Right. Here."

Dr. Foster slipped his stethoscope under her hospital gown and listened to her chest, then looked up, spoke directly to her. "I was worried about your lungs, but you sound fine and the scan is normal. You can go home tomorrow, but you'll need plenty of help. We'll have to arrange for home care . . . unless . . . ." He looked directly at Riley. "Unless you can take care of her full-time."

"No." Riley exhaled the word with more force than she'd meant to show.

"Absolutely not," Kitsy said in unison. "We can hire help. Riley has a son, a store to run and a week's worth of parties to finish arranging."

Dr. Foster looked down at Kitsy over his glasses, which were perched on the end of his nose. "Now you be sweet to your daughter, and I'll send the social worker in to help make arrangements."

Kitsy batted her eyelashes at Dr. Foster—Riley swore her mother had just flirted with the doctor.

Kitsy's eyes filled with tears again and Riley saw, as she often did, the needy woman underneath the tough exterior. Mama had learned early how to use her wiles to get what she wanted. But there was another side to her that appeared when she and Riley discussed books and running the store together. If Riley lost the store, she feared that she would also lose that sweet connection with her mother. No matter what Mama said, Riley understood that saving this store was as important to Mama as it was to her.

The door swished shut and Riley sat down, pulled her chair up next to Mama. "You have to tell me everything about this chondrosarcoma. I will not let you ignore your health just for a party."

Kitsy looked toward the window. "Listen, Riley. Waiting a week or two to get treatment won't matter. It's a rare form of bone cancer." Kitsy smiled. "Of course I'd get the rare form. It's only stage one because we caught it early. I need surgery—that's the first step: remove it. I have decided to do it at a specialty sarcoma center. After that we're talking about other treatment, depending on how I do. Fiddle dee dee . . ." She made a gesture of dismissal.

"That's not funny, Mama."

"Of course it is."

"Where is this specialty center and when are you going? Why can't I tell Maisy and Adalee? Why can't you go now?"

Kitsy closed her eyes. "M. D. Anderson is in Houston, Texas. No, you can't tell your sisters and of course we can't go now. Maisy and Adalee are coming to see me." She opened her eyes. "Don't you see? They're coming here, now. All of us will be together."

"Okay," Riley whispered. "But why Texas?"

"Because they're the best, that's why. Of course"—Kitsy's voice lowered—"you know how we—you and me—choose the books we order for the store? How we know what the book clubs will want? You know how we don't talk about it to anyone else, ever?"

"Yes, Mama."

"This bone cancer is the same thing. It is ours to keep until we need to share it with everyone else. Okay?"

Riley nodded, swallowed the tears her mama hated to see fall. "That's just it. I can't run the store without you."

Kitsy's eyebrows lifted. "You have never, ever said that before, Riley."

"Said what?"

"That you can't do without me." Mama turned her head away.

"I'm sure I have. I definitely have told you that. The store is . . . hollow without you. You're its heart. I'm just its arms and legs."

Kitsy didn't look back at Riley. "You can go now, dear. I need to rest."

Riley didn't move, holding Mama's hand in her own. A nurse entered the room, pushed a clear liquid into the port of the IV. Kitsy looked back at Riley, squinted. "I think I'll sleep for a bit. Don't you dare go adding that stupid Create Bad Art Night to the week's events just because I'm laid up in bed. No decent bookstore has a Create Bad Art Night."

"Mama, relax. It's called Artist Night."

"That's what I said," Kitsy mumbled, and closed her eyes.

Riley gathered her belongings and kissed her mother on the

forehead before she left the room. Of course she'd already added Artist Night, in which all local artists would come to display and sell their art—just one more chance for the bookstore to make some profit.

On the walk back to the store, Riley stood on the sidewalk that ran parallel to the beach, where sprigs of grass sprouted through the cracked concrete. The number seven lifeguard stand stood in front of Riley, blocking her view to the water's edge. What if her mama was right? What if Riley hadn't gone out that night? Maybe she wouldn't have crawled into the vacant lifeguard stand while a bonfire roared farther down the beach, and inside her heart.

A broken heart, too much cold beer, ocean waves and a willing man were never a good combination, no matter what the country songs said. Riley walked to the lifeguard stand, touched its base and wondered if in every woman's life, there was a night she didn't talk about, a night that had changed everything.

FIVE

MAISY

aisy stared out the window, dropped her forehead onto the double-paned glass, her ears popping from the descent into Savannah. Winding waterways carved the land into marsh-bordered islands. The water reflected the setting sun, throwing the light back in glitter. The beauty here felt bound to her soul. Perhaps she had only fooled herself into believing she had severed the tie. The four-and-a-half-hour flight from Laguna to Atlanta, and then Atlanta to Savannah was more than a passage from coast to coast, more than a three-thousand-mile journey. It was a passage through time back to her childhood, back to when she left twelve years ago.

Even high in the sky, Maisy sensed the pungent air of her hometown, the salt smell of sea and marsh. She closed her eyes and imagined her California comfort points: her apartment decorated just the way she liked it, Peter holding her and telling her he loved her, the beautiful fabric and furniture in the store. She had longed for Peter to come with her on this trip; she'd even been foolish enough to ask. But he didn't know how to explain to his wife why he would make a trip to Georgia. Yes, his wife. Maybe, just maybe, this week away would make Peter miss Maisy enough to finally leave his wife.

Maisy reminded herself of all the reasons she'd left Palmetto Beach in the first place. Well, not *all* the reasons. First of all, who would want to live in a place that was practically empty three-quarters of the year? Her eyes swept to the east, toward Palmetto Beach, a blur on the horizon, a forty-minute drive from Savannah. Her hometown was meant for visiting. The population more than doubled by Memorial Day. Some of the houses where the townies lived full-time were smaller than those the summer people inhabited for three months.

Escape was all Maisy had wanted, yet she'd also loved the summer people because they made the town come alive. The school year had been a breath-holding wait for summer. Maisy had often wanted to be one of them—coming into town on Memorial Day with a car packed full of bikes, swimsuits, suitcases and beach toys on top of the car. She imagined they lived glittering, fabulous lives in Philadelphia, New York or Indiana in a mansion on a hill or a penthouse in the city.

The summer people came from *someplace else*, but in the end they all dug their toes into the same sand and bought ice-cream cones from the same shack next to the boardwalk. What was fleeting and dreamlike to the guests had once been Maisy's mainstay.

What had been their reprieve had been her permanent dockage. Not anymore.

When the cars would arrive on Memorial Day weekend—station wagons, Mercedes, Volvos, sometimes the dad following in his Porsche—the three sisters would gossip about each family, and joke about the silly names they called their cottages: Shore Thing; Big Chill; Merilee by the Sea; Sandity, etc. . . . .

"Ah, the crazy Whitmans are here. I wonder if their aunt will skinny-dip in the country club pool again," Adalee would say.

"The Murphy brothers came again. . . . I wonder if Danny is here or if he ended up in military school," Riley would say.

Maisy and her two sisters didn't need the movies; they had the summer people and their stories, their secrets: which wives cheated on their husbands when the men left for the week to work; whose "perfect" kids bought pot from the local boys; whose mother needed a scotch on the rocks by ten a.m.

To the vacationers, they had always been the Sheffield sisters, one entity. Back then Maisy would have followed Riley anywhere. And she had. . . . While the plane descended, Maisy remembered the night their sister Adalee was born and Maisy had followed Riley into the woods.

Ten and nine years old, Riley and Maisy had watched from the bedroom window as Mama and Daddy drove off to the hospital in the family wood-paneled Ford station wagon.

Maisy whispered to her older sister, who always knew what to do, where to go, who to be, "We're alone. We're not supposed to stay in the house alone. Not ever."

"No." Riley placed her hands on Maisy's shoulders. "They

wouldn't leave us alone in the house. They sent for Harriet. I'm sure Harriet is on her way."

They crouched beneath Riley's covers and waited as evening turned to deep night and Harriet didn't show. Maisy finally said the dreaded words: "They forgot about us."

"No," Riley said with a certainty that Maisy envied. She never felt certain about anything, always wavering.

Time passed and finally Riley threw off the covers. "Let's go. We aren't allowed home without a grown-up. Mama and Daddy said it's very dangerous."

"Where will we go?" Maisy fought back the sobs that wanted to rise from her stomach. She was counting on Riley to know the right thing to do.

"Outside. We'll go outside. We just can't be in this house alone."

Maisy had often felt alone in the Sheffield house, even when Daddy and Mama were in the drawing room reading or talking. Mama's attention went elsewhere after five p.m. when she had her first martini, while she waited for Daddy to come home. Daddy worked at the military base an hour away, and was often gone on trips. His absence was as palpable as his presence.

"We can't go outside in the middle of the night," Maisy said in a small voice, panic clamping her throat shut.

"We can't stay here." Riley sounded so like their mama that Maisy could only follow.

They took the quilt from Riley's bed and walked out the back door to the woods behind their house. "Why can't we go to the beach?" Maisy asked.

"Because we need to stay hidden," Riley said.

"Yes. Hidden." Maisy understood.

When the Palmetto Bluff police found them the next morning, curled into each other on a bed of pine straw under a quilt, the entire town had already begun a search. They returned to Daddy, who was standing on the back porch with fatigue and worry etched in deeper places on his face. "You have a new sister," he said, and walked away, leaving Maisy and Riley with two officers.

The taller man spoke first. "You scared your father to death. What were you thinking?"

Riley stepped toward the officer as if she were older, taller than she was. "It's quite simple, sir. We are not allowed to be home alone."

The two men looked at Maisy and she nodded. "We aren't."

The officer patted Riley on the back. "You're a good little girl, then, aren't you?"

Riley screwed up her face. "Of course I am."

Together Maisy and Riley walked into the house. Maisy reached for Riley's hand and Riley squeezed her sister's fingers. "Another sister. How much fun."

Maisy never asked her parents why they were left alone that night, and the subject was never brought up again. Adalee came home and life continued. Whenever Mama told the story of the night Adalee was born, she never mentioned the fact that the police were sent to look for her two older daughters; she merely spoke of the quick birth and her bravery in not requesting pain medication.

*   *   *

Those were the good days with her sister, Maisy thought, the days before the betrayal.

Maisy had been gone for many years now. Her excuses for not coming home were usually loud and insistent, but now they began to sound tinny, small, not really excuses at all. California had aided in her quest to stay away from Riley, from Palmetto Beach. The fact remained: Riley had betrayed Maisy and she had vowed never to speak to Riley again beyond what was required by family obligation. The anger she'd nurtured toward Riley now nestled dormant inside a corner of her heart.

The summer before Maisy ran away, right after high school graduation, while Mama and Daddy were preoccupied with buying the Logans' cottage and adoring baby Brayden, Maisy had wandered the beach and partied with friends, miserable because her first real love, Mack Logan, had not returned for her as he'd promised. The last summer in Palmetto Beach had culminated in a night of losing her virginity with her best friend's fiancé, Tucker Morgan, in the vacant Driftwood Cottage. Maybe she'd been looking for an excuse to leave Palmetto Beach; if so, she'd sure as hell given herself one. She'd done a terrible thing, and exile, self-imposed, was part penance, part pure running away.

Funny thing, she'd assumed the deed would eventually catch up with her. She didn't expect she'd be the one returning to the scene of her disgrace.

The plane skidded to a stop on the runway. Maisy was the last to disembark, allowing the other passengers out while she gathered her belongings. She dragged her carry-on down the aisle, then stopped outside the gate to call Peter before she faced her sister downstairs at the luggage carousel. Her cell phone was crammed into the bottom of her purse, and she sat on a chair while she dug it out. She dialed his number and held her breath. This was always the moment when her stomach clenched and her heart raced—would he answer? Would he be with his wife and pretend it was a business call? Would he be alone and able to speak the words of love she needed to hear?

She'd met Peter at a cocktail party for her friend Andy's thirtieth birthday. Peter had come up behind her, and when she'd turned, she'd walked right into him. She looked up to his face to apologize and found herself speechless, not because he was more beautiful than any man she'd seen but because of the kind way he smiled down at her. They'd talked for hours that night, and then kept in contact by phone before she realized he was married. She found out when she bumped into a girlfriend at the farmers' market while shopping for fresh fruit. The friend told her that of course Peter was planning on leaving his wife; he'd told everyone. But he hadn't left . . . yet.

Maisy had tried numerous times over the past six months to break off the relationship, but her heart wouldn't allow it. Peter was like an undertow that caught her over and over in the tumult of his words and touch. This was the second time she'd found herself caught in a wild ride of emotions with a married man. After the first one, she'd vowed never again—but this time she was in love before she knew about his wife.

Peter's kind words, his way of touching her, his knowing just what she needed to hear, pulled her back whenever she tried to walk away. The phone rang until his voice mail picked up. She slammed the cell phone shut and pulled the handle out on her rollaway to head down the hallway. She held her breath as she descended the escalator to the baggage-claim area. Maisy saw Riley before Riley saw her, offering Maisy the chance to take in her sister.

Riley stood near a pillar on her tiptoes, scanning the crowd. When had she lost her athletic, boyish look? When had she grown her blond hair halfway down her back? All this time Maisy had pictured the sister she'd left, not this one standing in the middle of the crowded airport.

Riley had always been the rock of the family. Still was. She made even unwed motherhood look responsible. Anger unwittingly rose inside Maisy. Suddenly she was—once again—irresponsible, young, wild.

With a deep breath, Maisy reminded herself of who she was *now*: a fabulous interior designer with a lovely, well-furnished apartment overlooking Laguna Bay. She was a capable woman. She had good friends, a creative job, a man who loved her, a full life.

"Maisy!" Riley's voice sang across the space.

Maisy raised her hand in a greeting, rolled her suitcase off the escalator, where it bumped the edge of the metal railing and tipped. Riley picked it up with one hand, but seemed awkward in her indecision over whether to offer a hug with her free arm. "I thought for a minute you changed your mind and didn't come."

"Almost," Maisy attempted to joke, returning the half hug.

Riley led them toward the luggage carousel. "You look great. A true California girl now, huh?"

Maisy glanced at her sister, her smile stiff. "You look fantastic, too." She stopped. "We don't need to wait for luggage." She tapped her carry-on. "This is all I brought."

Riley stopped, turned. Her hair fell across her face. "You only have one bag?"

"I'm not staying long, Riley. I can't. I just came to check on Mama and help you for a couple days. If I need anything, I'm sure you'll have something I can borrow."

"Maisy, I'm twice your size."

"Not anymore, big sister. Look at you. Is Mama working you to the bone?"

Riley looked down at her feet, as if the answer rested on the tile floor. "That's not the point. We have all got to help one another get this party off the ground, help Mama. . . ."

Maisy wheeled her luggage toward the electronic doors. "Let's go. I can't wait to get some sleep in my old bed. . . ."

They walked in silence toward the parking lot, Maisy behind Riley in some ritual of youth: following her big sister. Just landing on the tarmac of south Georgia had set her back twelve years.

She attempted conversation. "How's Mama?"

"Ornery. They've allowed her to come home, but she has a full-time nurse and Harriet."

"This should be fun."

"Oh, loads of fun. Thanks for coming. We really need you. You know how much this store means to Mama and how long she's planned this party."

"It shouldn't be my fault that Mama loves the bookstore more than she loves most people."

"That is ridiculous. Stop it. You've broken her heart by not visiting sooner."

Maisy held up her hand to stop the conversation. "No, Riley. We're not doing this. I'll do what I can to help, but I'm not getting dragged into family fights." Maisy took a breath. "So how is my adorable nephew?"

"He can't wait to see his aunt Maisy. He thinks you only exist in pictures."

"Kind of like a movie star, right?"

Riley laughed. "He's great; he's the light of my life. It's weird to think you haven't seen him since Daddy's funeral. He was only six years old then."

"I know." Maisy kept her words light to hide the emotion caught in her throat.

The car trip chatter was as shallow as the tidal pools on Palmetto Beach. Maisy felt like a stranger, discussing trivia as insignificant as job satisfaction, weather and lack of plane food. When Riley drove past the *Welcome to Palmetto Beach* sign, Maisy sighed out loud.

"Glad to be here?" Riley asked in a soft voice.

"No," Maisy answered. Damn Mama's martinis. Damn the family responsibility that had been so etched into her soul that she'd had no choice but to come.

"Well, so glad we'll have a happy Maisy while you're here. Can't you just pretend?"

"No."

Riley stopped the car at a red light. "Seriously, Maisy. There are worse things in life than coming to your childhood beach town to see your family."

Maisy rolled down the window. "I know. It just doesn't feel like it right now. I'm tired. I miss Peter." She stared through the open window.

The stoplight turned green and Riley drove down Palmetto Street before turning right into the gravel drive of Driftwood Cottage. "I have to grab Brayden before we go to Mama's. Okay?"

"I'll stay in the car," Maisy said.

"Of course you won't. Come on."

Anxiety and expectancy combined with Maisy's fatigue from the sleepless night she'd spent in anticipation of this: walking into the bookstore where townspeople would see her, know her, talk about her. . . .

Maisy looked up at a white banner taped across the front porch. *"WELCOME HOME MAISY"* said the sign, which was decorated along the edges in vivid drawings of starfish, sand dollars and a dolphin.

Maisy pointed to the sign. "Brayden?"

"Of course."

Maisy stepped out of the car, stretched and felt the stiff-boned ache of having sat in a plane seat for hours. Then the hometown coastal air filled her lungs, her heart; tears threatened. She shifted her gaze to the left and saw it: Driftwood Beach—that slip of sand in front of the cottage. Her life, in part, had been lived on that stretch of gray-white sand. How could she have believed she'd left it for good?

She turned away, climbed the front steps behind Riley and entered Driftwood Cottage.

A commotion at the front of the store grabbed Maisy's attention. "Time for the Driftwood Book Club," Riley told her. "This is the club that reads books suggested by the store. They're reading *Peachtree Road* by Anne Rivers Siddons." Riley's exhale made Maisy think of their mama, who could convey a world of emotion with a released breath. "Mrs. Lithgow must be here."

"What?" Maisy felt the sounds and sights of the cottage coming at her as if through cotton batting, muffled and cushioned: an upset lady; the aroma of coffee; faint music; soft laughter.

"I begged Verandah House to make sure she stayed home on book club day," Riley said, looking over her shoulder at Maisy. "She is an older woman who thinks she wrote every book I pick for the club. Since Verandah House is a retirement community and not a nursing home, its administrators won't take responsibility for Mrs. Lithgow walking the two blocks over here."

Maisy pushed past the other incoming sensations to hear an older, shaky voice. "My intent was to divulge the larger story of redemption, to write the Southern novel of our generation, not have it analyzed by women who have never even been to Atlanta. When I opened the book with 'The South killed Lucy . . .' I meant it both literally and metaphorically. It doesn't have to be either-or, does it?"

Riley sidled up behind the older woman, whose flailing arms sent her gold bracelets jangling. She placed her hand on the woman's shoulder. "Mrs. Lithgow, thank you so much for your input. Why don't we sit down and listen to what the others have to say on the subject?"

Mrs. Lithgow spun around on her loafers, pushed puffs of hair from her face. Her eyes misted with anger and confusion in a twitching glare at Riley. "Listen, missy. When I write these novels, I have something particular in mind and I don't like others offering their input like they're some kind of specialist on *my* work."

"Riley Sheffield." A woman who looked to be the leader of the group, with her leather folder and middle seat, stood when she spoke. "You promised this wouldn't happen again."

"I'm sorry. . . ." Riley guided Mrs. Lithgow to a club chair. "I can't control Verandah House."

Maisy watched the scene in a detached confusion: this was her sister running the family bookstore, living in Palmetto Beach. She'd understood this life went on without her, but she felt as though she were watching an ancient home movie on jumpy eight-millimeter film.

A sweet, soft voice filled the room then. "Don't worry, Riley. It's not that big a deal. Really. Right, ladies?"

The voice settled into the softer place of memory inside Maisy; she turned to see her old friend Lucy Morgan seated in a corner chair, her arm raised as though she'd asked permission to speak. Maisy backed up four steps, slammed into a cedar post and slid behind it. Lucy had not, as yet, looked her way.

The other twelve women nodded with suppressed smiles; a few laughs escaped.

"It is not funny at all." The angry leader's words sparked across the room. She slammed her hand on the side of the overstuffed chair she'd just risen from. "I read the book and spent many hours writing the commentary and researching subjects for us to discuss . . . and I don't need this disruption. We might have to find someplace else to meet if it continues."

Lucy laughed, a silvery sound. "Kind of hard to take the Driftwood Book Club to anywhere but Driftwood Cottage."

"Not really." The leader picked up her book and held it in front of her body like a shield.

Mrs. Lithgow pulled at Riley's sleeve. "What is that woman so angry about? Did she not like my book?"

"No," Lucy said, standing and walking toward Mrs. Lithgow, "she's just had a bad day."

"That's it." The leader waved her book at the group as though she were a Baptist preacher threatening fire and brimstone upon all those who didn't believe as she did. "I'm done with this." She walked off, then turned in a move that made her trip on a nail prodding from the hardwood floor. She grabbed the purse she'd forgotten and glared at the group. "If you can't take reading seriously, I'll find a group that can."

"Have fun," a redhead called after her. "We'll miss you."

Silence fell as the women in the circle of chairs and ottomans, coffee cups and scattered purses looked at one another for some sign of what would come next. Mrs. Lithgow spoke in a loud, firm voice. "Well, I for one am not going to miss her. She is impossibly arrogant, especially considering she is not the author of the book."

Lucy laughed first, and eleven other women joined her.

Riley stood in the middle of the circle as Maisy watched the scene—part of it, yet separate. Maisy did what she always had in moments of unease: she noticed the details of her surroundings, busying her mind with ways and means to improve the decor. A hand-painted sign hung over the area: Book Club Corner. There were mismatched chairs in many faded colors, plush ottomans in green and pink, tables crafted of driftwood. A delicate chandelier hung over the center of the space. Transparent lampshades made of gauze cast a cozy twilight.

"Sorry about that outburst, ladies," Riley said. "You just get on with your discussion."

"Have you read this one?" Lucy asked.

"Years ago," Riley said. "It's always held a special place in my book pile, and I thought it was time to share it with the group."

A clicking noise came from Mrs. Lithgow's chair as her tongue made sounds of disappointment. "My, my, Ms. Sheffield. You choose the books, you organize the clubs and you invite the author, yet you haven't read the book in years and years? You really must take better care of your store and its customers."

"Yes, Mrs. Lithgow. I will work harder to do so." Riley turned to the group, which was suppressing laughter in various forms of body contortions. "Now, while the club finishes talking, why don't you come with me and we'll set up your signing table?"

"That would be wonderful. Although I do not have a very large crowd. You must not have advertised well enough."

"My mistake," Riley said, and held out her hand to help Mrs. Lithgow.

The group began its discussion and Maisy thought she'd been successful at shrinking into the background, unnoticed, until Lucy looked up, settled back in her chair and found Maisy. A smile of recognition lit her face and she jumped up, her book falling to the floor.

Maisy smiled back and waved at Lucy while taking backward steps toward the counter, mouthing, *Later.* Lucy then turned her attention back to the book club.

Maisy sidled to the back of the store, and then climbed the back stairs. She opened the door at the top and saw Brayden sitting at the kitchen table, drawing.

"Hey, nephew," she said, attempting to ignore the trembling in her voice and body.

Brayden, this boy she hadn't seen in years, stared at her. "Aunt Maisy?" he asked.

"Yep, it's me."

He didn't stand for her, so she went to him, hugged him in the awkward way of family who are supposed to know one another in an intimate way yet don't. "What're you doing?" she asked.

"Drawing," he said. "Waiting on Mom. She said I had to wait here for y'all before we go to Gamma's. I'd rather be fishing."

Maisy nodded at him, yet her thoughts moved elsewhere: she'd been in town for only fifteen minutes and already she'd run into Lucy Morgan. This was not going to work out well at all.

The old panic overcame her—the reason she'd left this holiday town behind in the first place. Who in the living hell wanted to face their demons every single day?

"Did you hear what I said?" Brayden's voice rose.

"Of course." Maisy stared at her nephew and wondered for the millionth time what man had contributed to this child's beauty.

"Then what did I say?" he asked.

"That you'd rather be fishing than going to Gamma's. And guess what. I agree."

He laughed, a deeper sound than she would have expected from a child. "Then I guess we'll be fine—me and you." He looked past Maisy toward the staircase door. "Where's Mom?"

It took a moment or longer before Maisy realized Brayden meant her sister, Riley, not her own mama, Kitsy. "She's checking on the book clubs or something before we leave."

"You have the same mom as my mom."

"That's why I'm your aunt Maisy." She attempted to laugh and stared down into his gray eyes. She hadn't been back to visit in six years, and then only for Daddy's funeral, less than twenty-four hours. To Brayden she was just a name. Sorrow flowed upward from a place of regret.

He stared at her for long moments and then sharpened his pencil in the sharpener on the table. "Thanks for sending me all those Christmas and birthday presents."

"You're more than welcome. I hope they were things you wanted—I always asked your mom first. And I know she made you write all those thank-you notes, but I love them. I saved them all."

Brayden laughed, laid out his papers in neat rows and began to draw again, his fingers nimble, sea creatures taking shape under his hand.

"Wow, you're good at this. I used to know a boy who was really good at sketching, just like you. . . ."

"Who?" Brayden looked up underneath his bangs.

"His name was Mack . . . Logan." Maisy tasted his name on her tongue, felt the familiar yearning roll over her. She sighed and stood. "What is taking Riley so long?"

"She's been very busy since Gamma fell. You have to be a little bit patient." Maisy heard the parrot quality to his words, as if they'd been spoken to him only moments ago.

"I know. I know." Maisy paced the kitchen, then moved to the back hall to the sound of Brayden's scraping pencil, the creaks and songs of an old house she'd once known as "Mack's house."

She'd come to the house often in the summers the Logans had owned it, filling it with their own nautical gear and summer furniture. Seashell wallpaper still covered the hallway. Mack's family had hung it during that summer of her twelfth year. She had stood at the end of the hall, asked if she could help—she was bored and it was pouring rain. Mack and Riley had gone fishing, and hadn't returned. Those were the years when Mack thought of her as a pest, as Riley's little sister.

Now Maisy ran her hand over the sheet of paper Mr. Logan had allowed her to help hang before she got bored and went looking for someone to play Parcheesi with her. She laughed at the memory, and Brayden's voice came from the kitchen. "What's so funny?"

"Nothing," Maisy called out. She poked her head into Riley's bedroom, then stepped inside. The four-poster bed from Riley's childhood was covered in white chenille; a dark wood lamp stood on top of a pink bedside table. Books formed scattered piles throughout the room.

"Maisy." Riley's voice echoed down the hall.

She stepped from the bedroom as though she'd been caught smoking behind the Beach Club. "Hey, sis."

"You nosing around my place?" Riley softened her words with a smile.

"I think you have as many books in your room as you do in the bookstore." Maisy swept her hand across the area. "Have you read *all* of those?"

"Not all. I'm a little behind this month, what with the party and all. But I try. . . ."

"I guess that answers the question of what you do with your free time." Maisy picked up a hardcover of *The Stand* by Stephen King. "I read this in high school. It was one of those books that made me not want to read another book."

"Why not?" Riley took the book from Maisy, set it back on top of the pile at the edge of her dresser.

"Because I knew the next book I read wouldn't be nearly as good and I'd be disappointed. Are you reading it?"

Riley laughed. "I don't think I've ever quite heard that rationale for not reading. I have *The Stand* here because it's signed. . . . I don't want to lose it. I read it years ago. . . ." She led them into the hall and shut her bedroom door. "Let's go, okay?"

"You know, I could help you with decorating around here. I really could."

"I like it just the way it is." Riley's voice was tight, the way she spoke when she was insulted or defensive. Years could never erase Maisy's ability to read the subtle signals of sisterhood.

"You'd like it even better my way," Maisy said, and then put her hand up to her mouth. "That came out all wrong."

"Come on, let's go see Mama. She's called the store ten times."

Maisy followed Riley down the hall and back to the kitchen. "You have any medication I can take before we embark on this adventure?"

"What?" Riley spun around to see Maisy's teasing smile. "Oh . . . sarcasm. Your favorite form of communication."

"I call it joking. You call it sarcasm. Tomato, tom-ah-to. Whatever," Maisy said.

"Brayden, let's go," Riley called out.

The drive to the Sheffield home took less than five minutes, but Maisy felt that she was holding her breath the entire time. Together Maisy, Riley and Brayden walked into the drawing room, which had been turned into a quasi–hospital room. On a mechanical bed set up in the middle of the room lay Kitsy propped up on pillows. Her bedside tables had been arranged to suggest that she was in her master bedroom. A floral shop seemed to have dropped off an entire van full of arrangements. The curtains had been pulled back from the windows to expose the view of the expansive backyard with its hectic live oaks and lush grass. A tire swing hung from an oak branch. Maisy remembered leaning against that tree, waiting her turn to swing and thinking she was resting against God's shoulder.

Mama's eyes were closed, offering Maisy a moment to take in her appearance, to control her own reaction. She felt as if she'd just stepped onto a boat and needed her sea legs. As though Kitsy sensed her daughter in the room, her eyes flew open. "Maisy," she said with the inflection and endearment only a mother could utter. "My dear Maisy." Her hand rose to her chapped lips. "Come here and hug your mama."

"Hello, Mama," Maisy walked toward her, bent over for the embrace.

"Oh, darling. You look so well. So rested and tan and fit. California must suit you." Then Mama's eyes squinted. "I'm so glad you'll be here for a long time."

Maisy felt ten years old again; she was being told that she couldn't go to Lilly's sleepover because a family birthday took precedence. Family was always the first priority. How could she have forgotten that? Maisy took her mama's hand. "I've come to see you, to make sure you're okay. But I can't stay long." She glanced at Riley, who hung back in the doorway with Brayden.

Kitsy waved her hand through the air as if shooing flies from the back porch, Maisy's words like a trivial nuisance that could be run off with one swipe. "Of course you'll stay. Now sit down and we'll go over our duties." Kitsy bent from her waist, winced and pulled a bulging notebook from the bedside table. "Riley, dear, will you please go fetch Adalee from upstairs?"

"Adalee's here?" Maisy asked.

Riley's voice came muffled from the hallway. "Adalee Louise, get down here, please."

Pounding footsteps echoed across the upstairs hardwood floors, then down the stairs. Adalee's lithe figure appeared at the doorway, her mouth in a sullen pout. Her hair was blonder now than in the pictures she'd traded with Maisy via e-mail. She wore torn cutoff jean shorts and a red tank top with AU—for Auburn University—stamped across her tiny chest. Adalee was the youngest, and also the smallest, and always had been. Even her features were miniature.

While Maisy stared at her grown sister, Adalee met Maisy's gaze and her sullen expression turned to a wide smile. "Maisy!" She ran to her, and engulfed her in a hug. "I'm so glad you're here.

You'll defend me. . . . This is stupid, right? That we have to work all summer when I had other plans. This is ridiculous—tell Mama and Riley we are *not* doing this."

Maisy laughed, pushed the ragged-cut hair from Adalee's face. "I tried. Did you have plans?"

"Of course I did. This is my last summer before I have to get a real job. I was gonna hang out at the pool . . . spend time with my adorable boyfriend, Chad. You know, have fun."

Kitsy made a sound somewhere between a laugh and a snort. "So you believe you can fail out of three classes and then come home and celebrate your illustrious semester by partying all summer?"

Adalee's face contorted as though she were trying to decide whether to cry or vent her rage. "That is so mean, Mama. Maisy and Riley don't need to know everything. You didn't have to . . . say that."

Riley made a motion for Adalee to sit. "Not now, Adalee. Please." Riley went to Mama's bedside, fluffing her pillow, straightening her blankets.

"Mama started it." Adalee slumped into a chair, folded her arms. "And by the way, don't tell me what to do; you are not my mother." Adalee's voice took on the childish tones Maisy remembered as vividly as her sister's violet eyes.

The last time Maisy had seen Adalee she'd been fourteen years old—at Daddy's funeral. They'd talked through the years, texted and sent pictures, but the living, moving Adalee was vibrant and full of the nervous energy Maisy herself had. Her small body was kept thin by her manic movements and constant need for excitement—parties, friends and activity.

Maisy sat down on the chair next to Riley's. She'd do what she'd done as a child—pretend to be part of this family thing and then go do whatever the hell she pleased. "Go ahead, Mama. What do you need from us?" she asked.

"Traitor," Adalee said.

Kitsy attempted to straighten herself in the bed, applied pink-tinted lip gloss and cleared her throat. "Now, we all must chip in to salvage this party. I have been planning it for two years. We have every town dignitary, every previous owner of the cottage coming. Right now I have two hundred fifty RSVPs for yes—which of course means an outside tent—and that does not include the people who will just drop in. And we have a function or event every day next week leading up to the party: visiting authors, contests, book club giveaways, speakers, food. . . ." Kitsy handed out sheets of paper to her daughters. "Read this. . . . It's the schedule for the week. I have done all the work, made all the arrangements. You just have to make sure it happens. Follow up on each event. I wish I could do it . . . but . . ."

Adalee spoke, bitterness behind each word. "Yeah, but you fell down the stairs . . . drunk."

Kitsy glared at her daughter. "I was not drunk. I slipped." She lifted her chin in disregard. "Now, as for your individual duties . . ." Kitsy pulled more sheets from her leather-bound folder. "I have assigned each one of you a major duty to keep things going. Harriet typed this up for me. I should be out of this nightmare cast in six weeks. . . . Then we can move on with our lives."

Maisy glanced down at the thick paper in her hand—Mama's personal engraved stationery. Maisy's name was typed in bold, capital letters on the top of the page with her duties following: *in charge of all book clubs; follow-up on all RSVPs; work the morning shift at the bookstore.*

She looked up. "I can't do this. I don't work mornings. I'm not a party planner, and I have no idea what to do with a book club. I don't even belong to one. I don't even know what a book club *does*. . . . No, Mama. Hire someone to do it."

The glare that emanated from her mother struck silent all further protests. "I can't hire someone. We don't have the money."

Adalee stood. "What is that supposed to mean?"

"It means what I said. Listen carefully." Kitsy's voice rose. "This fall of mine could not have come at a worse time, but I trust you girls. I know what our family can do when we band together. The reality is that if we don't raise enough money during this anniversary celebration, we will have to sell the store." Mama glanced at Riley, and Maisy felt as if they were speaking to each other in secret code, unspoken words hidden below the spoken ones. "It is what it is. We must make this work. I promised your precious father that I would never deplete family money to keep the bookstore. Even with him gone, I will keep my promise. That is what we do in our family—keep our promises. Now sit down and tell me you understand your duties."

Adalee's eyes filled with tears. "Stop yelling. What is going on here? This is your bookstore, Riley. Not mine. Not Maisy's."

Mama tapped the metal bedside rail with her pen. "That is absolutely enough. What affects one affects us all. Family responsibility." Her voice turned soft, melodic. "That's what is going on. And you never, ever need to let the customers know we are in financial trouble. That is between us. And only us. They need to see and feel how much we love them, and the store, not the troubles we're facing. Do you understand?"

Maisy held up her piece of paper. "I don't see anyone trying to save my job or . . ." Her words were cut short by Mama's slicing look. She glanced over at Riley's list. *Run the store as usual; check on sisters; follow through on daily events for the week of the party.* She looked up at Adalee. "What are your jobs?"

Adalee swiped at her eyes, morphed from sadness to anger in that brief moment and waved her paper in the air. "I'm in charge of the history boards and timeline display for the house. Are you kidding? *And* work the afternoon shift at the store. *And* I'm in charge of the newsletter. I can't even write. . . ."

"I'll tell you what to put in the newsletter," Kitsy said. "You just have to design and print it. I'll do what I can from bed."

"This is crazy," Adalee whispered, looked at each sister in turn.

Mama dug through her folder, pulled out a newspaper article with ragged edges. "Riley, this article is great. Lodge Barton did a wonderful job. You must have given him a perfect interview."

"That's because Riley is perfect," Maisy said before she could cut the words short.

The air became full of unspoken retorts, replete with years' worth of hurt feelings.

Mama exhaled through the same pursed lips Maisy had already seen on Riley that morning. "Riley, will you please call and thank Lodge? And then ask if he'll do follow-ups all week. If you're sugar-sweet with the thank-you, he should say yes."

"Mama, he'd do it anyway." Riley stood, looked down at Mama. "You get some sleep. We've got everything under control."

Maisy smiled; she was well practiced at pretending to go along with family plans, yet she was surprised by how easily the motions returned to her after so long. *Run,* her mind screamed. *Far. Fast. Run.* "Yes, Mama, you rest. We have it all under control." Maisy smoothed a hand over the file stuffed with the RSVP list. She opened the manila folder, scanned the guest list without realizing who she was looking for until she found him: Mack Logan.

She smiled inside and looked up at Riley, who kissed Mama on the cheek, then turned to her sisters. "Come on, girls. We'll go to the back porch and talk. Then I have to get back to the store for the Budding Artists class." Riley motioned for her sisters to come with her.

"And"—Adalee raised her hand as though she were in a classroom—"I need to meet Chad at the Beach Club."

While the three sisters headed to the porch, Maisy tucked the knowledge of Mack Logan's imminent arrival inside her heart like a secret. Maybe, just maybe, this trip wouldn't be a total waste after all.

Six

RILEY

Riley's heart hurt already. She didn't want to head into a week of nonstop activity with a negative attitude, but her sisters weren't helping. The three of them walked onto the back porch after the meeting with Mama. Adalee sidled up from behind Riley, plopped onto the wicker divan, kicked off her flip-flops to put her feet on the glass-top coffee table. She pulled a cigarette from her purse and lit it.

"There is no way Mama would ever allow you to smoke in her house." Riley took the cigarette from Adalee and dropped it into a glass of water on the side table.

"Hey! You can't do that. . . . I'm not inside the house and you're not my mother."

"Yeah, you already told me that," Riley said. "I also don't want Brayden to see you smoking."

The screen door opened and Brayden's wide smile appeared. "Too late. Already saw Aunt Adalee smoking. You know you'll get lung cancer, don't you?"

"Now who is teaching this child to be judgmental at twelve years old?" Adalee crossed one leg over the other.

"Let's just get through all this." Riley pointed to the notebook Mama had given Maisy. "There's everything you need."

"Thanks." Maisy smiled at her sister, plotting her next move: a hot bath, a whiskey on the rocks and a solid ten hours' sleep.

Riley continued. "Adalee, here is the last newsletter and a draft of the one Mama wants for this week. Please ask me if you need any help. I'll show you where the template is on the computer."

Adalee nodded, but said nothing—her usual ploy. Most often this drew attention to her and prompted wheedling to get her to speak. No one wanted Adalee mad and silent. But Riley vowed not to let it get to her *this time*.

Riley spoke for fifteen more minutes about what they would need to accomplish in the next few days. Finally Maisy stood. "Listen, I can't do one more minute of this insanity without some sustenance."

"There's some fried chicken in the fridge. . . . It's from yesterday." Riley closed the notebook. "I'm done anyway."

"No, I meant a drink. Come on, girls. Up we go. Off to Bud's for a good old-fashioned cold draft beer." Maisy rubbed her hands together.

Riley waved her away. "Go ahead. I have Brayden, and I'm gonna head back to check on the store."

Maisy shrugged. "Okay, then. Come on, Adalee."

Adalee jumped off the couch, slipped her flip-flops onto her feet. "Totally awesome. Let me call Chad and tell him where I'll be. Maybe he can meet us there later."

Riley turned to face Maisy, whose full attention was on her cell phone screen. Riley stared at her sister in her preoccupation, her first opportunity to really look at Maisy. She still possessed a beauty that was difficult to define with words like pretty or pleasing. There was something unsettling about the combination of Maisy's features, which drew stares from men and women, even children. Her bronze hair had risen from the more obscure place in the Sheffield gene pool; their great-aunt Martha-Rose had had the same hair. Maisy's wide smile was juxtaposed against her tiny nose and round, sometimes green, sometimes blue eyes.

Maisy looked up. "Why are you staring at me like that? I'm just checking my e-mail. I do have a life."

"Yeah," Adalee spat out. "Unfortunately it's right here for the next week or more."

Riley ignored her sisters' comments. "Maisy, the morning shift starts at nine a.m. Anne comes in to open the café, but you need to be there for the bookstore. I'll be here with Mama tomorrow morning."

"No problem." Maisy stood, held her hand out for Adalee. They looped their arms at the elbow and entered the house with a slam of the screen door. Riley stood alone on the porch, her shoulders slumped under the weight of unspoken words, secrets and regrets. Would her sisters act any differently if they knew what she knew about Mama's cancer? Did it even matter?

Riley walked out to the backyard, called for Brayden, who

came from the east side of the lawn. He ran across the overgrown grass, dodging the massive trunks of mature oak trees and a puddle of standing water. He pushed the tire swing high into the air as he passed it, and then stopped short in front of Riley.

The sun fell behind her son, his hair and body backlit by an amber glow. Riley's heart swelled; she reached down and hugged him, felt his ribs beneath her fingers, his heart beating against her chest. There were times when for a few moments she was envious of others' freedoms, but when his small body fell against her chest, Riley loved her son and her life and was filled with overwhelming gratitude.

"Let's go check on Gamma and get some dinner." She took Brayden's hand in hers, squeezed the fingers that had grown in length and width when she wasn't noticing.

"Where'd the aunts go?" Brayden fell into stride with Riley, dropped her hand.

"They need to catch up. They haven't seen each other in a while."

"Gamma says Maisy is wild—that she'll be in trouble before the week is out."

Riley looked down at him. "Gamma is taking too much pain medication. She shouldn't tell you crazy things like that."

Brayden rolled his eyes as only a twelve-year-old could pull off.

They entered the front foyer; Riley glanced up at an oil portrait of the three sisters when they were young: three, twelve and thirteen years old. Riley had stood behind her sisters, large, gawky, her legs and arms too long for her boyish body. Maisy had stared at the camera as if seducing it even at that young age, and adorable Adalee held a daisy between her fingers, which the artist had drawn in instead of the dandelion she'd actually been holding during the formal sitting.

It was Mama's way to rewrite the past—to turn a dandelion into a fresh white daisy. Their childhood was this: Daddy gone so many nights for his work in the Air Force that Riley barely remembered him being home; Mama's slurred words every evening; Maisy's police escorts home on more than one summer evening. But Mama remembered, or attempted to make them remember, their life as a fairy tale on the beaches of coastal Georgia. If Mama were to write the book, to pass along the family stories, there would be a million daisies.

The Sheffield children each seemed to be born with roles as defined as the seasons of the year. Riley had mutely accepted hers—she was to be an example for the other girls, a rock of steadfast strength. She was the oldest: responsible, a tomboy athlete with her bigger-boned body and strong muscles. Maisy was the middle sister: beautiful, fragile and lithe. Adalee was the youngest: pampered and naive, even now unaware what had happened that last summer before Maisy left, of the break in the family bonds.

Riley turned from the family oil painting, from the memories, and lifted her cell phone from her back pocket to call Lodge, as Mama had requested.

"Hey," he said after the first ring. "Riley, what's up?"

"I hate caller ID," she said. "Now I can't prank call you like I used to."

"Okay, pretend I don't know who you are."

"Too late," she said. "You already know."

"Yes, I do," he said. "I do know who you are."

The way he said it made her smile. "I'm just calling to thank you for the article. It's wonderful. Have I told you what a terrific writer you are?"

"No, and you can tell me whenever you like."

"You're a terrific writer."

"Thank you, Riley Sheffield." Shuffling noises came across the line, and then his voice. "Sorry—dropped the phone. Hey, listen, wanna go grab some dinner?"

Riley stared up at the portrait of the girl Lodge had once known. "Oh, I can't. My sisters are here. Mama is laid up. I have Brayden. . . ."

"I know, I know. You're busy. I just thought . . . we could do a follow-up article to come out when the festivities start."

"Oh. Yes. That would be great. I was actually going to beg for just that. Why don't you stop by the store tomorrow?"

"Sure."

Riley hung up and put her arm around Brayden's shoulders. "Who was that?" he asked.

Riley grabbed the pile of opened mail off the front table, leafed through the letters paper clipped to their envelopes as she answered, "The newspaper guy—you know, Mr. Barton, who you fish with sometimes."

Brayden opened his mouth to speak, but the home phone rang in the hallway. He made a grunting noise. "I hate the phone. Every time I think we're leaving or doing something—the stupid phone rings."

"This is a terribly busy time, Brayden. I promise it will get better."

A voice, both familiar and distant, spoke. "May I please speak with Ms. Sheffield?"

"Speaking," Riley said, made a motion for Brayden to hold on a minute. He sat slumped on the bottom step of the curving staircase and propped his elbows onto his knees.

"Kitsy Sheffield?"

"No, this is Riley." She made a face at Brayden.

"Well, hello, Riley. This is Sheppard Logan. I know I'm a bit late with this question, but Mack and I are coming to town to-morrow and we can't seem to find a place to stay. I don't know why we didn't expect it—but in the old days we wouldn't have had any difficulty finding a room there. Times have changed, eh?"

Riley attempted a laugh, which came out more like a cough. "Yes, the summers are crazy here now. But there is a new place. Have you called the Seaside Inn?"

"No. Do you have their number?"

Riley rattled it off. "I am so glad you're coming. There will be events every day leading up to the party, so please take full advantage of the festivities." Riley repeated the words she'd said to at least a hundred customers over the phone, yet this time her voice shook.

"Hold on. I need some paper."

Silence filled the line; then Riley heard it: Mack Logan's voice calling out to his father, "Here, Dad." She closed her eyes, tried to imagine a Mack Logan who was thirty-two years old, in his parents' house. She couldn't do it. Nothing came to mind except the tanned, tall boy of summer.

Mr. Logan came back on the line. "Go ahead. I'm ready."

Riley gave him the number again, and then paused before speaking in her most controlled voice. "Please tell Mrs. Logan and the boys that I said hello."

"I will, dear. And I so look forward to seeing your family again."

"Thank you, Mr. Logan."

Riley held the receiver in her hand, the buzz of disconnection humming across the foyer.

"Mommm . . . hello. They hung up." Brayden's irritation was obvious.

Riley glanced over at her precious son, sitting on the bottom step of her childhood staircase looking at her holding a dead receiver in her hand. In a way, in a distorted and fantastic way, even though he wasn't Brayden's father, Mack Logan was one of the reasons this child sat in front of her. She hung up the phone and hugged Brayden too tight.

"Stop, Mom. You can be so embarrassing."

"Yes, for the throngs of people watching you right now, I am humiliating."

"I'm going to see Gamma." He ran off down the hall.

She allowed the sweet thrill of hearing Mack Logan's voice, even in the background, run through her before she dismissed it as another childhood fantasy. When they'd been best friends as children, she'd had an unbounded belief in mermaids and fairies, in fairy tales and nature's mysteries. She'd believed she could fly with Peter Pan, breathe underwater, walk without touching the ground. And she'd believed that Mack Logan loved her.

Reality had a way of ruining a girl's dreams. Her life with Brayden above a coastal bookshop was all she dreamed of now. Riley climbed the curved staircase, took a left at the top of the stairs. Photos of the Sheffield sisters lined the entire hallway: Halloween night dressed in princess costumes; first days of school; Christmas morning with the stockings—all snapshots that could never capture the internal workings of who they were then and whom they would become. Riley stopped at a photo of Maisy with her homecoming queen banner hung across her pale yellow dress. Riley reached up, wiped dust off the bottom of the frame and then opened the door to her own childhood bedroom.

The room was empty save for a queen-sized bed and dresser used for guests. Riley sat on the bed, closed her eyes; she allowed the last memory of Mack Logan to take shape in her mind's eye.

Mack had been Riley's best friend since the day they were seven years old and had met on Pearson's fishing pier. Riley showed him what type of bait to use for the redfish, and he showed her how to throw a cast net. A friendship formed that would remain, or so she'd thought. All those years ago, she'd been able to forget about Mack during the school year until his family's Volvo station wagon pulled into Palmetto Beach on Memorial Day weekend, bikes clipped to the back of the car, a large plastic carrier that looked like a purple turtle with its head hidden strapped to the top. Mack, his brother, Joe, and their parents would get out of the car at Driftwood Cottage and summer would begin.

For eleven years they came.

That last summer arrived with record-breaking high temperatures. Heat rose from the pavement in waves, and the summer people ran across the sand screeching and jumping, using towels as stepping-stones. Large multicolored umbrellas dotted the beach, parents underneath fanning themselves while children ran at the water's edge, oblivious of the ninety-eight percent humidity and over-hundred-degree temperatures. The ceiling fans in the Beach Club porch whirred incessantly and ineffectively.

Mack and Riley came together on the pier as they always had. After the awkward greetings, which followed a school year apart, they dropped their fishing lines into the gray-blue water. Riley pulled her baseball cap lower on her forehead, yanked her T-shirt off to fish in her bathing suit. Mack was quiet; he hadn't said much since he'd arrived. They were eighteen years old now, high school graduates—a new world.

Riley couldn't take his silence much longer. It was usually less than ten minutes before the natural rhythms of their summer friendship resumed. "Okay," she said, placing her fishing pole in a metal loop. "You're mad at me. What did I do?"

He backed away from her. "No . . . no. Why do you say that?"

"You're acting totally weird."

"Just because I'm quiet doesn't mean I'm weird."

She leaned against the pier's cracked wooden railing. "Okay, not weird." She tilted her head at him. "You sure got a lot taller this year."

He laughed. "Pizza. That was pretty much my diet. I don't think I'm any taller, just bigger maybe."

Riley felt the natural camaraderie of their decadelong friendship begin to return.

His eyes traveled down her body, the leaner body she hadn't possessed the summer before. Then he turned away. "Yeah, you changed, too."

"Whatever." She picked up her fishing pole, cast the line into the water.

"You're . . . smaller."

"No, I'm two inches taller." She poked at his side with the pole.

"Yeah, I guess." He blushed.

She laughed, a small, nervous sound. Maybe, just maybe this would be the summer he loved her as much as she loved him. She'd been willing to remain his best friend these last years with the remote hope that one day he'd turn to her and see her: Riley Sheffield, the girl almost a woman. Maybe it was happening now.

The next days were the best. They flirted around the edges of attraction, touching fingertips while fishing or baiting hooks, looping legs and arms in a wrestling match in the pool—seeking out any reason to touch without appearing to want to do more than roughhouse.

Riley floated through those days with an expectation of love finally fulfilled. Her mother was right; some things were worth waiting for. Mack Logan was one of them. She wasn't the most beautiful sister—that was Maisy. Yet thankfully, Maisy seemed to irritate Mack: her high voice, her clumsy way at sports.

Well into the third week of summer, Riley waited for Mack on the front porch; they were going to the movie on the lawn, a weekly event in the park where the teenagers congregated without supervision while their parents drank scotch and vodka at the

Beach Club. This was the site of first kisses, first tastes of cheap wine and first puffs on cigarettes. Riley had spent more than her usual five minutes getting ready that night, suffering a sudden indecisiveness. Hair in a ponytail, and then down over her shoulders; a tank top, and then a T-shirt; a jeans miniskirt, then shorts. It was simpler when Mack hadn't noticed her as anything more than a buddy, but still she wouldn't change the anticipation she'd felt the last few weeks.

Her heart sped; her skin flushed. Everything seemed more possible, as though the world had shifted into the orbit it was always meant to have.

Maisy came out onto the porch, where Riley was leaning against a post watching the sidewalk for Mack. She dropped her tall body into a chair and somehow made the simple gesture look seductive. "Whatcha doing?"

"Waiting for someone." Riley turned away from her sister's beauty, not wanting anything to ruin how she felt about herself at that moment.

"Who?" Maisy was sixteen now, and her adolescence had increased her radiance.

"None of your business." Riley saw Mack turn the corner to Sixth Avenue. "Gotta go." She ran down the front steps and met Mack on the sidewalk.

He smiled at Riley. "I brought a blanket and a cooler."

She wanted to bask in this moment, to enjoy his smile for her, his preparation for an evening under a night sky watching a movie, skin touching skin in innocence and promise.

Maisy's voice shattered the night. "Hey, Mack," she hollered.

He stopped, looked over his shoulder at Maisy running toward them, then at Riley.

Riley sensed the shift before it actually happened: Mack turning his smile, his focus on Maisy. She felt the desperate desire to rewind time, to undo the act of Maisy running toward them. Even before the change occurred, Riley knew that it would happen eventually, so why not now? Riley was bland gray compared to Maisy's radiant light.

Riley took a deep breath, sensing the end of something that had barely begun. She looked at Mack. "She's here to irritate the hell out of me. That's essentially her life goal."

"It always has been," he said, yet his gaze followed the sixteen-year-old girl coming toward them. He laughed, looked at Riley. "You wanna ditch her?"

He'd said these words a hundred times over the years when Maisy had found them at the pier or asked to go out on the sailboat or to join them at the pool—*Let's ditch her*. It had been easy then. It would be impossible now.

Maisy arrived breathless at their side. "Hey, y'all on your way to the movie on the lawn?"

"Yes," Riley said. "Why don't you go find that boyfriend of yours and head that way?" Her words were a dull sword compared to the sharp impact Maisy's beauty was having on Mack.

The slow turning of his affection wasn't completed that night, or the next morning, but the beginning of Mack and Maisy's summer romance began at the exact moment that Mack and Riley's ended. Of course Riley pretended that it had never begun, that his preoccupation with Maisy was of no concern to her. They'd been friends and always would be. Yet inside, her heart broke in places that remained permanently jagged, places where the most casual graze of memory catches in pain.

Hate for Maisy began to grow inside Riley's heart, tangling the emotions of love and sisterhood. An ally became an enemy. A friend turned foe. Riley hid these feelings for Maisy as she hid most feelings behind her happy-go-lucky, Riley-loves-everyone persona.

Once Mack noticed Maisy, what was simple became complex and confusing. He'd arrive at the house, and Riley would think it was to fish or boat, and instead he'd take Maisy to the movies or the ice-cream stand. Maisy stepped out of her role as tag-along sister into a new one: competition.

The months passed until the bonfire on that last night in celebration of the end of summer. All the teens in Palmetto Beach were frenetic with the need to take in and consume this last night before they all returned home. The music was loud, the voices high-pitched, the laughter almost hysterical.

Riley would leave for college in a week. The blazing bonfire, and the burning hole in her gut from the lemonade-vodka surprise she'd drunk with Lodge Barton behind the lifeguard station allowed the bitterness toward her sister to grow, as the fire did with each log added.

This last night—this night of the fire—Maisy had gone home. She was sixteen years old and her curfew was an hour ago. Daddy was strict about this in a way he wasn't about other things. Freedom reigned in almost all other aspects of their lives, as though someone had told him you get to pick one rule to enforce in your daughters' lives, and he'd said, "Fine, curfew it is."

Mack stood on the other side of the bonfire, laughing with his brother, Joe, his head back and the fire lighting his chin. He caught Riley's gaze across the flames and smiled, motioned for her to join them.

Maybe, she'd thought, just maybe this would be the night he'd really see her. She'd once believed in this kind of equilibrium: in a single moment in which the world turned right, in which things worked out for the best, in perfect destiny. In the balanced world in which she'd lived—where the tide breathed in and then exhaled back out twice a day every day, where wild-winged ospreys returned to the same nests every year, where the rising moon mirrored the setting sun over the marsh—it was utterly impossible for someone to love another person as much as she loved Mack Logan and not feel that love returned.

Logs had been arranged to form a perimeter separating fire from sand, and she walked around it to Mack, to happy endings and new beginnings. Lodge stopped her, offered her another swig of his alcoholic concoction. She shook her head no.

Then the world became off-kilter somehow, tilted and backward. Mack's arm was draped around a girl. Riley stumbled in the sand, moved forward.

Maisy.

Mack was holding her and they were moving toward the lifeguard station, laughing. Riley caught Joe staring at her; he shrugged and Riley ran. Her rushed steps took her home without her own full understanding of what she was doing or why. The Sheffield house was only one block down and one block back from the beach. "Second row," the summer people called these homes.

Riley burst through the front door. Mama and Daddy were sitting in their usual chairs, Mama cross-stitching a dining room chair cover for the Historical Foundation, Daddy reading a novel.

"Maisy is at the bonfire," Riley said, her calm tone belying her inner panic and anger, her bitterness.

Daddy's face turned the purple shade that Riley often imagined he used when yelling at the cadets at the flight academy. A military man, he was not one for discussion or debate, only action. His novel fell to the ground as he bolted from the room without asking any questions.

Mama shook her head. "Now was that necessary, Riley?"

"Yes, it was." Riley ran to her room, imagining the scene at the bonfire until she could no longer stay herself. She bolted down the back stairs, returned to the beach. Her toes sank into the sand and she felt something shift, something now unalterable in the Sheffield family.

She reached the beach again, easing her way back to the party. She slid into the group around the bonfire. "Ooh," Betsy Miller, from Connecticut, said, "you missed it big-time. Your daddy came in here and dragged your sister home. She was totally freaking out."

"Oh?" Riley raised her eyebrows, scanned the crowd for Mack. Where was he?

She spun in a circle.

There.

He stood alone, his face blank and full of flame's shadows. For the first time in memory, she could not feel his emotions. She tucked her hair behind her ear and walked toward him, slow, steady. He looked up at her across the night, across their years as best friends. He held her gaze for only a moment as she begged, in her mind, for him not to turn away.

But he did.

She called his name. His steps were deliberate as he moved away from the fire and into the night.

Away from her.

Away from Palmetto Beach.

Despair overcame her. She stood below lifeguard station number seven. Footsteps fell behind her, and she turned to face Sheldon Rutledge.

She'd known Sheldon since her summer memories had begun. An only child of older parents who doted on him, he was often the host of the parties, oyster roasts, sailing races, and he possessed a wit that kept them all laughing. He was good-looking in the casual way of a boy who doesn't care, yet draws girls to his side: his dark hair always falling into his eyes, his laughter heard across the water.

"Riley, what's up?"

Without a real answer, she shook her head.

Sheldon placed his hands on her shoulders. "Last night of the summer. Then college," he said.

She nodded.

"So I am going to do something I've promised myself I'd do since I was ten years old."

Riley laughed, expecting him to do something funny and relieve her suffering. "I, Sheldon Rutledge, am going to kiss you, Riley Sheffield. Right now."

And he did. In a slow, gorgeous way that made Riley forget, if only for a brief respite, the pain of despair. In the dark night, they whispered about their future—about Sheldon's plans to enter the Air Force right out of college and live a life of freedom and flying; of her dreams of college and a master's in English literature. She allowed herself to float into this relief, to become part of something that didn't have anything to do with Mack Logan or Maisy Sheffield. Nothing to do with love at all, really.

Sheldon asked, "Now what?"

She answered, "I go to college; you go live your dreams." He cuddled close to her and agreed. His next kiss was deeper; she immersed herself in the comfort and hunger of a boy she'd known and adored.

Later she would be haunted by the shame that her first and last time with a man was a search for relief and from heartbreak, and not an act of love.

Late that night, Riley knocked on Maisy's bedroom door, wanting to say something, anything to reverse the night of betrayal on both their parts.

Maisy called from inside, "Go away. I hate you and I always will."

Riley opened her sister's door anyway, stepped into her room. Maisy lay on the bed sobbing, her face red and blotchy. She looked up. "You did that on purpose because you love Mack. You've faked all summer that you didn't care, but you do. You love him, and you can't stand for me to be happy with him."

Riley answered in anger and stunned pain. "You're the one who stole my best friend."

Maisy sat up in bed, pointed at Riley. "You are a mean, ugly sister. He never would have loved you. Just because you took him away from me tonight doesn't mean you can take him away from me forever. He only liked you because you knew how to do boy things. Just because you love someone doesn't mean they love you back. He'll never want you the way he wants me. Never."

Something in these words sounded to Riley like the truth and made them more painful than any lie Maisy could have uttered. Riley tripped on a pair of flip-flops as she backed out of the room, her gut clenched, her heart hollowed out. She'd lost her best friend's adoration. She'd lost her sister's love. She'd lost her innocence.

A week later, she left for college, and then halfway through her first semester discovered she was pregnant. She dropped out of school and retreated home. Nine months passed, and Brayden Collins Sheffield entered the world. Riley started Driftwood Cottage Bookstore with her mama—a major detour in her life's plans after one impetuous act.

Since that night thirteen years ago, Riley had spoken to her sister only when necessary. The gulf in their relationship was easy to blame on Maisy—after all, she'd been the one to leave Palmetto Beach and move to California, then refuse to come visit. But Riley understood that mere physical distance was not what kept them apart; their bitterness and anger did.

SEVEN

Maisy was always most comfortable when men noticed her in bars. She felt in her element, like an animal in its natural habitat. Bud's was the main gathering place in Palmetto Beach—combination restaurant, bar, pool hall, teen hangout on the outdoor patio. Peanut shells covered the floor of the bar area and shellac lay an inch thick on the tables. Maisy spotted an old boyfriend, Billy-Joe Caulfield; she waved at him across the room, remembered the night he'd begged her to leave with him when his former girlfriend, Candy, had sat two tables over on the patio. Maisy had once heard he'd eventually married Candy, even had a couple kids.

His eyebrows lifted in recognition, and he rose from his table and made his way toward where Maisy and Adalee were sitting at the far end of the bar. Maisy maintained eye contact with him until he reached her.

"Well, well, Maisy Sheffield is back to join us in little ol' Palmetto Beach, Georgia. What brings you from the far coast?"

Maisy stood and threw her arms around Billy-Joe, maybe a little too close, a little too tight for a married man. She expected him to hug her back, but he didn't. He kept his arms at his sides while she clung to his neck. Embarrassed and slightly annoyed, Maisy stepped aside, almost knocked her barstool over.

"So good to see you, too. How are you?" Maisy forced a formal tone into her voice, yet even she heard the alcohol slur behind the words.

"I'm just fine. Are you in town for the big celebration?"

"Of course. I wouldn't miss it for the world." Billy-Joe looked over his shoulder at the table full of men he'd just left. They all five stared at Maisy. "Is there a particular reason they're staring at us like I have horns growing out of my head?" she asked.

Being noticed but not admired was ruining Maisy's evening and putting her in a foul mood. She'd wanted to come here with Adalee and remember the better times, have a couple drinks before bed. The time difference would make it nearly impossible for her to fall asleep until much later.

"They're just wondering if it's really you." Billy-Joe's hand wandered through the air as if he couldn't find a place to settle it, as if he wanted to touch her but couldn't. This thought soothed Maisy.

"Yes, it's really me." She smiled with a slight tilt to her chin.

Movement out of the right side of her vision caused Maisy to twist and stumble, and stare into the face of Lila Carter, who was holding a full beer mug and a sarcastic grin. "Look who's come back to town to grace us with her presence. Ms. Homecoming Queen, Prom Queen, and all-around most-admired girl in Palmetto Beach, Maisy Sheffield." Lila bowed in a mock gesture, spilled beer onto the sticky hardwood floor.

Maisy took two steps backward on the crushed peanuts to avoid the spillage. "Charming, Lila. Absolutely charming. All class, as usual."

Lila spun to face six women seated at a round table, called out, "All right, girls, lock up your men. Maisy Sheffield is back in town."

Maisy's stomach plummeted. She hid her embarrassment behind bravado. Her reputation—which had obviously not changed since she'd left—now grabbed her by the heels and tripped her up.

She sat and glanced at her sister, who was leaning against the bar watching with a slight grin of amusement. Maisy wanted to fade into the background, but fading away was not one of her best skills. Sarcasm won out. "So lovely to see you also, Lila. It's always a pleasure to return home to such warmth and admiration."

Lila made an odd snorting sound and returned to her table of women. Billy-Joe waved goodbye over his shoulder and returned to his table, to the card game and other men. Adalee laughed.

"You thought that was funny?" Maisy asked.

"A little, yes. Come on, Maisy, you gotta admit that you didn't expect that. Man, Billy-Joe was in love with you for, like, ten years. He didn't even hug you back. What'd you do to piss him off?"

"Nothing. That's the problem. I didn't do anything with him."

"No, I think the problem is that you made him *think* you would do something with him, and then you didn't."

"You think I can control what they think I will and will not do?"

"Of course you can. You're the almighty Maisy Sheffield."

"And Lila Carter has always hated me. She was a mean girl in high school. . . . I'm not even sure how she has friends." Maisy held her hand up to order another drink when her cell phone buzzed; she reached into her bag, hoping to hear from Peter. He would be sweet to her and soothe this jangled feeling that left her out of sorts and distracted.

She answered without glancing at the caller ID, then wished she hadn't when Riley's voice came across the line to remind her that she had the morning shift, and to tell her that Mama's night nurse was there now and she was leaving.

"Great," Maisy said. "Then I'll see you in the morning at the cottage." She looked at Adalee. "I have it all under control."

She hung up and stared out over the crowd, wondering when Mack Logan would arrive. Who the hell cared what anyone else thought of her? Mack was coming. Maybe he was the reason for her forced return to Palmetto Beach. It all seemed to make sense now, to fall into some plan. Her thoughts had flitted from Lucy and Tucker to Billy-Joe and then to Lila, and then to Peter with his wife. Now they settled calm and secure on one person: Mack Logan.

The bartender placed another whiskey in front of Maisy and she thanked him, smiled and watched him respond. Now she was herself again.

Adalee glanced at her cell phone for the hundredth time. "I wonder why he hasn't called or shown up yet."

"Who?" Maisy was still smiling.

"Chad. He said he'd call when he got off work and then meet me here." Her eyes filled with tears.

"Whoa, no crying over boys, Adalee. Lesson one. You are in control."

"We were supposed to hang out all summer. I got him a job at the Beach Club, and now I'll barely see him since I have to work at the bookstore. My whole summer is ruined."

"No, it's not. There are ways around this. I know I left for California when you were only ten, but now I can teach you the things an older sister should pass on."

Adalee laughed. "Like how to get grounded, or make every girl in town hate me?"

"Hey, not every girl. I have, well, *had* a lot of friends. Most of them have moved on." Maisy stood. "Come on, let's play some pool."

"The tables are full." Adalee sat back. "And I'm not in the mood."

"You can*not* allow some guy to put you in a foul mood. Lesson two. You can put them in a foul or lonesome mood, but not the other way around. Do you understand your first and second lessons so far?"

Adalee jumped off her stool. "Understood." She walked toward the pool table, set two quarters on the side to indicate theirs was the next game.

Maisy chose pool cues from the slots and handed one to

Adalee. They leaned against the wall, drinks in one hand, pool cues in the other, waiting their turn. The crowd in the bar grew larger; Maisy avoided eye contact with Billy-Joe's table and Lila's gaggle of women. She scanned the tables and bar over the top of her glass with each sip she took. She mentally ticked off the names of people she recognized who hadn't seen her yet. Others she recognized but couldn't name—librarian, teacher, babysitter.

Adalee's laughter caused Maisy to turn: Adalee was hanging on to a tall guy with too-long blond curls and a torn T-shirt. Yuck. This must be the boyfriend.

The guy turned around, nodded at Maisy. "Hi, I'm Chad."

"I figured. Nice to meet you," Maisy said.

Adalee put her beer down on the side bar, handed her pool cue to Maisy. "I'm going to take a walk on the beach with Chad. I haven't seen him in, like, twenty-four hours."

"Oh." Maisy glanced around. "There went our pool game."

"Rain check?" Adalee asked.

"Sure, go on." Maisy slid Adalee's pool cue back into the wall hanger.

Chad took Adalee's hand and they walked toward the front door. Maisy shifted her purse up on her shoulder and moved to leave.

A hand landed on her elbow. "Don't you have the table next? If you don't want it, we're waiting." A man stood beside her; his eyes met hers.

"You can have the table." She smiled and took two steps around the pool table, sidled past the crowd at the bar until she shoved the front door open with her foot. Rich, humid coastal Georgia air lodged itself in her lungs.

She dug the keys to Mama's pickup truck out of her purse. Mama had forbidden Maisy from taking the Volvo, as she would most certainly move the driver's seat and Mama would never get it in the right position again. The street wavered in front of Maisy as she slid behind the wheel. She rested her head on the steering wheel and longed for her apartment in Laguna Beach overlooking the bay, where her pictures were neatly hung in silver-and-crystal frames, her books covered in white paper to give the bookshelves a clean look. A knock on the window startled her and she looked up to see Billy-Joe.

She rolled down the window.

"You can't drive, Maisy. Sheriff Mason sits at the end of this road every night waiting for people to leave the bar. It's his newest source of town income." Billy-Joe smiled. "Get out." He opened her door.

Defeat and humiliation left her weary. She climbed out of the truck. "I'm just really tired. I flew in from California today and I haven't eaten."

"Come on, we'll walk over to the Waffle House and get you a patty melt and a coffee."

Maisy smiled at him, remembering the better times with Billy-Joe, which seemed to be mixed with the bad times in a bitter cocktail. "That's probably not a great idea . . . for you. I'll call a cab or walk home."

Billy-Joe pointed to his truck. "Come on, I'll drop you off. I think I know where you live."

Maisy followed him. "You gonna get in trouble for this?"

"Get in the truck."

She climbed in the passenger seat and stared at the side of his face, at his stubble and thick eyelashes. "How's Candy?"

"Great." He started the engine, looked over at her. "We have two wild boys. Six and two years old."

"Wow." Maisy closed her eyes. "Life just keeps going, doesn't it?"

"Yes, it does." He pulled out into the road, waved as he drove past Sheriff Mason, and in minutes pulled into Maisy's driveway.

She sat there for a moment, then shifted in her seat and looked at Billy-Joe. "Was I really that bad? I mean . . . bad enough to have everyone hate me?"

He smiled at her. "I don't know anyone who hates you."

"Candy?"

"Okay, maybe she did once. But I can damn sure tell you she's forgotten about it by now, what with the kids and diapers and school. . . ."

"Yeah." Maisy opened her door. "Do you hate me?"

"Of course not, Maisy. We have great memories. Did I want to hate you? Sure. Any guy whose ego has been hurt wants to be mad. But you are, without a doubt, the hardest woman in the world to stay angry with."

"Really?"

"Really. Now get out of my truck." He grinned that wide country-boy grin that had first inspired her crush on him. Why hadn't she followed through with him? *Because he wasn't Mack Logan—that's why.*

The thought raised the hairs on her arms; she jumped from the truck. "Thanks for the ride."

He nodded and drove off while she stood in the driveway, stared at the front door of her childhood home. "Welcome home, Maisy," she said out loud, the whiskey making the three words into one.

She walked up to the front porch, sat down on a rocking chair. This was where she'd first fallen in love with Mack. The first place she'd known he was the one.

At the beginning of every summer since Maisy could remember, Mack Logan had arrived in his family's Volvo station wagon with his brother and parents. Riley would run down to Pearson's Pier to meet him, and Maisy would hardly see her again until Labor Day. Mack stole Maisy's role as Riley's best friend and became the primary source of her jealousy; each Memorial Day he kidnapped her sister and released her for only leftover moments with Maisy.

A few weeks into that last summer, Mack walked up to the front porch, where Riley stood waiting to go with him to the movie on the lawn, and something about the way he moved made Maisy stop, stare. She watched as he stepped onto the bottom step, and in the space between one breath and the next, her jealousy turned to desire. She knew Mack Logan was the boy she'd been waiting for all along.

She waited for a moment and then ran after Riley, set her gaze on Mack, and their summer romance began.

Even then there had been emptiness in Maisy, a need that she was convinced was unique to her, and she had sought to fill it with constant fun, beautifying, socializing. But during that last summer with Mack, she pulled away from all else and focused on him, making him her source of fulfillment.

One afternoon they sat above the county dam, watching water splash over the spillway. She gathered her courage and told him about the empty place in her, the yearning. He laughed and said that of course everyone had that place, that feeling, and if they claimed they didn't, they were lying. In the silence that followed, she realized that he knew her as no one else ever had, and she loved him.

Uncertain in this new first love, she was cautious, wary, afraid to mess it up, hesitant to jump too far or too fast into what she wanted. She withheld words of love and of the future in the faith that she would know the right time, the right place to speak them. As the summer neared its end, she understood—like a good ending in a novel—that the night of the bonfire would be the right time and place. They would make plans. He would go off to college while she finished her last year of high school, and then she would join him. Her mother had always told her that all good things were worth waiting for.

That night Maisy defied her father's curfew to join Mack at the fire. They moved away from the flames and under the lifeguard station, her skin prickling with sunburn and the need for his touch. Heat from the fire wafted toward the dark space in which they stood, and she lifted her arms to lay her palms flat on the underside of the guards' perch. Mack ran his hand down the inside of her arm, from her wrist to her torso. No other man would adore her as Mack adored her. No one would understand her as he did.

"I think I love you," he said, the words she'd wanted to hear all summer long.

It was here, in this scrap of time, that her memory failed her. She could not remember exactly what she said in return or what happened next. She wanted to believe she said, "I love you, too," but she wasn't sure.

And then there were torn images—Daddy coming toward her in a rage, calling Mack terrible names and grabbing her. Faces appeared before her as a crowd gathered around them. The realization that Riley had seen her and Mack at the fire and run home to tell their father hit her like a blow: betrayal.

Next thing she knew she was in her room sobbing, and Riley entered. Why, she couldn't remember. All she knew was that Riley's presence only compounded her rage. Cruel, hate-filled words spewed from her mouth, words that could never be recanted, a vow that could never be recalled.

She cried herself to sleep and woke early the next morning to listen to the cars of the summer people as they clogged the main road, heading home. The Logans' Volvo would be among the others pulling out onto the highway. But Mack would return next summer. She just had to make it through her senior year, and wait for him. She would stay true to him, and never let on to anyone how much it cost her. After all, all good things were worth waiting for.

That year, the emptiness inside Maisy returned and grew. She tried to obliterate it with constant motion—classes, cheerleading, dances, boys' attention and homecoming queen. By Memorial Day, all she could think of was Mack's return.

And then she learned that the Logans had put Driftwood Cottage up for sale. They were never coming back.

With nothing left to lose, Maisy let herself go wild over the summer in a round of nonstop partying, frantic with a need that she believed only Mack could satisfy. Yet every time she considered trying to contact him, the pain of his possible rejection stopped her. Then, while grasping for a feeling she had found only with Mack, she slept with Tucker Morgan, and before she knew it, she was on a plane headed for California.

During the thirteen years that followed, she had continued to believe that Mack was her first and only love.

EIGHT

RILEY

*D*awn light filled the observation tower with its sweet blessing. Riley hadn't been able to sleep past six a.m. in days. She'd climbed up the ladder and was sitting in the single wicker rocking chair looking over the beach, sea and horizon. She held *Walking on Water* by Madeleine L'Engle in her hand, but it was futile to pretend that she had enough presence of mind to start the book chosen by the Writers with Wit book club. Her mind filled to overflowing with thoughts of the week's festivities, Mama's illness. . . .

The ringing phone down in the kitchen startled her. She glanced at her watch: six twenty-five. Nothing good came from a phone call so early in the morning. She stumbled down the spiral steps, grabbed the receiver. "Hello." Her voice cracked on the day's first spoken words.

Sobbing was evident on the phone, gulping sobs. "Riley . . . I need you to come get me."

Confusion and weariness were washed away in a sudden flood of understanding: *Adalee was in trouble.* "Where are you? What happened?"

"Stupid Sheriff Mason had a speed trap at the end of Broad and I got . . . caught."

"Speeding?"

"Yes." Adalee's voice faded as though other words hid behind them.

"There's more," Riley guessed.

"I was driving Chad's car because he had too much to drink. I didn't think I'd had too much. I mean . . . really, only a couple beers."

"Oh, shit, Adalee. You got a DUI." Riley felt the truth crawl up her arms, over her gut in a nauseating clampdown.

"I have to hang up now. Can you come . . . get me?"

"How long do you have to stay there?" Riley stood, headed for the bedroom, holding the phone between her ear and shoulder. She grabbed her jeans off the floor.

"I've been here most of the night. I can go now if someone . . . bails me out. I thought Chad would, but he never came back."

"I can't leave Brayden by himself. Let me call Maisy to stay with him while I come get you."

Adalee's voice broke. "I am so, so sorry. Sheriff Mason told me Daddy would be ashamed of me. Please do *not* tell Mama. You just can't."

Riley promised, understanding that this was Palmetto Beach

and Mama would know anyway within the next few hours. She hung up on Adalee and poked her head in Brayden's room; he was sound asleep.

In the kitchen she called Maisy's cell phone five times before she answered with a groggy, "For God's sake, what do you want? It's six thirty in the morning."

"Your sister—the one you took to the bar last night—is in jail with a DUI. I need you to come here and stay with Brayden while I go bail her out."

"Oh, shit."

"Those were my exact words. Did you leave her at the bar by herself? She's barely even legal to drink."

"No, she left me. Her too-smooth boyfriend came and they went off together."

Riley exhaled.

"Don't go judging me. You couldn't have stopped her either."

"I'm not judging you. I'm exhausted and this is not the best way to start a new day."

"I left Mama's truck at Bud's last night."

"Then use the Volvo," Riley said.

"I'm on my way." Maisy's phone went dead. Riley brewed a pot of coffee; she needed it and she had a feeling Maisy would, too. She watched the coffee drip into the glass container—an old Mr. Coffee from Mama's house. She ran her fingers along a crack in the countertop and longed to update the kitchen. While the coffee dripped, Riley ran downstairs and unlocked the back door for Maisy.

Riley knew every sound and movement that this house made

in its waking and in its sleeping. She felt when the floorboards shifted, when the children's section was full, when Anne opened the bakery, when Brayden turned the water on for his shower.

Even when the Logans summered here more than thirteen years ago, she had known many of the house's sounds: Mr. Logan coming in from fishing, a storm blowing the shutters in a *smack-smack* song against the clapboard shingles, Mrs. Logan opening and closing the cupboards as she cooked dinner, Mack's door slamming before he came down the same back stairs Riley now came down every morning. The third stair from the bottom groaned the loudest on the left side.

The only rooms she'd never entered when the Logans lived here were the bedrooms: Mack's, Joe's, their parents'. Now she lived in the master bedroom and Brayden slept in one large room created out of two smaller bedrooms. She didn't think of it often—that she now lived and worked in the Logan house, that their life stories were entwined with hers.

Finally the floor shook as Maisy ran up the back stairs, shoved open the door into the kitchen. A tattered Southern Cal baseball cap covered her chestnut red hair. She wore a chocolate-colored velour Juicy Couture sweat suit and had the green look of a hangover around her eyes.

Riley swallowed her intended words of condemnation and regret. Instead she grabbed her purse. "I'll be back as soon as I can. How long can it take? I've never bailed anyone out before. . . . Brayden needs to get up by seven fifteen to meet Wes' parents, Jean and Art White, at the dock at eight. They're taking him out on their boat today. He'll kill me if he misses it. And you need to be at the front desk by nine, when the Blonde Book Club meets."

"The Blonde Book Club? You're kidding, right?"

"Nope. Totally serious."

"What do they read? Picture books?"

"This coming from a wannabe blonde?" Riley laughed, dug her car keys out of her purse.

"Just because I put lemon juice in my hair in the nineties doesn't make me a wannabe." Maisy smiled at Riley. "But really, why would they call themselves that?"

"Ask them." Riley set out toward the door, then turned. "Thanks for helping. I know Mama will find out eventually, but let's try to keep it between us for a while. She's stressed out enough."

"Oh, the joy of returning home." Maisy pouted. "I am so sorry about this. Even though it's not really my fault, I somehow feel like it is."

Riley nodded, opened the door to the stairwell and called over her shoulder, "There's a fresh pot of coffee on the counter. Brayden knows what to do for breakfast." Riley waved over her shoulder and ran down the back stairs.

The jail and the bond house were conveniently located next to each other on Tenth Street. Riley wrote out a check and handed it to Gentry Wallace—a boy she'd known since second grade. He told her he'd always known Adalee would have to be bailed out someday. Riley didn't laugh.

The Palmetto Beach precinct and jailhouse weren't exactly

built for hardened criminals, and Gentry took Riley back to where Adalee sat on a metal cot sobbing into her hands. She looked up when Riley entered the gray concrete hallway. "Thank God you're here." She jumped up, rubbed her face. "I was afraid you were going to make me stay to teach me a lesson."

"Let's go," Riley said.

Adalee followed her out, didn't speak a word during the drive to Mama's. When Riley pulled into the driveway, Adalee started the tears again. "Go ahead. Give me my lecture."

"Enough with the tears, Adalee. They don't work on me. And I'm not going to lecture you. You're twenty-one years old. You've lost your license until your court date—which is months away."

"Can't you call Daddy's friend—Tom something-or-other, the lawyer?"

"You want me to call on Daddy's old friend to get your license back?"

"How am I gonna get around all summer? Working for you is terrible enough without having to bum rides, too."

Riley stared at her younger sister for a long moment before she spoke. "Who are you? I don't even know this girl I'm looking at. What or who has changed you so much that you can't even see your own responsibility in this?"

Adalee opened the passenger-side door, climbed out and slammed the door harder than necessary. Riley watched her walk through the front door and spoke out loud to the empty car. "You're welcome."

The clock in the car blinked eight fifteen as Riley backed out of the driveway and worked her way back to the cottage, hoping that Brayden hadn't told Maisy that chocolate Pop-Tarts were an adequate breakfast.

The parking lot to one side of the bookstore was usually full of various SUVs and station wagons—the signature cars of the carpool moms who came straight to the bookstore from the school bus stop for coffee, gossip and book club. Riley couldn't have planned the bus stop location any better if she'd bribed the superintendant.

The back door was locked, and Riley fished her key out of her purse to let herself in through the beachside doorway. The ocean called to her, but she turned from it, and ran up the back stairs to grab a quick shower.

Quiet morning sounds filled the rooms: the swish of a window air conditioner, the cry of seagulls and far off, a boat horn. She walked over, turned off the air conditioner and opened the back window to listen to the waves, to let the fresh breeze of morning move through the rooms.

Riley looked at the clock—eight twenty-five a.m. Maisy would have dropped Brayden at the dock by now and should be on her way back. Riley liked to account for her son's whereabouts. During school, she had Brayden's schedule memorized and often closed her eyes and pictured him seated at various desks in the middle school that she herself had once attended. She imagined that her visions of him sent protection.

Walking toward her bedroom and bathroom, Riley unzipped her jeans. Bradyen's cracked door made her pause in the thin strip of light falling onto the hardwood floor. Riley leaned into the room, and felt their presence before she saw them: Brayden asleep in the bed; Maisy asleep on the beanbag chair in the corner.

"Maisy." Riley's voice echoed across the room, shattered sleep.

Maisy startled, rubbed at her face. Brayden sat up. "Hey, Mom. What time is it?"

"Almost eight thirty."

Brayden threw off his covers, jumped out of bed. "Mom, I was supposed to be at the dock a half hour ago. Why didn't you wake me up?" On the run for the bathroom, he tripped over his sneakers in the middle of the room.

"Maisy was supposed to wake you." Riley turned to her sister. "What in the . . . ?" She bit her bottom lip to stop the cuss word.

"I'm sorry. . . . I'm so messed up with the time zones. It was, like, three in the morning my time when I came over. . . . I thought I'd just lie down on this beanbag for a minute until I woke him up. I'm sorry." Maisy turned to Brayden. "I am so sorry, sweetie. It's my fault. I screwed up. Again."

Maisy's hair stuck out in several directions, her baseball cap on the floor.

Riley sighed. "Okay, let's figure this out. I don't have their cell phone number." She paced the room while Brayden ran to the hall bathroom, turned on the shower. "You take Brayden to the dock, see if they're still there. Then go back to Mama's and shower. I'll run the store until you get back. . . ."

"Damn, do you always think in such logical and sequential order? Do you have a five-minute-by-five-minute schedule for each and every day?"

Riley's shoulders sagged. "That is mean, Maisy. I'm just trying to—"

"Keep it all together. I know." Maisy turned away, walked to the window. She yanked her baseball cap over her hair. "You've always been the one to keep it all together. Make sure everyone does the right thing."

Riley stared at her sister's back. "I'll meet you in the bookstore in an hour or so."

"I'm sorry," Maisy repeated, but Riley thought she might be speaking to herself.

In her bedroom, Riley ran a brush through her hair, smoothed on lip gloss, slipped on a white linen shirt over her jeans. There was no time to worry about the perfect outfit or hairdo when the book clubs would be gathering and the store filling up with only Anne to handle everything until Ethel arrived in half an hour. "Damn," she mumbled and ran down the back stairs with her coffee cup in her hand.

"Hey, Anne," Riley called. "Is everything okay?"

Anne poked her head up from under the counter, her auburn hair bobbing in its ponytail, her T-shirt displaying a multicolored peace sign with the words *BOOKS NOT BOMBS* underneath. She sang along to Brad Paisley playing over the sound system. "Yeah, but I haven't unlocked the front door or checked out front for messages or deliveries." Anne tilted her head at Riley. "You okay?"

"Not one of my best mornings. I just want to make it to lunch and then I'll take a shower."

After Riley spent half an hour doing the automatic tasks of opening the store, assisting customers and welcoming early members of the book club, Ethel bustled through the front door. Her flowing skirt swept along the floor, carrying a dust bunny in its hem. Her right glove was larger than the left, making her hands look disproportionate. Riley hugged her. "What would I do without you?"

"Go crazy, most probably." Ethel pulled at a chain around her neck from which dangled the key for the old-fashioned cash register. "Most definitely."

Riley was grateful for Ethel's sense of humor, a grace note to her day. She walked back to the café. "Anne, I'm stealing a muffin. Put it on my bill."

Anne laughed. "Yeah, that bill is starting to look like the national debt."

Footsteps sounded behind Riley and she moved toward a customer she hadn't heard enter the store. His voice seemed to come from far away, and yet was right behind her. "I'll take one of those muffins, too," he said. "You can put it on *her* bill."

Riley felt the voice vibrate below her ribs. She turned quickly on her heels, stumbled and righted herself with her palm on the counter. Coffee splashed out of her mug and slid across the linoleum surface. He smiled; her heart emptied and filled in a single moment. "Mack," she said.

Like a vivid dream, he stood in the middle of her bookstore. His brown curls fell across his forehead. Hints of a boy's face showed beneath the mature bone structure and the stubble on his cheeks and chin. The lines around his eyes and mouth had deepened, but his smile was the same, wide and ready for fun. He wasn't any taller than the last time she'd seen him, six feet at the most, yet somehow she'd pictured him still growing.

She nodded, unable to find the words she'd stored up to say to him. "Hey," she said.

"That's it?" He reached forward and pulled her into a hug. "Hey? That's all I get after thirteen years?"

She hugged him back—too hard, too long, her cheek landing higher on his chest than it had all those years ago. He let go first. "I'm so glad you decided to come to this celebration," she said, her words sounding stiff. Thoughts flew through her mind like a flock of sandpipers startled off the shoreline: she hadn't taken a shower; she looked tired; she wasn't prepared.

"Well, thank you, ma'am." He smiled at her. "When did you get so formal?"

She punched the side of his arm.

"There she is, the girl who thinks she can beat me up."

"When did you get into town?"

"Late last night."

The back door opened, slammed against the wall, and a fresh wind burst through the café. Brayden stood in the hallway. "They left me," he said.

"Oh, Brayden."

Riley moved toward him, but he held up his hand. "Now my entire day is ruined. And it's all your fault."

Mack laughed. "Now this must be your son because only a mom can ruin a boy's entire day," he said.

Riley nodded. "Brayden Collins Sheffield."

Mack walked toward him. "Hello, I'm Mack Logan, an old friend of your mom's. There is no way she ruined your day."

"Yeah, right. She didn't wake me up in time and I missed the boat and now I can't go fishing."

Mack said something to Brayden, but Riley couldn't hear the words. Was she in a dream in which Mack Logan stood talking to her son about boats, fishing and tides? Dizziness threatened. She took a long sip of coffee, and then a deep breath. She attempted to smooth the hair back from her face. They both turned to her.

"Sorry, Mom. I didn't mean it."

"I know, cutie." She smiled at him.

"Ah, don't call me that. Can I go fishing with this guy?" Brayden pointed at Mack.

Riley felt momentarily confused by the question. What world was this?

Mack made eye contact with her while still talking to Brayden. "I'll take you fishing, to the same place I won every bet against your mother, but only after she shows me around my old house."

"Your house?" Brayden asked.

"The Logan family lived here before Gamma bought the building and made it into the store," Riley explained.

"You're a Logan?" Brayden squinted at Mack.

Mack narrowed his eyes back at Brayden. "Depends what you've heard about us."

Riley held her breath—what *had* Brayden absorbed through the years?

"Nothing, really. Just heard the name, that's all."

"Then you don't know how I beat your mom at the fishing tournament, at the sailing race, at the badminton competition?"

"Like she'd be hard to beat." Brayden rolled his eyes.

Mack laughed. "Actually, she was. And I'm exaggerating a bit. She's just being polite not mentioning how many times she beat me."

Brayden looked at his mother as if he didn't know her. "You did?"

"Of course."

Mack touched her elbow. "You too busy to show me around right now?"

She shook her head. "Just let me check on the book club and Ethel, and then I'm all yours."

He laughed. "Yeah, right."

The subtlety of the flirting words, the deeper laugh, combined to make her feel as though her feet had been put on the opposite legs, making her clumsy. "Have a muffin on me. The chocolate-chip ones are the best. I'll be right back." She turned to Brayden. "Where's Aunt Maisy?"

"She said there was no way she was going through the day without a shower. She went back to Gamma's and said to tell you she'll be here as soon as she can."

"Oh." Riley forced a smile despite her irritation with Maisy for contributing to her crazy morning. "Let me check on the book club." She walked toward the gathered Blonde Book Club, felt Mack's gaze follow her. Her mind went to questions she rarely considered: were her jeans too tight? Her shirt wrinkled? Her hair knotted?

The book club members waved in unison, like homecoming queens in a parade, which all of them appeared to be. "You all okay?" Riley asked the group.

"Yeah," Kiki Anderson answered. "We're just waiting on our coffee and muffins." She sounded like a whining child, and Riley forced herself to smile.

"I'll have Anne send them right over, and then my sister Maisy will stop by. You'll love her."

Kiki clapped her hands together. "Oh, I know who she is. It'll be fun to see her."

"Yes," Riley said. "Fun."

A fervent desire for a long hot shower came over Riley. She rejoined Mack and Brayden, her heart lifting at the thought of Mack being here. Someone called her name: she turned to see Lodge come through the front door with his camera, satchel and a wide smile. He waved.

The morning was coming at her too fast; she couldn't seem to keep up. Lodge arrived at her side, pushed his glasses up on his nose. "Morning, Riley."

"Hey."

"You forgot," he said.

She grimaced. "A little. I'm having a weird day—going to the bondman's office is never a good way to start."

"What?"

"Forget it," she said.

Lodge followed her glance to the café. "Am I imagining it or is that Mack Logan?"

"It's him," she said. "He just got into town."

"Oh, this is great. I can take a picture of two owners together—it'll make a great follow-up piece."

Riley swiped at her hair. "No way. No pictures of me looking like this. Maisy will be here in a minute—take her photo this time."

Lodge shook his head. "You never have understood how cute you are. You look fine, Riley. Maisy can't compare."

She turned away. "Yeah, right."

"To me," he said, and walked away as he said it so she wasn't absolutely sure he had.

Lodge and Riley entered the café, where Brayden and Mack were sitting at a table sharing a large muffin. Mack recognized Lodge, and his face broke into a smile. He stood up and shook his hand. "Man, it's good to see you."

Lodge laughed. "Good to see you, too." He turned to Brayden. "Hey, buddy, how's it going?"

"Hey, Mr. Barton. I'm good. You?"

"Just fine."

Brayden had chocolate in the corner of his mouth. "Mom, I'm going to check out the new magazines." He waved toward the periodical section. "Tell me when Mr. Logan is ready, okay?"

"Sure thing," Riley said.

Mack shook his head. "This is crazy, seeing all of you. So many great memories, huh? Those days were only thirteen years ago, but a lifetime, you know?"

"Yeah," Lodge said. "Somehow time marches on. Jobs, families."

"Do you have a family now?" Mack sat, motioned for Lodge to sit also.

Lodge shook his head, and set his camera on the table. "Lost my wife, Tibbie, to a rare blood disease years ago."

Mack shook his head. "I am so sorry. Any kids?"

Lodge shook his head again, and an awkward silence followed until Mack cleared his throat and said, "I wish I hadn't lost touch with everyone. I didn't . . . mean to."

"We never do," Lodge said. "And hell, you haven't missed much. You can probably catch up in about fifteen minutes."

"Maybe." He turned to Riley. "Are you . . . married?"

"No," she said, shifted her feet. Finding nowhere to put her hands, she clasped them in her lap. "Never . . . have been." Her skin flushed at relating facts she wasn't accustomed to speaking aloud.

Lodge filled the awkward pause. "So, Mack, tell us about life on the other side of Palmetto Beach."

"Life on the other side . . . hmm . . . it's good. I have a degree in architecture, work for a firm in Manhattan. Still single, but my brother, Joe, is married now; they're about to have their first kid." Mack leaned back in his chair. "We definitely have changed, haven't we? We aren't those kids who spent summers on this beach learning to fish, sail, smoke cigarettes, fall in love and get our hearts broken by the local girls."

Logan laughed. "Some of us still get our hearts broken by the local girls."

"I can imagine," Mack said.

"So, man, when was the last time we saw you?" Lodge asked.

"The bonfire the last night of summer," Mack said without hesitation.

"Yeah, yeah, I remember now." Lodge leaned back in his chair. "Crazy night. At least what I remember of it. That was right before we all left for college."

Mack nodded. "Yep." He glanced up at Riley. "You ready for that tour?"

Riley felt as though she'd been watching the scene from far away, and now that her attention was needed, she landed with a thud in the middle of the room—large and awkward. "Great. Let's go."

Lodge stood, lifted his camera. "Photo first?"

Riley shook her head.

Mack threw his arm around her, pulled her close. She looked up at him to tell him to let go, and Lodge's flash went off. Torn between wanting to stay, and wanting to throw Lodge's camera into the trash, she became immobile.

Lodge set the camera on the café table. "I'll wait until Maisy gets here, and take one more shot for the Sunday edition. You two go on. I'll get a cup of coffee while I wait."

"You sure?" Riley stepped out from under Mack's arm.

"Positive. Go give your tour."

Riley led Mack through the cottage rooms, one by one, explaining where they'd knocked down walls, what the rooms were used for. They stopped in the Kids' Corner, where a group of children was sitting on beanbag chairs, entranced as Ethel read *Treasure Island* out loud.

Mack leaned close to Riley and whispered, "This is so sweet. My mom would love to see it. She adores knowing that her old cottage is a bookstore."

Riley motioned for them to move away; they walked to the main section in the middle of the store. "I think your mom read about a hundred novels every summer. She could probably start a bookstore with all her old books."

His face held a shadow of sorrow; she recognized it because she'd seen it before. "Is your mom okay?" She touched his arm, then quickly withdrew her hand.

"She's fine." He looked out the window. "It's Dad who's not doing well. He has lymphoma. We're taking this trip to . . . get away, remember better days."

"Oh." Riley's eyes filled. "I am so, so sorry."

"It's been hard. I'm taking a couple weeks off work."

"Where exactly are you working?"

"I've been terrible about keeping in touch, but that doesn't mean I don't think about you . . . and your family. I do." He sat down in a club chair; Riley took a seat in the ladder-back chair next to him. "I design mostly commercial space for a small firm, Harbinger Associates."

"So you put your drawing skill to use."

"You remember?"

She smiled at him, shook her head. "Are you kidding? I remember everything about those summers." Embarrassment at her sudden confession made her stand. "But for some reason I thought you wanted to design houses. Did I make that up?"

"No, you remember right. I somehow got . . . sidetracked. Dad is good friends with the president and well . . . here I am."

"Yes, here you are. Come on, I'll show you the upstairs. It's not clean—we've had an insane morning—but I'll show you around."

Together they walked up the back stairs and entered the kitchen. She tried to see the house through Mack's eye. The upstairs part of the house had once held all four bedrooms, yet Riley had transformed it into one tiny kitchen with a table and a sitting area open to it, and two good-sized bedrooms. She moved through the rooms, fluffing pillows, straightening baskets of books and Brayden's schoolwork, his sports equipment. But the place still looked cluttered, worn. Yet she loved these rooms. They had held her and Brayden close.

Mack stood in the middle of the kitchen and took a deep breath. "This is amazing, Riley. My family loves books, and now our old cottage is a bookstore—and you live in it." He looked at her. "This is why I love life. It does make for some surprising coincidences, doesn't it?"

"Yes, it does. Connections," she said, "surprising connections."

"That, too," he said, and laughed.

Yes, they were connected, bound together by the past and the present. And for the first time in a long while Riley's life seemed more interesting to her than the novel on her bedside table.

NINE

MAISY

*M*aisy's clothes were strewn across her childhood bedroom. The room had changed very little since the day she left for California. The bulletin board held dried corsages; the pale pink walls whispered of adolescence; from the bottom right post of the bed hung one blue and one green pom-pom. Of course Mama had removed the R.E.M. band poster. Maisy walked over to the window and opened it in the hope that the breeze of an incoming storm would wash her mind clean.

It didn't work.

She showered and dressed, regret slowing her movements—for new and old mistakes. She hadn't been home twenty-four hours and she'd already screwed up. After dressing, she poked her head into Adalee's room, where she was sound asleep in a curled-up position. Maisy woke Adalee, told her to get up, get dressed and go see Mama and pretend nothing had happened. Now. And she was expected at the bookstore in an hour.

When Maisy entered the drawing room moments later, Mama was sitting up in bed with a large piece of white graph paper on her lap, her breakfast tray on the side table. Uneaten eggs had congealed on the plate, a single bite of English muffin had been taken and a few strawberries were scattered across the family china. Maisy walked over and kissed her mama on the cheek. "Good morning, Mama."

"Well, hello, sweet girl. Aren't you running a little late?"

"Yes, I am. The time zone messed me up. Riley's at the store. All is well."

Mama pointed to the graph paper with codes and numbers that looked like a strategic military chart. "You see, you're supposed to be at the book club meeting and Adalee is supposed to be here with me for the next hour, going over the . . ."

Maisy picked up the sheet of paper, and saw it was a grid schedule with the initials RS, MS and AS filling blocks of time. "Well, this is impressive."

"Riley did it. I'm just revising it."

Maisy looked around the room. "Where's your nurse? You hardly ate any of your breakfast."

"I told her to leave me alone, that I was sure my youngest daughter would be down any minute to eat with me."

Maisy looked away from her mother's penetrating blue eyes. Mama would know she was lying if she said everything was okay with Adalee—Mama always knew when her girls weren't being truthful. "I'm sorry I missed breakfast; I've got to go help Riley." Maisy shrugged. "But I'll see you this afternoon, okay?"

Maisy kissed her mama goodbye and somehow made it out of the house without having to explain why Adalee was still in bed. Maisy parked in the rear of the bookstore lot and entered through the back door. Morning light fell through the windows onto the scarred hardwood floors. She did love this place.

Riley's voice came from the other end of the store. The aroma of coffee and cinnamon wafted from the bakery. Women's laughter filtered from the book club corner.

Maisy looked toward the side room where the door was shut: the former library in the Logan home—now a storage area. The wooden double doors were closed. A bright red ribbon was tied around the two glass doorknobs with a calligraphy sign saying "*Do Not Enter.*" If that sign had been there the night she'd come here with Tucker Morgan, would it have stopped her? Could anything have stopped her in those days when she seemed bent on self-destruction?

She moved toward the doors, ran her hand over the glass knobs, felt their ridges in her palm.

Familiar voices made chill bumps run down her arms. She spun around and saw them—Mack Logan and Riley. Maisy froze, her heart—already battered with memory—stopped, then started with a stutter. They were laughing; Mack's arm was draped over Riley's shoulders. A man she didn't recognize stood in front of the group with a camera slung over his shoulder.

Ancient anger rose from a place Maisy had pretended didn't exist. In slow steps she moved toward them.

Mack saw her first and smiled. That heartbreaking smile. The one she'd remembered exactly right. His hair fell across his forehead and she knew that underneath was a thin scar from a boat accident.

"Maisy."

She went to him, threw her arms around him with an abandon she immediately regretted, yet couldn't seem to stop. "Mack," she said, then stepped back to look at him.

At last she recognized Lodge, hugged him, too. They stood in a semicircle, and Maisy said, "We look like we're about to perform some primitive dance to the Driftwood gods."

Lodge lifted his camera. "Hey, let me get a quick shot and then I'll go finish this follow-up article. I think I have everything I need, right?" He glanced at Riley.

"The newsletter I gave you has the details," she said.

Maisy watched her sister's nervous movements, knowing them as well as she knew her own: the toss of the hair, the rub of the eyes and the shuffle of the feet.

Riley called Brayden over and they lined up in a row: Brayden, Maisy, Mack and Riley smiled for the camera.

Logan shook his head after he snapped a few more pictures. "Time warp," he said.

Maisy laughed. "Yeah, wouldn't that be nice."

Brayden moved back to his seat at a nearby table, but he continued to observe them through squinted eyes. Riley went to him and Maisy wondered for the hundredth time which man had given this child his quiet spirit. Did whoever it was even know that Brayden existed? She glanced at Mack. She wouldn't imagine it could be him—Riley had denied it vehemently ever since the day she came home from college.

"Maisy," Riley said, "will you take the tray of coffee and muffins to the book club?"

"Yes, ma'am." Maisy heard the bite of resentment underneath her own words.

Riley exhaled, that damn disapproving exhale. "Forget it. I'll do it."

Maisy held up her hand. "I said I'd do it. I woke Adalee and told her to be here in an hour."

"Thank you," Riley said. "Thank you so much." Then her face went expressionless, flat. "Damn."

"What?" Maisy followed her sister's gaze.

"Poor Ethel is having to deal with Mrs. Winter again. She keeps buying hardcover novels and then returning them, pretending she's never read them . . . and gets another."

"Does she think this is a library?" Maisy took a step toward the front counter.

Riley put her hand on Maisy's arm. "Don't say anything. It's just not worth it. Her son is a local police deputy and she'll throw a monumental fit, and then we'll get a call from the sheriff's office, and then he'll come in here wanting to know why we'd embarrass his mother in that disgraceful way."

Maisy laughed. "Sounds like you know what you're talking about."

"It's happened too many times."

"Good ol' Palmetto Beach."

Riley turned to Mack. "Okay, I've absolutely got to get to work. But we'll see you later this weekend, won't we?"

"Absolutely," he said.

Maisy studied Riley, watching for signs of attraction, lust, even love. When Riley left to wait on customers, Maisy sidled up to Mack. "Hey," she said.

He smiled. "It is so weird to see my old home like this. But it's like it was meant to be."

She nodded, and then blurted out, "Want to meet for lunch or something? Riley and Mama have me working nonstop, but I do get a lunch hour."

"I'm headed to the pier to fish with Brayden and Dad, but we can meet for a late lunch. One o'clock at the Beach Club?"

She nodded again, her usual quick wit failing.

"Great," he said, motioning to Brayden that he was ready to go.

Maisy stood immobile while her nephew and Mack walked out the back door toward the beach. Anne stood behind the bakery counter, piling muffins on a wicker tray. Maisy approached the counter, broke off a piece of a banana-nut muffin. "Thank God for the bakery."

"Yeah, I've heard that one before. Coffee?" Anne asked.

"Please." Maisy picked up the full tray Anne had prepared. "I'll take this over to the book club and be right back."

The six women sat in a circle, purses and tote bags scattered on the floor. "Hi, ladies." Maisy entered the group, stood in the center. "I'm Maisy Sheffield. I'll be helping with the book clubs for the next week or so while Mama is laid up. Please let me know if you need anything." She set the tray on the large and, in her opinion, heinous-looking coffee table. It was made of pressed wood, something she hated with the same fervor their childhood preacher had hated dancing.

A tall blonde stood up. "Hi, I'm Betty Oberman. This"—she ran her manicured hand in a circle—"is the Blonde Book Club. We meet every Friday morning."

"You read a book a week?" Maisy asked. She took a quick glance at each woman, trying not to be obvious. Yes, each was a different shade of blond.

"No . . . but we talk about lots more than just books."

"Great." Maisy looked over her shoulder at the cash register, where Ethel had a long line. "Can I ask you a question?"

"Sure." Betty smiled.

"Do you have to be a blonde to be in the book club?"

Betty's smile grew larger. "Oh, no. Definitely not. We called it that because we were all friends in high school—and we all had blond hair back then. Of course we all have to fake it now, so we thought it was funny. Millie's not here—but she has black-as-a-raven hair."

These women were younger than Maisy, so she wouldn't have known them in high school. "You all went to Palmetto High?"

They nodded in agreement. Betty answered for them all. "We graduated six years ago."

"Go, Dolphins." Maisy faked a rah-rah sound. "I graduated from there also."

"We know," Betty said. "You were only seven years ahead of us. Everyone knows who you are."

Maisy studied the woman's face, and found a sweet smile.

"You know, we are much more than a book club. We are part of a group called PEO, which is Philanthropic Education Organization. We raise money to give to women to continue their education. Books are just our reward and excuse to get together."

"That's wonderful," Maisy said.

"When you're free, why don't you sit with us a while? Whenever she's here, your mama always joins us at the end."

"Okay, that would be nice."

Maisy grabbed her coffee cup from Anne, checked the book club time slots and updated the RSVP list for the party. When she finished, she scanned the store; it needed help—aesthetic help. Some paint, a floor polish, new furniture, bookshelves that didn't sag. She'd have to talk to Riley about it. In her mind she saw exactly what she could do to this place. It had good bones, but the wide plank floors were worn and chipped, the open beams dull and dusty, the furniture covered in horrid faded paisley and floral prints that reminded her of the formal living room in Mama's house, which was probably where most of this stuff had come from.

Maisy sat outside the Blonde Book Club circle. They had, after all, invited her. They smiled at her, but continued their conversation about Kelly-Anne's unnamed boyfriend. From the gist of the conversation, Maisy determined that Kelly-Anne wouldn't offer his name, she was distraught because he told her he loved her, yet he stayed with his wife. Obviously this group of women was best friends.

Maisy made a cynical *huff* without realizing it.

"Excuse me?" Kelly-Anne turned to Maisy. "Did you say something?"

"No, sorry."

Another woman leaned forward. "I know exactly what you're going through. You want to tell yourself not to love a man who is unavailable—it is wrong and terrible and hurtful, *but* you just can*not* tell your heart what to feel and what *not* to feel."

Kelly-Anne wiped at her eyes. "Exactly. It just sucks. I know I have to walk away from him. I am not this kind of woman."

Another blonde exhaled, shook her head. "Doesn't being in love with someone you can't have just make you crazy?"

Kelly-Anne nodded. "Crazy."

"I know." A murmur of agreement went up around the circle. Betty held up the book they'd just read: *Wuthering Heights*. "I think Emily Brontë agrees. Love can make you crazy. Literally in this case."

Maisy couldn't resist. Riley had put her in charge of book clubs, so she'd step up to the job. "Okay," she said, "what is the craziest thing you've ever done for love?"

Laughter filled the circle. Kelly-Anne went first. "Well, I had my brother remove the wheels on the car belonging to my lover's wife so that when she went out the next morning, she found the car sitting on cinder blocks."

Betty took a sharp inhale. "Oh, Kelly-Anne, that was so mean. It's not her fault."

Kelly-Anne dropped her head. "I know, I know. I felt desperate and weird all at the same time. I wouldn't do it again. I didn't steal the wheels. I just had to do something, anything to vent my frustration. It was so stupid and doesn't even make any sense."

Maisy nodded. "We all do the stupidest things for love."

"I bet you've never done anything that stupid. Or dated a married man."

Maisy laughed. "Oh, don't be so sure."

The conversation switched in an abrupt turn-around when Kiki clapped her hands. "Okay, who wants to call the library about the fund-raiser?"

"I will," said a woman in a tank top and frayed jeans.

"Hey, everyone," Riley called out. Maisy twisted her neck to stare at her sister, now showered and changed into a skirt and linen shirt. The women looked up at her as if blinking into the sunlight. "Just checking in on you."

Kiki stood. "Hey, Riley. Where have you been hiding your sister? We just love her. . . ."

"Of course you do. Everyone does," Riley said, her smile only half formed as Adalee came to her side. "This is my younger sister Adalee."

Adalee nodded and pulled on Riley's sleeve. "I need your help," she whispered. "I don't know where to start on this stupid project."

Riley's smile stayed in place. "I'll leave you all to your discussion. I'm sure Maisy has it all under control."

"Nice to meet you, Adalee," the group chorused.

Maisy fidgeted in her chair, uncomfortable now in the midst of these women. She stood. "So wonderful to meet all of you. Please let me know if I can do anything. And I hope to see you at the festivities this week."

"Wouldn't miss it for the world," Betty said.

Maisy glanced up at the clock. Soon she'd meet Mack for lunch. Maybe, just maybe, this trip home would be bearable after all. Maybe the house did connect people, bringing happiness to all who passed through its doors. Now, finally, she and Mack could finish what they had started.

R I L E Y

*D*espite the rocky start to the morning, Riley felt the bookstore come more alive as the day progressed, as if the presence of her sisters and Mack Logan had unleashed a new energy within the cottage. Maisy went out for lunch, pretending to go alone, yet Riley had heard her invite Mack.

As usual, keeping busy at the store helped Riley keep her emotions from wreaking havoc on her heart. Now that school was out, the store filled with teenagers guzzling coffee and listening to music. Younger kids came in with frazzled mothers not yet accustomed to the school-free days. Riley had asked Adalee to spend some of her time fixing up the children's section, which was left in constant disarray by unsupervised children whose mothers browsed the other sections.

Ethel called Riley over to check on some new orders. She took the order form and fall catalog into her office, shut the door and scanned the titles. She shut her eyes and whispered out loud, "Oh, Mama, I need you here." Mama was the one who knew intuitively what the Palmetto Beach community wanted to read. Riley used to argue with her about certain titles, and been wrong once too often, left with unsold inventory. Now she relied on Mama's un-erring choices. Riley stuck the order form in her bag and decided to take it to Mama that evening.

For the rest of the day, Riley attempted to keep up a cheerful front for the customers. Inside she felt jittery and unsettled as she prepared for that evening. Nick Martin, the bestselling adventure novelist, would be signing and reading from his recent book, *Gold Hunt.*

The book clubs that gathered that day adored Maisy, which didn't surprise Riley. Adalee stayed in the back room, working on a timeline for the house. When she came out she talked constantly about Chad and where he was, how much fun he was having without her. Riley didn't know how to convince her sister that there were more important things than who did or did not go to the beach party, who hooked up with whom. Adalee's lack of a driver's license didn't do much to improve her attitude.

By some miracle, Kitsy had still not learned about Adalee's night spent in jail, and in her phone calls, she was calm. Late that afternoon, Riley stood in the shop's storage room, surrounded by unopened boxes. The poster-board presentation of the timeline of the house was set against the wall. Despite her complaints, Adalee had taken the box of pictures and information about the house's history, which Riley had handed over, and produced a clear pictorial history. She'd divided the board into decades, with a picture of the house from each period and a list of the family or families that had owned it during that time, including pertinent information about the town. Black-and-white photos created a frame around the board. Adalee had stopped in 1996—the year the Logan family sold the house to Kitsy.

"Ethel," Riley hollered out the door. "Do you know where Adalee is?"

"How am I s'posed to keep track of the Sheffield sisters? For God's sake, even their mama can't do that."

Riley laughed, closed the storage room door. So many families had come and gone through this house. She did not want to have to sell out to still another family. This was *her* home, her refuge.

The door to the storage room opened, and Ethel poked her head in. "There's a long line forming for Nick Martin's book signing, and it's still two hours away. This is great news. . . ."

Riley forced her thoughts to the evening ahead. "Did we order enough books?"

"Oh, yes. I anticipated a great turnout."

Riley brushed her hair back, and entered the store to make sure everything was ready for the author's signing. It was a huge coup to get Nick Martin to come to Driftwood Cottage to kick off the week of anniversary festivities. He didn't go on tour often anymore—his adventure novels hit the bestseller lists the week they were released.

Riley had gone all-out for this signing. The gourmet store across the street had provided free wine; the podium was set up for his talk; the chairs were organized in neat rows. There would be a raffle to win a stack of signed books and a bottle of Frei Brothers wine, from the winery where the climactic scene in the novel took place. Riley always made sure to read the book before the author arrived, to have a special giveaway that tied to the novel's plot. If effort equaled success, she and the store would survive. Unfortunately this was not always the case in the book world. Rarely were they able to predict what would sell well. Mama was better than most at this guessing game.

Riley fixed the crooked tablecloth at the book-signing table and was startled by Anne's hand on her shoulder. "Hey." Riley hugged her. "You didn't have to come tonight. You have the night off, remember?"

"I know, but I thought you might need some help and I brought you a little something." Anne had her hand behind her back. Her T-shirt read: *Lead me not into temptation. I can find it myself.*

"What is it?"

Anne withdrew a piece of pottery from behind her back. "Wings."

Delicate and thin, these angel wings were smaller than most of the ones Anne crafted. Riley flipped them over to see what word she had carved: REST. "Oh . . . they are beautiful. So sweet and . . . I don't . . ."

Anne held up her hand. "I know what you're going to say— that you don't need these wings. But you do. You most definitely do. And I made them for you. I knew you had to have them."

"I am so grateful." Riley hugged Anne. "Now go take your night off. Okay?"

"Nope, I'm here to help." Anne headed back to the front desk.

Riley slipped the pottery wings behind the café counter, where they would be safe from damage. Anne had last made Riley wings five years ago, when Brayden had broken his arm. They had said HEAL. Riley ran her fingers over the word REST and took a deep breath. Not yet, not just yet.

Maisy and Adalee came through the front door, wound their way around the line of people waiting for Nick Martin. They'd obviously gone home to shower and change. Adalee's kinetic energy sparked across the room. Maisy's smile seemed to be lit from within, her hair catching the leftover light.

Lodge came in behind them, fulfilling his promise to cover the first night's event. He stood against the back wall. Riley sensed his presence as she brushed crumbs from the podium, placed a water bottle under the stand. She waved at him. He gave a single nod.

Adalee tapped her hand on the podium. "Someone should tell Mama about this great crowd."

Riley hugged her. "Great idea. Why don't you let her know? Maisy, would you hand out numbers to the people in line so they can browse the store without losing their place? Adalee, you pile the books up on the signing table while I check on the wine. Okay?"

Maisy bowed in mock submission. "Okay, boss. But I'm keeping my eye out for Nick. If he's as cute as his picture in the book, I'm sitting in the front row."

Riley narrowed her eyes. "Do not flirt with the author. I'm begging you."

Maisy rolled her eyes. "We wouldn't want anyone to have any fun now, would we?"

Riley ignored the sarcasm and scanned the room for anything amiss. Maisy wrapped her arm around her shoulder. "I'm sorry, really. You're just trying to do your job. I know that. But can I offer a small suggestion?"

"What?" Riley shrugged off Maisy's arm.

"Since you made me leave my job for more than a week, and come here to help you—we need to do something about the decor in this place. Really. Make it more comfortable."

"And with what money would you like to do that?"

"Family money? I have so many ideas about how to fix this place up—we can Beach Chic the entire place on wholesale. . . ."

Riley held up her hand. "Let's just get through this week."

Adalee leaned up against the counter and sighed. "Chad said he was coming, but I don't see him."

"Please," Maisy said. "Can we talk about something besides Chad and his whereabouts?"

Adalee's eyes filled with tears. "That is so mean."

Riley hugged her little sister. "Let's concentrate on this book signing, and then we'll find Chad. How's that?"

"Great. But can I ask you a quick question that is making me crazy?"

"Of course."

"Why does Ethel wear those white gloves?" Adalee leaned closer to Riley and whispered, "They're dirty."

Riley pulled on her sister's ear in a reminder of the days when Mama would flick their ears when they were being too loud at dinner: an annoying punishment the sisters had made fun of throughout their adolescence. "I've never asked," Riley said. "I figure she has her reasons."

"Don't you think it's a little weird?"

"I guess sometimes you get so used to things that you don't even notice them anymore. So, no, I don't think it's weird at all."

"I do." Adalee glanced at the front desk. "And I bet the customers do, too."

"The customers love her, Adalee. Adore her. Maybe they know that appearances don't matter as much as other things. . . ."

"Why do I always feel . . . so judged by you?"

"I have no idea. . . . I'm sorry."

Adalee stamped her foot. "God, I just want to go to the party at the Beach Club."

"Well, while I'm ruining your life, will you run upstairs and tell Brayden he can spend an hour at the beach before dark? I told him to finish cleaning his room and then . . ."

Adalee nodded, turned on her flip-flops. "Whatever," she said as she ran toward the back of the store.

An older couple approached Riley and Maisy; Riley smiled at them in vague recognition. This always happened at the beginning of the summer—it took her a moment to remember the summer people's names.

The man, his hair white, wrinkles embedded in his smile, held out his hand. "Riley Sheffield. It is so good to see you again. Mark and Lauren Rutledge."

The room wavered as though Riley were being held underwater. A tremor ran through her middle, where Brayden had once grown inside her womb. Resolved not to give away her trembling, Riley held out her hand for Mr. Rutledge to shake. "It is so nice to see you again. You haven't been back in years."

Mrs. Rutledge offered a tender hug, which Riley returned. "Thirteen to be exact. When we received the invitation, we just knew we had to come celebrate with Kitsy and see the store. We love this town. It holds so many dear and wonderful memories."

"Wonderful memories," Riley agreed. She took two steps backward. "Thank you so much for coming. Excuse me a moment? Hopefully you'll be here all week?"

The older couple nodded.

Riley sensed she was being rude, yet escape seemed her only option. She allowed Maisy to take over the conversation, and ran up the back stairs. Brayden had already left for the beach and Adalee was gone, too; the apartment was empty. Riley dropped into a kitchen chair. The Rutledges had raised one son, Sheldon. Last Riley had heard, he was in Iraq with the Air Force. Mr. and Mrs. Rutledge had no clue that their grandson was playing with his friends on the beach a few yards away.

With the motions of a deeply ingrained habit, Riley climbed the spiral stairs to the observation tower, where she breathed in the fresh breeze. She needed air—deep gulps of it. The sea spread toward the horizon in a wash of blues with Brayden at its tattered edge. He bent over to pick something up off the sand. His blond curls, his tanned skin and his gangly body seemed a natural part of the sand, sea and waves. This miracle of a child she had kept to herself—her secret. By refusing to name Brayden's father, she had intended to preserve Sheldon's freedom, yet she had failed to consider Mr. and Mrs. Rutledge, Brayden's grandparents.

Brayden was hers to protect. To love. But now, with the Rutledges in the store below, her well thought-out reasons for secrecy echoed hollow, vacant and selfish.

As though he felt his mother's gaze upon him, Brayden looked up and waved at her. *Hey, Mom,* his lips mouthed the words—no twelve-year-old boy wanted to be caught hollering at his mom. He turned and threw something into the ocean. Two men approached him: one younger and tall, one older and frail—Mack and Sheppard Logan. Brayden spoke to them, laughed: past and present blurred together.

Riley climbed down the ladder, obligation the moving force now. There were a hundred people downstairs, a *New York Times* bestselling author on the way to speak and two sisters who needed supervision. She went to the bathroom, wiped her face clean of regret and disorientation, and descended the back stairs to host the evening with warm efficiency.

Eleven

Maisy

_M_aisy watched Mr. and Mrs. Rutledge browse among the bookshelves, pausing occasionally to greet people they knew. What was wrong with Riley, walking away from old family friends?

Maisy greeted each patron with a smile and a slip of paper with a number on it. "You'll be able to get right in line with this number. Please feel free to enjoy a glass of wine."

"Number thirty-seven," Maisy said, handing a yellow slip to a woman who was reading a book in line.

The woman looked up with a smile. "Hey, Maisy." Her hand fluttered.

"Oh, Lucy . . . hi." Maisy fought her sudden panic. "How are you?"

"Good. You?"

"Great. Just great. It's wonderful to see you. . . . Can we catch up later? I have to hand out all these numbers."

"Of course." Lucy nodded, and gazed after her, the best high school friend who ran away to California practically on her wedding day, leaving her short one bridesmaid.

The line turned around the corner and Maisy handed numbers out to the last patrons. *Run. Just run.* Her internal voice screamed in furious words that she swore others must be able to hear. She glanced around the room, hoping to see Mack. They'd had a quick lunch that afternoon, like one note in a song she was dying to hear in its entirety. If she found him, she'd grab on to him like a life preserver—wasn't that what she always used men for? The thought made her dizzy, it was so true. She snatched up a bottle of the Frei Brothers wine.

The storage room doors were unlocked. Maisy slipped inside, slid to the floor against the wall. A few drops of wine spilled onto the floor. She glanced around the room for a plastic glass or Styrofoam coffee cup, but saw only boxes of books, stationery, a chair with a broken leg. . . .

"Great, everything but what I need." She took a long swallow of wine straight from the bottle and closed her eyes.

This was a nightmare. How had she thought she could avoid Lucy Morgan, Tucker's wife? She would not hide in here with her pitiful bottle of wine and recoil in fear like the coward she was. This shameful, cringing girl was not the woman who lived in Laguna Beach.

The only decent thing about returning here was Mack. Their lunch today had proved that he was still as she'd remembered. He

had looked at her across the table with the same wide-eyed wonder
he'd had all those years ago. In a mood of quiet intimacy they had
talked about their lives in New York and California. She hoped
that maybe this would bond them together—the knowledge that
they had experienced a wider world beyond Palmetto Beach.

Maisy swallowed more wine and then took inventory of the
room, yet saw only what it had looked like then—the night she'd
come here with Tucker. The difference one decision could make
in a life, one moronic decision . . .

It was a year after Mack had left; Maisy had graduated in May.
Riley had given birth to Brayden in June. Lucy and Tucker were
engaged. Months before the wedding, Lucy had asked Maisy to
be a bridesmaid and she'd done her duties—helped pick out the
dresses, choose the flowers, stamp the invitations. Lucy was the
first of their group of friends to get married straight out of high
school. The week before the big event, Maisy ran into Tucker
at Bud's. She joined him and his friends, keeping up with the
whiskey-laced Coke drinks, which they'd snuck onto the outside
patio where the Ping-Pong tables would have to do until they
were twenty-one and could go into the bar area. She prided herself
on her ability to keep up with the boys; she was one of them.

The night wore on, and the alcohol had settled like a dull
haze over her senses. She and Tucker played Ping-Pong until
she dropped the paddle to admit she could barely see the ball
anymore.

"You excited about the wedding next weekend?" she asked,
leaning against the table.

He shrugged. "I can't believe it's come up so fast. . . ."

"You'll be a married man by this time next week," Maisy teased. She meant it innocently, didn't she?

They left the bar together, walked toward his home on Ninth Avenue. The floating feeling born of liquor, the closeness of an old friend who was marrying another friend, allowed Maisy's words to come easy and light as they passed the Logan house.

She pointed at Driftwood Cottage. "He was the only guy I would have married."

"Pining after a summer love? Doesn't seem your style, Maisy."

"My style?" She stopped, stared up at the empty dark house the Logans had put up for sale.

"Yeah, you seem more like the live-and-let-live type, the kind that loves and leaves."

"Why would you say that?"

"Because I've known you forever."

"You *don't* know me." Maisy stamped her foot. "Nobody around this hick town really knows me."

In the moonlight, in the dark of the night with Mack Logan on her mind, Maisy heard Tucker Morgan say, "I'd like to really know you."

Until that point she'd avoided loneliness with frenzied partying, but now the emotion settled deeply into her gut. "Then come on," she whispered. "The house is for sale. Mama's trying to buy it. Let's see if it's open."

The front door swung inward without resistance. They tiptoed around unsold objects belonging to the Logan family. Heartbreak followed her step for step through the living room, past the kitchen, into the front study, where moonlight fell in bands on the sea grass rug. She whispered, "This was Mr. Logan's library."

"I wonder why they didn't come back this year," Tucker said in a whisper.

"Mama told me that with their last child in college, they didn't know when they'd ever come back, and they just didn't want to hold on to it. I've never heard from Mack. . . . I guess he's probably finished his freshman year by now."

"He broke your heart," Tucker said.

The truth of his words brought unbidden tears. "I hate him," she said. "He never called. He never wrote. He left last summer with . . . promises to keep in touch."

"You only think you love him because he might be the only guy who didn't chase after you."

"Not true."

Tucker came toward her then. "I'm sorry," he said. "If you want me to go find him and kick his ass, I will."

"That'll do me a lot of good." She smiled at him, and then his hand was behind her head, in her hair, and he drew her toward him. Her first thought was that there was no way she was going to kiss him. The second thought was obliterated by confusion, and then dull desire.

In the Logan study, in the room in which she'd read and hung out with the family, longing replaced rational thought. The desire for Mack was channeled into another and distant yearning—for someone to hold her, to comfort her.

On an old sea grass rug, Maisy lost herself in fantasy that this union was what should have happened between her and Mack.

The dark night and the empty house echoed their desire as she and Tucker came together for entirely different reasons.

It was her first time.

The act itself was brief and empty; she regretted it before it was over. She lay on the floor in the quiet night with the painful understanding that no one save Mack could fill the emptiness inside her. When Tucker fell asleep with whiskey breath on her cheek, she cried silent tears and slipped out into the night. She walked for hours on the beach and wished on every star that the night could begin again—that she could erase what had just happened in Mack Logan's old house with her best friend's fiancé.

She went home to spend a sleepless night, and the next morning, she knew with an iron certainty that she had to get out of this place, where her worst self lived. She packed two bags with her favorite clothes, her best makeup and all the cash she'd made working at the Beach Club serving overweight businessmen who thought they had a chance with the bikini-clad girls jumping on and off the boats in the marina.

She didn't call her family until she'd landed in Los Angeles. She imagined the wailing and gnashing of teeth that ensued. Mama went to bed for days; Riley reeled while adjusting to single motherhood—she called Maisy's cell phone five, six times a day, begging her to come to her senses. By God, she was supposed to be a bridesmaid in her best friend's wedding. Adalee was only ten years old at the time, and she pleaded with Maisy to come get her, let her live with her in California.

Maisy couldn't explain to Adalee that she didn't really "live" in

LA yet—she moved among youth hostels while making money as a waitress until she found the town of Laguna Beach and the Beach Chic store, where she'd worked ever since.

Those days seemed a million years gone. A different person existed now. Or so she had thought. Yet here she sat in the same damn room, and she was the same damn person. She hadn't erased anything; what she'd thought was gone had been waiting here for her.

She leaned against the wall, took another swig of wine and attempted to ignore Riley's voice calling her. She could not go out there and see Lucy. She'd never heard from her friend except for one brief voice mail full of tears saying she couldn't believe what Maisy had done; she'd never have expected *that* of her. Surely, then, Tucker had told her. But they'd married anyway.

"Maisy." Riley's voice was closer now, and the door opened. "What in the hell are you doing?" She grabbed the wine bottle.

"Hiding," Maisy said. "I can't go back out there." She sat up.

"Why?"

"Ten million reasons."

Riley held out her hand to bring Maisy to her feet. "I don't care what your reasons are. I need your help. The place is packed."

Maisy shook her head.

"You are so selfish. Whatever your problem is, it's not as important—"

Maisy stood, planted her hands on her hips. "You're not gonna say *as family*, are you? Family? You don't mean the entire family now, do you, Riley? When you say family, you mean you and Mama. I'm just an extra, an added bonus when you need a helping hand. Because who is all this work benefiting? Not me. This is all about you and Mama and your precious store. Because it sure ain't about me, or my job, or my life."

Riley's face hardened. "I can't even . . . answer that right now. I can't . . ." She turned away. "If you need to leave, go ahead, Maisy." Riley's back was straight as she walked away; then her head tilted to the right as she greeted someone who'd come through the front door.

Maisy stood in the opening of the storage room, her empty stomach sick from the wine, her heart heavy with her cruel words and crueler memories. She would go grab her bags and return to Laguna Beach right now, get out of here, out of this house, out of this town. She moved in slow motion to the back door, across the porch. She took off her shoes, allowed her feet to sink into the soft sand.

She wiped at her face, felt tears she didn't know she'd cried. Brayden and two men stood at the water's edge, their backs to her while Brayden cast a net. In the twilight, they pulled the net in to find a stingray writhing inside the nylon. They released the sea creature, laughter echoing across the beach. She couldn't see their faces, but she knew the sound: Mack Logan's laugh.

She smiled, hung on to the thought and image of him to buoy her in the midst of memories that threatened to sink her.

He was here.

Now.

Maisy would stay, all right. But not for the reasons her family thought.

There were enough people in that store to keep her from coming face-to-face with Lucy. She could do it. Absolutely. She was stronger than the girl who had left years ago.

She pulled her hair back, wiped her face, attempted to separate her mashed eyelashes with her pinky nail and walked back toward the bookstore. A man joined her on the porch: tall, dark haired. She hadn't met him before, yet he looked familiar. They collided as she attempted to open the door to let him in.

He laughed. "Hey, I was trying to open the door for *you.*" He gave a slight bow. "I was told to come in the back door. . . ."

"Got it," she said, and held the door open with her foot. "I'm Maisy Sheffield." She held out her hand.

He shook it. "Nick Martin."

"I knew you looked familiar. My family owns the store. . . . We are so glad you've come."

"My pleasure." He gestured for her to walk through.

"Follow me," she said, and gave him her best smile.

"Anytime." He laughed, and she looked over her shoulder at him while she led him to the front of the store.

"Riley." Maisy tapped her sister on the shoulder. "Nick Martin is here."

Riley turned; she was now a different woman from the one who had come into the storage room and berated her younger sister. "It is so lovely to meet you," she said, held out her hand. "As you can see, you've drawn a huge crowd. We're ready to get started whenever you are."

"Let's go then," he said. He turned to Maisy. "I always panic when I get close to a signing, thinking this will be the time no one shows up."

"I'm sure that never happens to you."

"Hey," he said. "It happens to everyone."

She pointed toward the podium. "Once everyone is seated, I'll introduce you."

"Great."

Riley followed Maisy to the podium, whispered, "I was going to introduce him."

Maisy spun around. "You said you wanted my help."

Riley held up her hands, whispered in harsh words, "You smell like you've been drinking."

"I had a few sips of wine, that's all. If you call that drinking, you've obviously not been living with Mama."

"Then go for it." Riley stepped back, made a gesture toward the podium. "Have fun."

Maisy tapped the microphone, and the crowd moved to their chairs. "Welcome to the Driftwood Cottage Bookstore event for *New York Times* bestselling adventure writer Nick Martin."

The crowd applauded and Maisy gestured toward the author standing behind her. She read from Riley's typed introduction on the podium, added her own comments, which brought laughter, and then stepped aside for Nick. She took a seat in the first row. She focused on Nick, on his talk about his writing journey and how he'd come to this place. His story was inspiring and funny, filled with witty, self-deprecating descriptions of embarrassing moments on the road.

After he told about a night when he arrived at the wrong bookstore in St. Louis, an older woman stood in the back row. "Excuse me," she called out.

"Yes?" Nick asked.

"I don't know why you are up there blathering on about a book you know nothing about. I never meant to flaunt this book about as if it were a show pony. This is a fine piece of literature meant to inspire, not be joked about."

"Excuse me?" His look of confusion ended with a nervous laugh as he glanced at Maisy, who shrugged.

Riley went to Nick's side, whispered in his ear. He nodded, then answered the woman. "Well, I, too, believe this is a fine piece of literature. You've done a wonderful job."

Maisy jumped up, realizing it was the same woman who had disrupted the book club earlier that day. Mrs. Lithgow—the lady who thought she'd written all the novels being discussed.

Nick took the microphone out of the stand, and walked toward one side of the room. Maisy saw that the old woman was coming toward him, her heavy shoes clacking on the hard wood. Nick smiled at her, spoke directly into the microphone. "Can you tell us your motivation for writing this novel?"

She took the microphone from him, spoke with force. "Yes. Although it appears to only be about adventure and mystery, it's really about searching for something that can't be found in life, only in death."

Nick nodded at her. "Very astute."

Adalee reached their side before Riley and Maisy could get there. "Mrs. Lithgow, your signing table is ready. Why don't we get set up while everyone is still seated?" The microphone squealed as the woman handed it to Adalee.

"Well, that's just fine, young lady. You know I can only sign for an hour. That is my limit—my agent should have told you that."

"Oh, she did. Why don't we get going so you can finish in time?"

"Thank you, but will you please tell this gentleman to stop talking about my book like he wrote it? He's very good-looking, you know. But he really has no idea what he is talking about."

"Oh, I agree," Adalee said.

Riley and Maisy joined them. Maisy took Mrs. Lithgow's arm and led her to the back of the room. Maisy grimaced at Nick. *I'm sorry*, she mouthed.

He covered the microphone. "No worries. That's more fun than I've had in a while." He approached the podium. "Well, I really want to thank all of you for coming. You've been an indulgent and wonderful audience. Nothing more I can say unless you have some questions."

Hands shot up. Nick laughed, pointed at Lucy Morgan. "Yes?"

Lucy stood; Maisy turned away, walked toward the rear of the room, where Riley was seating Mrs. Lithgow at a signing table. Nick's voice echoed through the room during a Q&A session. Maisy leaned down to Riley. "Okay, how cute and sweet can one man be all at the same time?"

Riley held her hand up to Maisy in a phoning gesture. "Please call Verandah House while I set this table up for Mrs. Lithgow and let them know that she will need a ride home." Riley's eyes rolled toward the phone. "Now."

"Yeah, yeah, I got it," Maisy said. Adalee kept Mrs. Lithgow preoccupied with aimless chatter about the weather, fishing and summer people while Maisy grabbed the phone.

All at once, Mrs. Lithgow stood up and glanced around the room, her opaque blue eyes filled with tears. "What has happened to my house?"

Adalee looked over at Maisy, who shrugged and mouthed, *I have no idea.*

Adalee took the older woman's hand. "What do you mean, Mrs. Lithgow?"

"This is where the couch usually is. Why are there so many books, and why are the floors ruined, when Mama just had them done?" Mrs. Lithgow's voice grew louder.

Adalee led her across the foyer and into the café, where the music drowned out their words.

Maisy entered the front room, where Nick's session was just ending, to much applause, and all the patrons lined up according to the numbers they'd received earlier. She stood at Nick's side, and opened the books to the title page as Riley had told her to do. He was kind to every person in line, signed every book they handed him—old or new release.

When the crowd was gone, the doors were locked and Riley had gone up to check on Brayden, Nick smiled at Maisy. "I'm assuming you know this town a bit better than I do," he said. "Any chance I can talk you into going out for a quick drink?"

"I know the perfect place." She led him out the back door, locking it behind her. "It's only five blocks down. You up for a walk?"

"Absolutely. You know, you have a wonderful family, and the store is amazing. I wish all my events went as well as this one."

"I bet you say that to all the store owners."

He returned her laugh and Maisy's spirit lifted like a helium-filled balloon.

TWELVE

RILEY

Riley stood over the coffeepot, waited for it to fill, focused only on the dripping liquid. It was the Saturday morning after Nick Martin's book signing and she refused to think about what had haunted her all night—the arrival of Sheldon's parents; Maisy leaving with Nick; Mama's cancer, which might be spreading; the six thousand things to be done during this week. And then there was Mack. Mack and his ill father. Mack possibly starting up with Maisy again.

Her thoughts turned to more practical matters; what would she do if she had to close down the bookstore? She pulled out a pad of paper and made a list while the coffee machine did its job. She and Brayden could move back in with Mama until Riley saved enough money to get an apartment. She could go back to school and get her degree in English lit and then teach, or work at the library. Water running through the pipes in the back of the house distracted her. Brayden entered the kitchen, rubbing his face, his curls tangled.

"Morning, Mom." He opened a cabinet, pulled out the Pop-Tarts.

"Morning, baby. Pop-Tarts aren't breakfast."

"They are in the summer." He smiled, and his beauty overwhelmed Riley.

"Why are you up so early? You can sleep in today."

He ripped open the wrapper, took a bite of pastry. "Going fishing with the Logans. Pearson's Pier. Mr. Logan wanted to know if the jetty's still the best place to catch redfish, and I told him it isn't, that Pearson's Pier is the best place, so now we have a bet."

Riley's eyes narrowed. "You didn't invite yourself, did you?"

"Please, Mom, chill-lax."

"Okay . . . but only go to the pier. I'll stop by after my morning powwow with Gamma."

He shrugged. "Please don't embarrass me."

"That's my job," she said, and kissed his forehead.

Someone banged on the kitchen door; Riley opened it to Adalee, sweaty and disheveled. "How'd you get here?"

"I jogged." Adalee held out her hands as if to say, *Isn't it self-evident?* She wore a pair of pink nylon shorts, a faded gray T-shirt and running sneakers. "I needed to get out of the house, and I really wanted to talk to you before our morning torture with Mama."

Riley laughed. "Torture?"

"Yes," Adalee said, opened the refrigerator and pulled out the milk. "I can't believe she doesn't make you as crazy as she makes me. You got any cereal?"

Riley wanted to explain to her sister how the knowledge of *one* thing can change *everything*. Maybe if Adalee knew Mama was sick, or realized how she'd saved Riley and Brayden with the bookstore . . .

Brayden pulled down a box of Raisin Bran. "Hey, Aunt Adalee. How's this?"

"Morning, good-looking." She poured a bowl full, sat down at the kitchen table. "Listen, Riley, what do you know about that crazy old lady who always comes in here thinking she's the author?"

Riley joined them at the table, took a long swig of coffee. "She lives at Verandah House—she's in her nineties, part of a group of women called the nifty nineties."

"Well, how does she keep getting here if she lives in a nursing home?"

"It's not a nursing home. It's a community for the elderly. She actually lives alone, and has private nurses and aides who check in on her, but if she wants to walk, she is only two blocks away. We've asked Verandah House to help us with the problem, but they say it's not their job. I think she's always lived in Palmetto Beach, but I didn't meet her until recently."

Adalee took a bite of Raisin Bran, wiped her mouth. "I think she used to live in this cottage, in its old location, maybe eighty years ago. Isn't that crazy?"

"Really?"

Brayden laughed. "No one lived here eighty years ago. That's like the age of . . . dinosaurs."

"Yeah, pretty much." Adalee poked at her nephew. "Anyway, that's why she comes here all the time and why she gets confused about the bookshelves and furniture, you know? I talked to her for a long time last night while I waited for someone to come get her. I guess it was her nurse."

"Probably. They usually call her private nurse to come get her. The nurse doesn't live there full-time, but do you know for sure that she used to live here?"

"No, I was hoping you could help me. Would Mama know? I'm almost done working on the history boards and I'd like to include Mrs. Lithgow. Then I'm working on the decor of this place."

"You sound like Maisy. And what about Chad?"

Adalee's face filled with a smile. "I met him at the Beach Club after the signing last night. He's great."

Brayden looked up at the clock. "Hey, I gotta go. Yes, Mom, I'll take my cell phone." He ran back to his room to change into his bathing suit.

"Okay," Riley said, and then turned her attention to Adalee. "Let's check out the display before we go see Mama."

Together they entered the back storage room, where Adalee had cleared a work space for her project. She had lined the boards up side by side to create a timeline. More work had been done on them since Riley had looked yesterday, and photos were now surrounded by fabric or with frames made of driftwood sticks. Adalee smiled, bowed. "You like?"

"Adalee, this is amazing. How did you know how to do this?"

"Well, for one, I am studying interior design—the only class I'm passing—and I have to do board projects all the time."

"Did you use all that research I gave you?"

"Yep. I can't figure out who lived there in eighteen ninety-two, when the house was still on the plantation. . . . Maybe it sat empty."

"When do you think Mrs. Lithgow lived here?"

Adalee pointed to a black-and-white picture of the cottage with an ancient black car parked in front, headlights glaring at the camera. "That is a nineteen twenty-six Plymouth sedan. I looked it up on the Internet. I think she was part of the Wentworth family. I can't figure out if she was a cousin or child. . . . I thought maybe we could ask the people at Verandah House if they know her maiden name."

"Good work." Riley studied each picture, each family name. "You've completely surprised me. You've done an incredible job."

"Thanks. I stopped at the Logan family. I called and left a message for Mrs. Logan and she faxed me one picture." She pointed to an empty square surrounded by bright green fabric. "I haven't put it up yet."

"Yeah. And what about us? Aren't you going to include the bookstore?"

"I'm thinking . . . well, just thinking here. It might be fun to make a board about just our family."

"Brilliant. Well, let's go so we don't keep Mama waiting. Have you seen Maisy?"

"No, but her bedroom door was closed, so I know she came home last night."

"Well, that's something, right?" Riley placed her hand on Adalee's arm. "Thank you for your help. I know this has been a hectic time and I've been a little uptight, but I can't tell you how much I appreciate what you've done here."

"You know, it really was a lot more fun than I thought it would be."

"Things don't always have to be fun, you know."

Adalee shook her head. "Maybe not for you. Really, Riley, everything doesn't have to be a total bore and chore either."

"No, but some things just are. You want a ride back home, or are you gonna jog?"

"Not if I can help it. A ride would be great."

Riley checked on the store, told Ethel that she'd be back in an hour and that Maisy would be there to entertain the book clubs by ten a.m.

"I think she's good at entertaining our visitors." Ethel laughed at her own innuendo.

Riley sighed. "What am I supposed to do with Maisy?"

"Can't fire her now, can you?" Ethel stuck a key in the cash register, began to count the money.

"Very funny, Ethel. See you in a bit; let me know the totals for last night."

Together Riley and Adalee walked out the back door and got in the car. Riley forced herself to think about the upcoming meeting with Mama, who was bound to be in a foul mood over missing Nick Martin last night.

Riley looked over at her sister. "Let the fun begin," she said.

Adalee leaned her head back on the car seat. "Your definition of fun is skewed."

Riley laughed. "Yeah, maybe."

"But seriously, when did you get so worried about upsetting Mama? Seems to me that for most of your life, your goal has been the opposite—to cause 'affliction and agony.'" Adalee repeated their mama's words said once at a dinner table when Riley had refused to eat the liver and onions being served. For years afterward the sisters had walked around the house bemoaning the "affliction and agony" of life.

Riley felt defensive, explanatory words rise from her gut. "I don't know what to say, Adalee. Life changes. Knowing and living through certain things changed me. Fighting with Mama, or trying to outwit her, doesn't seem . . . worth it. Maybe you could try a little tenderness."

"Me? Are you lecturing me?"

Riley was silent until they pulled into the driveway. "No, I am absolutely not lecturing you, Adalee. You asked why I was so worried about not upsetting Mama. The best answer I can come up with is that life changes."

Adalee stared out the front window. "Sometimes I want life to stay exactly the way it is; and other times I just can't wait to get onto the next thing."

"I know," Riley said. "Like a novel where sometimes you're dying to know what happens next, but other times you just don't want the book to end."

Adalee shook her head. "You and your books." She opened

the passenger-side door, hesitated. "I *am* glad I'm here even when I don't seem like it."

Riley smiled at her little sister. "I'm glad you're here, too."

Adalee jumped out of the car, hollered over her shoulder, "But I hate these meetings. Hate with a capital H."

Riley laughed and followed her into their childhood home.

ℭℓℓ THIRTEEN

MAISY

*M*aisy stood on the screened-in porch and stared out over the backyard. Her sisters were five minutes late, and she listened for the car. She anticipated every word and gesture Riley would make. She wouldn't mention Maisy's leaving with Nick Martin, but she would send a clear message of distaste without speaking a word. It hadn't always been this way—once, Riley had been her best friend. Mama had been the one who conveyed her disapproval with one look, one comment. Maisy had decided long ago that even if Mama could make her feel bad about herself, she couldn't control her behavior. She had chosen in her early years to *do* whatever she wanted. Mama couldn't make her stay home at night, or not kiss that boy, or not drink that beer at seventeen.

Only her father had been able to stop her. One word from him and she halted whatever she was doing. She never understood why she needed his love and approval more than she needed her mama's, but it was true. To lose his admiration would have been worse than being grounded for a thousand weekends. The last time she'd defied him had been the night with Mack at the bonfire.

Mack.

Since the moment she'd seen Mack across the bookstore, her thoughts about Peter had receded like a fever that had run its course. She hadn't even tried to call him again.

The crunch of gravel against tires drew Maisy out the screen door and onto the lawn. Adalee and Riley climbed out of the car, laughing.

"What's so damn funny?" Maisy asked.

They both stared at her. Adalee spoke first. "Why are you in a foul mood? You're the one who had the hookup last night."

"Now why would you say that, Adalee? That's ridiculous."

"That's enough." Riley spoke in a soft voice. "Let's go talk to Mama. We're seven minutes late."

Together the three sisters entered the drawing room turned hospital room, where a physical therapist was assisting Kitsy's morning stretches. Each sister kissed their mama and then sat in what had become their designated chairs. Riley cleared the bedside table, leaned closer to Kitsy. "Did you finish your breakfast?"

"Yes," Kitsy said. "Stop fussing over me."

"You need the protein to heal. I'm not fussing." Riley helped Kitsy scoot up in the bed.

Kitsy settled back on her pillow. "Okay, I want to start by getting something out of the way."

The sisters looked at one another.

"Adalee Louise Sheffield. I want you to know that you can't hide anything from me. I have told you this since you were a little girl and I found that broken china cup in your underwear drawer. I know about your DUI. I have arranged for legal counsel. You will pay me back, and we will deal with the other repercussions after the party is over."

Adalee stared at the floor. "Yes, ma'am. And I'm sorry. It wasn't . . . I need you to know it was not entirely my fault."

Mama interrupted. "Don't even begin to try to excuse your behavior. I absolutely don't want to hear it. You do not choose to drink and then drive. Do you understand me? And you're forbidden from going anywhere but the bookstore and the house."

Adalee looked up, tears in her eyes. "I'm sorry. I'm terribly sorry, but you have to let me see Chad. I was driving his car. . . . Please, Mama. He only got a job here so he could be with me."

"Maybe you should have thought about that when you got behind the wheel of the car after drinking."

"I didn't think I was . . ." Adalee dropped her head into her hands. "Don't stop me from seeing Chad."

"Mama, please don't be so hard on her," Maisy said, uncomfortable seeing Adalee take the brunt of her mama's anger.

"You do not choose to drink and drive without consequences."

Maisy's sleepless night made the next words come out. "Yeah, you just choose to drink and try to walk down the staircase."

Kitsy's lips drew inward until only a thin, bloodless line was set where her mouth had been. "You may leave now, Maisy. You may go back to California and get on with your life. If that is what you are so angry about, that we took you from your fabulous life, go back to it now."

Maisy stood. "Great. If I'd known that one sarcastic comment would get me back to California, I would've said it a long time ago."

Riley held up her hand. "Please don't do this," she said. "Maisy, sit down. No one is going anywhere. Please stop this fighting. We have so much to get through this week. There is something every single day. Maisy, the book clubs adore you." Riley stood, walked toward Kitsy's bedside. "Mama, you should see the history boards Adalee made. The book signing last night may have been our most successful ever, and Maisy and Adalee were a huge part of that. Let's please pull together this week, enjoy the party and then you can fight all day long. Or leave, or whatever you want."

Kitsy closed her eyes for a long moment, and when she opened them, she had a smile on her face. "Okay, tell me about these history boards. And then let's talk about Book Club Celebration tonight."

"Yes. The speaker, Mrs. Guthridge, is the local librarian. She is going to talk about how book clubs enrich our lives. I'm hoping that members from all twenty book clubs will show up, and then buy their books for the next month. We'll have a trivia contest and of course wine and cheese."

When they were finished with business, Adalee went to her Mama's bedside. Maisy sat in the chair wishing for another afternoon with Mack—escape.

"Mama," Adalee said, "do you know Mrs. Lithgow?"

"Only from the bookstore. Why?"

"I think she used to live in the cottage."

"I wouldn't know; she's about fifty years older than me."

Adalee laughed. "She's a hundred and thirty years old?"

"Funny. Now go about your business. I have a wheelchair to pick out for my birthday party."

"You're gonna make it to the party?" Riley looked up from packing papers into her satchel.

"Yep, that is my surprise for this morning. Doc says I can go *if* I do my physical therapy twice a day without complaining."

"Great. Just great." Riley kissed her on the cheek. "Listen, I gotta run. I'm checking on Brayden and then getting back to the store. Maisy, I told Ethel you'd be there for the Page Turners Club by ten."

"Okay," Maisy said.

"By the way, you have a phone message." Kitsy pointed at Maisy. "It's in the kitchen; the housekeeper said she couldn't find you last night to tell you." She squinted at her daughter. "Where were you?"

"At the bookstore," Maisy said.

"No," Mama said. "This was late—maybe ten."

"I was entertaining Nick Martin."

Maisy walked away, allowing her statement to linger in the room. Let them believe what they wanted—maybe they'd imagine a better night than the one she'd had. She'd actually spent most of the evening looking for Mack Logan instead of enjoying Nick's company.

"Maisy." Riley's sharp voice made her turn before she reached the kitchen.

"I am not in the mood for a lecture." Maisy tossed her words over her shoulder, disdain underlying every syllable.

"I just want to ask you to please be nicer to Mama. You don't have to make this so hard."

Maisy stopped in the hallway, turned to face Riley, took two steps toward her. "When did you turn into this perfect little princess trying to make everything right for Mama? This store, this week, this life . . . it's all about her. All about you."

"You don't . . . understand. And you never take the time to try," Riley whispered, her voice shaking as she turned to walk away and leave Maisy alone in the hallway.

Maisy flinched and walked toward the message in the kitchen: maybe Mack wanted to see her again.

The notepaper lay next to the phone on the far counter. These marble counters had been installed when Maisy was in high school and they still gleamed from Mama's constant care. *Lucy Morgan called—would like to meet you for coffee at 11 a.m. at the bookstore.*

Maisy's breath caught in the back of her throat. There would be no way to avoid Lucy. Maybe she should have walked out of this house, this town, when she had a chance a few moments ago; she'd be halfway to the airport by now.

Damn.

When she arrived at the cottage in Mama's pickup truck, she walked straight back to the book club corner where the Page Turners Club was taking their seats. They started the morning by complaining that the coffee was cold, the muffins smaller than usual and the air-conditioning too chilly. Maisy smiled, made new coffee, set out more muffins and walked behind the counter to adjust the thermostat. Ethel smiled at her. "They giving you a hard time?"

Maisy shrugged. "Nothing seems to be right for them this morning."

"Nothing is ever right for them," Ethel said. "Don't be taking it all personal now, okay?"

"Okay. Ethel, how long have you worked here?"

"Since your mama and sister opened the doors twelve years ago."

"You love this place, don't you?"

"I do. I love it more than I like most people." Ethel let out a long, deep laugh. "And I'm not kidding."

Maisy laughed, too. "At least more than the Page Turners Club."

Ethel nodded. "But never more than your mama and Riley. Never. I love them with all my heart."

"Me, too," Maisy said, let the truth of the words warm her before she turned back to Ethel. "I'm renaming this book club."

"Oh?"

"The Complaining Companions. You like that?"

"Perfect." Ethel waved at a book club member who was motioning for Maisy.

"Wish me luck," she said as she headed back and asked the women how they felt about the book they were reading—*Gone With the Wind.* They launched into a heated critique of Margaret Mitchell's writing style. Maisy wanted to tell them to stop wasting their time tearing apart one of the bestselling novels of all times, but she smiled, asked, "Is the room temperature okay now?"

A dark-haired woman glanced up. "Getting there. Have you read this novel?"

Maisy shrugged. "Saw the movie. Does that count?"

The woman rolled her eyes. "No, it does not."

"So," Maisy said, needing a quick change of subject. "What are you reading after this?"

"We read classics only. *To Kill a Mockingbird* is next on our list. We compare the writing styles of different time periods and discuss sentence structure and plot development."

"Okay." Maisy stifled a laugh. "Sounds like . . . loads of fun."

The woman stared at Riley for a moment, and made a huffing noise. "We'd like more chocolate-chip muffins, please. None of us likes the blueberry."

"Yes, ma'am." Maisy glanced at the antique wall clock, hoping that the club would end before eleven, when Lucy Morgan was due to arrive. Maisy's gaze wandered to the front door, to the coffee bar and then back to the club. She busied herself fulfilling the Page Turners' requests until ten fifty-eight a.m., when she excused herself and headed toward the checkout counter, where Adalee stood talking with Ethel about glue and tape for her history boards. Behind the counter, sagging plywood shelves held the current book club choices; handwritten signs were posted in front of each chosen book. A copy of Ethel's monthly pick, *Where or When* by Anita Shreve, was displayed on a wire stand. Maisy recited the names of the clubs in an attempt to stay the prickle of panic that was forming in her stomach: "Beach Babes Book Club; Blonde Book Club; Classics Only; New Moms; Fabulous and Forty; Out-of-the-House Wives; Kindred Spirits . . ."

Adalee poked at Maisy. "You okay? You're mumbling."

"I'm fine."

"You know, we should really do something about this place." Adalee swept her arm to encompass the entire cottage.

"What do you mean?" Maisy glanced at the opening front door.

"I mean it's stuck in, like, nineteen seventy. Really. We could fix it up. It would be . . . fun. If Riley has to ruin our summer, the least we can do is have fun."

"You and your fun," Maisy said. A shaft of light fell across the hardwood floors and two women walked in; neither was Lucy. Maisy looked back at her sister. "Riley said we can't make any changes. No money."

"We could surprise them. The Antique Mart and Flea Market is in town for two days. Come on, let's go see what they've got, just like old times."

Maisy's heart filled with memory: she and Adalee used to go to the flea market, find old furniture, paint it and redecorate their bedrooms at least every six months. It drove their mama out of her mind. All the family antiques and fine furniture, and she and Adalee would come home with "someone else's trash." They tried a different theme each time: hippie, punk rock, Laura Ashley . . .

Adalee lifted her palms in the air. "Oh, my gosh, remember when we tried to do a Lilly Pulitzer theme with all red and pink, and it looked like someone had thrown up Pepto-Bismol all over our rooms?"

"It was a good idea, but we should have gone with the blues instead of the pinks. I still think a Lilly-inspired room would be pretty awesome."

Maisy felt that dangerous feeling—this was where she could be fooled into staying, into remembering the better aspects of life with her sisters. Alliances between the three of them had shifted with the seasons: Riley and Adalee building a fort in the woods, then Maisy and Adalee scanning flea markets, then Maisy and Riley sneaking out for a party at the old lighthouse. She'd almost forgotten.

"And," Adalee said, her voice rising, "Riley would never let us touch her room. She had the exact same room, with her furniture in the exact same place, forever. In fact, it's still like that. Even down to the white chenille bedspread."

"I love white chenille," Maisy said. "Funny how some things are timeless."

"Like old friends." A voice came from behind Maisy, and she turned to face Lucy.

Her heart quickened, her stomach gripped in anxiety. She attempted a smile, her words caught in her clenched throat.

Lucy backed up a step. "You don't want to see me, do you?"

"Yes, yes. I just thought . . ."

"Just thought what?"

Maisy glanced at her sister. "I'll be in the coffee shop. Come get me when you're ready to go to the Antique Mart."

Adalee clapped her hands together. "Awesome. I thought you said . . ."

Maisy held up her hand. "Just come get me in a few."

Lucy and Maisy walked to the café and sat down at a far table next to a display of luxury gift soaps made by a local artisan. Anne brought over Maisy's regular latte, then asked Lucy for her order.

Lucy ordered a hot tea and folded her hands on the table, tilted her head at Maisy. "I know we haven't talked in, like, twelve years, but I want you to know I'm not mad . . . anymore about what you did. And I miss you. When I saw you in the bookstore the other day, all my reasons for not talking to you washed away. I remembered all the good times."

Maisy stared into her coffee cup, avoiding Lucy's brown eyes.

Lucy sighed. "You never told me why you did what you did."

Maisy lifted her head, panic rising like acid. Was she truly supposed to explain to her ex–best friend why she'd slept with her then fiancé, now husband? "I don't . . . know what to say."

"Tucker thinks you didn't show up because you got in a fight with your family . . . your sister or someone. He said I shouldn't take it personally. But how was I supposed to take it? You didn't show up at my wedding, and you never answered any of my phone calls. I wanted to hate you, but I only missed you."

"Oh . . . Lucy. I am so . . . so sorry." Maisy released a deep breath of relief and regret; Lucy didn't know about her and Tucker.

"Why did you leave?" Lucy asked again.

"I had to. I don't know how to explain it. I had to get out of this town, away from this place. I should have called you. I needed to get away from my family. Away from Riley. Away from . . ."

"What did Riley do?"

Anne arrived with Lucy's tea and Maisy waited until she walked away before she answered. "It doesn't matter now. I am just so sorry. How's your family?"

Lucy smiled now. "Great. Tucker and I moved to Bartow just

down the road. We don't have kids . . . yet. He wants to wait a bit longer. I come here at least once a week to see friends, go to book club, catch up. I worked at the local real estate office, but Tucker wants me home when he gets there, so now I'm thinking about what to do next."

"You don't live in town anymore? I thought . . ."

Lucy laughed. "Things don't stay the same just because you left. No, we moved years ago."

"I've missed . . . a lot, haven't I?"

"Yes," Lucy said. "Riley and your mama have done an amazing job with this store. It's a gathering place for the whole area. I don't know what we'd do without it. I almost didn't make it last week because something weird happened to my car, but I never miss book club. I don't know what went on between you and Riley, but you should be proud of what she's done here."

"I am." Maisy turned away. "It was a long time ago. . . . Change of subject. So, what happened to your car?"

"Some prankster took off all the tires and left them in a pile on the sidewalk. The car was on cinder blocks."

Maisy stared at the wall behind Lucy's head, seeing the sobbing book club blonde talking about the crazy thing she'd done to her lover's wife. "Oh," Maisy said.

Lucy shrugged. "Stupid teenagers or something. A ridiculous dare by one of those high school clubs, I'm sure."

"Probably." Maisy nodded and forced herself to look at Lucy.

"Tell me about your glamorous life in California." Lucy still had that sweet smile, full and genuine. "I bet you love it there. You look great, by the way. Then again, you always did."

"I do love it there. Part of me regrets not going to college . . . but I'd probably be doing the same thing I'm doing now, just with a degree."

"We all thought you were so brave when you ran off to California. Was it scary?" Lucy leaned forward, folded her hands around her mug.

"Yes." Maisy nodded. "At first it was, but just like anywhere else, you meet people, you get a job, you find a life. And it has been years, so it's hard to remember everything about that early time."

"I remember what it was like when you left." Lucy tucked a stray curl behind her ear, stared up at the ceiling. "It was sad. No one knew why you went, and your family was distraught. I couldn't believe that my best friend wouldn't be in my wedding."

Maisy exhaled. "I am so sorry. I never, ever meant to hurt you. It was all . . . terrible."

The smile returned to Lucy's face. "Well, it turned out all right, didn't it? Just like a good book or something. You have a great life. Tucker and I are married. And now you're home and we can catch up, hang out before you go back."

"Sure." Maisy smiled, glanced up at her sister coming toward them. "Adalee wants to go to the Antique Mart and Flea Market." Then Maisy's heart opened up to her best friend: the girl who had stayed over most weekends, who had listened to her cry and confess her loves and fears; the girl who had hidden the homecoming wine bottle in her own car and taken the blame. Maybe it would be okay; she could keep her secret, start off where she had left off with Lucy like nothing had ever happened. The past was buried, gone.

Lucy retrieved her purse from the floor. "It was really great to see you. I know this week is crazy." She tapped the newsletter listing the events. "I'll try to come to everything—I do want to support your family."

Maisy took Lucy's hand across the table, a silent confession and asking of forgiveness concealed in her next question. "You want to come to the flea market with us? We aren't going for long. I have to be back for this evening's event."

"That is so sweet, but I volunteer at the History Center at noon on Saturdays."

"Okay . . . I'll see you tonight?" Maisy asked.

"Absolutely."

Adalee shifted her feet. "Maybe you can go next time." She turned to Maisy. "Let's totally get moving before the best stuff is gone."

The three women walked out the front door of Driftwood Cottage, laughing over a story Lucy was telling about a woman they saw coming in from the parking lot, a local neighbor whose dog constantly humped Lucy and Tucker's concrete bunny in the garden. Relieved, Maisy basked in the comfort of Lucy's friendship even while guilt and regret lay below the surface of her smile.

FOURTEEN

RILEY

Regret buzzed through Riley like a fly she couldn't swat. Why had she spent so much time being irritated with Mama when she should have been appreciative? And why did it take the storm of illness to awaken the need to cherish Mama? She walked down Pearson's Pier, and then lifted her hand to stop her hat from flying off in a quick breeze. Her eyes locked on Brayden and she waved.

He turned away and she imagined him rolling his eyes at Mack, fishing next to him. As a child Brayden had come to her in the middle of the night with bad dreams. Now he didn't seem to need her at all. When she was twelve years old, and summer had released her from the grip of homework and team sports, she, too, had spent hours and hours on this pier. She'd run around with a couple of dollars in her pocket—enough for lunch at the

Burger Shack and an ice cream in the late afternoon. Sometimes she'd pick up loose change on the boardwalk for extra bait at the Pier House. If she didn't have the change, old Mr. Henson would sneak her a bag of chum.

Riley came up behind the two males and they turned in response to her greeting. A cloud moved from the sun, and vivid sunlight struck Mack's face. Riley lifted her hand to shield her eyes.

"Hey, Minnow," he said.

Brayden answered, "No, her name is Riley."

Mack laughed. "There was an entire summer when she wanted to be called Minnow."

Riley shook her head at Mack, pulled her hat lower and spoke to Brayden. "I never wanted to be called Minnow."

Brayden made a snorting noise in the back of his throat. "Then why did he call you that?"

"Because"—Mack bent closer to Brayden—"she thought she had this huge, really huge fish on the line. Thought the bet was won. She reeled it in and there was this very, very tiny fish—a minnow really—and a very, very large hunting boot."

"Which, for your information, Brayden, was full of wet sand and muck, making it heavy," Riley said.

She looked up at Mack, and for a brief moment, Riley saw the young Mack on the other side of a bonfire. She smiled past the memory. "Hey, thanks for fishing with Brayden, but no more childhood stories. And I haven't seen your dad yet. . . . Is he here?"

Mack turned, called out to his father. Sheppard Logan, standing at the other end of the pier, turned at his son's call. He walked toward them, and Riley remembered everything good about her childhood summers, everything pure and right. She didn't hesitate to hug Mack's father, held him for a moment and then leaned back to look at him. "It is so wonderful to see you."

"You, too, Riley. How in the world did you grow up? Get married? Have a son? Just yesterday you were a twelve-year-old girl outsailing and outfishing my sons, to their dismay."

It was true—all those years she'd been Mack's equal in the activities of a Palmetto Beach summer. She'd kept up with him on the sailboat, at the fishing pier; at badminton, pool races and beach games.

Riley laughed. "I only outsailed and outfished them for the first two weeks of every summer. They always beat me in the end. They just had to get out of their big-city skin to catch up with me." She ignored the assumption that she was married.

"Ah, yes. That's exactly why we're here. To get out of our big-city skin. Your son." Sheppard pointed to Brayden, who was staring at them as if they were aliens.

"Yes," Riley said. "So." She smiled at Mack and Sheppard, placed her arm around her son. "Is he holding up the family tradition? Did he kick your butt fishing this morning?"

Brayden pulled away from her. "You are so embarrassing. And Mack caught the first fish. I owe him an ice-cream cone." Brayden held out his hand for money.

Riley laughed through her nervousness, wondered what her hair looked like, if the straw hat was covering her new wrinkles. "You conning a twelve-year-old?"

"I was attempting to con him out of more than an ice-cream cone," Mack said. "Maybe pizza and a Coke on top of it." To Brayden he added, "Sorry, but you must also repay old family dues now." A buzzing noise caused him to pause; he pulled a cell phone from his back pocket. "Sorry, work. I'll be just a minute." He flipped open his phone and Riley heard a barrage of angry words she couldn't quite catch.

Riley, Sheppard and Brayden looked at one another, and stepped back from Mack and his phone call.

Mack turned his back on them, his hard reply clear in the silence. "Mr. Harbinger, I am more than sorry for any problems my absence is causing. I promise to be back by next Monday. I need some time with my family. I'm sorry you don't understand. I thought you would."

More words came from the other end, and then Mack said, "I understand." He hung up without saying goodbye, closed his eyes and lifted his face to the sun.

"Boss doesn't sound too happy," Sheppard said to Riley. "My fault. I talked Mack into coming."

"I think Mack is here because he wants to be here," Brayden said, sounding awfully grown-up all of a sudden.

"Absolutely." Mack was at their side, a smile on his face. "I wouldn't want to be anywhere else. Now back to the important stuff—oh yeah, Brayden, your mom owes me for all her unpaid bets through the years."

Brayden looked at Riley. "Really?"

"Don't believe anything this guy says," she answered. A sudden breeze caught them by surprise and took Riley's hat down the wooden dock. Mack ran down the dock, attempted three times to nail it down—stomping at it and eventually grabbing it before it flew over the side.

He returned to a laughing group, and handed the hat to Riley. "Thanks," she said, and yanked it back over her tousled hair.

"Do you have some time to spend with an old friend today, maybe walk around the newly improved Palmetto Beach?" Mack asked.

She stared down the pier. "Well . . ." She looked at Brayden.

"Go ahead, Mom. I'm meeting Wes at the jetty anyway."

She looked at Sheppard, who shooed her away. "You two go on now. I'm meeting my friend Norman Fuller here in twenty minutes."

"Okay," she told Mack. "Let me check on the bookstore, and I'll meet you back here in thirty minutes?"

"Sounds good."

After checking that all was in order at the store, then running a brush through her hair and applying lipstick, Riley walked back to the pier. Along the way, sunlight filtered through the Spanish moss of the live oak trees, its beauty calming her breath to a smooth pace. She glanced toward Pearson's Pier for Mack, and then he walked toward her in his wrinkled khaki shorts and faded Palmetto Beach T-shirt. A baseball hat was pulled low on his forehead to the top of his Ray-Ban sunglasses. He lifted his arm to wave, his freckled skin against the blue sky. The same arm that had once lay against hers in the simple days of childhood. She lifted her hand to wave, knocked over someone's fishing pole to the left. The pole's end dipped into a bait bucket, splashing water onto her legs and exposed toes. She stepped away, and knocked into a father with a child on his shoulder, who laughed and nodded at her, content in their own world. Riley stared at the child: a small girl with brown curls wet and sticky in the humidity, a circle of red around her mouth from a Popsicle. The child seemed to exude the pure joy of the moment, and the sight wrung Riley's heart with longing.

Mack came to her side. "Remember those simple pleasures?" Riley asked, pointing at the father and child.

He nodded. "That's why I'm here. For those simple pleasures." He looked over the beach. "The water, the smell of bait, the slow days."

"That smell of bait would be me." Riley laughed, shook her foot.

He tapped the bill of her baseball hat. "Who would you be without the sweet scent of fishing?"

Riley stared at him for a long moment. "Okay, you asked for a tour. Tell me where you want to go, what you want to do." So close to him now, she saw the places he'd missed with the sunblock: a patch on his neck, a thin strip on his forearm, the susceptible places left exposed to the sun. She almost reached out and touched the reddened skin, but then withdrew her hand before she remembered her own lessons of life: not to mistake one's own feelings of closeness for another's.

"I want to go wherever you want to take me. I want to see Palmetto Beach as it is now, through Riley Sheffield's eyes. Because if I look back, Palmetto Beach always has you in it."

"Let's go," she said.

"Where to first?"

"Follow me."

She walked back down the dock, looked over her shoulder at him. He took two long strides to catch up with her. His arm rubbed against hers. She smiled up at him and halted. "Bait shop, first stop." She gestured to the door of the shack. "It is now owned by a man named Arthur Smack."

Mack held up his hand. "What happened to old man Silvers?"

"He passed away years ago. Probably five or six."

Mack stared off. "Wow." He took a seat on a metal bench at the end of the pier, motioned for Riley to sit with him. "And all this time I imagined old man Silvers running the bait shop, just like always."

"Yes," she said.

"And look at you with a twelve-year-old son. Maisy in California. Adalee, who was like eight or nine years old the last time I saw her, now in college."

Riley smiled, nodded.

"The last time I saw you was at the bonfire. We didn't even get to . . . say goodbye."

Riley flinched. "I don't think you were too happy . . . with me."

"What?"

"You know, Dad coming to get Maisy and all that."

"Yeah, that was embarrassing. I figured I needed to hightail it out of there before the remainder of the armed forces showed up." He laughed, shaking his head.

"That was . . . my fault," Riley whispered, looked away.

Mack shrugged. "What was?"

"That Dad came and grabbed Maisy."

"Riley, that was a long time ago. I felt bad that I never said goodbye to either of you. I did hear . . . that you came home from college. That must have been when you had Brayden."

Riley watched a seagull peck at a French fry stuck between the wooden boards. She pushed her sunglasses against her nose as if they had slipped down, which they hadn't, and she struggled to find something, anything to say. In her mind, Mack had represented something of innocence and sweetness, of a past that could never be lived again. If she had imagined seeing him at all, she had imagined him as he was then, not this man sitting next to her asking about her son.

"I'm sorry," he said. "That came out judgmental or something, didn't it? I just wanted to . . ." He took his baseball hat off, and then put it back on again. "I just meant that I haven't seen you since then and I didn't even know . . ."

She took in his awkward gestures, his crooked grin. "Mack, it's okay. I left college my first semester, when I found out I was carrying Brayden. I came home and after Mama and Daddy screamed about me behind closed doors, they came out with smiling faces and told me we would consider our options. And we did. Mama bought your old cottage and made her dream of owning a bookstore come true. Maybe she merely used me as an excuse, but I was more than willing to go along with the plan. So I moved in when Brayden was a few weeks old and I've been there ever since. So, yes, my illustrious college career lasted half a semester, but I had a four-oh when I left." She laughed.

"Of course you did." He touched her hand, and then quickly withdrew his.

She leaned into the bench back, beginning to feel some of the old camaraderie with him. "So I am sure that you had a more notable college career than I did. Tell me all about it."

He shook his head. "It's almost weird to me that you don't know. It still feels like you should know everything."

She shrugged. "Hey, it usually took us at least one day to catch up every summer—so let's start now."

"Every summer," he said, and sighed. "What would I have done without you?"

"Caught less fish," she said.

He laughed. "Okay, real life. I went to Brown undergrad. You already knew that, didn't you?"

"Yup."

"Afterward I got a degree in architecture from Syracuse. Harbinger Associates hired me right out of school." He shrugged. "Sounds like a big deal, and it was since I still had to earn the job, but you know he and Dad have been friends since college."

A group of teens walked past, laughing, passing a cigarette among them. "That's it?" Riley asked. "Thirteen years and that's it?"

He shook his head. "In a summary, yes. I guess. Doesn't sound very exciting, does it?"

"You've left a lot out, Mack. Where do you live? Do you have a girlfriend? How's Joe? How are your parents, really?"

He stood, held out his hand. "Come on, let's walk and talk. I want to see the Beach Club, the jetty. I want to eat a cheeseburger at Archie's and then have a red Icee that will stain my teeth and lips."

"All worthy goals," Riley said, and stood.

"I'll start with Dad," he said as she fell into stride next to him. "He was diagnosed with lymphoma two years ago. He's had every treatment he can have, but it just keeps coming back. When we received the bookstore invitation, we knew we had to come."

Riley stopped, her breath taken with the singular thought of Sheppard Logan sick, dying. "It's so hard to wrap my head around the image of your dad sick. He's always been such a rock."

"He doesn't have much longer, they say."

His words slammed into her stomach. "Mack, don't say that."

"To you I can. I've always been able to say anything to you. It isn't something we talk about. But it is true. And terrible." He didn't look at Riley when he answered, but continued to walk, staring straight ahead through his sunglasses. "So really, the bookstore party is just an excuse. We're here to remember more happy times." He stopped, lifted his sunglasses and looked at Riley. "If that is even possible, it is possible here. I want to see old friends. . . ."

She nodded, condolences gone into that place where words wouldn't suffice, where there was nothing to say.

They began to walk again. She heard the long inhale before he continued. "So, here we are. As far as the other questions . . . Joe's wife, Maggie, is pregnant, after trying for four years. I live in Manhattan in an apartment as big as my old closet in Boston. I have been dating a woman—Olivia—but am not quite sure if I will be when I get back. Things weren't going very . . . well, and she was none too happy that I left for a couple weeks. We both work at Harbinger. . . ."

As the afternoon passed, their first awkward steps together after so many years apart became the smoother dance of an old friendship. After they'd downed cheeseburgers and red Icees, they'd reached the back entrance of the bookstore. Riley stopped on the bottom porch step. "I really have to get back to work. I'm so happy you came for all these celebrations, but it means that I am insanely busy."

"I know," he said. "I'm glad I got some time with you. After the bookstore event tonight, I'll take Dad back to rest and then I'm going to an oyster roast with the Murphy brothers."

"Well, that should be interesting." Riley laughed. "Trust me, they aren't much different all these years later."

"Which means one of us will end up being thrown in the river. Worst-case scenario—it's me."

They hugged goodbye and she touched the sunburned place on his forearm. "I'm sorry about your dad and all you're going through."

He placed his hand on top of hers and smiled. "I'll see you tonight." With a wave he walked away.

Riley entered the bookstore, where Ethel told her that Adalee and Maisy had gone on some secret surprise errand that had something to do with fleas. Riley ran upstairs, stared at her flushed face in the mirror and took a deep breath before she returned to work. She reminded herself to never, ever believe that a man wanted more than friendship; it only led to heartache and betrayal. Only friendship. He'd already said it: *I am here to see old friends. . . .*

Fifteen

Maisy

*M*aisy and Adalee walked down the aisles of the Antique Mart, the air pungent with dust, mildew and furniture polish. Now that they were alone together, doing something they loved, the natural bond of sisterhood returned, each step they took between old dining tables and whitewashed dressers erasing the years Maisy had been gone. Their laughter rose in excitement; their exchanges speeded up with each lacy doily they picked up, with each scrap of chenille or damask they held.

Adalee checked her cell phone every five minutes until Maisy told her to put it away. "Don't you have a boyfriend?" Adalee asked. "I mean, really. It's normal to want to talk to your boyfriend."

Maisy picked up a silver teapot. "This is beautiful."

"You don't like tea. And you didn't answer my question."

"I like tea now, and I don't want to answer your question." Maisy placed the pot back on the table.

"Come on, I'll tell you anything you want to know about Chad. Tell me about your guys. I bet you're dating more than one." Adalee bent down to look at the price on a pink-washed side table. "When I was little, I used to think that when I grew up, I'd be as pretty as you. But it never happened. I always thought that one day I'd get all the guys like you do." Adalee straightened up. "Oh, well."

"But you *are* beautiful." Maisy put her hand on Adalee's shoulders. "You always were."

Adalee shrugged. "Not like you."

"Well, it's not like I have any great luck with men."

"Really?"

Maisy nodded. "I haven't found the one yet, so don't be wishing you looked like me or were me. You have so much ahead of you." She grinned and leaned toward Adalee. "But I do have another lesson for you—don't love someone who is impossible to have. That seems to be what I'm good at—loving the ones who aren't available." She attempted a laugh and walked away from Adalee, toward the far end of the aisle. She looked over her shoulder. "Come on, they're unloading a huge pile of pine furniture back here."

Together they sorted through furniture, fabrics, lamps and knickknacks, commenting on how they would use each item. Adalee finally sat on an unpainted chair. Maisy lifted a folded piece of cream overwashed linen. "Look at this. Feel how soft it is." She held out the material.

"You know, I can't figure out what is wrong with Riley." Adalee rubbed the fabric between her fingers. "She's acting like she has to protect Mama from everything. Like Mama is frail and naive. We all know Mama could run the store or the world, even from her bed."

"Riley has her whole life invested in that place. It just feels like Mama and she are so wrapped up in it, all that matters to them is the store." Maisy stared off toward the back loading dock. "I have an idea."

"What?"

"Let's surprise them. . . ."

Adalee grinned back at her sister. "Like it's our bedrooms years ago."

"Exactly." Maisy lifted the bolt of soft linen, handed it to Adalee and then yanked her cell phone from her purse. "I can get Beach Chic to overnight us some slipcovers. You negotiate for this bolt of linen—you're better at that than me."

The afternoon passed with Maisy engaged in her favorite activity: foraging for finds in the bins and tables of flea-market objects. Her head filled with ideas and images. Peter's call halfway through the excursion was not enough to make her stop and talk. It wasn't until Riley's text reminder came through that Maisy remembered she was due back for the Book Club Celebration.

Covered in dust and dirt, she and Adalee stuffed their finds in the back of Mama's pickup truck and drove too fast back to Palmetto Beach. They ran through the front door of the bookstore, laughing.

Riley stood at the cash register, waved at them over the crowd, which was double what it had been the night before for Nick Martin. "Look at all these people!" Maisy said.

Together they worked their way to Riley's side. "Glad you could make it," she said. "You look . . . great?" She raised her eyebrows, taking in their disheveled appearance.

"Sorry," Adalee said. "We lost track of time."

Riley brushed dirt from Adalee's face, tucked hair behind her ear. "Will you please set up the table for the name tags? I have them ready by the front door. As the women come through the line, write each one's name and then the name of their book club underneath."

"Aren't you exhausted?" Adalee blew a piece of hair off her forehead.

"Tomorrow is a half day—can't open until after church—we can all rest up for Cookbook Club. They use the café kitchen here every Sunday afternoon to prepare recipes from the cookbook they picked that month. This time we've invited the public to come and watch. . . . We sold tickets for dinner."

"What a cute idea. I didn't know we had that book club, too. You think of everything."

"It was Mama's idea," Riley said, and turned to Maisy. "Will you please announce that the trivia game will start in twenty minutes? Here are the questions. The book clubs are divided up in those chair groupings." Riley pointed at the round circles of chairs.

Maisy nodded. "Sure, sure."

"You might want to go wash your face. . . . Where have you been?"

"The Antique Mart."

"Ah, okay." Riley lifted a notebook, tucked it under her arm.

Maisy glanced down at the floor, noticed her flip-flops were covered in dust. She'd lost herself in the thrill of the hunt. Imagining and decorating a room or an entire home caused her to detach from herself, flying high above her own angst, but now she realized she was covered in dirt. "I'm a mess," she said. "Do I have time to run home and change, get cleaned up?"

"No, but why don't you use the bathroom upstairs? I'm sure I have something you can wear."

"I doubt it," Maisy said.

"What is that supposed to mean?" Riley's face closed in.

"I just meant that— "

"Go on," Riley said. "You're welcome to borrow whatever you want, but you don't have to. You always look good." Riley walked away, headed toward Brayden, who was in the back of the Kids' Corner.

Maisy wished she could take back the words she'd just said— they'd come out all wrong. Often the leftover anger flooded back and Maisy remembered the way Riley had looked when she'd come in to apologize after sending their father onto the beach that night of the bonfire. Standing in Maisy's bedroom doorway, Riley had looked victorious . . . or it could have been regretful—Maisy had been too distraught to know for sure.

Riley tousled Brayden's hair. Maisy noticed how her nephew had grown almost as tall as his mom. Mack came over to stand next to Brayden, his laughter resounding.

Maisy's joy billowed upward, joining the sweetness of the af-

ternoon she'd spent with Adalee. She allowed every sensation she
felt with Mack Logan to pass through her: the sound of his voice,
his presence here. As though he heard her thoughts, he lifted his
head and stared at her. He moved toward her, and she stood still
at the counter, wishing she didn't have dirt on her face, in her hair
and on her clothes. He reached her side.

"Maisy," he said. "Hi."

"Hey, you." Her voice came out nervous and shaky. She smiled
her best smile, the one with the tilt of the head, the flirty eyes.

He brushed dust off her cheek. "You been crawling around in
the dirt?"

"Adalee and I went to the Flea Market."

"Same as ever."

"Sort of," she said. "Yes, sort of."

An older gentleman whom Maisy recognized as Sheppard
walked toward them with Brayden at his side. "You've met my
nephew?" she asked.

"We've been fishing."

Maisy tore her gaze from Mack's gray eyes to watch Brayden
and Mr. Logan move around the set-up chairs and wooden pillars.
She took fast steps toward them, navigated the food table covered
in a white cloth and threw her arms around Mr. Logan. "Oh, it is
so good to see you." Maisy hugged him hard, noting the dimin-
ished frame beneath her arms. Mack had told her at lunch that
he was sick, and as she hugged him, she found herself fighting a
feeling of loss, of passing time. This man had once been a tower,
a pillar of strength.

His voice came out as strong as she remembered. "Well, well, little Maisy Sheffield. I heard you moved to California or some other such country."

Her laughter came from the deeper place of contentment: Mr. Logan was here talking to her as if she were still the innocent girl she'd once been. She wasn't a woman dating a married man, or a woman who slept with her best friend's fiancé; she was little Maisy Rose.

"Yes, I do live in California, but I'm home for a bit now."

Mr. Logan took her hand. "It is good that you came home to help your family."

Maisy could have argued that point, but instead she smiled and squeezed his hand in return.

Riley joined them. "We have to get this night going. Do you want me to do the announcements and trivia game, Maisy?"

"No, no, I said I'd do them and I will."

Brayden and Mr. Logan walked to the back of the room, leaving Maisy and Riley face-to-face. "You can't even let me have a decent conversation," Maisy accused. "All you care about are these freaking parties."

"What?" Riley had started to walk toward the food table, but now turned and stared at her sister.

"You sent Mack fishing with your son. You're the same girl, the same jealous girl who took him away from me that night, and used our father to do it. First Dad, now Brayden."

"What are you talking about?" Riley's jaw clenched, her hands balled at her sides. "I didn't send him anywhere."

Maisy took a deep breath, noticed a tight group of women staring at them. A soft voice said, "Those are the Sheffield sisters."

Riley exhaled; her shoulders sank and she moved close to whisper, "Maisy, please. That was so long ago. I said I was sorry fifty thousand times in fifty thousand ways. If you wanted Mack Logan, you should have gone after him instead of running to California."

"You have no idea what you're talking about." Maisy spoke with closed lips.

"Please drop this. You can go out with him every day and every night. Just please get the trivia game started before the book clubs leave."

Maisy straightened, brushed dust off her cotton blouse. "Of course."

Riley joined a group of women calling her name. Maisy turned her thoughts to the one thing that brought her peace: Mack Logan was here, in Palmetto Beach, in Driftwood Cottage.

A quiet but persistent voice reminded her that she didn't even know how he felt about her. She'd only had a brief lunch with him, caught up on the facts of life. All these years she'd nurtured her own memories, imagining that the last thing he had said to her—*I love you*—would be the first thing he'd say if she ever saw him again.

Back then, she'd decided to wait for him. She was still waiting.

Sixteen

RILEY

For the first time in weeks, Riley didn't wake up exhausted. The Sunday morning sun had already whispered across her hardwood floors and onto her white chenille bedspread. She stretched and smiled. Last night had gone well. Despite Maisy's anger and lateness, she'd done a brilliant job as emcee. Adalee had bounced around, greeting every guest like royalty. Her sisters might grumble behind the scenes, but they knew how to be charming hostesses—a Sheffield gift.

The cruel words Maisy had thrown at Riley last night—words about how she was a jealous sister who had used their father and then her son to keep Mack away from Maisy—had continued to eat at her. Riley took a deep breath past the pain of knowing that Maisy was still holding on to the anger of that long-ago night, yet wanting and needing things to be different between them.

She redirected her thoughts to Mack and Sheppard at the party. Father and son had sat, laughed, drunk the free wine and challenged each other over the trivia questions on classic literature. Mack had caught her gaze in the middle of the contest, smiled and mouthed *Thank you* as though she had done something for him.

And maybe she had. She'd brought Mr. Logan back to his beach cottage.

A loud banging from below sent Riley bolting out of bed. She grabbed her robe and slippers and hurried to Brayden's room. He was asleep with the covers thrown off. She opened the doorway to the back stairs and stepped so the treads wouldn't creak. She opened the bottom door to see that the café light was on. Behind the counter Adalee stood watching coffee drip into the coffeepot. "What are you doing?" Riley asked, flicking on another light.

Adalee startled, dropped the mug in her hand. Shards of pottery flew across the hardwood floor, onto Riley's slippers. "Oh, oh." Adalee's eyes overflowed with tears.

"What's wrong?" Riley dodged the broken pieces, and went to her sister, put her arms around her.

Adalee shook her head. "Nothing. I'm okay. You just scared me, that's all." But her eyes were swollen, her face red and blotchy with yesterday's makeup.

"You don't look okay. It's me, your sister. What is wrong? And why aren't you at Mama's on Sunday morning? You know she'll be frantic."

"I told her I was spending the night with you."

"Where *did* you spend the night?"

"Here." Adalee motioned toward the open door of the storage room. "I used the pillows from the couch in the Book Club Corner."

"Oh, Adalee, why didn't you come get me? You could have slept with us upstairs."

"I didn't mean to . . . spend the night in there. I thought I was going to be with Chad . . . but when I got to the beach party after the book club celebration, I couldn't find him. Kimmie told me he left with some girl visiting from Atlanta." Adalee turned away, her shoulders dropping. "I thought he loved me. I really did."

"Oh, sweetie. Are you sure?"

"I never saw him at all. He wasn't there."

"So you came back here?"

"Yes, I didn't know what else to do. I didn't want to go back to Mama's. Then I started working on some . . . stuff in the storage room and I finally fell asleep."

"What are you working on? I thought the history boards were done."

Adalee smiled as if the storm of Chad had passed. "Surprise. Can't tell you."

"Come on," Riley begged, heading toward the storage room.

Adalee sprinted past her, slammed the old library door shut. "No."

Riley tried to dodge around her, laughing. "This is my house. Show me."

"Upstairs is your house. This part belongs to all of us." She smiled. "And today you cannot go in there."

Riley feigned pulling on the doorknobs. "It smells like paint."

"Yes, it does."

Riley dropped her hands from the door. "You win. I'm going up to wake my son and get ready for late church service. Want to go with us?"

Adalee shrugged. "Sure, if it'll keep Mama off my back." She glanced around the store. "You'll tell her I stayed here, right?"

"You did, didn't you?"

Adalee nodded and then followed Riley toward the café, where they poured themselves cups of coffee.

"Last night went great," Adalee said. "You must be so happy."

"What I'm happy about is that the store is closed until one o'clock today. I need some rest, some time with my son and a long walk on the beach."

They headed up the back stairs together to find Brayden sitting at the kitchen table with a box of opened Pop-Tarts. Riley kissed the top of his tousled head, picked a pastry out of the box and took a bite. "I'm gonna shower. We'll leave in half an hour."

Brayden hollered after her, "Hey, those are *my* Pop-Tarts."

Riley, Adalee and Brayden stepped out of the church sanctuary into the bright noonday sun, and strolled down the sidewalk back toward Driftwood Cottage. Brayden, walking ahead of them, looked over his shoulder. "Come on, the day is wasting," he said, mimicking his mother's oft-spoken words.

Riley lifted her face to the sun. "We need to go see Mama for lunch."

Adalee groaned. "Oh, Riley, I don't know how you can stand

living here. Her constant demands and need for attention make
me crazy. Truly crazy."

Riley stopped on the sidewalk to look at her sister. "I couldn't
do what I do if it weren't for Mama. I'm raising a son alone. And
I'm doing what I love—running a small bookstore. To do that, I'll
put up with almost anything. Mama is not that bad, except when
she feels out of control, which of course she does, sitting in a bed
in her drawing room, unable to be here for all the events she's
planned for well over a year. So, I know that she can make us all a
bit insane, but just tolerate it for a little bit longer, won't you?"

Adalee nodded. "Okay. I get it. But can I ask you a question?"

"Sure."

"It's sort of off subject." She pointed to Brayden already halfway down the sidewalk. "Why won't you tell us who his dad is?
Why won't you tell *him*? Don't you think it would make things so
much . . . easier? You wouldn't have to raise him alone."

Riley stared after her son running toward the cottage. "Why
are you bringing this up now?"

Adalee shrugged. "I just thought it would be better to know."

"Better for who? Me? Maybe. The dad? No. I couldn't do that
to him. I made a terrible mistake and I can't . . . ruin his life."

"Have you ever thought that maybe, just maybe, it wouldn't
ruin his life? That he might *want* to know?"

Riley stared at her sister, sadness running through her like a
slow-moving river. As with all her decisions, she'd made this one
and moved on. She didn't like revisiting her reasons or motives.
Still, her heart ached at the thought of Brayden's grandparents
here visiting without knowing.

Adalee pointed to Brayden. "If he were my son, I'd sure want to know him. He is the coolest kid ever."

"It's more complicated than that, Adalee."

"I'm sure it is. I wasn't questioning you. I just always wondered, and well, you never talk about it."

"And I don't want to talk about it now, either." Riley stopped. "And you have your own problems to worry about."

"Like?"

"Passing your senior year. Will Auburn even let you return?"

"You didn't go to college. Maisy didn't either. And you're both just fine, aren't you?"

"Fine? Adalee, think of all the other opportunities I might have if I had a degree. Here I am, thirtysomething years old, and trying to decide if now is the time to go back to school."

"I'm not here to live the life you didn't." Adalee stamped her foot like a child refused an ice cream.

Riley sighed.

"I hate, hate, hate when you do that. You look like Mama when you blow your air out like that."

Riley smiled, withheld her laugh with a hand over her mouth.

"You're laughing at me," Adalee said, her voice breaking.

"I'm not laughing at you. I'm laughing at me. Exhaling like Mama? Really?"

Adalee plunked herself down on an iron bench along the sidewalk. "Riley, I didn't mean to *fail*. I just went out of town for the weekend with Chad, and then stayed a few extra days, and then got too far behind."

"So what have you been doing with your time?"

"I did get an A in my design class. I've made a bunch of design boards. It wasn't like I wasn't doing anything. I did work on my portfolio."

"And hung out with Chad."

"Yes." Adalee pouted. "I really, really like him. My friends don't, but they don't know him like I do."

"Oh, Adalee. You let a guy—"

"Don't say it. I hear it enough from them."

"Okay. But you have to finish school. Promise me."

Adalee held up her right hand. "I promise. I can be done in two semesters."

Riley stood up. "Let's go." She glanced down the sidewalk to where Brayden stood with his legs apart and his hands on his hips, impatient for his mom and aunt to get moving. Riley asked her sister, "Do you know where Maisy went or what she did after the bookstore last night?"

Adalee shook her head. "Who knows where Maisy goes, or what she does? I swear, she's like a wisp of smoke—here and then gone." She took a few more steps, then laughed. "But we sure do know when she's here, don't we?"

Riley put her arm around her little sister. "We sure do."

SEVENTEEN

MAISY

*M*aisy awoke with a memory of the previous night: she'd stopped Mack before he left the bookstore to go to the oyster roast at the Murphy brothers' river house. She'd been nervous, though she made her words casual when she asked him if he'd meet her at the Beach Club for brunch today. She was not going to let Mack leave Palmetto Beach without knowing she'd at least tried to find a way back to the words of love he'd once spoken.

The shower ran hot and hard on her back and thighs. She scrubbed her hair, allowed the conditioner to stay in a few minutes longer before she rinsed. She wanted Mack to see her smiling and shining, not dirty and flustered as she'd been last night. The clock on the bedside table said ten-oh-six. She could only use the time-zone difference as an excuse for so long. Now Mama would be mad as a trapped hornet because she was supposed to be down by nine a.m. to eat breakfast with her, and tell her everything about the previous night: who'd been there, who hadn't, and how the event had gone, how many books they'd sold.

Maisy yanked on a pair of jean shorts and a tank top, pulled her wet hair into a ponytail and ran downstairs to the drawing room, where Mama was sitting up in bed, her lips a thin line, her face pale and set. Maisy kissed her, sat on the chair next to the bed. "Morning, Mama. What's for breakfast?"

She pointed to two covered plates on the rolling metal table. "Cold eggs."

"Sounds good."

"They were fifteen minutes ago."

"Mama, I'm sorry. I was so tired after last night, I just slept in a bit, that's all."

Mama met Maisy's eyes, her face coming to life with her question. "How did it go? Were there a lot of people? Who won the basket of signed books?"

"Whoa." Maisy pulled the breakfast tray toward them. "I'm starving. Can I eat my cold eggs first?"

This comment brought a smile to Mama's face. "Yeah, sure. I just forget how hard you girls are working. I hate being cooped up in this damn bed. I just want out. . . . I want to come to the store. . . ."

"I know." Maisy lifted her fork. "We miss having you there. It's like a missing lightbulb in a beautiful chandelier."

Mama turned to Maisy. "You've always had that gift—that gift of being able to make everyone feel good. You know just the right thing to say. No wonder all the boys fall in love with you."

"That's not true," Maisy said. "You want to hear about last night or not?"

In between bites of Harriet's chive-and-feta-cheese scrambled eggs and brown sugar–covered bacon, Maisy told her mama about the night, who'd come and left, who'd won the trivia and who'd drunk too much of the free wine. She took another bite of bacon, sat back. "When I go home to California, I'm gonna weigh six hundred pounds."

Mama leaned back on her pillow, closed her eyes. "I am so blessed to have you girls here. The store sounds like it can go on without me."

"Of course it can." Maisy placed her hand on her mama's arm. "But I know they wish you were there. And I can't stay forever."

Mama opened her eyes, stared at Maisy. "You're going back to California?"

"Not today, but of course I am. I live there, Mama."

"I was hoping you'd remember. . . ."

"Remember what?"

"How great it is to live here. To be around your sisters. To be . . . with me."

"Oh, Mama." Maisy laid her head on the thin cashmere throw covering her mama's legs. "I didn't leave to get away from you."

"Then who did you leave to get away from?"

"Me." Maisy attempted a laugh, a lighthearted answer that held more truth than she'd meant to convey.

"But, Maisy, you take you with you," Mama said.

"Yes, I did. But I also left some of me here."

Mama placed her hand on top of Maisy's wet hair. "You can

never leave a part of yourself somewhere. That is impossible. You just think you did."

"I was kiddin'. Of course I can't leave me here; if I did, you wouldn't be asking after me, now, would you?" Maisy closed her eyes and felt the warmth of her mama's hand on her head. She was a child again—a child who needed to be told that everything would be okay.

Maisy lifted her head. "You always said things work out for the best."

"Yes, I did. But you always took that to mean that things would work out the best for *you*. I never said that. I just said they work out for the good of all. Somehow when it didn't work out for you, you didn't think it worked out at all."

"Why does that sound like an insult?"

Mama shook her head. "It wasn't. You are my heart, Maisy. I do love you."

"I love you, too. And it sure is nice to have a half day off. I'm having brunch with Mack Logan, and then I'll help the Cookbook Club get set up. . . ."

"First tell me all about last night." Mama settled back into her bed.

Maisy rattled off names, funny stories and how Mrs. Lithgow got confused about how many of the books she'd written. When she was finished, Maisy stood, kissing her mother on the cheek. "Riley and Adalee should be here by one. So you get your rest and they'll check in."

"Maisy?"

She stopped halfway to the door. "Yes?"

"I didn't mean to make you feel guilty for leaving. I know you have to live your own life. I just never understood it . . . and I miss you."

Maisy's heart rolled with the sweet honesty of her mama's words. She smiled. "That is the second time I've heard that in two days. Glad to know I've been missed."

Mama turned away, closed her eyes. Maisy ran up the stairs to dry her hair, pick out something to wear to meet Mack. Maybe her mama was right—maybe things did work out for the good of all.

By noon Maisy was sitting at a corner table at the Beach Club, her hair smooth and flat, sunglasses pushed on top of her head. Her white linen shirt was unbuttoned just enough to reveal a hint of her bright pink bikini bathing suit top, and the thin white cotton skirt flowed over her thighs. Her left flip-flop smacked back and forth against her heel as she waited. She'd been early on purpose, wanting to watch Mack walk in and move toward her as she sat still and waiting. The entire scenario was planned—much better than being found dusty and dirty with her mouth open in stupid surprise. Today she would redo the bad impressions she'd made yesterday.

The waiter placed an iced tea with an orange straw on the table; Maisy took a long sip and thanked him, stared out toward the beach, where the Sunday-morning crowd was unpacking their coolers and unrolling their bright beach towels. A family battled a large umbrella, laughing until they had it upright and open over a baby in a portable playpen. Maisy dropped an elbow onto the table, settled her chin in her palm. She turned her face away from the beach to take another sip of iced tea; the straw missed her mouth and settled directly up her left nostril.

She attempted a slight shake of her head to free the straw. When that didn't work, she covered her face with her right hand and lifted her left to yank the straw free from her nose. A deep laugh made her shoot her head up. Mack stood there, his smile broad.

She dropped her head into her hands and moaned.

Mack sat catty-corner to her. "You know you couldn't have done that better if you'd tried."

Maisy peeked at him from between her fingers. "Can we do that again, and this time I'll be sitting here looking poised and elegant, like a woman in a Bloomingdale's catalog?"

"No way. I much prefer the imperfect Maisy with a straw stuck up her nose."

She dropped her hands, and feigned a punch to his arm. "If you tell a soul, I will personally kill you. I have a reputation to uphold."

"You do?"

She sighed. "Or maybe it's a reputation I don't want to uphold. Either way, can you just not tell anyone?"

He reached over and gave her a salt-and-sand-scented hug. She remembered him in a rush of sensation: how he smelled and the comfort of his warmth. "It's been so great to see you the past couple days," he said, "and you look absolutely amazing. It's as if time hasn't passed at all for you."

She touched his temples, brushed the short hair with her forefinger. "You look very sophisticated with your business haircut."

"Well, that's because I am sophisticated."

"When did that happen?" Maisy pulled her sunglasses over her eyes as the noonday sun became too strong.

The waiter's arrival cut Mack's answer short. They ordered their

food and talked about their lives as the sun moved westward and
Maisy's heart moved toward Mack Logan. When their food was
gone, they both ordered Bloody Marys, sat in the quiet of a Sunday afternoon and looked out over the porch of the Beach Club,
past the sand buckets, laughing kids and sunburned tourists.

Maisy leaned her head back on the chair's headrest. She wanted
to stay right here for hours with Mack, the sun warm on her face
and the hope of things to come flirting with her heart.

"Want to take a swim?" Mack asked.

Maisy opened her eyes. "No. I want to stay right here for days
and days."

He smiled. "Sounds good, but I think the hostess is trying to
seat some more people."

Maisy looked up at a long line of impatient, hungry people
staring at them. "Okay, but let's go down to the beach in front of
Driftwood Cottage. It's never as crowded there."

"You read my mind."

They walked in silence, Mack stopping every now and then to
bend over, pick up a shell, dig his toes deeper into the sand. Maisy
brushed up against him as if she were that same sixteen-year-old
wanting one touch, one brush of his arm or leg against her skin;
the adolescent who'd tagged along behind her sister and Mack to
the movie on the lawn, staring at Mack Logan with the full force
of her desire, and then moving her blanket closer to his. Her mind
scrambled for the words to ask him if he was dating someone, or
worse engaged; this subject hadn't come up yet. But she held tight
to the question that might change everything about the dream-
saturated afternoon.

When they reached the beach behind Driftwood Cottage, Maisy threw her straw beach bag down on the sand. Mack yanked his T-shirt over his head. "I haven't been in the water yet. Let's go."

She slipped off her cotton skirt to reveal her bikini bottoms, unbuttoned her shirt and removed her sunglasses to drop them inside her beach bag. "You know . . . I haven't been in the water yet, either. So it's the first time for both of us."

She realized how that sounded and her heart quickened at his smile. He ran toward the water, hollering over his shoulder, "Beat you to it."

She ran behind him, laughing and pumping her legs to catch up with him. They ran through the shallows, then ducked under the deeper waves. Together they swam farther out, then parallel to the beach. Out of breath, Maisy stood in the chest-high waves, watched Mack dive and surface, float on his back. She lifted water in her palms, let it trickle between her fingers as she bounced up and down on the tips of her toes with the waves.

Mack dove, stayed there. Maisy scanned the surface, called his name. A hand grabbed her ankle, and in an instant, she was under, too, her parted lips taking in a mouthful of seawater. She allowed Mack to pull her deeper, wrap his arms around her waist, their bodies melding hip to shoulder, skin on skin. He released her and she sputtered to the surface, pretended to be angry and spitting water. She splashed him. "That was mean."

He stood close to her, wiped a strand of hair from the side of her mouth. She turned in response. He smiled that sweet smile. "Do you remember what you said when I told you I loved you all those years ago?"

This was what Maisy had been waiting for—this exact moment with Mack, her chance to make it all come right this time. "I said I loved you back."

"No, you said, 'I know.' That was the last thing you said to me. 'I know.'"

Maisy felt warmth wash her insides, beginning at her heart and rushing down to her feet, her blood flowing to the truth: she'd had a chance to tell this man—then a boy—that she loved him, and back then it would have been true. "But I did . . ." She bit her lower lip on the certainty, the unequivocal truth.

"Some things are just better and bigger in memory, aren't they?"

"No. Not you." Maisy fought the need to throw her arms around this man she barely knew anymore and tell him that she loved him. She'd loved him then and he was just as wonderful now, but she didn't want to push him away with her desperate need.

Mack released her, dove under the water and swam toward shore. She watched in awe as water sluiced off his body. He stopped, stood waist-deep and waited for her to catch up.

Together they waded back to shore. He shook his head, salt water spraying over her. She inhaled his scent and then smiled at him, hoping that he could hear her unspoken words of desire. "Can I see you later?" she asked.

"Absolutely," he said. "Do you have to go somewhere now?"

She nodded. "I have to help the Cookbook Club cook something, but the truth is, the last thing I made was macaroni and cheese from a box."

"Just smile and they won't even notice you can't cook," Mack said, and walked toward their shirts and towels.

A child's voice echoing across the water reached them. "Mr. Mack . . . hey, hey, over here."

Mack and Maisy turned together to see Brayden jumping up and down on the beach.

"Hey, Brayden," Mack called, backed a few feet away from Maisy.

Brayden ran up to them. "Hey, Aunt Maisy, what's up?"

"Not much, buddy. What's up with you?"

"Just finished a boring meeting with Gamma and Mom and Adalee. How come you got out of it?"

"I had my interrogation this morning." Maisy slipped her shirt back on over her bathing suit, buttoned it.

Brayden turned his attention to Mack. "Okay, your turn. Let's see if you can really catch more redfish off the jetty than off Pearson's Pier. I'm telling you, you can't. Maybe in the old days, but not now."

"Who you calling old?"

"You . . ." Brayden ran off, calling over his shoulder, "I'll get the poles. Meet you at the jetty."

Mack smiled at Maisy. "Guess I'm going fishing. I promised Dad, too."

"Yeah, and I gotta . . ." She motioned toward the house.

"God, it's great to be here." Mack headed off, and Maisy turned toward the cottage, hoping no one could see the big, goofy smile on her face.

EIGHTEEN

RILEY

The sun warmed Riley's shoulders, the afternoon hazy with languid humidity as she relaxed, knowing that Maisy was preparing for the Cookbook Club. She'd walked to the jetty pier to meet Brayden and bring him home before the public arrived for the cooking demonstration. Next to her on the pier stood Mack, Brayden and Sheppard, their fishing poles appendages that hung over the slapping waves. The men continued their bets about the best place to fish.

Mack hollered toward Brayden. "Take a couple steps back, buddy. Your mom will kill me if you fall in."

Sheppard flung his line to the right, toward the marsh area. His fishing hat hung loose on his head, his thinner hair poking out underneath the rim. Mack leaned toward Riley. "He's had that hat since I can remember. Even the stains have stories. Every lure is the one that got away. I don't have a summer memory of him that doesn't include that hat."

Riley smiled, laid her hand on top of Mack's resting on the warm wooden railing. The sun seemed to hum as it pressed down on them, spreading lassitude and warmth. A sad thought crossed Riley's mind—what would Mack do with that hat when his father was gone? What did one do with the most important memories held in material possessions? Display them? Bury them?

Riley turned away from Mack's frail father, away from her morbid thoughts, and watched Brayden reel in his line to show them a tangle of marsh grass. Mack hollered, "Told you this wasn't near as good a place to fish."

Then Sheppard let out a shout. "I got me a big one here."

Brayden dropped his pole on the dock, ran over to Sheppard's side. Holding up his pole, Sheppard smiled. "Ta-da." A large redfish dangled on the end of the line, sunlight glinting off the silvered scales.

Together they unhooked the fish. Sheppard was holding it over the water to release it when Brayden placed his hand on the old man's arm. "My mom is a really good cook. She can fry that thing up for you in about a second."

Mack laughed. "And I bet she can clean it faster than anyone you know."

Brayden nodded. "Except me. I can do it faster."

Riley leaned against the rail and shook her head. "Go ahead and release the fish, Mr. Sheppard. There is no way I'm going to have time to fry that up tonight."

Another hour passed in quiet companionship before Mack put

his pole down and sat with Riley on the wooden bench attached to the railing. "Is it like this when you live here?" he asked.

"What do you mean?"

"Are you at peace like this all the time? Like now? Or is it only this way if you visit. . . . At this moment, I feel no need to contact the outside world. It doesn't exist anymore."

Riley shrugged. "I'm not sure about the peaceful part. I do have to work and face all those other problems that can make life hard. But yes, sometimes I feel that the outside world doesn't really exist. It's hard for me to picture you in New York or Boston or anywhere but on the end of a Lowcountry dock."

"Maybe because that's where I belong."

An older couple—hand in hand—walked slowly down the dock. The woman leaned her head against the shoulder of the taller man, who carried a parcel or box of some sort. As they drew closer, Riley recognized them—Mr. and Mrs. Rutledge, Sheldon's parents. A whisper passed her lips. "The Rutledge family," she said.

Mack waved at them, but the couple stared past him and Riley, almost through them. It wasn't until the couple reached the end of the dock that their faces flickered with recognition. Mrs. Rutledge formed her mouth into a round O of surprise, and said their names. Riley realized that Mrs. Rutledge was crying, her eyes swollen and full of tears.

Sheppard placed his pole in a round brass holder and shook Mr. Rutledge's hand, offered greetings, and then gave Mrs. Rutledge a hug. Brayden turned toward them, but didn't come closer.

Mrs. Rutledge hugged Mack. "I am so sorry I didn't recognize you for a minute. This is a hard day for us."

Mack looked at his father, who spoke to him in soft words. "I heard yesterday and meant to tell you this morning. Sheldon was . . ."

Mr. Rutledge finished Sheppard's sentence. "Sheldon died with honor for our country on a mission in Iraq. It's been months, but we wanted to bring . . . bring him here."

Riley backed away, grabbed Brayden's arm, heard the ensuing conversation as though she were a bug trapped in a Mason jar, the sounds muffled.

Mack spoke to the older couple. "I am so sorry. I have so many wonderful memories of Sheldon. He was one of a kind, a true gentle and yet tough spirit."

"Yes," Mrs. Rutledge said. "This was his favorite place in the world. And you were one of his favorite friends from those beach days. I know he regrets . . . regretted not keeping in better touch."

"Me, too," Mack said, and bowed his head to stare at the dock.

Mr. Rutledge spoke with a tremor in his voice. "We are here to toss his ashes into the sea. It is what he wanted. It is what he asked for. Our only son."

Sheppard placed his hand on Mr. Rutledge's shoulder.

Brayden looked up at Riley. "Mom, you're hurting me."

She realized she was squeezing his arm so hard that the impression of her fingers remained when she jerked her hand away. Mack came to their side.

"What's going on?" Brayden asked him. His eyes were wide and his gaze flickered from Sheppard to the Rutledges and back to Mack.

Mack bent so that he was eye to eye with Brayden. "This sweet couple are old friends of ours and they are here to say goodbye to their son. Do you want to run down to the ice-cream shack and we'll join you in a few minutes?"

Brayden reeled in his line and leaned toward Mack. "How are they going to say goodbye if he's not here?"

Mack looked to Riley with a question on his face. She understood she needed to answer her son, yet the words were locked inside her.

Mack explained. "Their son died in Iraq. That box contains his ashes."

"Oh." Brayden nodded.

Mack's hand went to the small of Riley's back; she swayed beneath him, her eyes closed. He grabbed her with both arms, and she fell into him, her face against his chest, her arms limp at his side. "Oh . . . It can't be."

"I know," he whispered into her hair. "It's terrible."

Riley's body shook; her breathing became shallow. "Are you okay?" Mack asked, lifted her chin.

"I don't know. . . . I can't . . ."

"Mom?" Brayden's voice seemed to contain a multitude of questions.

Riley didn't answer or look up, just buried her face in Mack's chest. She felt his hand in her hair. "Riley?"

She lifted her face. Mack's voice was like a jackhammer to the glass jar surrounding her; shards of slivered glass seemed to fly through the air in brilliance; she saw Brayden in the light. He shifted his baseball cap on his head, twisted his feet on the dock as if trying to decide which way to turn in this uncertain world in which his mother wouldn't answer him.

Riley stepped away from Mack and straightened to her full height, finding a new strength in her guilty heart. She looked directly at Brayden. "This couple is here to say goodbye to their son. We will stay and add a prayer for his soul."

Mack lifted his eyebrows in question. "Are you sure?"

"Yes," she said.

Together the three of them joined Sheppard and the Rutledges. Riley hugged Mrs. Rutledge, then her husband. "I am so sorry about Sheldon. He was an amazing boy. I have so many great memories of him."

"Thank you, dear. He spoke very fondly of you also."

Riley held her hand out for her son. Brayden stepped to her side and she placed her arm over his shoulders. "This is my son, Brayden Sheffield. If you don't mind, we would like to stay and help you say goodbye to Sheldon." With each word Riley felt something in her world shift, as if broken pieces of reality were trying to come together but didn't quite fit.

Mr. Rutledge sat down on a bench to look Brayden in the eyes. "Son, do you understand what we are doing?"

"Yes, sir," he said.

"My son died for our country, and we are here to honor him. Are you sure you want to stay?"

Brayden nodded, his eyes wide. Mrs. Rutledge looked at them all. "This is a small miracle. We thought we would be saying goodbye to him alone and now . . . look, you're here. More people who loved him."

"Everyone who knew Sheldon loved him," Mack said.

"Yes." Mr. Rutledge stood, Mrs. Rutledge at his side. Mack

placed his hand in Riley's and together with Brayden and Sheppard they walked to the end of the dock with Sheldon Rutledge's
mourning parents.

Late-afternoon light shimmered across the walls of Riley's bedroom. A breeze from the open window lifted the sheer curtains,
creating uneven shadow patterns across the hardwood floors. Riley's body still shook with a fever of grief and guilt. She wrapped a
quilt around her legs, curled into a ball on her bed.

Images without words tumbled through her mind: Sheldon
laughing in front of a bonfire; Sheldon above her telling her how
beautiful she was and how he'd wanted her since the first time he
saw her punch Lilly-Mae for bullying a little boy; Brayden's face
and eyes as Sheldon's ashes flowed across the air and into the waters off Palmetto Beach.

She longed to tell everyone and yet no one that Brayden's father had just been honored at the end of a jetty pier. She craved to
cry and yet feel nothing at all.

She ignored the soft knock on her door, and then Maisy entered without permission. "Riley? Are you okay?" Her voice was
soft.

Maisy's footsteps stopped next to Riley's bed, but she didn't
open her eyes. Maisy's hand came to rest upon her forehead.
"You're sick." Riley nodded without otherwise answering. "You've
been working too hard . . . too long." The bed tilted under Maisy's
weight. Riley curled tighter into herself.

"Maisy, did you know that Sheldon Rutledge died in Iraq
months ago? Plane crash."

"God, no. That's awful. Is that what's wrong with you?"

In full protection of her secret, Riley sat up. "No. Listen, I'll get Brayden dinner after the Cookbook Club is done. They're coming now." She needed to find the strength to feed her son, check on the bookstore—all the responsibilities that made her get up each morning. This was not the time for self-pity, for regret and selfish tears. She'd made her choices and she'd live with them. She'd decided to keep her secret about Brayden, and a promise to herself was the same as to any other—you didn't break it just because it didn't feel good anymore.

Use your logic, her mind screamed. This afternoon, this death, was a reminder to keep her head on straight and move forward. Romantic notions of Mack Logan were a silly waste of time. She felt like an idiot for even letting the prickling warmth of desire return.

A breeze floated into the room. Riley forced a smile. "I'm fine, Maisy. Go on and enjoy your evening. I'll finish with the Cookbook Club. You go . . . on now."

"You sound really weird, Riley. I think you need some sleep or something. Why don't you spend the night with Mama? Adalee and I will take care of everything here. Brayden has been promising to play Monopoly with me—every time I try to nail him down, he's running off to the pier. Let me help you with him."

Riley wished with a sudden and fervent desire that Maisy was the kind of sister she could confide in—the kind of sister who would understand her guilt and grief and offer comfort in return. The kind of sister she used to be.

Riley got out of bed and stood straight and firm. "That is sweet of you, Maisy. Yes, you take over the Cookbook Club, but

I'll bring Brayden to Mama's. He likes playing with the boy who lives next door."

Yes, it was a good idea for her to spend the night with Mama. She'd be back in the morning—first thing. Riley gathered an overnight bag, rounded up her son and drove to her mother's house.

She had tried to tell Maisy about Sheldon on the night of the bonfire. Later, she'd wanted to tell Maisy how the events of that one night had not only broken apart their relationship, but also formed a new life in Brayden.

In the days before that last summer, Maisy had been the kind of sister to whom Riley would have confided this story of Sheldon. Once upon a time they'd have hidden beneath the canoe stored on the side of the Beach Club and whispered secrets. In that sweet past they'd tiptoed down the hall and sequestered themselves beneath the blankets on Maisy's bed and told each other about the boys who wanted to kiss them.

Tears filled Riley's eyes at these memories from before she'd betrayed her sister in jealousy. She understood why Maisy had left town, why she hated her, but she didn't understand why Maisy had never pursued Mack, why she had never gone after him or told him of her love. When Mack didn't return the following summer, Maisy had run away instead of going after him.

Brayden touched Riley's shoulder as she pulled the car into the driveway. "Mom, is something wrong?"

She smiled down at him. "I don't feel all that well. I'm gonna go lie down for a while. You can play with Tommy next door, or hang with Gamma."

"Got it," he said, jumped from the car's passenger seat and

ran through the hedges to the next-door neighbor's house, calling Tommy's name.

The car idled, and Riley rested her head on the headrest. Walking into the house, talking to Mama and then retreating to her own bedroom seemed too monumental a task compared to just closing her eyes. The sun's warmth filling the car pressed her toward the comfort of dreams.

A loud thump startled Riley and she opened her eyes, realized she'd fallen asleep with the motor running. Adalee stood outside the car, her eyebrows furrowed. Riley shut off the engine and opened the door to stand and face her sister. "Hey, Adalee."

"Are you okay?"

"I'm fine, but I can't believe I fell asleep just now."

"I'm headed over to the bookstore. I was hoping you could drive me." Adalee glanced back toward the house. "If Mama thinks I drove, she'll lose her mind. She is madder at me about that DUI than she's ever been about anything ever."

"Oh, Adalee. I just left the bookstore. Can Maisy come get you?"

"No, she's working on . . ." Adalee stopped her words short. "Forget it. I'll get Harriet to take me." She turned on her heels and ran back into the house. Riley stretched, lifted her face to the sun's warmth, wanting to absorb it into her heart and mind, let it wash the mourning and regret from her body.

Riley slipped through the back door, ignored Mama and tiptoed up the stairway to her old bedroom, where she curled into her childhood bed and slept.

Nineteen

Maisy was filled with the frantic need to create something beautiful. She knew to take advantage of this drive. It was when she did her best work—when love's promise appeared before her and it seemed as if her dreams might just work out . . . this time. Her creative work reflected the promise of fulfillment. As soon as the cookbook ladies went home, she'd head for the storage room and the project she was working on with Adalee, but now she sat at the café bar and chatted with the club members about their latest dish—shrimp and grits from Nathalie Dupree's cookbook.

A crowd sat in rows of chairs where the café tables were usually arranged. Cookbooks were displayed on iron stands throughout the area. The aroma of garlic, shrimp and a spice Maisy couldn't name wafted across the room. Classical music, chosen by the club members, brought a sense of peace. Maisy stood behind the counter as the club cooked, and the leader, Sharon Martin, spoke to the audience about the process. When the public had had its fill of food, and Ethel had rung up the cookbook sales, Maisy took a seat on a barstool and smiled at the club. "You all did a fantastic job. I think I might even be able to cook that dish now."

"It's an easy one," Sharon said. "Now that everyone else is gone, we get to have our own party."

Eventually the discussion turned from the dish they had prepared to issues within the community and the personal problems in their lives.

Sharon placed a clean plate in front of Maisy, dropped a ladleful of steaming shrimp and grits onto it. "This is for you," she said.

"Thanks." Maisy dug in. "Delicious," she said. The discussions continued: children who hadn't visited from college; grandkids who needed tending; husbands who had lost their jobs or their sex drive. The women shared their joys and pains as Maisy helped them clean up and pour more wine, listening and laughing with them.

Sharon was complaining about her teen daughter, who barely spoke to the family anymore. A beautiful woman, tall and thin, replied, "Well, Carla is still talking to us, but only in country music lyrics."

Maisy laughed. "What?"

"She's not making that up," Sharon said. "Her daughter thinks that if she only speaks in lyrics, her country music career will finally take off. It's some weird superstition."

"Has she thought about maybe just moving to Nashville and

breaking into the music scene? Seems a lot less complicated than talking in lyric-only language."

"Well, I'll just let 'Jesus Take the Wheel,'" the woman said with a laugh, then explained to Maisy, "That's a Carrie Underwood song."

"I know, but maybe you should tell her to find a 'Good Friend and a Glass of Wine.'" That was the title of a LeAnn Rimes song.

"Ooh . . . that was a good one." The woman laughed with her head back, wine almost spilling from her glass. "By the way, I'm Barbara." She held out her hand and shook Maisy's free one. "So nice to have you here."

"Thanks," Maisy said, and thought of a song title she'd like to recite to Mack: "If You Ever Have Forever in Mind" by Vince Gill.

Adalee came through the front door, iPod buds in her ears, singing too loud to a beat only she could hear. "Oh, to be young again," Sharon said. "To not care that you're singing off-key."

Adalee noticed the women staring at her, placed a hand over her mouth and popped her ear buds out. "Oh . . . hey. I'm sorry."

The women waved at her to join them and returned to their discussions while *ooh*ing and *ahh*ing over the food. Adalee whispered to Maisy, "Can I go out with Chad? I know you want me to spend the night here with you, but this is the perfect chance for me to get out and see him. Living in Mama's jailhouse, I'm going to lose my mind."

Maisy leaned closer to Adalee. "I thought you were gonna help me with the furniture and stuff tonight. That's the main reason we got Riley to leave."

Adalee made a cute pouty face. "Just for a bit?"

Remembering when she'd been twenty-two and in love beyond reason, Maisy nodded. "I'm going to regret this, aren't I?"

"Not at all," Adalee said, jumped off the barstool and ran upstairs, a duffel bag slung over her shoulder.

Once the dishes were clean, and the café back in order, the Cookbook Club sat down to rate the food in their Big-Book-of-Recipes notebook. Each woman wrote down her comments in a special section. Comparing their remarks inspired as much laughter and conversation as the cooking itself had. Sharon wrote: *Reminds me of my first date with Bill when he took me to the Boathouse in Isle of Palms.* Barbara scribbled across the page and then showed her comment to everyone: *Wish we had My Keylime Pie.*

"Get it?" she asked.

They all shook their heads.

"I get it," Maisy said. "'My Keylime Pie'—you know, that Kenny Chesney song."

Laughter filled the room as each woman continued to fill the comment section.

After they had hugged one another goodbye and the club had gone home, Maisy unlocked the storage room and began to move the furniture she and Adalee had bought and were hiding from Riley. Maisy could now sit in this room, her music blaring, and not imagine she saw Tucker Morgan. Instead she imagined only the beauty that would emerge from this old furniture and the odd knickknacks. She had to admit Adalee did have a great talent for decorating, maybe bigger than her own. They were taking a chance that Riley and Mama would love the transformation without having contributed to it.

The history boards were tucked neatly behind a screen of cane chairs, still sticky with new paint. Another set of boards, ones Adalee had made about their family, were propped on the other side of the room.

Maisy laughed, turned her music all the way up and began to paint another set of chairs in the sage green Adalee had chosen. Perfect color. The slipcovers from Beach Chic should arrive in the morning, and the linen she'd dropped off at Mama's seamstress should be ready by the afternoon. Maisy realized she was smiling even as she worked.

This was where she felt most at peace: in the midst of a consuming project. Her smile grew wider as she recalled the day with Mack; the way he'd touched her face. She reached her hand up, caressed her own cheek, closed her eyes and sighed. "Please," she whispered out loud. "Let it happen this time."

Maybe it was true that happy endings were formed here at Driftwood Cottage. Maybe that was the real reason the cottage was now full to overflowing with books, stories, clubs and gossip. Maisy approached the history boards and read what Adalee had written in calligraphy below photos from when the Logan family had lived here: *Legend says that Driftwood Cottage is a place where people connect and all stories have happy endings. But maybe Driftwood Cottage is a place where all of our stories are played out over and over, again and again, none of them ever really ending, just continuing. . . .*

Maisy touched the picture of the Logan family sitting on the front porch. She stared into a young Mack's eyes. "Or," Maisy whispered under the music, "maybe this is a place where happy endings come true for me."

An hour later, she was engrossed in painting when her cell phone vibrated on the hardwood floor; Peter's name appeared on the screen. She took a deep breath, and decided not to answer him. Yet, by the time she'd reached over to turn off the ringer, she found she'd already taken the call.

"Hey, baby." Peter's soft voice traveled over the airwaves. Maisy sat down on the floor, leaned up against the closed doors and felt her stomach clench with rising longing. She hadn't spoken to him in three days, and at the mere sound of his voice, every emotion she felt for him returned full force.

"Hey, Peter," she said.

"When are you coming home? I miss you terribly."

Maisy stared up at the old brass chandelier that had once hung over Mr. Logan's desk, when this room was the library. "What am I supposed to say now?" She thought of Mack, his wet hair on his forehead.

"You're supposed to say you miss me, too," he said in a whisper so quiet she barely heard him.

"Why are you whispering? Where are you?"

"In the back bedroom . . . well, in the bathroom."

"Is Sue home?"

"She's in the kitchen. . . . She can't hear me. I just had to hear your voice."

Maisy recalled the woman in the Blonde Book Club, the one who loved the married man. She heard Lucy speak of her husband as if he were faithful and true. Maisy's breath caught as she realized who she was in this scenario: the pitiful one who believed that the married man really loved her and would eventually leave his wife. She didn't want to be *that* girl.

Peter's voice came across in a breathless murmur. "Are you there? I need you."

Oh, Maisy thought with her eyes shut, his voice seemed close, as if he were lying next to her. He still had the power to conjure up in her the terrible need to be needed. "I'm here," she said.

"I wish."

Over the phone line, Maisy heard someone banging on the door and a voice saying something she couldn't make out, followed by the distinct click of disconnection. He was gone. Desire and need receded like a retreating wave, leaving Maisy with a familiar sense of loss. She snapped her phone shut. She was tired of wanting what she couldn't have, tired of waiting for something she would never get.

She dialed information, found the number for the Seaside Inn and asked for Mack Logan's room. The phone rang until the call went through to voice mail—he was out eating with his dad; he'd told her that. But she wanted, no, needed to see him. She stood, paced the room. Where would he go to eat? There weren't a lot of options besides the Beach Club and Bud's. She would try Bud's.

She laid the paintbrush on the drop cloth, slammed the top back on the paint can. She needed a break anyway, didn't she?

Her rationalizations continued on her walk to Bud's, where a crowd spilled onto the sidewalk. Maisy greeted a few familiar faces and entered the bar. She scanned the crowd, no longer fooling herself into believing that she wasn't chasing Mack.

She wound her way through the room, around the pool table, where a young couple melded in a tight embrace blocked her way. She tried to squeeze past and ended up knocking the two into the table. "Sorry," she said. The young man looked straight at her.

Chad.

Maisy stopped in her tracks and confronted him. "Where is Adalee?"

The girl tilted her head at him. "Who's Adalee?"

Chad squinted at Maisy as if he were trying to place her. "Huh?"

Maisy took a step closer and spoke slowly, deliberately. "Where's Adalee?"

"How am I s'posed to know?"

The girl made some adolescent cooing noise, cuddled up next to Chad. "Who's that?" She nodded in Maisy's direction.

Maisy answered for him. "His girlfriend's sister—the girlfriend who got him his summer job." Maisy didn't wait to see their reactions. She turned toward the front of the restaurant. If Chad was here, where had Adalee gone?

"Maisy?" She turned to see Mack and Sheppard sitting in a far booth. Her anger immediately dissipated. She smiled, and went toward the table, conscious of every movement of her body: where she held her hands, where her hair fell across her forehead, where her jeans rubbed against her stomach.

Mack rose to meet her, and kissed her cheek; she turned quickly enough to allow him to catch the edge of her lips. Sheppard stood too, and hugged her. "You eating here?" Mack asked.

"No," she said, her reason for coming now seeming foolish and transparent. "I . . ."

Mack pointed behind her. "You looking for your sister?"

Maisy spun around, saw Adalee headed toward the back of the restaurant. "Adalee!" she called out too loudly.

Adalee turned and waved, then came over. "Hey, whatcha' doing here? I thought—"

"I thought you were with Chad."

"It's weird. I can't find him. I thought we were meeting at the Beach Club, but he didn't show up. Maybe he said Bud's, and I got confused."

Maisy's feet felt stuck in sinking ground. "Why don't we go back and finish our project? Maybe he got . . . busy. He'll call later."

"Oh . . . well, I guess." Adalee glanced around the bar. "I'll just take one look around, and then I might as well go back with you."

Maisy looked at Mack, and found all her reasons for coming here in his face: his love for his father, his willingness to acknowledge what had passed between them all those years ago. She could steer her sister out of this bar and away from her cheating boyfriend, or stay and bask in the company Mack offered.

Mack's gaze flickered from Maisy to Adalee, an unspoken question forming.

"Well," Maisy said, "it was really good to run into y'all. Guess I'll see you tomorrow."

"Absolutely," Mack said, looked down at his dad.

"You got it," Sheppard confirmed. "We'll be at the evening party. We're going deep-sea fishing in the morning, but we should be back by late afternoon."

"Great." Maisy placed her hand on Adalee's back and led her

out of the restaurant. Together they reached the corner before either spoke, and then their words overlapped.

"Where else did you look for Chad tonight?"

"Were you looking for me?" Adalee asked, her hands on her hips as she stood in a wide stance at the corner. "I can take care of myself."

"I wasn't looking for you," Maisy said. "Were you running around town looking for your boyfriend?"

"I wasn't running around town. I just thought I got the Beach Club and Bud's mixed up. That's all."

Maisy began the walk back to Driftwood Cottage. "You didn't get anything mixed up. You should never run after a guy—you're too good for that."

Adalee caught up to Maisy. "Maybe you are, but I guess I'm not."

Maisy stopped and stared at her sister, who looked like she couldn't decide whether to be angry, upset or some confused combination of both. Maisy let out a long sigh. "I'm not too good for it, either. I guess I just think we *should* be."

Adalee's shoulders slumped. "Whatever."

Maisy draped her arm around her sister's shoulder. "I know a cure for the blues."

"What?"

"A can of sage green paint, soft white linen and cane chairs . . ."

"I get it," Adalee interrupted. "Okay, let's finish what we started."

"Yes," Maisy said, her mind not exactly on chairs and paint, "let's finish what we started."

Ce~ TWENTY

RILEY

The doctor's office smelled of flower-scented cleaner mixed with antiseptic. Riley sat in the waiting room with Mama, who sat perched in her wheelchair as if it were a throne. Today, Monday, was the first time Kitsy had left the house since her accident, and she was done up as if she were attending a black-tie event for her friend the Guvnah, whom she'd gone to high school with, of course.

Riley reached over and dabbed at an errant spot of Mama's lipstick. Kitsy pushed her hand away. "I am not a child."

"I was just . . ." Riley exhaled in frustration and fatigue. "Sorry, Mama. I was just wiping off some stray lipstick."

"I can do that myself." Kitsy formed her mouth into a round O and wiped around her lips with a manicured pinky finger.

How her Mama could be confined to bed and still make sure

the manicurist and hairdresser visited the house on schedule was beyond Riley's understanding. "Mama, you look great."

"Of course. Bed rest is no excuse for being slovenly and lazy. I'm not sure why you insist on wearing those jeans and loose tops. At least put on some lipstick."

"Thanks, Mama. I'm fine. And by the way, these tops are very much in style." Riley smiled at her mother, and then reached down and answered her ringing cell phone.

"Hey, sis."

Maisy's voice made Riley's stomach clench. "What's going on?" She should never have left the store for so long; God only knew what her sisters had done or, worse, not done.

"Okay, so here's the deal," Maisy told her. "You are not allowed to return to this store until three o'clock this afternoon. At eleven you have a hair appointment and facial at Michael's that I have arranged and paid for. You can't argue—just go and then keep yourself occupied. You understand me?" Maisy laughed as if they were twelve years old and had just raided Mama's forbidden Estée Lauder cosmetics together.

Riley pulled the phone from her ear and looked at it as if this were a prank call. She replaced it. "You know I can't do that. Brayden is home alone until I'm finished with Mama's X-rays. I haven't set up for tonight. Someone needs to make follow-up phone calls. The posters of the authors need to be hung. . . ."

"Whoa," Maisy interrupted her. "We've got it all under control. Right after you left, Mack and Sheppard stopped by and asked if Brayden could go deep-sea fishing with them. I knew it would be okay with you."

"I didn't give him permission to go anywhere."

"But you would have, right?"

"Ummm. Yes, I would have."

"Ethel is stacking the books. I already tacked up the posters. Adalee is setting up the chairs in the arrangement Mama sketched. I'll make the phone calls. Do not return here until three o'clock."

"This is crazy. And sweet. Thank you so much, Maisy. But why?"

"Because I said so." She hung up without saying goodbye.

Riley stuffed her phone back in her purse as the nurse called Kitsy back to the X-ray room. "What was that all about?" Kitsy asked.

"Your crazy daughter. Nothing important."

Kitsy smiled. "It is so wonderful having you girls together."

Riley agreed. The sister who had just called her was the sister from well before thirteen years ago: the one who laughed fully, behaved without pretense and loved with her whole heart. It was nice to pretend for a minute, or even for a day, that things were the way they used to be.

After the follow-up X-rays, Riley settled her mama back at the house with a cup of chamomile tea, a painkiller (almost as good as a martini) and Harriet and the nurse tending to her every need. "Mama, please tell me what the doctor had to say today."

Riley both feared and wanted to hear about chemo and treatment and rehab. But Mama closed her eyes and leaned back on her lavender-scented pillows. "Not now. I'm going to sleep. You go on, Riley."

She backed out of the room, stared at her mama in wonderment. This was a woman who couldn't keep a secret for more than fifteen minutes, a woman who used prayer requests as a means to tell horrid secrets, and yet she could lie in bed with all her daughters surrounding her and remain silent about her serious illness.

Riley shook her head and headed for Michael's Salon—the only one in town aside from the barbershop.

Michael's was shut tight when Riley arrived. She groaned. Of course it was closed: it was Monday. She shouldn't have believed Maisy. She was digging into her purse for the car keys when a man appeared at the glass doors, unlocked and opened them. "You must be Riley."

"Yes, and you are?"

"I am Frederick. Your sister has arranged for a makeover, and I'm here to serve." He bowed.

"Where . . . ?"

"I work in Savannah, but your sister called, and I came running."

"How do you know Maisy?" Riley followed Frederick into the salon, where she usually came twice a year to have her ends trimmed.

"I knew her in Laguna Beach. I moved back to Savannah a few years ago—that's where I'm from."

Riley shook her head. "This is crazy."

Frederick threw his hands in the air. "Isn't she amazing?"

Riley laughed. "Okay, you may not give me orange hair, or chop it all off or give me bangs, or . . ."

He held up his hands to stay her words. "Just sit in the chair and allow me to work my magic," he said.

Riley dropped her purse on the floor and stared at herself in the mirror as Frederick walked through the salon, turning on lights and music. "How did you get Michael to allow you to use his place?" she asked.

"I didn't. Maisy did." Frederick wheeled out a trayful of coloring and cutting paraphernalia. "Now, let me see the damage." He stood behind her, ran his hands through her hair. "You have a gorgeous wave to your hair. We should work with the natural curls. . . ." His voice trailed off and Riley gave herself over to his ministration. As he folded foil into her hair, he talked nonstop about the state of the world, the changing attitudes in the South, corrupt local politics, and living in Savannah after having been in Laguna Beach.

Riley never did more than laugh or agree with all he said. Under the dryer she fell asleep. While his hands rinsed her hair and massaged her scalp, she realized she'd finally put aside her worries about the store, and Mama, and Sheldon, and what Mack Logan did or did not think about her. Frederick blew dry her hair using a large round brush and finally spun her chair around. "Now, who is that gorgeous woman in the mirror?"

Riley stared at herself, then looked up from her reflection to Frederick. "I don't know." Her blond hair now had lighter streaks that made it look as though she'd spent a month on the beach. Her hair curled in layers that landed just below her shoulders. Her new bangs slanted to the right.

Frederick laughed. "You are a beautiful woman, Riley Shef-

field. All I did was improve on what was already there." He spun
her chair around again. "Listen, I see this all the time with women.
Stop thinking you are only a mom. Really. You are gorgeous. Let
your light shine, baby."

Riley laughed. "Did Maisy tell you to give me a pep talk along
with a haircut?"

Frederick shook his head, suddenly serious. "She loves you."

Riley looked away, tears threatening. She swallowed over the
lump in her throat. "I doubt she said that, but thank you."

"She didn't have to say it." Frederick glanced at his watch.
"Your makeup artist—who will complete your makeover—will
be here in a few minutes. I, on the other hand, must return to
Savannah."

Riley reached for her purse. "What do I owe you? And even
more—how do I keep this up? Will you tell Michael how to do
it?" She pulled at a strand of hair.

"Savannah is only an hour away, dear."

Riley smiled. "You're right."

"And you don't owe me a thing. This time." He smiled. "I
owed Maisy a big favor. So what goes around comes around."

"For what?"

Frederick winked. "I'll never tell."

Riley dropped her purse to the floor. "Thank you so much. I
really do love it, even if I have no idea how to make it look this
way again."

"I cut it so you can let it dry naturally, or for a smoother look,
you can blow-dry it with this large barrel brush. It's yours now."

"I have some hot curlers at home."

He groaned. "This is not the seventies. Only seventies music is allowed—not clothing or hairdos. You own scrunchies, don't you?"

Riley grinned. "Of course. In every color. I don't use them . . . anymore."

"Oh, please throw them away. If you don't, you'll be tempted."

A singsong voice called out a greeting, and Frederick and Riley turned to see a young woman with dreadlocks coming through the door. "Hey, Celia." Frederick went to her, kissed her full on the mouth. "Come meet the amazing Riley."

The next hour passed under Celia's gifted hands as she gave Riley a full facial, then made up her face, adding instructions about how to achieve the same look on her own. With Celia fussing over her, Riley forgot her responsibilities, but as soon as she inhaled the moist outside air, her flip-flops slapping against the pavement, she yanked out her cell phone, and called the bookstore.

Ethel reprimanded her for checking on them, and told her not to return for at least another hour. Riley walked past the coffee shop, the gift shop and the knitting store. Townspeople and summer people waved or called her name. When she reached Confetti Boutique, she stared at the window display. She hadn't shopped here in years: she couldn't afford it, and she had no need for anything but her jeans, cotton skirts and tops. She moved down the sidewalk, dreamlike, enjoying a certain laziness born of relaxation and the spent grief of the previous night.

"Riley Anne Sheffield." She turned in slow motion. Lodge Barton stood in front of the scarred wooden door leading to the newspaper offices. "You look beautiful. Got a date?"

She laughed. "Yeah, with a bookstore."

He came toward her, his glasses reflecting her own smile. "You headed to the cottage?"

"No, they won't let me back for an hour. So I'm just wandering the streets."

He glanced up at the large clock tower in the middle of the square. "Past lunchtime. Come eat with me."

She noticed that for the first time, he didn't ask—he told. She nodded in agreement.

"The Patio," he said, once again decisive.

"Sounds great. I can't remember the last time I ate there. I am not getting chicken salad. That's all I ever have at the bookstore café."

He laughed, placed his arm over her shoulder and gave her a squeeze before releasing her. "This is like a miracle on Broad Street—finding Riley Sheffield with an hour to spare."

They walked the block to the Patio and Riley paused at the front door. "Do I really seem that way to you—like I don't ever have an hour to spare?"

"You are the most preoccupied, busy woman I know. It's hard to pin you down for more than a two-second conversation before someone or something needs your attention."

"Really?" Riley tried to see the woman he saw, yet she only envisioned a tired female running through the bookstore in a frantic need to save a business that had once saved her.

"Really." He opened the Patio's glass door, held his hand out for her to enter.

The tinkling of glass, quiet laughter and murmured voices

filled the subdued restaurant, which was packed with what Mama called the "ladies who lunch" crowd.

Lodge looked over his shoulder. "Maybe we should have gone to Bud's. I seem to be a little out of place here, the only man."

A high school girl with terrible acne who had once worked at Driftwood Cottage came to the hostess podium. She ignored them for a full minute, pretending to study her seating chart before finally saying, "Oh, hello, Ms. Sheffield. Two for lunch?"

"Yes, please," Riley said. "Hello, Cami."

She felt herself blush as she remembered the sobbing scene in which she'd fired this girl for coming in stoned one afternoon.

"Follow me," Cami murmured, turning her cool gaze away from Riley's.

Lodge shrugged his shoulders and they followed the bobbing ponytail to a far back table next to the bathrooms. They sat, and when Cami walked away, they burst into laughter. "What did you do to that girl?" Lodge asked. "Ice is warmer than she is, and this might be the worst table in the restaurant."

"How do you know she's mad at me and not you?"

"She didn't say, 'Hello, Mr. Barton' with barbs of hate attached." He grinned and leaned toward Riley. "I would absolutely love to know what you could have done to piss someone off that badly."

"I fired her."

"Ah, got it." He reached for a menu. "Oh, I almost forgot—I have pictures for you. The second one will go in tomorrow's paper with the article about the events at the bookstore." He leaned down, pulled two photos from his satchel, handed them across the table.

Riley looked down at the first black-and-white photo, show-ing her and Mack. She was looking up at him while he smiled at the camera. "Oh, I hope you don't use this one. I look . . . terrible. I'd had a terrible morning, not even a shower."

"No, you look adorable, and quite adoring also."

"Thanks, Lodge, but please don't put it in the paper. And I wasn't adoring him. I was talking."

"Of course."

Riley looked at the second picture: her, Mack, Maisy and Brayden smiling at the camera. "If someone told me when I was a kid that one day I would be in this picture, with my son, I wouldn't have believed them."

"That's why life is so . . . interesting," Lodge said. "Now, how are things coming for the party?"

"There are so many answers to that one question, I don't even know where to start. Can we talk about you for a little bit? I'm tired of me, my sisters, my family, and my bookstore. They're ex-hausting." Riley reached for the end of her hair to move it off her shoulder, and found only air.

Lodge's warm smile made Riley want to curl up right there and take a nap. "Your hair is shorter," he said, as if he knew what she'd meant to do with her hand.

"Yes, Maisy had someone give me a . . . makeover."

"You didn't need one. You were fine just the way you were, but you look great now, too."

"Obviously she didn't think so." Riley smiled back at him. "But I am not complaining. I don't care about her motivations. So how is the newspaper business?"

Over plates of shrimp scampi and glasses of white wine, Riley became lost in conversation with her old friend. She leaned forward on her elbows, breaking Ms. Dixie's rule of etiquette. "Has it been . . . easier for you lately? I mean with Tibbie gone?"

"It's been five years, Riley."

"Wow. It doesn't seem that long ago."

"In another way it feels like a lifetime. Time is so . . . elastic. I mean, her last days seemed to pass too fast, and then the days after she was gone seemed to drag on forever."

"I'm sorry. I never knew what to do or say after she died. I wanted to come see you, talk to you, but I felt so inadequate."

"Everyone did. I did, too. I knew you cared. . . ."

"I hope so."

"You stopped by a lot, remember? You brought me all those casseroles." He laughed, looked away. "Everyone brought so much food."

"I guess I could have brought some fishing bait or a *Big Game Hunter* video. Would that have been better?"

He threw his head back and laughed. "Maybe. Maybe it would have been much better. I don't know anymore, though."

The lunch crowd had dissipated and Riley and Lodge lingered over their conversation. The waitress approached. "Anything else?"

"Yes." Lodge looked up. "One more chardonnay for the lady, please."

"No way," Riley said. "I have to go back to work."

"Yes, and one for me, too," Lodge said to the waitress, who nodded and walked off.

"Why'd you do that?"

"Because," he said, pulled her hand into his, "I want to have your full attention for at least another twenty minutes."

Something in the way he said it, in the pressure of his fingers, in the quiet of a table in the back of a restaurant resonated in Riley like an echo from another time—a time of desire. She blamed the wine. She needed to blame the wine because she didn't know what else to make of it. A response from her was needed; she knew that and yet she sat mute while Lodge Barton held her hand across the table.

He finally released her, and leaned back in his seat. She was unable for a long stretch of time to find chatty words of conversation. And this was the problem with want—with the desire for anything—it changed the way you acted. If he wanted her in the way she'd just felt, then there was a great irony in her life: all those years she'd wanted Mack and he had only desired friendship; and now here was a man who acted is if he wanted more and all she needed was a friend.

Her mind seized on a question, and she finally said, "Tell me about that case the paper is following on the mayor's wife . . . and—I don't know what the right word is. Fraternizing?"

The waitress came and placed glasses of chardonnay in front of them. Riley lifted the glass and sipped while Lodge told her the story about the wife who had been "allegedly" paying workmen at her house with "favors."

Warmth spread through Riley as she laughed along with Lodge. "You just can't make that stuff up," she said.

"Nope," he said. "Sometimes real life is better than any story."

"Yes," Riley said.

Lodge held her gaze across the table. "Funny," he said. "When I'm with you, I don't want to be anywhere else."

For a single moment Riley clearly saw that there were other possibilities in her life, a potential she hadn't noticed in her busy-ness and preoccupation. She took a moment before she said, "Thanks, Lodge. That's really . . . sweet."

He smiled, yet she felt his disappointment across the table; she couldn't and didn't return the words or sentiment. Something inside her rose and wanted to feel desire for this friend, to say the words he'd want to hear, but she couldn't find them. "Well, I guess we have to head back to our jobs. I know I have to get back to the bookstore."

"Of course you do. Big night tonight."

"Yes, big night." She smiled at Lodge, took his hand and squeezed it.

They stood and walked toward the front door, Lodge's hand on the small of her back as Riley wondered what else she hadn't noticed in her life, what else had slipped past her.

TWENTY-ONE

MAISY

*M*aisy and Adalee calculated that they had been awake for thirty hours. Their last can of Red Bull sat empty on top of a paint can. They lay down on the storage room floor, laughing so hard that Adalee began to cough. "I can't take anymore. I have to go to bed. Now."

"I'm right behind you." Maisy stood up, stretched. "But I have to see Riley's face. Don't you?"

Adalee stood up, glanced up at her watch. "She'll be here any minute. Let's get out there and then go to bed until Friday."

Maisy tucked a strand of Adalee's hair behind her ear. "That was the best night I've had since . . . Well, I'm not telling you since when."

Adalee pouted. "You still think I'm a little girl and you can't tell me stuff."

"Not true." Maisy hugged her sister. "I think you're brilliant, talented, funny and gorgeous. I just don't want you to know how terrible I really am. Why do you think I live so far away?"

"So you don't have to see us," Adalee said, turned away with a catch in her voice. "We're not stupid."

"Oh, Adalee, that is not true." Maisy turned her sister around. "That is not true at all. It has nothing to do with that. I just had to get away, and then, blink, it was twelve years later."

"Didn't seem like a blink to me. It feels like you've been gone a million years."

Maisy hugged her again. "I'm sorry. Let's get out there and admire our work, and then crash."

Adalee smiled, her face full again. "You have paint all over your cheek. It's in your hair, too."

"And you don't look a mess?" Maisy put her arm around her sister and they left the storage room, the central clearinghouse for their grand scheme.

Her eyes closed, Adalee plopped down in a plush lounge chair now draped with a pale rose trellis pattern slipcover from Beach Chic. Maisy leaned against the front counter, once Formica, now crafted from two antique doors laid flat across the surface, the cut-glass doorknobs still intact. This was her idea and it had worked brilliantly.

Her eyelids felt as though they were scratching her eyes with each blink. She yawned, checked the clock above the Kids' Corner. Three-oh-five. Riley would be here any minute.

Ethel stood in front of the store rearranging name tags for the evening. Then the door opened and Riley walked in. Sunlight followed her, and for a moment, Maisy forgot all about the total redo of the bookstore and only marveled at the redo of Riley Sheffield. Her hair fell in waves just past her shoulder, an Empire-cut sundress fell in pale blue folds and Riley's smile saturated her entire face with beauty.

This was the sister Maisy had left all those years ago. The sister with the full laugh and the face of an angel who was unaware of her beauty. Gone was the sister who pulled her hair back into a baseball cap, her eyes narrowed in concern. Maisy waved across the store.

Riley walked three steps into the store before she stopped, placed a hand over her mouth and let out a gasp. "Oh." She met Maisy's eyes, and continued toward her. With each step Riley took, her gaze wandered to another part of the store. Maisy couldn't read her reaction.

Riley reached Maisy, yet turned to the checkout counter, where the antique doors formed a new countertop. Riley ran her hand over the cut-glass doorknob, across the silken ancient wood. When she looked up at Maisy, she smiled, threw her arms around her. "What did you do? How did you get it done so fast? Where did you get the money?"

Maisy pointed to the sleeping Adalee. "It was all her idea. She has been working on it nonstop. Guess Mama should have grounded her years ago—maybe we would have known she was good at something besides partying. She made the design boards, picked all this stuff out at the Flea Market, and I ordered some slipcovers from my shop—I get a huge discount, so just consider it a gift from me."

Riley walked around the store, touching the slipcovers, the

painted cane chairs and side tables. The crystal chandelier had been cleaned and rehung over the Book Club Corner. Worn metal ceiling tiles now framed old book covers. Pictures of the Sheffield family during the childhood years had been set in peeling blue frames and set behind the checkout counter among the book club picks. The shelves holding the books had been replaced with new thick pine boards shiny with wax. Throughout the store soft cream linen hung in folds to the floor, separating spaces in the store without intruding.

"Those"—Maisy pointed to the blue frames—"are made of painted driftwood. Adalee found them in the bottom of a bin of discards."

Riley made a sweet sound in the back of her throat. "Oh, I love them. And the painted cane chairs, scattered everywhere like confetti. They're just adorable." Celtic flute music came over the sound system. "You even changed my music."

"It's a new band—the Unknown Souls. You like it?"

"I don't just like it." Riley spread her hands wide. "I love all of it. Everything. I can't believe how different and peaceful the place feels. How did you do all this in such a short time?"

"There's more to do, but not now. Let's just say I'm on my way to bed—upstairs. I won't even make it home. And you, by the way, look gorgeous."

"I know you did all that to keep me out of the store, but thank you. It was the nicest day I've had in a long time. I don't know why you did all this. . . ." Riley looked away.

Maisy hugged her sister, and then laughed out loud. "You've been drinking," she said.

Riley suppressed a smile. "If you call a glass . . . or two . . . drinking."

"Oh, I do," Maisy said, hugged her sister again, allowing this respite of anger to flow across the gap between them.

"Mom," Brayden called and both Riley and Maisy turned. He ran toward them, waving his sunburned arms and laughing. "Guess what."

"What?" Riley hugged him.

"I caught a cobia. Huge. The boat captain said it was the largest one caught all year. I have pictures." Brayden pointed at Mack and Sheppard lagging behind him.

Mack reached them first. "The store looks . . . different," he said, and smiled at Maisy.

She ran her hand through her paint-speckled hair, yet found nothing to say to the beautiful man standing before her like a fulfilled dream. Then he turned to Riley, and Maisy saw his face, his eyes light up in the way they had that summer thirteen years ago—before Maisy had made him look her way.

"Hey, Riley. Thanks for letting us take Brayden."

Riley nodded. "Thanks for taking him. Sounds like he had a good time."

Brayden interrupted. "What, are you kidding? I had the best time absolutely ever in my whole life. When I finish stupid school, I'm gonna be a deep-sea fishing captain."

Riley laughed. "You giving up on becoming a marine biologist?"

Brayden looked to each adult. "Can you be a marine biologist and quit school?"

They all shook their heads in unison. "Then, nope. I'm gonna be a boat captain." Brayden ran off toward the back of the house with a wave over his shoulder.

Mack grimaced. "Now I'll get blamed for the middle-school dropout, won't I?"

Riley laughed and even Maisy saw her beauty fill the room, lift all their spirits. Mack's smile widened, and his eyes never left Riley as she walked toward the counter, pulled out her purse. "What do I owe you for the deep-sea fishing? I know those excursions are expensive."

Maisy felt that weird, desperate need to have Mack move his eyes from Riley to her, and the words that came out were unintentional. "You don't always owe everyone something. For God's sake, Riley. Just let someone do something nice for you without making them feel guilty about it."

Riley's mouth opened, closed and then opened again. Mack filled the awkward moment with a laugh. "No need for payback. It was my treat. Really."

"Thanks," Riley said, looked down at the newly polished hardwood floors. "It means a lot to me that you took him. He would have been bored beyond tears today."

"No boy in Palmetto Beach is ever bored in summer." His gaze then turned to Maisy. "Did you do all this to the store?"

She nodded. "Me and Adalee." She pointed to her sleeping sister in the lounge chair. "And I'm off to do the exact same thing she's doing. You coming tonight?"

Mack nodded, looked across the store. "Where did Dad go?"

"He's in the biography section." Riley pointed at Sheppard sitting in a large lounge chair leafing through a book.

Mack's smile was sad, lifting only at the corners, not affecting his entire face. "That was . . . the living room. He sat there for days at a time reading. In that same spot." Then Mack laughed. "But usually he had a cold beer at his side, and sand on the bottom of his feet."

"Good days," Riley said.

Mack nodded. "Yes."

Maisy moved toward Adalee, lightly shook her. Adalee's eyes flew open; she jumped from the chair, slipped on the floor and fell on her bottom. She looked up at Riley, Maisy and Mack. "Oh, did I fall asleep?"

"A little, yes." Riley held her hand out to help Adalee off the floor.

She rubbed her eyes. "Oh, I wanted to see your face when you saw all this. Isn't it . . . amazing?"

Riley hugged Adalee, held her. "It is a miracle. I love it so much I can't find the words."

"Wow, you look great." Adalee pulled on the ends of Riley's hair. "You seriously look like . . . who's that actress whose mother is famous, too?"

"Kate Hudson," Mack said without hesitation.

Riley threw back her head and laughed. "Okay, she is about five feet tall and weighs about eighty pounds and is seriously adorable. I don't think that is who she means."

"That's exactly who I mean." Adalee looked at Maisy. "Doesn't she?"

Maisy looked at Riley and agreed, yet turned away before she answered.

A woman whom Maisy recognized approached the counter: Mrs. Winter, who always returned the hardcover books and
pretended she hadn't read them. Her posture was bent, her gaze
flickered, never resting on anything for a moment. She placed a
novel on the counter and spoke to Ethel, who was rearranging the
countertop. "I need to return this novel." She set another on the
counter. "And buy this one." She tapped the book she was returning: *The Secret Life of Bees.* "I had bought this one before I realized
I wanted to wait for the movie."

"Oh." Adalee approached the counter with a smile on her face.
"Isn't it great when they hide out in the river all night?"

Mrs. Winter's smile lifted. "Oh, yes, can you imagine a twelve-
year-old doing that?"

Adalee placed her hand on top of the novel. "Mrs. Winter, you
cannot return books that you have already read. You can donate
them to the library, or even check books out from the library, but
you can't return them here." Her sugar voice belied the words she
said.

The woman's face blanched. Her gaze, unsteady now, moved
from Maisy to Riley, to Mack and back to Adalee. "I didn't read
this one. I realized I already had it and needed to bring this copy
back. Are you accusing me of lying?"

"Oh, no," Adalee said. "I just figured you would know if you
bought a book you already owned, had read and loved as much
as this one."

"Of course," the woman said. She tucked the book under her
arm and bustled out of the store faster than she looked like she
was capable of doing.

When the front door swished shut, the five of them burst into laughter, holding on to the counter and slapping Adalee on the back. "Brilliant," Riley said. "I might get a call from her son, but hell, if she can lie to us and then lie to her son, I guess that's her problem."

Adalee smiled and placed her hands in a circle over her head. "Did I earn back my halo?"

"You never lost your halo. Now go to bed." Riley pointed to the back stairs. "Both of you."

Maisy stood still and silent, wanting to feel the joy that filled her sisters. She wanted to push past and through the loneliness that shrouded even the best moments, and at times she thought she had succeeded, but then it always returned without invitation.

She was following Adalee toward the back staircase when Anne called from behind the counter. "Maisy?"

"Hey, Anne, what's up?" Maisy rubbed her face.

"I wanted . . . well, I wanted to give you something I made for you. I know you didn't ask for one, but I saw you looking at the angel wings the other day and thought you might want one."

"Oh, I'd love one. But I'll . . . buy one."

Anne reached under the counter and held fragile white wings across to Maisy.

She took the wings, no more than eight inches across; pure white. She flipped them over to read the one word etched into the crease: PEACE. Maisy looked up at Anne. "Thank you. These are beautiful. And I'm glad you picked this one for me."

"I didn't just pick it for you. I made it for you. You seem to . . . need it."

Maisy, in her fatigue, fought the tears this truth brought. "Thank you." She turned away from Anne and went up the back stairs to Riley's apartment. She cupped the wings in her hand and felt sadness wash over her. It had been a long, long time since she'd felt peace. Yet she was always looking for it in someone, in something or somewhere.

Peace, she thought. *Yes, that would be nice.* She ran her pinky finger over the delicate word.

TWENTY-TWO

The next three days passed in the haze of busy-ness where Riley felt most comfortable when she wanted to avoid introspection. She kept her focus on the store, on getting through the week.

The Tuesday Poetry Night and the Wednesday Kids' Corner Night went as smoothly as she could have hoped. Lodge covered every party, showed up with his camera and placed a prominent article in the living section each day. Riley suspected that Mack and Maisy had restarted their romance, but she ignored this suspicion with grim determination: she would not stop them again. Adalee bounced and chattered through the events, and then ran off to find Chad. Mama became increasingly exhausted, even canceling a few meetings with her daughters, stating she understood everything was going well.

On Thursday evening a wild sunset filled the sky as Riley stood on the beach near the cottage, her back to the sea. The day after tomorrow was the big party and she went through a mental checklist in her mind, then paused to stare at the sky before she turned to look at the moon, its light stretching like a beacon across the waves, pointing to Driftwood Cottage.

Riley moved her hand up to curl the ends of her hair around her fingertips. She was still getting used to shorter hair and often her hand fell through the air as she reached for strands that were no longer there, like reaching for a memory and finding it gone, but knowing she was better off without it.

A stooped figure moved from the water's edge toward the cottage. Adalee came closer, sobbing. Riley ran to her. "Adalee, what's wrong?"

She looked up, gulped in air. "I just left the Beach Club. The damn Beach Club where I got Chad a job. The damn Beach Club where I found him making out with Kenzie Marshall with the awful boob job."

"If he's cheating on you, then he's not worth this angst."

Adalee glared at her. "That's always what people say when they catch boyfriends cheating. Always. *I've* said it to my friends."

"Sounds clichéd, huh? I'm so sorry. It hurts either way."

They reached the back steps and sat down together. Adalee rested her head on Riley's shoulder. "How come I always pick the biggest loser known to man?"

"If we could only make them love us as much as we love them," Riley said.

Adalee looked up at her. "Exactly."

Riley shrugged. "Not always possible."

Adalee leaned into her again. She sniffled, rubbed her nose with the back of her hand. "We—I mean me, you and Maisy—don't have very good luck with men, do we?"

"What do you mean?"

"I mean you—well, you won't even tell us who Brayden's dad is, so I don't really know about him. Maisy, well, she just picks guys who won't stay. And me, I always end up with the life of the party. Unfortunately he's always everyone's life of the party, if you know what I mean." Adalee sat up now, smoothed her face with both hands. "I will not cry over this. I will not."

Riley looked up at the sky. "I'm not sure if we have bad luck. That might be a stretch. Maybe we just make bad . . . choices."

"Don't get all lecturey on me."

"There is no such word as lecturey. But don't worry. I'm not up for a lecture. Too tired. I'm sorry about Chad. But I did see that cute artist making eyes at you at the party Tuesday night."

"Really?" Adalee's face brightened, then fell again. "Oh, never mind. Only three more nights of this and then we're free for the rest of the summer, right? Because I swear Chad cheated on me because I've been locked up like a prisoner. . . . This is all Mama's fault."

"Chad being a cheating scumbag is Mama's fault?" Riley stood up as her sister did, and laughed. "I can think of some things to blame Mama for, but not Chad's tendency to find the biggest boobs in the room."

They both turned when Maisy opened the back door, slammed the screen and held her hands out wide. "Am I missing out on something?"

"Loser Chad made out with Kenzie Marshall and I caught them," Adalee said.

"Oh." Maisy shook her head. "What is wrong with him?"

Together the three sisters shook their heads. "Men!"

They broke into laughter, and Riley felt it—the sweetness of sisters together, laughing and speaking in unison, in accord. Maisy glanced at Riley and she smiled. When Maisy smiled back, a small spot of past hurt was healed.

They walked into the bookstore to begin another night of festivities. Riley stopped short when she saw a new lounge chair set up in the Book Club Corner. "Oh, where did that come from?"

Maisy shrugged. "I have no idea. I thought you added it."

"No, you?" She turned to Adalee.

"No, Edith told me that a delivery truck dropped it off without any explanation."

"Oh, if I get a bill for this, Mama will kill me," Riley said.

"This is your store. Why do you get so worked up about what she thinks about every little thing?"

"Because the cottage is . . . well, hers."

"Either she gave it to you to run, or she didn't."

"It's not that simple, Maisy." Riley walked toward the front desk, smoothing her hand in automatic motions over the bookshelves, eyeing the counter for bookmarks and flyers. "Nothing is ever that simple. I don't want to upset her."

Maisy went over and put her hand on Riley's arm to stop her. "Why isn't it that simple? Because you made one mistake, you are indebted to Mama forever?"

"What mistake would that be?" Riley felt her hurt, just soothed, return as raw-nerved energy.

Maisy held up her hand. "Forget it." She walked away, then turned sharply on her heels and motioned to Riley's office. Riley hesitated, then followed her in, and Maisy shut the door. "What the hell is going on here? Why are you so desperate to protect Mama? Do you need her money? Do you want to be free of her, yet you want her store? So you appease her . . . say what she wants when she wants. You can't have it both ways, Riley. This store is killing Mama. I see it every day."

"It is not the financial worries that are killing her. The store saves her." Riley's voice was a mere whisper.

"Then what is it that drains her like this? The years of martinis? Missing Daddy? The boredom?"

"How would you know? You haven't been here."

"You probably don't need to remind me of that again. I think all of you have made the point just fine. Why don't you just sell the damn store? Then I could go back to my life."

"The store is all we have—me, Mama and Brayden."

"That is pitiful."

Riley's words turned cold. "Haven't you ever once thought about the bigger picture? About something other than you and the next guy you want? If we're forced to close the store, Edith and Anne will be out of jobs, and our town will lose far more than just a store."

"Our town?"

"Yes, our town. Do you know how many people come together here? How many events are held? How many hearts are healed? How much good is done?" Riley shook her head. "Sometimes I feel I just don't know you at all. When did you become so self-centered?"

"If I'm self-centered, maybe it's because I don't want to become you—sacrificing your life to keep Mama happy. You slave away at the store, so ready to fulfill every one of Mama's endless demands."

Riley's anger rose with a fury she hadn't felt in years. "You have absolutely no idea what the hell you're talking about. You're so blind, you can't even see all the good that Mama has done this town and me. You complain about having to give up a few days of your time, and you have no idea what sacrifice she's making. Wake up, Maisy. The world does not revolve around you. You are so angry that you can't even see that Mama might be dying, that for once, this is *not* about you."

Riley slammed the office door on her way out. She couldn't bear to see Maisy's reaction to her harsh words, couldn't believe she'd broken her promise to Mama.

From far away, someone called her name and Riley brought her attention back to the store, to Mrs. Harper, waving a large book in her hand. "Ooooh, Riley?"

She placed a weary smile on her face, whispered to Edith to please have Anne bring over a latte and then went to Mrs. Harper. "Hi, ma'am. How are you?" Her body shook inside with the remnants of her unaccustomed fury, and she held her hands behind her back to still them.

"I am thinking of going to Italy this summer. Would you say this is the best book to get?"

Riley glanced down at the book. Mrs. Harper would never leave the confines of Palmetto Beach, much less travel to Italy. She'd bought more than fifteen travel guides in the past five years, and had yet to leave the town limits to drive to her granddaughter's house an hour away. Sympathy for this woman billowed inside Riley.

"Mrs. Harper," she said over the lump in her throat, "you've made an excellent choice. Why don't you have a seat here in this new chair and take some time to scan the pages? If the book still interests you, I'll ring it up for you. Take your time."

"Really?" Her penciled-in eyebrows rose above her eyeglasses.

"Sure." Riley patted the cushion. "You might even be the first person to sit here."

Mrs. Harper sat, and when she looked up with a smile, Riley had to turn away for fear the old woman would see the tears in her eyes. When she reached the edge of the front counter, Adalee squinted at her. "You okay?"

Riley nodded. "I must be exhausted. Sweet old lady Harper makes me want to cry."

"Why?" Adalee looked over Riley's shoulder while she fingered the name tags for the night.

"She has been buying travel guides for five years, yet she hasn't left the town limits since her husband passed away. I don't know why, but it just hurts my heart today."

"Because," Adalee said, and bent closer, "maybe she reminds you of a woman who reads books about other women's lives, but barely lives her own."

Riley pulled away, startled, then hurt. "You've always done that, Adalee. Always."

"Done what?" Adalee spread her arms, opened her red-rimmed eyes wide.

"Tried to shove your hurt off on other people. I'm sorry you're having trouble with your boyfriend, but don't let it out on me."

"I just meant . . . just meant that you read all these books. I've never seen anyone read so many books. But you never do anything except work and take care of Brayden. I mean, surely you must want to go out and have a date, or travel, or—"

"Just because you don't like the way I live my life doesn't mean *I* don't like it."

"What? You adore jumping to Mama's every call?"

Adalee's words, coming on the heels of Maisy's accusation, made Riley's stomach rise. "This doesn't sound like you, Adalee. You're quoting Maisy. I can hear her words coming out of your mouth. And if you two want to psychoanalyze me, do it on your own time." Riley turned on her heels, and walked toward the front of the store to greet incoming guests for the evening. When she dared to glance at the entranced face of Mrs. Harper in the lounge chair, her heart hurt where Adalee had probed into her worst fears. Maisy had still not come out of the office, and with each breath she took, Riley regretted more and more the news she'd dropped on her sister.

Mack and Sheppard entered through the front door; Riley leaned against a pillar and watched them. If she just stood still and breathed, took in the details of her store, of her life, she would be fine in a moment. Then Mack's eyes caught hers and Riley felt her insides vibrate like a tuning fork. She turned away; she must have been exhausted for her sister's words to be affecting her so strongly. Or maybe she was getting sick. She needed to get through the next couple of days and then move on with her life.

Then Mack was at her side. She held her hands behind her back to stop herself from running her fingers through his hair, throwing her arms around him. Sheppard wandered off to a lounge chair, sat and leaned his head back with his eyes closed.

"When I see him like that," Mack said, nodding toward his dad, "I can pretend that we're back here when the cottage was ours, when the world was right and Dad was healthy. . . ."

"I know," Riley said, a note of understanding echoing between them.

"I can see the Scrabble game on the coffee table, the thousand-piece puzzle set up all summer. Mom would be humming along to the local radio station. Joe would be on the back porch rinsing the salt water off the fishing poles. . . ."

As Mack spoke to her, Riley felt as if the room had faded and the books disappeared.

He laughed, a low, soft sound. "I remember one day—me and you. We must have been nine or ten years old. You came running in the back door straight from church, hollering all about how there was only an hour left of the tide, and if we wanted to take the Sailfish out, we better do it right then.

"I looked at you in your Sunday dress, your hair pulled back with a white satin ribbon and said, 'You look like a girl.' You stared at me like I was the biggest moron in the world and said, 'That's because I am one, you idiot.' Mama proceeded to tell me I was a brilliant ladies' man."

Riley had no such memory. "Then what?"

He shrugged. "We went out on the Sailfish, I assume."

Riley pressed her hand into the pillar to bring herself back into this world, to this present moment. That was the thing about memory—each person carried their own scraps of the past. Mack remembered events that she didn't, or had his own version of events that they shared. He had some memories, and his father had others, her mother still others. If they combined all the remembrances together, could they form an entire summer from them?

Mack spoke into her silence. "Let's let Dad sleep for a minute or so. Want a cup of coffee?" He pointed toward the café.

Riley looked toward the front desk. "The party starts in an hour. . . ."

He wound his arm through hers. "That sounds like an excuse to me. Come on. One cup of coffee."

"Sure," she said, squeezed his arm. She followed him into the cafe, motioning to Anne behind the counter. A minute later, Anne plunked two scones and two cups of coffee on the table.

Mack took a bite of the pastry and a long sip of coffee before he leaned back in his chair. "Okay, old friend. Tell me how your mama is doing."

"She's healing. And cranky. It makes her crazy to be laid up in bed, missing all the events she planned. She pretends this store is her hobby, but it's more like an obsession. That's why my sisters are here. . . . Otherwise Mama would be doing all the work. It takes two of them to do what she would do." Riley settled back in her chair. "But I gotta tell you, I can't believe how they've re-decorated. I've dreamed of making over the bookstore like this . . .

but, well, I didn't have the money, and decorating is not exactly my gift. Mama is gonna love it."

"More important—tell me about Brayden. Can you tell me about his dad?"

Riley turned away from him, her gaze flitting about the store.

"I'm sorry. . . . That was none of my business. I shouldn't have asked."

"It's okay. It's just that I've never told anyone who his dad is. Anyway . . ." She took a deep breath, exhaled her question. "So how is your sweet mom?"

"She's worried about Dad, but she encouraged this trip. And it's been great. Coming here and remembering those quieter, timeless days. I've been to the Murphy brothers' oyster roast—they're still crazy—played poker with Dad's old buddies. I've run the length of the town and watched the sunrise off the jetty. All the good stuff."

Mack squinted at her through the late-afternoon sunlight falling through the old windows. Her heart filled with another memory—full and complete. He was walking her to the movie on the lawn when Maisy ran up behind them, begged to come with them. Had he wanted her, Riley, then, even for a moment?

Mack reached across the table, took her hand. For a while he seemed to struggle to find the right words and then settled for, "It is really great to see you."

"You, too," she said, squeezing his fingers, wondering what he'd really meant to say.

Sheppard appeared beside them. "You two gonna let an old man sleep in the middle of the biography section, snoring like a fool?"

"Just thought we wore you out today, Dad." Mack stood. "Let's go get something to eat and then come back for the party tonight. You up for it?"

"I am," Sheppard said. "I guarantee we're smelling up this pretty shop with our fishy selves. Let's go."

Mack hugged Riley goodbye and walked out of Driftwood Cottage. "We'll be back for the party in an hour or so," Mack promised.

"Great." Riley held the door open and watched them walk down the cobbled pathway.

Lodge came to her side. "Hey."

Riley startled. "Hey, when did you get here?"

"A few minutes ago." He nodded toward Mack and Sheppard. "Time may have passed, but some things don't change, do they? You've always . . . had a thing for him."

Riley shook her head. "Why would you say that?"

He shrugged, motioned to Mack and Sheppard.

"Lodge, everything has changed," Riley said. "And is still changing."

"Maybe you're right," Lodge said, and together they watched Mack and Sheppard walk down the cobbled pathway, memories of summer following them.

Twenty-three

When the readings were finished, and the last goodbye had been offered, Maisy stacked folding chairs against the wall. Riley had gone upstairs for the night, and now Maisy glanced around the cottage for Mack—she'd asked him to come back and see her when the party was over. The past two days he'd disappeared to catch up with old friends, go fishing and hang out with his dad. The same desperate need for him that had consumed her on the night of the bonfire had returned now and Maisy's stomach danced with nervousness.

Adalee slammed a chair shut. "Who are you looking for?"

"What do you mean?" Maisy stopped, squinted at Adalee.

"You've only looked back at the café, like, two hundred times. And you're totally preoccupied."

Adalee and Maisy both turned to the slam of a screen door, then saw Mack enter through the back door.

"Over here," Maisy said.

"Oh! I get it now," Adalee said. "You go on. I'll finish here tonight. I owe you one."

"Thanks, sis." Maisy walked toward Mack, folding a table-cloth into a neat square just like Mama had taught her.

The music still played: Alison Krauss singing "Stay." "I love this song," she said.

"Yeah, Alison can break your heart, can't she?"

Maisy nodded.

Mack smiled at her. "You done with your work for the night?"

She nodded yes. This was it, she thought. This was when the past ran so fast, it caught up with the present.

For Maisy, the walk from the cottage to the beach seemed to erase the time that had passed between now and the summer of his leaving; the bonfire might still be burning and she might still be standing underneath the lifeguard station with every nerve on fire.

They stood in silence at the edge of the sea, shoes in their hands, the full moon lighting a path on the water. Maisy sought perfect words to say in this moment full of possibility.

Mack stopped, stared out over the waves. "Being here makes time almost stand still."

Unable to speak, Maisy merely nodded.

Mack looked back over the water. "Like we're all in our teens and life has every chance of becoming perfect."

"Yes," Maisy whispered, shifted her weight in the sand so her upper arm rubbed against his.

He moved his arm away, and for a brief moment, she felt the sting of his rejection. Then his arm dropped over her shoulder, pulled her closer to his side. Far off a foghorn called; laughter from a party rang across the beach. Maisy leaned into him.

"I've imagined this a million times," she said.

"Imagined me?"

"You . . . with me. Here."

He turned to her, placed his hands on her shoulders and stared at her for so long she thought he might be waiting for her to say something, do something. But she waited . . . waited for his kiss. Instead he stepped away, grimaced. "Sorry, my cell phone." He grabbed it from his back pocket.

Confusion overcame her. "Mack?"

He glanced at the screen, then at her. "It's Dad."

"Huh?"

"A text from the hospital. Something's happened. I've got to go. . . ."

"I'll come with you," she said, tried to clasp his hand but he slipped it free.

He shook his head. "No, you don't need to do that. I'll call the bookstore . . . let y'all know what's going on. . . ." He hurried off without another word.

Understanding flooded Maisy's heart—he didn't want her with him. He'd torn his hand from hers as though she'd held on for too long.

Maybe she *had* held on to him and his memory for too long.

She stared at her empty hand, pale in the moonlight. An off-shore breeze lifted her hair, isolation and loneliness her companions once more. She'd been the fool again—holding on too hard, showing her heart too soon, needing too much.

She sat down in the wet sand, felt the dampness seep through her thin skirt, her sadness swelling—for Sheppard, who might be seriously ill; for Mack, who was losing his father; for herself for clinging to men who didn't want her.

Maisy curled over her legs, stared out at the dark waters. The beach grew silent as the last stragglers went home. Porch lights turned off. The moon moved across the sky and she understood: Mack did not and would not fill the place of emptiness inside her; his touch was not what she really wanted. This was not a fairy tale and he was not here to save her. The one person she had thought would finally mend the frazzled edges of her broken heart had left her feeling more alone.

Twenty-four

Friday morning, Riley woke to find Maisy seated at her kitchen table, a mug of coffee cradled in her palms.

"I have to tell you something," Maisy said. "Sheppard Logan was admitted to General last night. I don't know what happened, just that he texted the news to Mack, who took off." Maisy's shoulders slumped forward, her gaze on the table.

Riley didn't hesitate. "Will you keep an eye on Brayden?"

Maisy nodded, and Riley was at Sheppard's bedside before she gave any thought of calling first. She stared down at father and son: Mack asleep on a chair; Sheppard hooked to an oxygen tube, an IV in his hand.

Mack startled as though Riley had made a noise. His smile was tired and closed-lipped. "Hey," he whispered.

"Hey, you." Riley walked to the foot of the bed.

Mack stood and they hugged, held each other for a moment. "How is he?" she asked.

Sheppard made a sound vaguely like a cough. Mack was at his bedside in a half breath.

"Dad?"

Sheppard opened one eye. "Hey, son." He took a ragged breath. "I'm sorry I messed up your night. One minute I'm playing poker with some old buddies. The next I'm in the ER."

The door opened and a tall man in a lab coat came to stand next to Mack. His face hung in weary folds, and behind glasses his eyes were faded with fatigue. The doctor held out his hand. "Hello, I'm Dr. Steinman. Are you Mr. Logan's son?"

Mack shook his hand. "Yes, I'm Mack Logan. What's going on? I talked to the doctor last night, but I haven't heard anything since then."

Riley's small steps took her, inch by inch, to the back wall, where she tried to be inconspicuous, wanting to give them privacy.

"Well, from the brief history we've gathered from your dad and his doctor in Boston, and the lab tests we just got back—he has neutropenia."

"What's that?"

"His white blood cell count has dropped." The doctor walked over, lifted Sheppard's right hand. "He received a cut a few days ago, and it's become infected; he has a fever of one hundred and three and the infection is spreading up his arm. He fainted, as I assume you heard. His doctor in Boston did not approve his travel here. In his condition, considering the advanced stage of his cancer—he should be resting at home, and he most certainly should not have let this wound go untreated."

Mack turned to his dad. "You didn't tell me you got cut. And did you know you weren't supposed to travel?"

Sheppard turned away. "I felt great . . . and sometimes the doctor's advice and my needs don't match."

Dr. Steinman sat down on a metal stool. "We'll need to keep him for at least twenty-four hours to allow the IV antibiotic to bring down the infection. Then we'll work with his doctor in Boston and arrange to transfer him back to his home hospital."

"You should have told me you were cut," Mack said.

"I felt fine. I didn't even notice the cut was infected." Sheppard turned away, his eyes moist as he spoke with a slight quaver in his voice. "These have been the best days in years and I almost forgot . . . almost forgot."

"I know, Dad. Me, too." Mack patted his father's back.

Riley slipped out of the room. In the hall, she exhaled the breath she'd been holding. Then Mack's hand was cupping her elbow. "Riley."

She looked up at him. "I should leave you two alone. . . . I just thought you might . . . I have no idea what I thought."

"That I might want my best friend from Palmetto Beach to be here?"

"That was a long time ago." She looked at the shut door to Sheppard's room. "Go take care of your dad."

Mack placed his hands on either side of her face, and kissed her forehead. "Thanks, Minnow. I'll catch up with you later."

*   *   *

When Riley returned to Mama's house, she was summoned straight to the drawing room, where Mama rose proudly in front of her new walker. Riley laughed out loud. "Mama, you're walking. You look great!"

"I look like hell, but give me two hours with my hairdresser, and an hour with the manicurist, an hour with the makeup artist, and I'll be ready to go." With that, she collapsed back onto her bed. "I'll have to stay in my wheelchair for most of the party tomorrow night, but I insist on standing for the announcements and speeches."

Riley helped her mama situate herself under her favorite linen sheet. "Whether you're sitting or standing, it'll just be great to have you there."

"Let's go over the list once more, okay?" She scooted up against the headboard, and then yanked a folder off the cluttered bedside table.

Riley was convinced that if she went over the arrangements one more time, her head would spin. *Patience, Riley, patience.* "Okay, Mama. Once more."

They reviewed the schedule in minute detail until they reached the raffle announcements. Mama pointed to the list of prizes. "Where did all this stuff come from? I never solicited a weekend trip to Charleston or a free makeover. . . ."

"Adalee got all that donated. She went from store to store in town. People have been buying tickets for ten dollars apiece. The store will make money from it."

"Are you sure we're not paying for it?"

"I'm very sure." Riley patted the sheet smooth around her

mother's legs. "Trust me. I know how to run the store. It has been an incredible week. Everything is right on track. Adalee and Maisy have worked so hard. Ethel and Anne must be angels. We just can't see their wings."

"I'm quite sure some details have fallen through the cracks. I'm just going to have to learn to let go of things I can't control. Not everything can get done without me." Mama fluttered her eyes as if a gnat had stuck to her eyelashes.

Defensiveness rose up like a wave inside Riley. "Mama, nothing fell through the cracks. I promise."

Mama leaned forward. "What about the singer for later in the night? I never called one."

"Maisy hired the daughter of one of the Cookbook Club's members. Country music, I think."

Kitsy groaned. "Oh, please don't tell me she hired some twangy redneck girl to sing bad karaoke."

"Let's hope not. . . ." Riley stood. "Listen, I know Harriet will get you to the store on time, but call me if you need something."

"I won't need anything."

Riley stood, and then hesitated. "Mama, did you know that Sheldon Rutledge was killed in Iraq?"

"Yes, I'd heard about that at the garden club a few weeks ago."

"Why didn't you tell me?"

"Guess I forgot."

"He was a good friend, Mama. I wish I'd known before. . . ."

"Sorry, dear. Sometimes an old woman forgets things."

"You don't forget anything." Riley leaned over to kiss her mother on the forehead. "I'll see you later."

"Darling," Mama called out as Riley walked out of the room. Riley looked over her shoulder. "Yes?"

"I like your haircut."

"I had it cut days ago."

"I know. I just kept forgetting to say something."

Riley nodded and closed the door to the drawing room. The weight of responsibility pushed down on her shoulders, making them ache along with the pounding in her head. After tomorrow night it would all be over.

Riley drove back to the cottage, and entered with a breeze that sent sand across the hardwood floors.

Ethel waved a white-gloved hand from the front counter. Maisy stood on a ladder in the Book Club Corner, stringing white lights through the rafters. Riley called out to her, "What are you doing?"

"Lights—you always have to have glittering lights when you give a party."

Riley stood under the ladder, looked up at her beautiful sister. "Where's Adalee?"

Maisy pointed to the storage room. "Locked in there."

"What's she doing?"

Maisy shrugged. "She just yells at me to go away."

Riley rubbed her temples, fought the urge to ask about Maisy's night with Mack. "It's time to finish setting up. I'll need her history boards—so let me grab the key from Ethel. I'm so glad we don't have an event tonight. I still don't know how we're gonna be ready by tomorrow."

"We'll be fine, Riley."

Riley was halfway across the room when she felt Maisy's stare. She turned. "What?" She held her hands up in question.

Maisy averted her gaze. "Nothing."

Riley asked Ethel for the key to the storage room, and Anne for a large mug of coffee.

The key to the old library turned in the lock but the door remained bolted from the inside. "Adalee," Riley called through the crack.

The bolt slid open and Adalee stood before Riley. Her hair was pulled into a loose ponytail, and dark circles ringed her eyes.

"You okay?" Riley asked, maneuvering around Adalee to enter the room.

"Yes. I know I don't look like it, but I'm really great."

Riley squinted at her sister, but didn't have time to probe into the issue of Chad. "Are the history boards done?"

"Yep, and I even have two surprise ones. So, you can't see them yet."

Riley put an arm around her sister. "I'm sorry I hollered. I'm . . . exhausted."

"I know," Adalee said. "But it's almost over."

Riley nodded. "Almost over." She left the storage room; the mug of coffee Anne handed her was exactly what she needed. She leaned against the pine wall, cradling her mug.

Maisy walked toward her, whispered, "Tell me what you meant about Mama last night. And tell me now. Please." Maisy's pupils were shadowed with a fear Riley hadn't seen since childhood.

"Let's go outside. Okay?" Riley set her mug on the café counter before walking out the back door.

Together they stood on the back porch, silent until Maisy said, "Please tell me Mama isn't really dying."

"I was angry. I shouldn't have said that."

"Answer the question. What did you mean?"

"I don't know everything yet." Riley explained what she'd learned from Mama and Doc Foster about the cancer, ending with, "I promised not to tell anyone, and I'm really sorry I broke that promise."

"You mean . . . Mama has cancer of some terrible sort and you haven't said a word about it? What the hell is going on? Have you researched this?"

"A little, yes. Mama and Doc promise to tell us all their plans when the party is over. Mama begged me to not talk about it, to allow her this celebration with her daughters. . . ."

"Dear God, Riley. This explains so much. . . ." Tears broke free from Maisy's wide eyes. "Damn." She swiped at them as if she were angry that they'd betrayed her emotions.

"Please, I am begging you: don't say a word. Just act like . . . you don't know."

"How?"

She shrugged. "Like you have been . . ."

"But I would have been . . . different if I'd known." She turned away from Riley. "Isn't that terrible? Absolutely horrid. I would have acted differently if I'd known. What kind of a daughter am I?" She dropped into a rocking chair and bent over.

Riley placed her hand on the top of Maisy's copper-colored head, on top of the hair she'd been so envious of at six years old that she'd used a red Magic Marker to try to draw highlights in her own hair.

"Please, please, go inside, Riley." Maisy pushed her hand off her head.

Riley backed away from Maisy, who wouldn't accept her comfort, and entered the cottage, which offered her the only consolation she knew.

TWENTY-FIVE

MAISY

*S*aturday morning Maisy stood in front of the full-length mirror and stared at herself, a woman in a girl's bedroom. After Riley had told her about Mama's illness yesterday, she'd run from the cottage and even from Palmetto Beach, driving Mama's pickup truck down the coastal roads that wound through the Lowcountry. On a dirt road in nowhere south Georgia, she'd parked the truck and wept for her vanished dreams of Mack, for her betrayal with Tucker, for her lost years with her sisters, for her idiocy with Peter, for the fear of losing Mama. Especially for Mama, whom she'd never imagined as sick, or worse, gone. When darkness was complete, she drove home and crawled into bed, empty of feeling, hollowed of emotion.

She awoke once in the night and reached for the fantasy of Mack, her consolation, only to sense the void where the dream had vanished. Sleep came dreamless and deep until her cell phone rang and she jumped. Lucy Morgan's voice sounded soft and sleep-filled. "Hey, Maisy . . ."

"What's up, Lucy. You okay?"

"Yeah . . . I was just hoping you might have some free time to see me today before the party. I figure you'll be leaving first thing the day after."

"Well, not first thing."

"Can I see you before you go?"

"I'd love that," she said, and meant it. A smile came to her face before she realized. "Coffee is what I need right now. A lot of coffee."

"You want to head this way toward Bartow?"

"Why not?" Maisy stood and walked toward the closet. "I'll get out of here before Mama wakes. It's the best plan."

Lucy laughed and Maisy hung up, pulled on a pair of frayed jeans and a Rolling Stones T-shirt she found in the bottom drawer of her childhood dresser.

The drive to Bartow proved to Maisy that life had changed here in small-town Georgia. Resort-style homes had spread into the surrounding towns like kudzu overtaking the landscape. With each passing block the beach "cottages" grew until mansions crowded the beach and corner lots. Bartow, on the other hand, hadn't changed much. The sign made of worn wood, the letter "a" faded from the town's name, suggested that encroaching development had so far bypassed this town.

The ancient coffee shop was situated on a corner. Lucy waited for Maisy on an iron bench. A Braves baseball cap covered her brown curls and large sunglasses hid the top half of her face. Maisy parked the pickup truck and joined her.

"Oh, Maisy." Lucy hugged her friend. "When are you going back?"

She shrugged, placed a hand over her eyes to shield her face from the sun. "I've got to call . . ." she said, then stumbled over her words when she noticed the snail track of tearstains on Lucy's face. "Is something wrong? Are you okay?"

"Tucker didn't come home last night."

Maisy felt it again—the guilt and panic that she had carried inside for thirteen years now rising with gale force. "Oh, God. I'm sorry . . ." Maisy said, meaning more than Lucy could understand.

"It's not your fault. . . . I shouldn't have said anything. I'm sure he just drank too much during his weekly boys' night out and fell asleep at Bobby's house. That's what happened last time." She gave a shaky smile.

"This has happened before?" Maisy asked before she could stop herself from probing. The sobbing woman of the Blonde Book Club was as clear to her as if she stood there at that very moment.

Lucy nodded, wiped at her face as if to erase all evidence of heartbreak.

"Let's take a walk," Maisy said, her heart somewhere near her throat, the morning sun bearing down on her.

Lucy stood, lifted her sunglasses to look at her. "I thought you needed coffee in a big way."

"I need to talk more," Maisy said. "If we're going to dig up the good parts of our past, I have to unearth the bad parts, too. Come on." She moved down the sidewalk, pretending to notice each boutique and store on the main street.

Finally Lucy put her hand on Maisy's arm. "What is it?"

"I need to tell you something. It's terrible and horrible, and this will probably be the last time you ever talk to me. But I have to tell you, not only because I love you and always have, but because Tucker is still . . ."

"Still what?"

"Cheating on you."

Lucy pulled her hand from Maisy's arm as if burned. "No. He might drink too much, and be too controlling and a jerk sometimes . . . but not that. I know he wouldn't do that."

"I ran off to California and missed your wedding because I'd slept with Tucker. I didn't love him, Lucy. It wasn't . . . that, which might make it worse. I wanted to get back at Mack for never calling, for never coming back. I was . . . drunk. We walked past Mack's old house and went inside . . . and it just happened. God, I am so sorry. I used him to fill that empty place inside me that I never could fill. I never, ever wanted you to know, but I think he is still . . . cheating."

Lucy bent over, put her hands on her knees to steady herself. "No . . ."

"I will never be able to make up for this. I thought I could leave behind that dreadful part of me, that terrible part that uses men to make myself feel better. But I took it with me and didn't even know it. I know you can't forgive me, but I need you to know anyway. He doesn't deserve you. You are the most amazing, smart, talented woman. He is . . . sleeping with a woman in a book club at Driftwood Cottage." Maisy made no attempt to cover her tears this time.

Lucy looked up now, and although Maisy couldn't see her eyes through the shaded glasses, she felt the hate coming from them like heat: hate she deserved. "How the hell could you know something like that? You're trying to make him into something evil when it is you who is the cheating . . ."

"Say it."

"No."

"Yes," Maisy whispered. "I am. But there is a woman in the Blonde Book Club. Her name is Kelly-Anne. I don't know her last name. She is having an affair with a married man who promised to leave his wife, but never has. She had her brother take all the tires off the car belonging to her lover's wife."

Lucy faced Maisy. "I hate you. All these years I missed you so badly, I thought I would be sick. I thought I did something wrong to end our friendship, when it was you. It was always you who ended everything. I hate you."

"I know. I deserve it." Maisy reached out to touch Lucy's arm.

Lucy shoved at Maisy's hand. "Get away from me. Go back to California. I will never again waste another minute missing you or your friendship."

"I am so, so sorry."

"Leave," Lucy whispered.

"Please let me . . . help you or do something."

"You've done enough," Lucy said, and turned so fast she lost her balance, tripped over a root coming through the cracked side-walk and then ran toward the corner, to disappear behind the coffee shop to the parking lot.

Maisy leaned against a light post and understood that this truth was more important than what she had thought was the comfort of hidden deceit. No more illusions. The fantasy of Mack Logan, of the perfect life was gone. It was time for reality. Time for honesty.

Driftwood Cottage was lit from within, activity evident in every window. Candles flickered in lanterns hung from wrought-iron poles leading up the walkway. A white tent had been erected to one side—donated by the local party-rental facility—where extra food and a bar had been set up to relieve the congestion inside. Two young girls from the local high school stood at the door, handing out pamphlets and greeting early arrivals. Maisy parked around back, entered through the rear door and immediately went into action.

Guests were scattered around the store, leafing through books and lounging in the newly slipcovered chairs while the caterers placed appetizers on burlap-covered tables. Maisy checked the sound system and front check-in table while Ethel and Anne scurried around not quite knowing what to do.

The rear staircase door opened and Maisy turned to see Riley and Brayden hurry through the café into the bookstore. Maisy's hand paused in midair with a name tag dangling from her fingers—Riley's hair fell in soft waves over her bare shoulders and a sundress, cornflower blue with an Empire waist, hugged her body. A long, multilayered beaded necklace hung from her neck.

Maisy stared at Riley as she walked through the store: there she was; there was her sister. The one who'd been hiding behind books and a son. The one who'd been her best friend and always won the race across the beach and pool. The one who'd listened to her cry in the middle of the night, who'd held her when the nightmares came and Mama was too deeply asleep to wake.

Riley caught Maisy's eye and smiled. The thing between them—the anger or jealousy or whatever she wanted to label it—no longer seemed to matter. Her anger was not directed at this sister, who had made a life for herself above a bookstore, but at herself. The thought brought nausea and grief. Maisy had hated herself for the things she'd done and somehow she'd allowed herself to believe she hated Riley.

Riley hadn't slept with Tucker on a hardwood floor in a vacant house. Riley hadn't stolen Mack from her. Riley hadn't run away from the family and hidden from her own sin. Maisy dropped into a chair.

A hand came to rest on her shoulder and Maisy gazed up into Mack's face, lined with fatigue. For the first time, he looked older to her than the college boy she'd loved all these years. Or maybe she was finally seeing him as he really was, and not as she'd imagined him. Maisy stood. She hugged him. "How's your dad?"

"Not good, Maisy. Not good. His blood counts are bad. . . . It's complicated. But they'll fly him home in the morning. He has to stabilize first." Mack dropped into the chair next to hers. She sat too and faced him as he continued. "I'm sorry I left so abruptly last night."

"It's okay," she said, placed her hand on his knee. "It really is. I understand."

"I need to say something. . . ."

She nodded.

"I shouldn't have . . ." He took her hand, wound his fingers through hers. "Being here made me lose track of real life."

She squeezed his hand. "I know. . . . This place does that." She attempted to inject a levity in her voice that she couldn't find in her heart; her smile felt as false as it probably looked to him.

"I'm not sure what happened, but I shouldn't have brought you into my confusion."

"You can bring me into your confusion anytime," she said, felt the lump in the back of her throat melt.

"Oh, adorable Maisy," he said.

"Mack, go take care of your dad."

"I forgot to tell you," he said, pointed to the new chair across the room. "Mother sent that as a gift. When I told her about what y'all had done here, what the place had become, she wanted to be part of it."

"Sometimes," Maisy said, "life comes together in the most beautiful ways."

Mack placed his hand on her cheek. "Yes, it does."

"Maisy?" Riley called from across the room.

"Over here," she said.

Mack stood with her. "I can't stay long. I just wanted to . . ."

His words halted when Riley came to their side. And it happened again—his eyes, his smile, his attention became riveted on her.

This time, Maisy didn't feel the rise of bitterness. This time, she saw the truth: Mack wanted Riley Sheffield. Perhaps he always had. To Mack she, Maisy, was just what she'd been for Tucker and for Peter: a substitute, a stand-in. When he'd said he loved her under that lifeguard stand, it had been an adolescent desire for a connection that had probably dissipated in the heat of the morning sun.

Riley looked at him. "Mack, what's wrong?"

Maisy took two steps back as Mack spoke to Riley about the doctor's news and their next steps. The cottage began to fill with partygoers, the sound level rising. Maisy went to the café and turned up the music, made sure the bartender and caterer were ready in the tent. She sought out Adalee, and found her dragging the history boards from the storage room. "Let me help you," Maisy said, and grabbed a falling board.

"Thanks." Adalee's smile seemed to light up her face. "I can't wait until Mama and Riley see these. If you'll put them on that table there, and line them up against the stand, I'll get the other two, which go on those tables." Adalee pointed to two more tables covered in sand and pieces of driftwood and set up catty-corner to the large table.

"Got it," Maisy said, lining up the boards.

Adalee returned as Maisy straightened out the last board. "Ta-da," she said, and held up a large hard-back poster board of the Sheffield family history.

"Oh," Maisy whispered.

Adalee set the board on the table, rearranged the driftwood, seashells and sand as Maisy scanned the board from the top left to the bottom right, starting with Mama and Daddy's wedding, followed by all three births, first school days, family vacations, proms, Christmases, homecomings, graduations. The double board told of all the significant moments in their shared history, including Daddy's illness and death. "This is what you've been doing while hiding in that room? I thought you were mourning Chad."

"He's not worth it," Adalee said. "Do you like it?"

Maisy hugged her. "Beautiful. Perfect. I forgot . . . about some of these times."

"Me, too." Adalee pointed to a Christmas picture in which Riley, Maisy and Adalee sat in a go-kart in their Santa pajamas, waving at the camera. "I don't even remember that go-kart," Adalee said.

"I do," Maisy said. "You fell out a few moments later. Mama freaked and gave the cart to the Foster boys."

"Blame it on me," Adalee said, and laughed. "I have one more board." She hurried back to the storage room.

Maisy continued to run her gaze over each photo, and gradually the hollow places in her body filled with love—for Mama, for Daddy, for the love, for Riley and Adalee. . . .

"Last one," Adalee said. She plopped a board on the remaining table, then arranged it to one side. A chair was pushed up to the table, a pen and a large pile of photos ready as if for a book signing.

"What's this?" Maisy studied this new board, not recognizing the young girl in the sepia-tinted photo standing in front of what appeared to be a much earlier version of the cottage.

"You know the lady who always thinks she wrote the books we discuss?"

Maisy nodded.

"Well, I figured out that she lived here in nineteen twenty-six when the house was still located on the river plantation. That's why she gets so agitated when she's here—it's her house. She's ninety now, but she lived here when she was ten years old. Tonight she'll be signing photos of the house—see." Adalee pointed to the stack of photographs.

"Adalee, you're amazing. What a great way to honor her."

Commotion and loud voices came from the front of the book-store. Together they turned to see Riley pushing Mama through the door in her wheelchair.

"Kitsy Sheffield has arrived. Let the fun begin," Maisy said.

Adalee moved toward the door, and Maisy swept the cottage with a single glance, looking for Lucy. Deep sadness came over her—Lucy wouldn't come to the party. What was said could not be taken back, just as what was done could not be undone. Maisy looked toward the front door, at her mother motioning for her to come. She smiled above her sorrow and went to join her sisters and mother.

Twenty-six

RILEY

The party had been going on for hours, overlapping voices, music and laughter filling Driftwood Cottage and the tent outside as Riley moved through the space, talking with old friends and meeting new people. Sorrow followed her like an unseen guest; this might be the last party the bookstore ever held. Despite the success of the week's events, first tallies hinted that they hadn't brought in enough to pay off the debts and balance the books.

Brayden ran around the store with his friends until Riley grabbed him by the shirt collar, whispered in his ear, "No roughhousing in the store. Take it outside."

In a quiet moment, Riley stood in the back of the Book Club Corner and observed the party. Maisy seemed to be chatting up every book club member in the room, recalling details about their lives and the books they were reading. Her movements were hectic, suggesting she was trying a bit too hard. In the far corner, a young woman was busy setting up an amp, guitar and microphone. A line of people waiting to view the history boards and obtain Mrs. Lithgow's signed photo wound around the room.

Riley didn't know how her heart could be so empty and yet so full at the same time. In one moment she felt she might burst with joy, and then she was swamped with sorrow, like waves that came one after the other.

A receiving line had formed at Mama's wheelchair near the checkout counter. Harriet stood at her side. A table nearby overflowed with birthday presents.

Adalee stood at the history boards answering questions. The sea green furniture and strings of white lights looked warm and inviting next to the new slipcovers and rows of bookshelves. Why, Riley wondered, did things always seem to reach their very best just before they were lost?

Mack.

Daddy.

Innocence.

Love.

Then her mind grabbed on to the best thing in her life: Brayden. Fear formed like a blooming blackness. She scanned the room for her son, and then remembered telling him to go outside. At a run, she hurried to the back porch and hollered his name.

He didn't answer from the beach; nausea rose in the back of her throat. She called his name louder. She ran out onto the sand, toward the water. Where was he?

Her flying thoughts told her that of course he was okay. He

was an expert swimmer, knew this beach and every curve of it. Her feet flew out from underneath her body as she tripped over a pair of shoes lying in the sand. She regained her balance, yet in the twilight, she imagined she saw only Mr. and Mrs. Rutledge tossing Sheldon's ashes and sobbing over their regret and loss.

Voices from the cottage drifted out onto the beach, but Riley listened for only one: Brayden's.

It was his laughter she heard above the others as a group of teens moved toward the cottage with their shoes in their hands, their arms and legs loose and gangly in the way typical of adolescence. A girl giggled; a boy said something Riley didn't catch.

She stood there as the group came toward her. They stopped when they noticed her.

Brayden stepped forward. "You're not looking for me, are you?"

"No, I just needed some fresh air. . . ."

"We're going to the pier to avoid this party . . ." Brayden said.

"Sorry, son. Not tonight. It's Gamma's birthday and there are a lot of people here who want to see you."

"You've got to be kidding." He moaned.

A boy dropped his hand on Brayden's shoulder. "We'll catch up with you tomorrow."

A blond girl dug her toes in the sand and touched Brayden's arm. "See you at Pearson's Pier at noon?"

Brayden nodded at her, and then stomped back to the cottage, the best one can stomp in sand. Riley followed. Her fear of a moment ago had put her worries in perspective. . . . Losing the bookstore would be nothing compared to losing her only son.

Like the Rutledges had just lost their only son.

She entered through the back door. A loud squawk came from the microphone as Maisy tapped it. "Can I have your attention?"

The room grew quiet with a few murmured voices at the edge. "It's time for the raffle."

A spattering of applause filled the room, and one by one Maisy drew names out of the bowl. She gave away signed books, manicures and various other services offered by the small businesses around town. She gave away a handcrafted driftwood centerpiece. Then she whistled and announced, "Now for the big prize: a trip to Charleston for the weekend."

Loud applause followed her announcement. Adalee ran up behind Maisy and whispered in her ear. She nodded, spoke again into the microphone. "Okay, my sister is going to pick the last name."

Leaning against the checkout counter, Riley was situated behind Adalee and only she saw her sister slip a scrap of paper from her back pocket, pretend to pull it from the bowl, and then hand it to Maisy. "Mrs. Harper," Maisy shouted into the microphone.

Silence filled the room as everyone waited for the ticket owner to come forward. Riley shouted the name again. A cry came from the back of the room. "Mom, that's you."

The crowd turned to stare at Mrs. Harper, who stood in the far back corner with her hand over her mouth. "I won?" she asked.

Maisy motioned for Mrs. Harper to come up as she read about the trip out loud. "You have won a two-night stay at the Vendue Inn, plus a tour of the aquarium and sea turtle hospital, a dinner at High Cotton and . . ."

Mrs. Harper reached Maisy's side and spoke into her ear.

Maisy smiled at the older woman, and took her hand. "This trip is for two."

Mrs. Harper's daughter appeared at her mother's side. "Mom, of course you can take this trip. I'll go with you. We can do it together."

With large tears and shaking hands, the old woman took her daughter's arm. "I haven't been anywhere since Frank died. I just don't think . . ."

Maisy turned away from mother and daughter, but Riley heard her voice crack with emotion as she made her last announcement. "Today is not only a celebration of Driftwood Cottage and its two-hundred-year history, but also a celebration of my mother and our family. Mama, will you come up here so we can sing to you?"

"Oh, no . . . no . . ." Mama called from her wheelchair at the side of the small staged area. But her smile betrayed her joy as the crowd broke into "Happy Birthday to You." Riley stepped forward, resolved to enjoy the remainder of the evening. If she ran hard enough and fast enough, if she dove deep enough into the loud voices and rhythmic music, the knowledge of impending loss could be denied until tomorrow.

The birthday song was sung to Mama twice and once to the house before Mama grabbed the microphone. She struggled to her feet without help as she'd planned, and in a Southern accent cultivated through several generations, she said, "My, my, that was lovely. Thank you so much for caring about me, my family and our little cottage bookstore."

In a strong voice that convinced Riley there could be no illness, Mama thanked the local businessmen and -women who had contributed so much to the week's events. Once she had officially recognized representatives from the families who had once lived in the cottage, Maisy took the microphone and handed the night over to the live music. Riley and Adalee were sitting together in a large lounge chair, squashed together with their legs tangled to the floor. "That was nice," Riley whispered to Adalee.

"Yes, she did a good job."

"No, you. I saw what you did for Mrs. Harper. Your heart is bigger than this whole town."

Adalee's eyes opened wide. "Oh, please don't tell Mama I cheated on the raffle."

Riley laughed. "Are you kidding me?" She held out her pinky for the ancient promise-keepers' vow. They linked fingers. "I swear."

A young woman dressed in torn jeans, a loose white linen top and turquoise jewelry around her neck and up her arms approached the sisters. Red cowboy boots matched her leather belt. "Hey," Maisy said. "I want y'all to meet Brooks. She is one of our singers for the night. You're going to love her work. I heard her sing live at Bud's last week and just had to invite her. Her mother is in the Cookbook Club."

"Hi, Brooks. That's a lovely name." Adalee shook her hand.

Riley stared at her. "I'm sorry. I thought you were Nancy. Is she your sister?"

The girl looked at Maisy, who answered for her. "She recently changed her name to Brooks, after Garth Brooks."

"Oh . . ." Adalee laughed, jumped up. "Are you the one who only speaks in country music lyrics?"

The girl nodded.

"'Shameless,'" Adalee said, and then glanced between her sisters. "That's a Garth Brooks song."

"Oh . . . you 'Shoulda Been a Cowboy,'" Maisy answered with raised eyebrows. "Come on, who can name it?"

"Toby Keith," Brooks answered.

"Okay, I'm going to lose at this game," Riley said. "The only thing I can think of is a song by Alan Jackson: 'Everything I Love Is Killing Me.'"

Brooks smiled. "'Love Is a Sweet, Sweet Thing.'"

Riley looked to Maisy. "Faith Hill, right?"

Brooks laughed. "'I Believe There Is Magic Here. . . .'" She bowed and moved toward the microphone.

Maisy resumed her seat on the edge of the lounge chair. "That was Kenny Chesney," she said.

"Okay, it's really scary that you know song titles and lyrics like that," Riley said. "How do you know everything she's quoting?"

"I didn't leave everything behind when I moved to California. . . . I took my country music with me."

Adalee whispered, "You left us behind."

Maisy turned to her. "I'm sorry. I didn't mean to. It was like I was drowning and I grabbed on to the first life preserver I saw, then swam as far and fast as I could. It was wrong. I was wrong. I'm sorry."

Riley pressed her fingers at the edges of her eyes. "Don't you dare make me cry when I spent so long putting on makeup."

Maisy took a long, deep breath. "I am such an idiot."

"No . . . no. You're not." Adalee pulled her into a hug, and

Riley wrapped her arms around both of them, clinging to the tender moment. She felt the warmth of someone's gaze on her before she realized why she'd turned. Lodge snapped a picture of the three sisters just releasing from their hug.

"Hey, Lodge." They all called his name in overlapping voices.

Riley said, "Thanks for coming. Did you get enough food?"

He laughed. "Plenty. I've been here for an hour."

"You have?"

"I tend to be invisible to you sometimes, don't I?"

"What? No. I've just been . . . preoccupied with all this chaos." She searched his face for pain, but found only his open smile. "You shaved," she said.

He shrugged. "Guess I thought this occasion deserved a good clean shave."

Riley wondered if he thought *she* was worth a good clean shave or if it really was just the occasion. How unfair to let him believe she felt something else for him besides camaraderie. Her own pain had come from believing someone else felt something more for her than friendship, and she couldn't allow this to come between her and Lodge. He laughed, pushed his glasses up his nose. "I'll go get some quotes and pictures from other people. . . . We'll talk later. Okay?"

Riley motioned to the corner of the book club area. "Can we talk for a second before you take off?"

He shrugged. "Sure."

Facing Lodge underneath the string of white lights, Riley took a deep breath. "I wanted to talk about . . . well, us."

"Us?" he said.

"Our friendship."

He set his camera and notebook on a side table, took her hand. "You do know I want it to be more than friendship, right? You've figured that out by now, haven't you?"

She nodded, squeezed his fingers. "Yes, but I don't think it's a good . . . idea. I enjoy our friendship. I enjoy you. I just don't want anything . . . else."

He released her hand, attempted a laugh. "Is this a 'we can be friends' speech? I don't think I've heard one of those since high school."

"What I said . . . it came out all wrong, didn't it?"

"No, it came out right, Riley. We'll be friends. We always have been. You can't make someone love you back, you know?"

She nodded. "But friendship—it can be enough, right? There are so many wonderful things about us. We still have . . . those, right? We're okay?"

He nodded. "Yes, we're okay." He hugged her, held on a moment longer, then released her. "I'm off to work. It's a great party."

"Thanks, Lodge," she said.

He waved over his shoulder when she saw Mr. and Mrs. Rutledge move through the crowd. No matter where she looked, her eyes were drawn to this couple, as though their loss had become a ghost that followed them wherever they went. Finally Riley leaned against a table and closed her eyes, gathering the courage to say hello, but when she opened them again, the Rutledges were gone.

The party lasted past the ten o'clock written on the engraved invitations. Riley found Maisy on a rose trellis slipcovered chair, staring at the crumpled napkins, the half-full plastic cups, and the sand covering the hardwood floors, as if a wind had blown the beach into the bookstore. Adalee stood at the front door waving goodbye to the last guests. Ethel pushed Mama's wheelchair around a chair and brought her next to Maisy.

"You holding up okay?" Maisy asked her mother.

"I'm fine, and the party was perfect. I can't think of the last time I had so much fun."

"Well, considering you've been laid up in bed, I'd guess so."

Mama's rouge shone too bright on her pale face. Her lipstick had bled into the small lines around her mouth and her silk skirt had crumpled up around her knees, exposing her thin legs and swollen ankles.

"What are you thinking?" Mama asked Maisy. "I know that look on your face."

"How I've missed you." Maisy took her hand, squeezed it.

"My, aren't you being a softy." Mama's voice shook, and she looked away. "I'm really tired. Where is Harriet to take me home?"

"She is loading up your heap of presents."

"Guess opening them will give me something to do over the next few days." Mama stared off toward the front windows for so long that Riley thought her exhaustion had caught up with her, but she must have been gathering her courage to ask the next question. Without looking at Maisy she asked, "Are you leaving now that the party is over?"

"Well, I'll go home in a bit, but I have to help Riley clean up first."

"No." Mama turned back to her, met her gaze. "I meant are you going back to California now? Are you leaving . . . again?"

"I don't know. . . . I have a job."

"I know," Mama said, closed her eyes. "I do know that."

Harriet bustled in beside the two of them. "Okay, Kitsy, time to get you to bed. Doc Foster is going to kill me for allowing you to stay out so long."

Mama looked up at Harriet, and her smile was back in place, her laughter hiding the pain Maisy had just inflicted. "What he doesn't know won't hurt him, now, will it?"

Maisy stopped the wheelchair with her foot. "Is there anything you want to tell us, Mama? While we're here together tonight?"

Riley's eyes widened in surprise at Maisy's obvious probe.

"Oh, yes, of course," Mama said.

The air separated in front of Riley, leaving a blank space for Mama's words that could change everything.

"Thank you for all your hard work," she said, and then motioned for Harriet to wheel her out the front door.

Maisy looked at Riley with a question on her face, but not spoken. Riley slid away to hide in the quiet of the back porch, where the sounds of the sea eased her down from her party high. Maisy joined her at the railing.

"It was a great night," Riley said. "Thank you for everything."

"It was great, wasn't it?"

"If you want—you can go out now. You know, with Mack or whatever you want. Adalee and I can clean all this up tomorrow when we're closed."

Maisy shook her head. "Mack doesn't . . . There isn't anything . . ." Emotion seemed finally to surge upward from a hidden place inside Maisy, but Riley couldn't be sure since she couldn't see her sister's full face. "It's not just Mack who doesn't really want me. It's any man I've ever chosen."

"Oh, Maisy, don't talk like that. You're just exhausted."

Adalee came onto the porch. "Talk like what?"

"I'm fine," Maisy said. "Come here and let me tell you how proud I am of all you've done this week."

Together the three of them stood with arms linked, staring out over the dark beach and the whispering sea. Adalee's head dropped onto Maisy's shoulder. "Could it be any better than this?"

Maisy's answer was to hold on to her sisters more tightly, on to everything that seemed sure on the back porch of Driftwood Cottage. Finally she yawned. "Bed. I need my bed."

"I'm right behind you." Adalee took her sister's hand and the screen door slammed after them as they bid Riley good night.

Riley entered the nearly empty bookstore, and went up the back stairs, checked on her son, then found herself in the observation tower, staring out into the night. For all the joy at the party, she was now free to acknowledge her underlying sorrow. She had to let go—and she was not very good at that.

Maybe this was the lesson she had to learn: to release what she could not control. She couldn't make the sun rise in the morning. She hadn't been able to make Mack love her all those years ago. She couldn't make the store survive financially. She couldn't force Brayden to stay hers forever.

She recalled words her father had once told her when they were fishing and Riley had cursed the sea for not offering her a fish. "There is a God, Riley, and you are not Him."

She leaned against the peeling banister surrounding the tower and stared out to where someone stood up from the sand and stretched. He must have fallen asleep on the beach after one too many. He walked toward the street, slow in gait. Riley felt her insides loosen as though a knot were untying without her permission. Maybe this was what letting go felt like.

The man looked up as if Riley had called his name. She took in a sweet breath: Mack.

"Riley?" he called in a soft voice from directly underneath the tower. "What are you doing?"

"Wait there," she said, and ran through the house barefoot, down the back stairs, through the store and out onto the porch before she could stop herself.

Mack stood in the sand, still staring up at the tower. She startled him when she appeared at his side and whispered his name.

He looked at her, and she saw his sorrow. Her insides quivered. He looked like the boy she'd known all along.

He spoke softly. "Hey, guess I fell asleep on the beach. A little embarrassing."

She laughed. "I can't count the times . . ."

"Riley, I'm headed home in the morning. It was nice to pretend I wouldn't have to go—but . . ."

"Ignoring the worst never stops it from happening, does it?"

He held out his arms and she laid her head on his chest, wrapped her arms around him: a place of rest. His hand ran through her hair, his fingers catching in the curls. "I hate that I have to leave, but I do."

He released her and smiled down, took her hands and lifted them to his lips, kissed the palms.

She stepped back from him, released him—let go—as she should have done all those years ago.

He touched her cheek. "You look like a girl."

"That's because I am one," she said.

"Yes, you are." He hesitated before he said, "I'm hoping I can come visit you again. I don't know when it will be. . . . Maybe in the next weeks or so. I have to see how Dad is doing. . . ."

"Mack." His name slipped past her lips.

"That sounded like a no," he said.

"Oh, that's not it. I want to see you. I'd love to see you. Come here anytime you want. But not for . . . me."

"Why not?" He stepped back in the dark. "I thought maybe . . ."

"No," Riley whispered, placed her finger over his lips. "You didn't, not really."

"You don't know that. . . ."

"I know where you are, Mack, because I'm there, too. Mom is sick. I'm losing the store. Life is changing and it's easy to grab on to something familiar and warm, something innocent and blameless . . . like the past. But it won't get us anywhere. Won't do us any good. Won't keep us safe or change reality."

"Damn, Minnow. Do you have an answer for everything?"

"No." She laughed. "I don't have answers for much of anything, but I want you to understand that it's okay by me to stay best friends. It's enough for me now. It's okay. All is well. Mack, I have a son; life is different now. So different."

"Brayden," he said. "He's a great kid."

Riley nodded, and the truth rose from the darkness inside her, from this sweet moment with her old best friend. "This was a hard week for me in many ways, but one of them was because his grandparents were here . . . and they don't know about Brayden . . . and Brayden doesn't know about them."

Mack held out his hand, took hers and pulled her close again. "Riley, you don't have to keep everything so close, so secret and tight."

"Yes, I do." Her voice shook.

He placed his hand on the back of her head, drew her in to rest again on his chest before he spoke. "It's Sheldon, isn't it? He's Brayden's father."

Riley nodded her head under Mack's hand. He held her for long moments; she heard his heartbeat, smelled the aroma of sea mixed with sweat and sleep. She shivered even in the heat of the summer night and held tighter to Mack until her breath evened out, until he released her. Telling him had unknotted something tangled in her soul. She looked at him. "Maybe I shouldn't have told you that. I've never told anyone."

"Yes, you should have told me. Didn't you just say it—best friends, right? We can tell each other anything."

She nodded. "I did, and it's enough, isn't it?"

"Yes, Minnow. Enough." He kissed her forehead. "I'll see you soon, okay?"

"Okay . . ." she said.

He walked off into the dark and Riley whispered again into the night, "It's enough."

TWENTY-SEVEN

MAISY

*M*aisy lay on her back in bed and let the emotions of the party wash over her once again. Watching her sisters give to others, Mama with her daughters, Mack coming to say goodbye—a real goodbye this time, one without empty promises. How would she incorporate all of these events into her life?

She rose from bed and stretched. She should be going home now, back to Laguna Beach, but now Mama was sick. "Home." She said the word out loud, but it sounded hollow.

Where was home? If it wasn't here in the place she'd left, or there in the place she'd been living, where the hell was it? She sat on the edge of the bed, dropped her head into her hands. She attempted to see her life in Laguna—her white condo, her beautiful store, the long, wide beach, the sunsets on the opposite shore.

When she'd originally left Palmetto Beach she'd believed that

Mack Logan was the answer to all her heartache, all her empti-ness. Over the years, she realized now, he'd become a fantasy that changed with her need, with the time and season, his image filling the vacant or hurting places. His adolescent adoration had once been enough and she'd attempted to make it last forever. But she'd only been fooling herself.

After taking a hot shower and getting dressed, Maisy stood outside the drawing room about to go in and hear if all this work had paid off, saved the store.

Riley came up behind her. "You okay?"

"Yes, I'm fine. Just exhausted. Aren't you?"

"Yes, but I want you to know that I couldn't have gotten through the week without you. I am so glad you came home—I hope it meant a lot of good things for you, too."

"What do you mean?"

"That you had fun. That you saw old friends. That you en-joyed being here."

Maisy turned away from her sister, away from the memory of Lucy walking away. Riley opened the French doors and went to their mama, who was propped up in bed in full makeup.

Maisy entered the room, sat in the corner chair. Adalee came running into the room, out of breath, flushed, her hair flying in curls around her face. "Sorry I'm late."

Riley laughed. "You're not late."

"I had so much fun yesterday." She plopped down in a large club chair, her feet on the ottoman.

"Did you get back together with Chad or something?" Maisy asked.

"Ooooh, no. My older sister taught me that I am too good for him." Adalee laughed. "Right?"

"Right." Maisy wondered how she could offer such good advice, but never take it herself.

"So how are my girls?" Mama asked. "I thought you'd sleep all day, considering how hard you worked all week."

Positive affirmations overlapped; they were all fine.

Mama clapped her hands together. "Okay, girls. I have something to say amidst all this hoopla." Mama exhaled through pursed lips. "You all did such an amazing job that I don't even know how to thank you." She turned to Riley. "I'll get straight to the point. Did we make enough money to save the store?"

Riley looked from her sisters to her mother. "Not enough, Mama. I'm so sorry. We can repay some of our debts, but not all of them and still make the payroll and mortgage." Riley dropped her gaze to the floor in defeat.

Mama closed her eyes, leaned her head back on the pillow. "Oh, Riley, I was really hoping we could save the store, but we just can't keep wishing, hoping and praying for some miracle. Hoping never made anything happen. We have to face the facts, don't we? We'll have to sell."

Maisy was shocked by the resignation in Mama's voice. It was so unlike her.

Adalee jumped to her feet. "No way. We can't lose Driftwood Cottage Bookstore. It means too much to this town. There has to be a way to save it."

Maisy stood also. "I agree with Adalee. We have to try harder to find a solution."

Mama cleared her throat. "There is no way to keep it. If we can't balance the books, or pay our employees, we can't keep it, period. You won't even be here to know anything about it. . . . You'll be back to your nice California life."

Anger flared in Maisy, burst and then simmered. "We'll figure something out. And I'm staying. Now I'm staying . . . for a while anyway."

Riley shook her head. "Maisy, of course I'd love it if you stayed, but it can't be with the crazy idea that you or anyone else can save Driftwood Cottage. This bookstore has been mine to run. I've tried for twelve years, and we are too far down the hole to make it work. You can't ask Mama to support Brayden and me. That is not her job. That is not her responsibility. And it's not yours either."

Adalee sat down in defeat. She spoke quietly. "I was gonna ask you if I could eventually open a design shop in the extra storage room."

Riley went to her, squatted next to her chair. "You didn't say anything."

"I was going to wait until the party was over. I mean, I graduate in two semesters. . . . I thought, well, I thought . . . we could work together and . . ."

Mama's voice filled the room. "Dreaming about things doesn't change them. Adalee, you can start your design business out of the house. You know that."

Maisy interrupted. "This is ridiculous. Are y'all going to just let it go?"

"You did." Mama said the words so sharply that Maisy fell to her chair as though she'd been slapped with an open hand.

"Please stop it," Riley said. "There is something else we need to discuss."

When silence fell, Maisy expected Mama to bring up the forbidden topic: cancer. Her insides were cold.

"This morning," Riley said, "I'm going over to visit Mr. and Mrs. Rutledge."

Maisy was having trouble following the redirected conversation.

"That is kind of you," Mama said. "They have suffered a great loss."

Riley's clear tones reverberated through the room. "I'm going to tell them that Brayden is their grandson."

Mama's shocked inhalation of breath was enough to make Maisy want to rise from her chair and slap her hand over her mama's mouth. All at once, she knew exactly what to do—she went to her sister and hugged her hard and long. "Oh, Riley, Sheldon was the nicest guy in the world."

"Yes," she said, and released her. "That's why I never told. Or at least that's why I *thought* I never told. I didn't want to ruin his life. Now I also know I didn't want to share Brayden."

"I didn't even know you dated him," Mama said through tight lips.

"I didn't, Mama. We spent one night together after I got my heart broken and drank too many lemonade surprises at the bonfire. Can you see why I never said anything? But I can't hide anymore. And it was cruel to keep Brayden from his grandparents. I'm sorry."

"For what?" Maisy asked, trying to assimilate that Riley had slept with Sheldon on the same night she broke up her and Mack. "Why are you sorry?"

Riley looked up. "I'm sorry for keeping this knowledge from all of you. I'm sorry I lost the store. I'm sorry . . . I took Mack away from you that night."

"Stop it," Maisy said. "We all, every single one of us, have done things we wish we didn't do. No more regrets."

"Isn't Sheldon"—Adalee hesitated before she said—"dead?"

"Adalee," Maisy said, the word sharp.

Mama spoke in a soft whisper. "Sheldon Rutledge."

"Yes," Riley said.

"Could be worse, I guess," Mama said, and shrugged her shoulders. "Now I need to get some rest."

The sisters kissed her one after the other and Maisy stared at Riley, envisioning the night of the last bonfire, their father sprinting onto the beach and pulling her and Mack apart, and she saw another deep bond between Riley and herself: Riley had slept with Sheldon for the same reasons she had slept with Tucker—to forget Mack Logan. One night—one sorrow-drenched night—had altered the course of many lives.

Twenty-eight

The cottage the Rutledges had rented for the week had cedar shingles painted white with bright blue shutters, and a tin roof. On a covered front porch the width of the house were a deep swing and three chairs painted in pastel blue, pink and green. A sign next to the front door read *Shore Thing*. Riley remembered a time when her uncle from Charleston had rented this very cottage; she'd fallen asleep on that swing.

During those last moments with Mack, when she'd told him the truth about Brayden's father, Riley had realized that she must also tell the Rutledges. For years she had convinced herself that she was keeping the identity of Brayden's father a secret for his sake, and that was partly true, but now she had a clearer understanding. If she told the grandparents, she would now introduce a new family into their lives.

She took a deep breath and walked up onto the porch, knocked on the front door.

A panicked inner voice told her to run. *Don't let them into your life.* Her hands clenched into fists at her sides; she shook them and held her palms up as if to offer herself the freedom to receive something new.

Mrs. Rutledge answered the door with a dishrag in her hand, a faded blue apron tied around her middle. Her dark brown bob was brushed and hair-sprayed into a perfect Vidal Sassoon look from the nineteen seventies. "Well, hello, Riley. What a wonderful surprise. Come on in, my dear." She opened the door wide. "I sure do miss those days when all the kids came to our cottage." She patted Riley's shoulder, which was higher than her own. "You'll always be kids to me."

Riley hesitated, not wanting to enter, but knowing she must. This news wasn't something one told a woman at her front door with a dishrag in her hand. She followed Mrs. Rutledge through the house, laughed when she passed through the living room. "This cottage is exactly the same as it was years ago when my uncle Sam rented it."

"It's a wonderful little place," Mrs. Rutledge said over her shoulder. "I loved owning our old place, but there sure is a great freedom in just locking up and leaving, in letting someone else worry about wood rot and painting the front porch."

They entered the kitchen together and Riley breathed in the distinct and comforting aroma of peach cobbler. "Oh, that smells wonderful. It brings back memories."

"Yes." Mrs. Rutledge sat in a ladder-back chair at the table, motioned for Riley to sit. "Everywhere I turn I find a memory. It's what I wanted from this trip, but I don't think I can do it again."

Riley closed her eyes and took a sustaining breath. "How many years has it been since you've been here?"

"The last time we came was the year Sheldon entered college. How long is that?" She glanced up at the wide plank-board ceiling as if it held the answer. "Probably thirteen years ago. It seemed like such a wonderful decision for him to enter the Air Force after college. Such a great opportunity. Who knew . . . ?"

Riley reached for Mrs. Rutledge's hand resting on the table, and squeezed it. "I am so sorry about Sheldon. We all just adored him."

"I know, and thank you."

Courage faded into panic, and Riley feared she wouldn't be able to tell the truth.

"If only . . ." Mrs. Rutledge looked into her eyes. "If only God had granted us more children, maybe this wouldn't be such a hard burden to bear." She shrugged, wiped her eyes on the dish towel she still held in her hand. "Or maybe not. We never know about 'could have beens,' do we?"

"No, we don't."

Mr. Rutledge entered the kitchen with a rolled-up newspaper tucked under his arm. His face broke into a wide grin. "Well, well, look who's here." Riley stood up, and he enfolded her in a hug, patted her back with his wide hand. "How are you, Riley?"

"I'm well, thank you."

"That sure was a fantastic party last night. We had such a wonderful time seeing old friends. That boy of yours is adorable. And funny. I enjoyed talking to him."

"You talked to Brayden last night?"

"Well, yes. We went out to the tent for a while when the store got too crowded. He told me all about the secret places to fish. I pretended I didn't know them already." Mr. Rutledge winked.

"He is absolutely obsessed with fishing," Riley said, unsure what to do with her hands, with her words, with her fear.

"I remember a young girl who was once obsessed with finding the best fishing hole every year. If she didn't win the summer's fishing contest, there was hell to pay."

Riley laughed.

"You still fish?" he asked.

She shook her head. "No time really, sir."

"What with running that bookstore and raising a son, I'm sure there's not. But I'd hate to think Riley Sheffield was not fishing out there on Pearson's Pier with her baseball hat on crooked and her feet dirty, her face stained red from the shaved ice."

Riley thought of the odd way in which memories were stored, a scent, a sound, a sight teasing the mind. This was Mr. Rutledge's memory of her: the girl who wouldn't let anyone beat her at anything, who could bait a hook faster than any boy she knew. And because he remembered that girl, she came alive in Riley. "I need to tell you something," she said.

They glanced at each other, and Mr. Rutledge motioned for Riley to sit. "Are you okay?"

"I am here to beg your forgiveness for not telling you sooner. That girl, the one Mr. Rutledge just described, left a long time ago. I don't know when she moved on, but she left behind a scared woman who was afraid to tell the truth."

"Forgive me for being a bit confused." Mrs. Rutledge wiped her dish towel in circles on the pine table.

"I'll try to explain, but I'm not sure how good a job I'll do, as I haven't planned this well. I've had my reasons for keeping this secret, but the excuses seem hollow now."

"What secret, my dear?" Mr. Rutledge continued to stand, as if he knew he'd need to brace himself for what was to come.

Riley took a deep breath. "My son, Brayden, is your grandson. Sheldon's son."

The silence that overcame the kitchen ballooned outward into the past, and then into the future, filling in the gaps and spaces of all their lives. Riley waited, as she knew she must, for the verdict of guilt and blame.

"We have a grandson, Mark. A grandson." Mrs. Rutledge's awed voice broke as her chair scraped across the hardwood floor.

Riley looked up at the older couple holding each other in the middle of the room.

"A grandson. Sheldon's son." Mr. Rutledge spoke in a sure and calm voice.

Riley sat as quietly as she could, wanting to leave these two people alone in their intimate moment. She felt like a voyeur, as if she had stumbled onto a scene that should never be shared beyond husband and wife.

She stood to tiptoe to the back door, which she knew led onto a dirt-and-gravel path that cut through shrubbery and scrubby pines, past two more cottages and then to the beach. This was her goal—the beach, silence.

A hand dropped onto her shoulder before she took two steps. Before she could formulate her response, she was enfolded into the arms of Brayden's grandparents.

"I'm sorry," Riley whispered.

Mr. Rutledge stepped back. "You have given us a great gift. How, oh, how can you apologize?"

This grace, this overwhelming grace, was more than Riley could take in. Their forgiveness filled her with joy and emptied her of fear. "I should have told you sooner. I should have told Sheldon, but I didn't want him to feel forced into doing anything except fulfilling his own dreams. I wanted to protect him . . . and you."

"No more. No more apologies." Mr. Rutledge spoke in a firm voice. "Gifts should not come with apologies."

Mrs. Rutledge clasped her hands before her as if in prayer. "Oh, Mark, we have so much to learn about him: his birthday, what he likes, what grade he's in. Oh, what if he doesn't like *us*?"

Riley took Mrs. Rutledge's hand. "He'll love you."

"Can we . . . ?" Mr. Rutledge's helpless gesture toward his wife revealed an uncertainty that Riley had never seen in him before, not even when he'd scattered his son's ashes.

"Can you what?" she asked.

"See him. Be . . . involved in his life?" His deep voice held a quaver.

"Oh, yes. Yes. I want you to know him—" She glanced between them. "But first I have to tell him."

Mrs. Rutledge took her husband's hand. "We've arranged to stay here until Saturday." She looked at Riley. "You know we live in Edisto now. We aren't that far from here—a few hours."

"I'm going to give you some privacy now." Riley placed her hand on the door handle. "Why don't you plan on coming for dinner tomorrow night? I have a tiny place, but we can eat in the café of the bookstore. . . ."

"Oh, dinner tomorrow would be wonderful." Mrs. Rutledge smiled, wiping her eyes.

Mr. Rutledge nodded without words, simply hugged Riley once more.

She took the path around the house to her car, and realized that her own smile was real, unfettered by fear. Possibilities seemed to be opening up as she allowed new people into her life, into Brayden's life.

The next day, Riley stood over her sleeping son and wondered if there was a book or instruction manual to help her tell her son that the dad he never knew was dead. There were probably a million wrong ways to say it, and she didn't know the single right way.

She sat on the edge of the rumpled bed and ran her forefinger over his cheek; he stirred beneath her. Brayden hadn't asked about his dad until he was five years old and they had donuts for Dad at school. She had told him then that his father was fighting in a faraway war—and it was the truth. She'd been prepared, over the years, to answer other questions—why she wasn't with his dad and why he'd never visited—but the only other time Brayden had asked was when he was six years old, after his granddad died. She'd tucked Brayden into bed and he'd whispered, "Is Dad fighting in a war so far away that he doesn't even know about me?"

"No, Brayden," she'd said, "he doesn't know."

"Do you love him?"

"I love him because he gave me you," she'd said, and kissed him good night.

Now Brayden opened his eyes, stared at Riley. "I thought I could sleep in," he said.

"I need to talk to you."

He sat up, his hair slanted to the left. He rubbed his face. "Is something wrong?"

"Meet me in the kitchen. I'll make your favorite gourmet breakfast of Pop-Tarts."

He squinted at her, and mumbled something that resembled an okay.

Riley sat at the scratched kitchen table and took inventory of all the things to which she would soon say goodbye: this kitchen she had always meant to have redone; the slanted, scratched hardwood floors; the familiar creak of the back steps; the sweet sound of the wind coming off the Atlantic. She pressed her fingers into her eyelids to stop the tears. She had to focus on Brayden now. . . .

"Mom . . . ?" His voice hesitated on the simple word.

She handed him a plate with two toasted Pop-Tarts. "I want to talk to you about your father."

He lifted the Pop-Tart, stared at it and then put it back onto the plate. "You already told me, Mom. We don't have to go over it again. He doesn't know about me; he's in a war. I get it. If you're starting to feel bad about me not having a dad for parents' day or something, it's no biggie, really." His response was so hard and sure that Riley felt the sting of her own neglect.

"Please, Brayden. Just give me a second here." She took a deep breath. "Your dad's name was Sheldon Rutledge."

He stared at her with a look she'd only seen once—when they'd had to evacuate for a hurricane: fear of the unknown.

"He was an incredible and wonderful man with a loud laugh and a big heart. He joined the Air Force to serve his country. All he ever wanted to do was fly planes. And he did. I made a huge mistake. . . ." She turned her face.

"Me," he said, his voice cracking.

Riley jumped up, wrapped her arms around her son. "No. Never. You are not a mistake. You are a gift. I made a mistake in not telling you who he is . . . who he was."

"Then why didn't you?"

The answers she'd dreaded saying all these years fell into her mouth. "I was scared. I didn't want him to . . . take you, or feel like he had to stay when he needed to go. But he would have loved you so much."

"Well, why don't we . . . ?"

"He died, Brayden. He died in a plane crash in Iraq."

"Just like that man whose parents scattered his ashes last week."

Riley closed her eyes. "Those were your dad's ashes, Brayden. That's why I made you stay."

He looked away, then stood. "Okay."

"His parents, Mr. and Mrs. Rutledge, are your grandparents. They're coming for dinner tonight, because even if you never knew your father, you can know them. They're an important part of your family, and they were very excited when I told them about you. They want to get to know you."

His blank stare brought panic rising in Riley's belly. She moved toward him; he held up his hand. "Leave me alone." He walked down the hall to his bedroom.

She stood in the kitchen aware of all she was losing: the bookstore, her home, and her son's trust. The hope that everything would work out seemed to fall into the gray realm of false dreams.

Brayden emerged an hour later and spent the rest of the day at Pearson's Pier, fishing by himself. Riley told herself she was just making sure he didn't run off, but after she caught herself driving past the pier for the seventh time that afternoon, she decided to go home and stay there. She subdued her panic with busy-ness, as she'd always done—setting out groceries for the Rutledge dinner, inviting Adalee, Mama and Maisy to join them, starting to prepare a Lowcountry boil while playing a CD of James Taylor.

Adalee arrived first at the bookstore café and gave Riley a long hug. "You okay?"

"I'm not sure. But I'm pretty sure I did the right thing. I might not have before . . ."

"Of course you did the right thing."

Maisy came in with an armful of flowers, a bottle of wine and a loud hello. "The party is here." She made a face at Riley. "Mama says she can't come. . . . She just isn't quite strong enough to go out another night." Maisy imitated their mother's practiced words. "Personally, I think she just needs a wee bit more time to process the . . . information."

Riley took the flowers from Maisy and filled a tall vase with water. "Thank you so much. I don't think I could do this dinner without you." She looked away as she trimmed the stems with scissors. "And we might have to do this without Brayden. He hasn't come home from fishing at the pier. I can't chase him down and drag him here."

"I guess he didn't take the news too well," Adalee said.

"He hasn't said a word. It's not his fault. It's mine."

Adalee poured a glass of wine. "This is for you. I'll be right back. I'm going to get that boy." She ran out the door.

Maisy grabbed the mismatched plates Riley had brought down from upstairs and set them on the table. "It'll work out, Riley. I promise."

She turned to her sister. "Yeah, I'll get to live with Mama in our old house with a son who hates me. Sounds awesome."

"You've read too many sad novels," Maisy said just as a knock sounded on the front door.

"Now I get to explain to the Rutledges why the grandson they came to meet isn't here. What the hell was I thinking?"

Maisy laid her hands on Riley's shoulders. "Put a smile on and answer that door."

Riley walked over feeling as if the life she'd been living was falling apart with each step she took.

Mr. and Mrs. Rutledge stood on the front porch holding hands, and Riley was struck by one certainty: she might have made a million and one mistakes in her life, but telling these kind people about their grandson was not one of them. She hugged each of them and invited them into the store.

Mrs. Rutledge spoke first. "This is such a precious place. It's just so comfortable and warm."

Riley nodded, swallowing over the lump of sorrow that seemed to be lodged in her throat. "Well, thanks to Maisy and Adalee, it looks better than it ever did."

The couple glanced around the store and Riley fought to find words to tell them that Brayden had run off, and she didn't have enough control over him to make him come to dinner. She motioned for them toward the café. "Would you like some wine?"

They shook their heads. "No, thank you, dear. We don't drink," Mrs. Rutledge said with a smile.

"Sorry . . ."

They grinned at each other in that knowing way of couples who have been together for decades. Riley thought of all the secrets between them, the private jokes. . . .

Together they all moved into the café, and Riley poured two tall glasses of Pellegrino and handed them to the couple. "I'm sorry Brayden isn't here yet. He often loses track of time while fishing. Adalee just left to drag him home."

Maisy greeted them and they stood around talking about the weather, the crowds and recent changes in the town. When the Rutledges asked about her job, Maisy made them laugh with her stories of customer eccentricities.

For Riley, time passed in increments of interminable embarrassment before she finally asked everyone to sit down and she'd serve the food. She scooped a portion of shrimp and crab onto each plate, set out corn on the cob and sausage.

"If Brayden is still out fishing, it looks like he inherited your love of the outdoors," Mr. Rutledge said.

Riley smiled at them. "Guess so, along with my stubborn refusal to come in when called."

"Well, I don't know about you all, but I'm starving," Maisy said. "Mr. and Mrs. Rutledge, please take your seats."

They sat, and the uncomfortable silence rang louder than any gong. Only James Taylor's voice singing about being a friend filled the room.

Finally Mrs. Rutledge laid down her corn on the cob. "This is delicious, Riley. I don't mean to be . . . nosy, but can you please tell us a little bit about Brayden? We . . ." She took her husband's hand. "We're dying to know all about him. What does he like to do? What is he good at?"

"Well, he's funny in that way that Sheldon was, knowing just what to say at the right time. He's an avid reader. He can fish all day . . . without realizing the time has passed. He seems to be popular at school. . . ."

"I am not." Brayden's voice came from the back door. Adalee entered with him while brushing sand off her feet.

Riley stood, relief flooding her body. "Hey, darling." She hugged her son, and was so glad when he hugged her back.

He turned to the table, walked over to Mr. and Mrs. Rutledge, shook their hands and said hello. He sat with a plate of food while Riley attempted to communicate her gratitude to Adalee without words.

Brayden broke a crab leg in half, pulled the meat from the shell. "I'm really not popular at all. My mama thinks so because she has no idea." He smiled when he said this, then put the entire length of meat into his mouth, and made a sound that resembled the word "awesome."

The conversation began to pick up as their words overlapped. Even as Riley ate and drank and offered her own comments, she was aware of hope rising like a buoy inside her. Maybe tonight was the start of something good.

TWENTY-NINE

MAISY

The evening with Sheldon's parents ended without promises or even future plans, but Maisy sensed the change in the air, like a spent storm leaving behind fresh, rain-washed skies. She finished washing the dishes while Adalee and Brayden played a long-promised game of Monopoly at a café table. As she listened to their sparring, a warm sense of belonging came over her. How had she ever thought it would be best to walk away from any of this?

When she couldn't find Riley, Maisy guessed where she had escaped to—the observation tower with a book. She slipped up the back stairs and found her sister seated in the wicker chair, bathed in a puddle of moonlight, staring out at the beach, an opposite shore from Maisy's own place in the world.

Maisy whispered from behind her, "I'm sorry, Riley."

Riley turned her head. "What? Isn't that my line?"

Maisy sat down on the splintered wooden deck next to her sister. "I always thought there was this life . . . you know, this other life. One where Mack and I were in love, married, living in some sitcom-perfect universe. I visualized our house, our kids. It was a life I thought existed in a parallel plane, and I couldn't get to it. One event had made it impossible for me to claim that life—you sending Daddy out to get me from the party."

Riley lifted her hands. "I already . . ."

Maisy pressed her forefinger to her sister's lips. "*Shhh* . . . I'm not done. So, I've gone around for years imagining this other life. When things went wrong, or love didn't work out, or I made a stupid choice, I thought, 'Well, there you go. I was supposed to live that *other* life.'" She looked up at the moon. "But that life never existed. And it's not your fault. Every choice has been mine. Every mistake has been mine.

"When Mack showed up here, I was convinced I'd now have a chance to start that other life. The life I'd been waiting for." Maisy sighed. "I went after him as if he was *the* answer."

"What happened?" Riley asked.

"Nothing at all. I chased him around Palmetto Beach, and just when I thought I had a chance, he was called to the hospital for his dad. And I realized you can't start where you stopped thirteen years ago. Or at least we couldn't. It was gone: whatever spark had been there before, whatever fantasy I had been carrying around, didn't exist anymore."

"I'm sorry," Riley said in a whisper.

"Don't pretend you're sorry. Don't pretend anything any longer, Riley. You love him. You always have. I knew it then and I know it now. I wanted to take your best friend away from you, and for a while, I did."

Riley looked away. "That's not it."

"Why don't you ever go after what you want? Why do you live like you're scared out of your mind? As a kid you used to live a loud, risky life. Tomboy Riley could get the best of anyone. Now you're a quiet bookseller trying not to make waves, trying to keep still enough so you won't disturb your own world."

"I have commitments, obligations."

"What alternate life do you think you could have lived? One where you finished college and went off to New York City to be a writer? Or one where you married some rich guy from Charleston and had a butler?"

"I don't imagine another life, Maisy. I'm not like you."

"Well, for someone who doesn't imagine another life, you're sure not living this one. If I wrote your story, I'd tell you to run off and find Mack Logan, throw your arms around him and let him do whatever he was thinking about doing when he stared at you across the room the other night."

"His dad is dying, Maisy."

"That sounds like an excuse."

"Maisy, it's different for me. You've always had men chasing you. I, on the other hand, need to know when a man has only feelings of friendship. I won't fool myself into believing there is more than that when there . . . isn't." Riley stood, leaned against the banister. "So much is changing—where I'll live; whether Mama will get better; what role Brayden's grandparents will play in our lives. I mean, maybe I wanted something Mack made me feel and not him at all."

"Or maybe you wanted him. Why not take *that* chance?"

"I can't go back to what we had in childhood. I can't relive those times, retrace my tracks and undo what's been done. It's not like writing a book and rewriting the ending to make it happier."

"You won't know unless you take the chance. Take a risk, sister. Like you used to."

Riley looked down at her. "Like I used to?"

"Yes. You were never scared of anything. Ever."

"Things change."

"Not the you inside. Not her."

"I'm glad at least you think so." Riley turned away. "Anyway, I hope Mama is okay being home alone tonight."

Maisy let Riley change the subject. "She's fine. Harriet is there." She took a deep breath. "When do you think she'll tell us about . . . the cancer? I can hardly say the word."

Riley shrugged. "We can't push it."

"Well, I'm not going back to Laguna Beach until she does." Maisy stood and leaned over the railing; she spoke to the sea more than to her sister. "I will not ever again allow the past to destroy the present. Right now is all we have. This . . ." She held out her hands to encompass the beach. "You go on to bed. I'll just stand here and stare at the stars and figure out what in the hell to do with the only life I have."

Riley hugged her. "I do need to check on Brayden."

Maisy nodded.

Riley walked down the steps to the apartment; Maisy felt

the floor shake with each step she took. She stood gazing out at the sea, and the emptiness inside her began to dissipate, to fill in around the edges. It might take a long time, perhaps even a lifetime, to fill the hollowness, but she would no longer clutter it with lies, fantasies or excuses.

Later that night, Maisy drove home with Adalee in the passenger seat, talking rapid-fire about how much fun the past week had been, how school would be terrible. Maisy laughed. "Is this the same girl who said we were ruining her life by making her come here?"

"Hmmm . . . I think that was you." Adalee rested her head back, and then sat up. "Who's that?"

"Who's who?" Maisy parked in the driveway, and then she saw what Adalee meant: a woman sitting on the back porch steps with three suitcases piled around her feet. Her elbows were propped on her knees, her head in her hands. "Lucy," Maisy whispered.

Adalee opened the passenger door. "What's she doing here?"

Maisy ran to her old friend's side and hugged her. "What happened?"

Lucy's voice shook. "You were right. I'm sorry for all the terrible things I said to you. I'm—"

"Don't. . . . You have absolutely nothing to apologize for."

"He was . . . Maisy, he was having an affair, but he says 'this time' he's in love with her. He even used the words 'this time.' I am such an idiot. Waiting to have kids, waiting on him . . . wasting my love."

Maisy hugged her friend and waited for the tears to finish before she asked, "What can I do to help?"

"Let me come to California with you."

"Well, I have a better idea—why don't you *stay* here with me?"

"You're not going back to California?"

"Not for a while."

Lucy smiled. "Really?"

"We will figure this out together, Lucy. We won't run away. . . ."

"Okay." She swiped at her face. "I promise I won't be a burden. You know, you said something the other day. When you told me the truth about Tucker, you said you'd always tried to fill up the empty place inside you with something outside."

"I said that?"

Lucy wiped her eyes again and laughed. "Yes, you did. And I know you were talking about yourself, but you were also talking about me. I have never believed I'm good enough on my own. It was never who I was—it was who I was with that made me feel worthwhile." Lucy slumped forward. "You know, he's never even let me have a real job—he said my real job was to be his wife. And I don't know what else to do. My mother insists that the Bible says I have to stay with him and pray, but I know I have to leave him. . . ."

Maisy lifted a suitcase, opened the back door and held it open for her oldest and dearest friend. "Stay for a while. Stay for as long as you need."

Four Sheffield women were gathered for breakfast in the formal dining room. Lucy was on the back porch meeting with the lawyer Mama had arranged to come to the house before the day even began. The night before, Maisy had already made two important phone calls: to Peter to tell him it was over and to Sheila at work to ask for more time off to sort through her family issues. Sheila told her to take as much time as she needed; Beach Chic would wait. Peter, on the other hand, didn't take the news so well.

Harriet had opened all the windows, shoved the curtains aside to allow the breeze from a gathering storm to enter the room. Adalee took a bite of brown sugar–coated bacon and leaned back in her seat, moaned. "This cannot be good for me."

In her wheelchair, Mama laughed with such joy that Maisy turned to make sure it was really she making the noise. "Listen, girls, I need to talk to you."

Adalee's moan became a groan. "Mama, the party is over."

"I know. But in some ways it has just begun."

"Huh?" Adalee scooted up in her chair, Riley closed her eyes and Maisy held her breath.

"I need to share something with you and I don't want you to panic, burst into tears or run for cover." Mama was laughing at her own joke as Dr. Foster entered through the side door and came to stand next to her.

Adalee jumped up. "Dr. Foster, why are you here?"

Mama cleared her throat, ran a finger across her lipstick and forced a smile. "A few weeks ago, after some tests, I discovered that I have this vile thing called chondrosarcoma. Dr. Foster found it when he forced me to have a CT scan of an annoying lump on the back of my knee." She took a breath, and held up her hand to let them know she was not to be interrupted.

Adalee went to Mama's side. "What does this mean?"

Riley and Maisy looked at each other.

"It means I have to have surgery for sure. Then maybe some radiation. And then lots and lots of tests. I'll need your love and care and, of course, your endless adulation."

Maisy laughed despite the fear closing her throat—Mama was still here, still alive, still making fun of her own need for attention. Now. Right now—it really was all they had.

Mama pursed her lips and squinted at Maisy. "You knew," she said.

Maisy stared ahead without admission or denial.

"Doc?" Mama looked up at Dr. Foster. He shook his head.

Riley grabbed Maisy's hand, and confessed, "I shouldn't have told Maisy, but I couldn't bear being the only one to know."

Mama pointed at Maisy. "That's why you're not going back to California. Well, I won't have it. You've always been very intent on living your own life and that's why I waited to tell you. I won't have you staying out of guilt. Only stay because you want to stay."

Maisy went to her mama's side. "I've always made my own decisions. And I'm making one now. I'm staying for a while. You can't talk me out of it."

Mama rolled her eyes with laughter. "When have I been able to talk you out of anything?"

Adalee glanced around the room. "Am I the only one who didn't know? Doc?" She turned to him, grabbing the sleeve of his suit jacket. "Tell us the truth. What does this mean?"

"Exactly what your mama told you."

"But . . . what about statistics and all that?" Adalee asked.

Dr. Foster took a step back. "Kitsy? You want to talk about this?"

"I don't believe in statistics." She made a motion of dismissal. "But the plan is that Doc and I will travel to M. D. Anderson in Houston, which is the best sarcoma center in the country. They will remove the tumor and then maybe I'll have to have proton therapy, which I don't fully understand yet. I won't be gone long. And I'll recover at home. I want Adalee to go with me while Riley takes care of selling the store. Maisy, I don't want you to lose your job. . . ."

"Mama, I won't lose my job. I'm here."

"We will not talk about percentages of survival or statistics or any of that—do you understand me? Right now, this moment, I have a one hundred percent chance of being here to drive you crazy, to love you, to listen to you bicker and holler and love and live in my house."

"That is good enough," Maisy said. "Absolutely good enough."

THIRTY

*B*ooks were scattered across the floor of the storage room. They would be packed and returned to the publisher. Riley's every new breath brought a combination of heartbreak and heart-healing thoughts. If only she could have saved this store . . . for Mama, for herself. But as she'd told Brayden when she'd explained that they'd have to move in with Grandma for a while, every ending also contained a new beginning.

Riley turned over each possibility, looked at it from all angles. She could ask Lodge for a job at the newspaper covering local events—who knew the town better than she did? She could register for classes at the local junior college and work on her English degree. She could offer her services to whoever bought Driftwood Cottage, if they kept it as a bookstore. New beginnings . . . she had to look at this time as a chance for exciting new beginnings.

She glanced out the window at the prominent for-sale sign on the lawn. The Realtor Mimi Bennett had pretended to be dismayed at having to slam the post into the ground, but Riley knew she was anticipating the commission. After two weeks, no one had put in an offer. Finally Mimi had told Riley to pack up some of the books so prospective buyers could better see the character of the house. They had hoped someone would buy the bookstore as a business, but some prospective buyers might want just the cottage.

Riley had left Adalee's history boards on display, and many customers came to read them over and over again, apparently finding something new in them each time. Just that morning, Riley had read the last line on the boards—*All connects. . . . The story continues. . . .*—and she'd realized that what she was going through now was just a new chapter in a never-ending story—her life story and the story of Driftwood Cottage.

The day after Mama's news, Adalee had run to the local USC satellite campus and registered for a huge load of classes with the intention of completing her degree by December. Maisy and Lucy had officially moved into Mama's house, and seemed to be having a great time together. Lucy was waiting for Tucker to sign the divorce papers, which he swore he would never do. His love for Lucy had suddenly and inexplicably returned two days after she left him. Her feelings for him had not.

Riley did her best to keep her spirits upbeat. Everything about the cottage took on greater import, more meaning than it ever had before. The dent in the hardwood floor where Brayden had dropped the iron urn while trying to help move it; the bookshelf with the crooked middle shelf that Daddy had built; the refreshed furniture and decorative touches her sisters had added. Anne had made Riley another pair of wings, larger ones that said *Believe*. They were prominently displayed on the front counter.

Afternoon sunlight fell across Riley's lap when Brayden ran in and dropped his tackle box on the floor. Summer seemed to live in his blond curls and brown cheeks. "I've decided what I want to do for my birthday that we never celebrated. Remember you said . . . after the book party?"

"Does this require extreme planning on my part?"

He sat next to her on the floor, crossed his legs one over the other and leaned back on his elbows. "I want to go visit Pops and Grams in Edisto. They say I'll love it and that the fishing there is just as good as here, and that there is a thirteen-year-old boy living next door, and Pops bought a Boston Whaler, and—"

Riley laughed. "Of course you can. But don't you want a party, too?"

"Am I allowed to have both?"

She poked at his propped arm so that he fell over. "Why wouldn't you?"

He sat back up. "Because we're, like, totally broke."

"What are you talking about?"

"That's what Susie Muller is telling everyone. She said her mother said that we have to sell the bookstore because we don't have any money and we'll be living on the streets. I told Susie we'll be living with Gamma."

Riley grinned at her gorgeous son. "Actually I'm considering a tent on the beach."

"Very funny, Mom."

"Brayden, we couldn't keep the store going, but there are other things we can do."

"Mom, I know. I know." He jumped up. "I'm gonna go fishing with Kenny." He ran off.

Ethel called across the store. "Riley, phone . . ."

"Can you bring it to me?" She pushed aside a pile of books.

Ethel walked up, looked down at her. "It's *that* woman."

Riley smiled at Ethel, knowing she meant Mimi, the real estate agent. "It's not her fault," she whispered to Ethel, her hand over the receiver.

Mimi's voice came over the line in rapid staccato. "Riley, you have just got to hear this. This is so fabulous. . . ."

"What?"

"We have an absolutely amazing and perfect and outrageous offer for the cottage."

Riley almost asked Mimi how many adjectives she could possibly use in one sentence. "We do?"

"Yes. I don't know why we didn't think to target this group, but one of the book clubs has been so distraught about losing this mainstay of the town that they got together, and they want to buy Driftwood Cottage. Dixie Plume is the main investor and they are going to run it together as a bookstore."

Riley closed her eyes. The Page Turners Book Club, the one whose members constantly complained about everything as if it were written in their club bylaws that they had to find at least six things that made them unhappy before they started each meeting. She had to sell, and she was grateful the bookstore could be saved, but she wished the new owner was someone she liked. But as her daddy told her after she'd traded her Schwinn for Macy Lane's Barbie dollhouse and then changed her mind, once you sell something, it ain't yours anymore.

"Well," Riley said, her eyes closed, "fax me over the offer and I'll look at it this evening."

Mimi's enthusiasm bubbled over. "I think you are going to be very pleased, and they want the store as soon as possible."

Riley stood and closed the phone, then walked it over to Ethel. "I'll be back in a little bit. Okay?"

Ethel nodded as Riley headed toward the back of the store, grabbed Brayden's fishing pole from the porch and slammed the screen door on her way out. She reached the end of Pearson's Pier without any memory of the fifteen-minute walk. She talked a man standing next to her into letting her have one piece of bait. She stood in bare feet. Her rolled-up jeans were covered in dust from sitting on the floor and the Driftwood Cottage Bookstore logo on her T-shirt was streaked with dirt.

Her fishing pole bobbed with the outgoing tide and Riley exhaled as though she'd been holding her breath for days, months, years.

Time rolled backward over hazy memories until she remembered the last time she'd fished here with her dad: the last day of summer before she left for college, before the night of the bonfire.

Was life like this for everyone? Inconsequential events, ordinary moments occurred all day, all year, and then the smallest decision shifted the course of your life?

The fishing pole pulled, and Riley jerked it backward in an instinctive maneuver. She held on with her left hand, turned the reel with her right. Riley felt something lift inside her, as though another part of her that had been hiding below, way below, now came bobbing to the surface even as she dragged her catch onto the pier.

The redfish's scales shimmered in the sunlight. The man who had given her the bait lifted his baseball cap in a salute. "Musta been the bait," he said.

"Oh, I think it was my expert fishing," she said with a smile. Bending over, she yanked the hook out of the fish's mouth and held it up by the gills. "You want it? I can't cook it tonight."

He shook his head. "Me neither. I'm just here for the peace and quiet."

"Me, too." She tossed the fish back into the water and watched it dive out of sight. Then she tucked her pole under her arm and thanked the man as she walked to the start of the pier and sat down on an iron bench until the pattern pressed into her thighs. Finally she stood and headed toward the cottage, where an offer to buy it would be waiting on her fax machine.

Thirty-one

Riley

The real estate attorney needed only two days to get the papers together and now she was due any minute at the bookstore. Riley waited in her office, which was full of boxes, and leafed through the newspaper until she found Lodge's last article about the bookstore. He summarized the good that had come out of Driftwood Cottage Bookstore, of the connections made and the beginnings fostered: how Mrs. Harper was traveling now; she'd planned a trip to Italy with her best friend. How Brooks had moved to Nashville to actively pursue her music career. How Mrs. Lithgow—in her lucid moments—was working with Adalee on a narrative of life in Palmetto Beach in the nineteen twenties. Lodge even wrote of Mama's cancer, of her recent trip to Texas with Adalee.

Riley put the newspaper down; she'd save this article for the last page of the Driftwood Cottage scrapbook. Even if the story of the bookstore was over, her own story was not. She reminded herself of this again and again. She would find new ways of living that weren't dependent on the past. Mama's tumor had been removed successfully and there was no metastasis. Mama and Adalee would come home in the next week, and therapy, nurses and home care would begin again.

The real estate attorney's cough made Riley look up from her desk. The woman gazed at Riley through bifocals, her bangs falling forward. "You ready?"

Riley nodded.

"Everything is in order. You have negotiated a wonderful deal here, Ms. Sheffield. You should be able to take this money and open any kind of store in any of the new storefronts downtown, but you do understand it can't be a bookstore, right?"

"Of course." Riley exhaled and attempted a smile, not wanting to explain that the money would go to repaying her debts. She took the papers from the lawyer. "I'll show these to Mama and return them to you in the next day or so."

"The buyers are anxious to close this deal. They'd like to take over in the next month."

"I know, I know. But Mama's name is on the ownership papers, so they'll have to wait until she can read them."

"But I thought she was . . . gone—you know, cancer treatment or something."

"She's fine now. She can read, for God's sake."

The attorney nodded, rose and left before Riley realized she had rudely not thanked her or said goodbye. She sat back on the café chair and folded the papers into a rectangle, shoved them into the manila envelope.

Anne stood behind the café counter wearing a T-shirt with a slogan Riley couldn't see under the apron. She called out, "Your cell phone has been ringing for a half hour back here. Your sister's name keeps popping up on the screen. You want to get it?"

Riley stood and tucked the envelope under her arm. She looked at Anne, sorrow grabbing her gut—how she would miss Anne and Ethel. Snatching up her phone, she shoved the papers under the counter and dialed her sister's number.

When Maisy answered, she was out of breath. "Where have you been?"

"Meeting with the attorney. What's up?"

"You didn't sell it, did you?"

"Maisy, we've been over this. I have to. Unless you know of buried pirate booty, the situation is what it is."

"I have booty, Riley."

"What?"

"It's not traditional buried treasure, but I think it counts. You listening?"

"Hmmm."

"Here it is," Maisy said, yet Riley heard another sound on the phone, a laugh.

"Are you on the phone, Adalee?" Riley asked.

"How did you know?"

"What is going on? Aren't you in Texas with Mama?"

"I am," Adalee said. "But I didn't want to miss this phone call. I've been working with Maisy and—"

Maisy spoke over Adalee's words. "Beach Chic wants to open their first East Coast store—a coastal satellite store. They will need a space for display and design work."

"Oh, that's great for you, isn't it?"

"What this means is that I will be opening a Beach Chic store and design center. Adalee will work there while finishing her degree here at the local college."

"Oh, Adalee, that is amazing. Where?"

"Driftwood Cottage."

Riley's breath caught on the possibility. "Does this mean what I think it means?"

"Yes!" Maisy screamed into the phone so loud that Riley pulled it away from her ear. "Beach Chic will pay half the mortgage for a full year as a test. Adalee will run the design section and I'll be training Lucy to run the retail section. You'll run a smaller version of the bookstore and still live upstairs. I have been working on this business plan day and night for two weeks. It's official. Do not sell Driftwood Cottage. We'll go over all the papers tonight; the Beach Chic lawyer drew up papers and it can work. It really can. Tons of details, but I know how to do this."

"I haven't . . . signed yet. I was waiting for Mama to read the offer."

"Tear it up. Now."

"Maisy, you can't leave your life, your job . . . all that. You can't leave California."

"Well, I only rented my apartment, so I'll end my lease and then go back and get my things. I have some logistics to work through, and who knows what the future holds . . . ? I'm just going to take it day by day. First thing is getting this store started and opened."

"Then," Riley said, "we did it. We, together. All of us."

"Meet me at the house in a couple hours, okay? We'll go over the specifics."

"I will. I will." Riley hung up, and then ran to the back of the house and shoved open the door to the shed. Rusted hinges scattered iron dust. She flicked on the overhanging naked bulb and squinted into the dancing dust motes until she found what she needed: the handsaw.

She ran to the front lawn, her bare feet pressing into the dew-soaked earth, and she made one phone call. Then she squatted in front of Mimi's wooden for-sale sign shoved deep into the ground. She began to saw the middle of the post. Laughter bubbled below the surface of her exertion, yet she would not allow its release until she heard the *thwack* of the sign falling into the grass.

Riley stood over the sign and her laughter rose sweet and soft. A small crowd had gathered without her noticing and she turned to their wide-eyed stares. There she stood with mud and grass on her jeans and tank top, her hair disheveled, her face sweaty.

"It's not for sale," she said, as if this explained her lunatic behavior.

Mrs. Lithgow came from behind a tall man. "Well, dear, I should hope not. Seeing as you are trespassing, I must insist that you leave as soon as possible."

Lodge's voice came from the back of the crowd. "Riley," he called, and then he was at her side. "You need some help with that?"

"Nope, I definitely got it."

Lodge turned to the crowd. "Show over, folks. Feel free to go on about your business." Then he turned to Riley. "Okay, this is why you called. You have to let me take a picture. I see the makings of a great article. What's up?"

"Well, Maisy convinced her company from California to open a satellite store here in the cottage. They'll take the storage room and probably some more space, but we'll rearrange."

"So where will you live?"

"Still here . . . for now."

"That's all we have, isn't it?" he asked, looking back at the cottage. "Now."

She nodded. "Yes, now. And then a little bit more of it each day."

He looked at her, smiling, pushing his glasses up his nose. "Exactly, my friend."

EPILOGUE

TWO MONTHS LATER

*H*umidity had moved into Palmetto Beach with its full August force; a haze settled over the town in somnolent heat. For months now, Riley, Maisy, Adalee and Lucy had been rearranging and redesigning the bookstore and design business in the cottage. Now Riley was taking a break with Brayden; they stood in silence at the end of Pearson's Pier, their fishing poles held over the water.

Riley reeled in her line, checking to make sure the bait was still on the hook. She spoke to Brayden over the far-off screech of a seagull. "You don't mind so much that I'm fishing with you today, do you?"

"Of course not." He rolled his eyes.

"You liked it better when I didn't?" she asked, and smiled at him from under her straw hat.

He lifted his baseball cap and rubbed his forehead. "Whatever, Mom." Then he tilted his head, squinted, yanking his cap back over his head. "Geez, that looks exactly like Mr. Logan over there."

Riley spun around and watched a man walk down Pearson's Pier, his stride long, a grin on his face.

Mack.

She smiled at him, feeling as buoyant as if she were floating above the wooden pier even as the voice in her head reminded her—*Only friends*. She'd imagined he'd return to visit someday, but that day always seemed in the future. Now he was here.

He reached her side. "Hey, Minnow." He turned to Brayden. "Hey, buddy, what's up?"

"Mr. Mack. How's it going?" He lifted his hand for a high five.

"Good. I'm glad to be here." Mack gave Brayden's hand a slap high in the air before he turned to Riley.

"Welcome back to Palmetto Beach," she said.

He held his arms wide, then gathered her into an embrace. She allowed her cheek to rest on his chest for a few moments, listening to the soft sound of his breath.

Mack released her, shuffling his feet as if unsure which way he wanted to go. "Hey, Brayden," he said. "Can I talk to your mom for a minute?"

"When a teacher says that, it means I'm in trouble."

Mack laughed. "You're not in trouble. We'll be right back."

"No problem." Brayden turned his attention back to his fishing pole.

Mack made a motion for Riley to follow him and they began walking down the pier.

"What's going on?" she asked him, her heart high in her throat, beating too fast.

"I came to see my best friend." He stopped at the end of the pier and turned to face her.

"That's sweet," she said. "How's your dad? And how are you?"

"Dad is stable; but he is at home with hospice care."

"This must be really hard on your mom." Riley paused, wanting to reach out, touch him. "I'm sorry your family is going through this."

"Thanks." He looked away, over the water, and then back at her. "Thing is, even though I don't want Dad to be sick, in a way his illness has been a gift to all of us, to our entire family. The trip here with him opened my eyes to parts of my life that were . . . off balance. The time with my family has made me realize that what is important has nothing to do with . . . things. I quit my job."

"Why?" She reached out to touch his hand, then withdrew it, still not understanding why he was here, what he needed.

"It wasn't what I really wanted, and well . . . being here reminded me of what I *do* want. And that has nothing to do with high-rises and corporate ladders and big accounts. I want to design and build houses. Always have. I don't know why I forgot what I already knew. . . ."

"Because life got in the way?"

"Yes." He paused. "You know, I've almost called you a million times, but I haven't been sure how to say what I need to say."

"You can say anything to me, right?" Riley said, her stomach rising and falling in a reminder of the time she rode the Tilt-a-Whirl with Brayden at the county fair.

"I know what's true," he said.

"And what is that?"

"When I left you on the beach a couple months ago, you said that being best friends was enough for you, but it's not enough for me anymore."

Riley stared at him. "It's not?"

He shook his head. "No. Is it really enough for you?"

"No," she admitted, hope and relief filling her. "I wanted it to be, but it's not. Definitely not with you standing here looking at me like that."

He held out his hand for her to take, smiling in a way that made her heart fill with the bright possibilities and profound joy promised by this new chapter of her life, which now included Mack Logan. The past and the future converged in that moment, and she stepped forward, entwined her fingers through his. Her story, all of their stories, would continue.

BOOKS MENTIONED IN *DRIFTWOOD SUMMER*

Howards End—E. M. Forster

The Screwtape Letters—C. S. Lewis

Beach Music—Pat Conroy

Peachtree Road—Anne Rivers Siddons

The Stand—Stephen King

To Kill a Mockingbird—Harper Lee

Wuthering Heights—Emily Brontë

Gone With the Wind—Margaret Mitchell

The Secret Life of Bees—Sue Monk Kidd

Walking on Water—Madeleine L'Engle

Treasure Island—Robert Louis Stevenson

Where or When—Anita Shreve

Shrimp & Grits Cookbook—Nathalie Dupree

Patti Callahan Henry lives with her husband and three children near Atlanta, Georgia, along the Chattahoochee River. Visit her Web site at www.patticallahanhenry.com.

Driftwood Summer

PATTI CALLAHAN HENRY

This Conversation Guide is intended to enrich the
individual reading experience, as well as encourage us
to explore these topics together—because books,
and life, are meant for sharing.

A CONVERSATION
WITH PATTI CALLAHAN HENRY

Q. What inspired this story?

A. During the past five years, I've traveled extensively for book tours, literary festivals and speaking events. I've listened to people's stories, and I've noticed recurring themes in some of the situations that touch our lives—our complicated relationships with family, the pain of lost love, the challenge of breaking free from the past and the sadness we feel at the disappearance of beloved community gathering places. Bookstores, libraries and book festivals seem to be places where, through the vehicle of books and book clubs, people talk more openly about their lives. I wanted to tell a story that integrated some of the concerns that matter most to us.

The sisters in this story relate to one another through the veil of past hurts, old loves and ingrained patterns of communication. Throwing three slightly estranged sisters into a situation in which they absolutely must work together allowed me to create a story of family and community healing.

Q. The beach and a bookstore—two of my favorite things. Are they among your favorites, too? Are any of the customers we meet in the bookstore based on real people?

A. I love beaches and bookstores, and figured my readers would, too! In my novels, none of the characters is based on real people, yet many are composites of people I've known. Some of the customers in the novel are also inspired by readers I've met over the years.

I set the novel in a bookstore because I am intrigued by the powerful influence of bookstores and libraries in my own life. Once inside a good bookstore, I lose track of time. Bookstores are more than places to buy merchandise. They are "gathering places" in many senses—where people gather, where I gather my thoughts. The endless stories in the books leave me with a full feeling, as if life will never be long enough to take in all the beauty of the written word. I am also fascinated with the role of books since they seem to be the perfect medium through which we share our hurts and pleasures, loves and lives.

Q. You're one of three sisters. Are you as different from your sisters as Riley is from Maisy and Adalee? What divides you and your sisters? What binds you together?

A. I didn't base the Sheffield girls on me and my sisters. Like most siblings, we're very much alike in some ways and profoundly different in others. I'm the oldest, which might make you think I'm the organized, type-A one in the family, but I'm not at all. My sisters, Barbi and Jeannie, are much more rational and organized, taking after our mother. I believe they tolerate my eccentric ways out of love. All that divides us right now is geographical distance and the all-encompassing needs of raising families with young children. What binds us together is shared history and love. . . . Our family is a very open and boisterous constellation. The past doesn't seem to have a hold on our relationships since we don't allow hurts to fester. As far as I know, none of us has ever loved the same boy. We talk through situations with a little sarcasm and a lot of honesty, hopefully keeping the past from influencing the present.

Q. This novel speaks to the importance of books in our lives. What role have they played in your life?

A. As a child I was a bookworm. I actually remember getting in trouble for ignoring the family because I was reading too much. My parents and sisters often teased me about always having my "nose in a book." We often cannot explain why we love someone or something or someplace; and I can't explain why I love to read. I just do. Always have. Of course I do believe it has something to do with the power of story.

When I was twelve years old, my family moved from our hometown up north to south Florida—and this is where my real love affair with novels began. For many years I didn't have many good friends. Books were some of my best friends. They still are.

Q. Memories of childhood summers spent at the beach are especially meaningful to Riley and Mack. Have you ever spent a whole summer at the beach? What was that experience like for you?

A. Growing up as a preacher's daughter, I was blessed each summer when Dad took a "reading month" in preparation for the busy fall church calendar. We escaped to Cape Cod, where we spent the entire summer running over dunes, through cranberry bogs and in and out of thick woods. These are my fondest memories of my childhood. I believe those were the days where my imagination grew, where my love of reading and nature was stitched into my soul.

There was more freedom in those summer days than during the school year. My sisters and I built forts, sailed our tiny Sunfish around the lake and only came back inside to eat. Once a week we went to the library—my favorite day. I would check out as many books as we were allowed to and read them all before we returned the next week. Those library days are a large part of why I write today; my love of books and story began there, in the long, languid days of childhood summers.

Q. In the novel, Driftwood Cottage Bookstore acts as a community gathering place. More than just a place to hang out and buy books, it serves to bring people together and foster meaningful relation-

ships. As you've visited bookstores to promote your work, what role have you seen real-life bookstores play in people's lives?

A. I've visited some of the most nurturing bookstores in the Southeast—places where people gather to talk about books and writing, to meet a friend for coffee, to buy a gift, or to chat with an author whose work they admire. They are places where a certain magic occurs. As people begin to talk about a story or the writing process, they also begin to talk about themselves. They connect. Acquaintances become friends, sometimes close friends. I love watching that process and being part of it.

It breaks my heart when I hear about another bookstore closing due to the financial challenges they face today. Libraries are also facing budget cuts and are hurting for funding. It is so important that, as readers and writers, we support our local bookstores and libraries. Sometimes we just don't know how much we value something until it's gone!

Q. Kitsy Sheffield seems to be a Southern woman of a certain generation, who places great importance on appearance, etiquette and gracious living. None of her daughters is quite following in that tradition. Does that reflect real changes between generations of women in the South today?

A. I think (or hope) that we, as women, are beginning to care less and less about what people think and care more and more about what we think, about our contribution to the world and to others. It's a challenge in any woman's life—balancing her own beliefs, needs and passions with the needs of her family. I wanted to touch on this subject while showing the sisters beginning to awaken to their own self-fulfillment.

Q. In several of your novels, including this one, you've explored the idea that each of our lives forms a story. Would you care to comment on this idea of life as story?

A. Ever since I was a young child, I've looked at my life and thought, "I wonder what will happen next." In this way, I've always looked at life through the lens of story. I don't believe anything happens by coincidence, and I often wonder what a chance encounter or new experience will mean in the long run of any life. If I pay attention, I often see threads in my life that intertwine, separate and come together again.

I also believe that our own experiences are better understood by hearing others' stories or in reading a story that touches our heart. Telling stories is the way we come to know and love one another. If we can look at the larger tapestry of life, instead of just the single threads of individual events, we begin to see how our lives intersect and connect. We notice meaningful patterns that weren't originally apparent. When life is viewed as an interesting story, it becomes an adventure. As the saying goes, truth is stranger than fiction.

QUESTIONS FOR DISCUSSION

1. Do you agree with Riley that book clubs foster compassion for others and a sense of community? What do you get out of your book club?

2. Patti Callahan Henry mentions some of her favorite novels in *Driftwood Summer*. What are some of your favorites?

3. The two older sisters—Riley and Maisy—suffer from an estrangement in their relationship that began when they both fell in love with the same boy. Have you ever had a relationship—with a sister, a brother or a best friend—that fell apart over a love interest?

4. Kitsy Sheffield, the girls' mother, asks Riley not to tell the other sisters about her illness until the party is over. Why do you think she wants to keep it secret? If you were Riley, could you have kept this information from your sisters?

5. At the end of the novel, Maisy says, "I always thought there was this life; you know, this other life. . . . It was a life I thought existed in a parallel plane, and I couldn't get to it." What do you think she means? Have you ever felt that way?

6. Many people in the novel talk about Riley's carefree confidence and tomboy ways as a girl, and how she has changed since high school. Why do you think she has changed so dramatically? Do you think she'll ever rediscover the less restrained Riley again? Is it inevitable that we bury certain parts of ourselves as we become adults?

7. Mama's cancer changes the way Riley looks at their relationship. Has impending death ever changed the way you looked at a particular relationship? At life in general?

8. To both older sisters, Mack Logan represents a youthful time in their lives. Do you have someone who represents such a time in your life? Do you feel you've idealized him or her? Do you keep in touch?

9. Maisy and Adalee both suggest that Riley lives vicariously through fiction rather than engaging fully in reality. Do you think the accusation is fair? Could you be accused of the same thing?

10. Describe what you think happens to each of the main characters during the year after *Driftwood Summer* ends. What happens to the bookstore?

11. Share some of your memories of spending summers at the beach.

12. Of the three sisters, which do you like best? Least? Why?